While the deputy watched, Tom's revolver swung toward him...

Sprawling back on his elbows, Longarm angled up his Colt and squeezed the trigger.

Big Tom cried out, dropping his drawn knife as Longarm's bullet shattered his collarbone. He was swaying now, like an old tree in a gale, but still he managed to stay on his feet, without dropping his gun.

And Longarm realized with a sinking sensation that he'd fired all five chambers of his own Colt.

Big Tom grinned as he read Longarm's thoughts by the look in his eyes.

"Looks like it's going to end up that we killed each other, Deputy," Tom said as he began to squeeze the trigger.

TABOR EVANS

LONGARM
AND THE
LONE STAR BOUNTY

A JOVE BOOK

LONGARM AND THE LONE STAR BOUNTY

A Jove Book/published by arrangement with
the author

PRINTING HISTORY
Jove edition/February 1984

ISBN: 0-515-07611-2

Jove Books are published by The Berkley Publishing Group,
200 Madison Avenue, New York, N.Y. 10016. The words
"A JOVE BOOK" and the "J" with sunburst are trademarks
belonging to Jove Publications, Inc.

PRINTED IN THE UNITED STATES OF AMERICA

Chapter 1

It was just past dawn on a dreary gray Denver morning when Longarm finally gave up on getting some sleep. He kicked back the covers and sat up on the side of the bed. Lord, he was weary! It was all he could do to plant his big feet on the scratchy, threadbare rug and scowl at his reflection in the blackened, blurry mirror hung lopsidedly above the chipped, scarred bureau.

He'd gotten back into Denver quite late last night—just a few hours ago, truth to tell. For the past thirty days he'd been chasing some mean old sons across the hard-as-nails country they called the Arizona Territory. About a week into the month that he'd spent in the saddle, Longarm had decided that his boss, Billy Vail, the Chief United States Marshal for the First District Court of Colorado, must truly hate him. Why else would Billy assign his best deputy to such ball-buster cases?

Longarm shook his sleepy head. He badly needed some rest, but it always took him a while to get used to being back in his rented room, especially after an extended period of camping out beneath the wide, starry skies. Hell, the little corner room was the best one that the boarding house near Cherry

1

Creek had to offer, but Custis Long, known to most folks as Longarm, was a big fellow, well over six feet tall. Walls had a way of making him uneasy, making him want to shrug them off, the way a wild stallion wants to bolt its corral.

Longarm stood up and stretched, arching his back until his bones stopped creaking and his thick, supple muscles rippled beneath his tanned skin. An old Sioux scout he'd come across at an army remount station a while back had clued him in on a couple of helpful hints about easing the hurt in a saddle-sore back. "Watch Brother Tomcat," the Sioux had advised him over a couple of tin cups of Longarm's Maryland rye. "Brother Tomcat starts each day with a wash and a stretch..."

Well, Longarm figured he could let the Indian's advice on personal hygiene slide, but he considered the idea of devoting a little time each morning to stretching out the kinks in his spine worth trying; once a fellow got past thirty, he had to start looking out for himself if he wanted to go on putting in long days in the saddle.

The deputy marshal padded across the carpet to take a closer look in the mirror. His lantern jaw, beneath his tobacco-brown longhorn mustache, was scratchy against his palm. He decided he could do with a shave before reporting in to Marshal Vail later this morning. Besides, a shave might help to wake him up, and maybe do something to rid his normally clear, blue-gray eyes of their bloodshot tinge.

He poured some water into the washbasin, worked up a poor excuse for lather off the granite-gray sliver of soap plastered to the side of the china bowl, and slapped the cold, wet mess of suds none too gently against his face. Time to get his blood circulating! He took his straight razor from the drawer and tested it with the ball of his callused thumb. It would do, he thought, sliding his thumb across the length of the edge. He didn't like an overly sharp razor; it had a way of making his face resemble the back forty acres of a sheepherder's pastures. Besides, the damned whiskers just grew back the next day...

After the shave, and an all-over wash utilizing the remainder of the lather and the scrap of rough towel next to the water pitcher, Longarm felt himself beginning to revive. A mug or two of black coffee, and he figured he'd have a fifty-fifty chance of making it through the day. He patted down his thick head of short-cut brown hair, scooped up some of the soapy water to rinse last night's residue from his mouth, and turned away from the washbasin.

He took a fresh gray flannel shirt out of his closet and shrugged it on. His black string tie was still looped around the collar of last night's shirt. He removed the damned foolish ribbon and tossed the old shirt back into the corner of the room, atop the rest of his soiled clothing. Later on today, his landlady, by prior arrangement, would see to it that his stuff found its way to Ho Quah's laundry on the corner. He spent a few muttering moments fiddling with the tie until it was approximately where it ought to be. The regulations stated that all deputies had to wear a tie while on duty, but the rule book didn't yet specify the width of the knot—or at least he didn't *think* it did, Longarm mused wryly. But give the bureaucrats time, he thought. Give 'em time . . .

With his tie in place, Longarm worked his bottom half into a clean pair of cotton longjohns, hitched on a pair of socks, then worked his long, lean legs into his skintight, brown tweed trousers. Next he stomped his feet into his low-heeled stovepipe boots. As a lawman, Longarm spent more time riding trains and walking around towns then he did working stirrups. Low-heeled boots let him move around a lot faster and easier than the average jasper shod in a pair of high-heeled range boots.

Longarm put on the brown tweed vest that matched his pants. He buttoned it up and then tucked his Ingersoll pocket watch into the left-hand pocket of the vest. The other end of the gold-washed watch chain was clipped to the butt of a double-barreled .44-caliber brass derringer, which went into his right vest pocket. Longarm glanced into the mirror to make sure the derringer wasn't making any tell-tale lumps, and then he arranged the glittering watch chain to drape between the two pockets.

The chain was the only gaudy thing about Longarm, but it served a very definite purpose. More than one ornery son of a bitch had drawn his pistol to demand that Longarm hand over that watch, and more than once Longarm had obligingly reached into his right-hand vest pocket . . .

Derringers were all right in a close-quarters, back-against-the-wall kind of pinch, but the main tool of his trade was his Colt. He fetched the double-action, .44-caliber pistol from beneath his pillow. The blue-steel Colt had a barrel cut down to five inches, eliminating the front blade sight. A front sight could cause more trouble than it was worth by snagging on the lip of an open-toed holster. It was Longarm's firmly held belief that any jasper who needed a sight in order to accurately shoot a pistol had no business getting himself into that kind of eyeball-to-eyeball shooting match.

He'd cleaned and oiled the revolver late last night, over a few swallows of rye. Longarm had hoped that the combination of hard whiskey and careful scrubbing and lubricating of the Colt's parts would serve to relax him after the long, rough, nighttime train ride into Denver. It hadn't, but at least the gun was loaded and ready for action. Out of habit, Longarm checked to make sure the hammer was resting on an empty chamber. There was nothing on this earth dumber than some old son with a fully loaded sixgun strapped to his hip, hopping down off his horse, jolting his pistol's hammer, and setting off a round. If the holster was pointing down, the man would lose some toes; if the holster had gotten twisted, he'd lose half of his ass; and then there were the poor souls who liked to carry their guns tucked into the front of their jeans...

Longarm's holster was waxed and heat-hardened. He strapped his smooth leather gunbelt around his narrow waist so that his Colt could ride butt forward, high on his left hip, the way he liked it. To make sure, Longarm reached across his belt buckle with his right hand, drawing the revolver in a whip-fast, rock-steady motion.

Returning the gun to its place on his hip, Longarm checked his pocket watch. It was just seven. He still had two hours before the Federal Building—and Marshal Vail's office—opened for business at nine. Longarm scowled as he looked around the close confines of his room. *Two hours*... If he was out on the trail, he could fix himself a pot of coffee and watch the world all around him, but here in town...

Well, he could always clean his rifle. He went to the closet to get the .44-40 Winchester and his gun-cleaning kit. That

4

was when he remembered that he'd run out of whale oil last night, while working on his Colt. He'd planned to buy a new can of the stuff this morning, after his briefing with Marshal Vail.

That settled that. He decided to go out and have himself some breakfast, and then meander over to Wilkerson's before continuing on to the Federal Building. The gunsmith opened up at eight, so Longarm knew he could make his purchase and arrive at Marshal Vail's office easily by nine. Billy Vail would be shocked; for once Longarm would be reporting to work early.

The deputy took his brown frock coat from its place in the closet and put it on, patting its pockets to make sure that he had a supply of spare cartridges, his handcuffs, and his wallet, inside of which was pinned his silver deputy's badge. Some lawmen liked to wear their badges all the time, but it had been Longarm's experience as a manhunter that he often got more information and cooperation out of folks when they didn't know he was a federal deputy marshal.

He checked the breast pocket of his coat to make sure he had enough cheroots and matches to get him through the day, then lifted his snuff-brown Stetson off its peg on the wall and set it dead center on his head. On the way out of his digs, he balled up his dirty laundry and stuck it underneath his arm. He set the bundle down in the hallway to be picked up by his landlady, and locked his door, taking the time to wedge a matchstick into the space between the door and jamb, and then break it off so that it was flush with the wood and not noticeable to anyone else. On his return later that day, Longarm would check to see if the bit of match was still there. If it wasn't, it would mean that during his absence somebody had been in the room—or was still in it. A lawman had a way of making enemies. Some of them would throw down on a man face to face, fair and square, but others liked to backshoot, popping up from beneath a fellow's bed, or out of his closet.

Quietly, for the benefit of those still sleeping, he made his way down the stairs and out of the rooming house, and headed up Colfax Avenue, his boots crunching against the cinder path that had to do for a sidewalk here on the poor side of town.

Above the low roofs of the houses Longarm could see the gold dome of the Colorado State Capitol, glittering against the gray sky like something very fine and very expensive in the velvet display case of a jeweler's window. It was over around Capitol Hill that the brown sandstone sidewalks and gas-illuminated streetlamps began, but that was also where the prices were so high that even a piss-poor breakfast of nothing but a couple of eggs, toast, and coffee could set a man back two bits!

Longarm shook his head. He'd be doing his breakfasting this side of Cherry Creek, where the spoons were a little greasier and the cook might not have shaved this morning, but where a man could get an honest, stick-to-his-ribs meal for a price he could afford to pay. President Hayes said that the depression of the seventies was well over, and that 1880 was going to start a new era of prosperity. Well, Longarm didn't think it was proper for him to argue with the President, but that prosperity hadn't yet seeped down to *his* monthly pay envelope.

He had his breakfast of steak and eggs, potatoes and toast, with plenty of refills of his coffee cup, and then paid a tab that wouldn't even have bought him the eggs if he'd waited until he'd crossed the Creek. On his way out of the eatery he fired up his first cheroot of the day. He'd smoked more expensive cigars, but his good old two-for-a-nickel stogies suited him just fine. The only thing that would have suited him better would be not to smoke at all. Longarm sighed and shrugged. He'd been working hard; he'd earned himself his smoking pleasure. Anyway, it was too early in the morning to start bothering himself about quitting. Again.

Puffing away on his smoke, Longarm headed along Larimer, past the early-morning quiet saloons and cheap hotels. It was about a quarter of eight. If he headed over to Wilkerson's now, he'd be no more than five minutes early. He could use the time to window-shop the gun store's wares until they were ready to let him in.

Longarm strolled back toward Capitol Hill, nodding good morning to the few yawning storekeepers who'd appeared with brooms in their hands to sweep away the night's dust from their doors. He crossed Cherry Creek and continued on up Colfax, turning right onto a narrow lane that led him past a row of shops devoted to serving the needs of the busy folks who worked in the Federal Building and the nearby United States Mint.

He passed a bakery, a general store, and a "guaranteed painless" dentist's office, before reaching Wilkerson's storefront. The gun shop's windows held a display of old weapons. There was a grouping of Kentucky rifles and Dixie "Brown Bess" muskets looking to be a mile long and as skinny as toothpicks; an ancient Dutch blunderbuss shotgun, its muzzle bell resembling a cook's funnel; a brace of Harper's Ferry .58-caliber horse pistols, designed to be carried in saddle holsters; and a bunch of engraved powder horns, leather pouches, and bullet molds to complete the assortment.

In all, it was just the kind of shop window to make a gun fancier stop and stare, and it was a hell of a lot more interesting than the standard assortment of factory-issue Colts, Smith & Wessons, and Winchesters. It was a very unusual display, but then, Alma Wilkerson was a very unusual gunsmith.

And not just because she was a woman. Her husband had started the business, but he'd passed away about ten years ago. Alma had been quite young when she'd married him, but even then she was the brains of the couple, or so folks said. Old man Wilkerson had been many years her senior. It wasn't too long before his eyes went bad, so that Alma had to take over the repair work and bookkeeping. Pretty soon she knew more about guns than her husband ever had. When he died, she'd decided to keep the business going. Longarm bought his ammunition and other gun supplies from her whenever he could. He liked the store's stock, the fair prices, and the way the pert, saucy brunette filled out her low-cut dresses . . .

Right now, Longarm was surprised to see that Alma already had four customers inside her store, even though it wasn't yet eight o'clock. He tried the front door, and found it locked.

That's odd, Longarm thought, his eyes narrowing. Now how did those four fellows get themselves inside?

Those in the shop had yet to notice him peering in at them. Longarm took the opportunity to take the measure of the four men with Alma. They were dressed "city style," in suits, satin vests, and ties, but their clothes were ill-fitting and as dusty

7

as all get-out. The men also needed shaves. They looked like fellows who'd just finished a long, hard ride.

Longarm checked his pocket watch. It was now a few minutes after eight. Why wasn't Alma unlocking the door?

Longarm rapped on the glass. As he watched, Alma whirled around to stare out at him, her eyes widening. The four men stared as well, standing as stock-still as scarecrows. Longarm grinned, rattled the doorknob, and then shrugged quizzically. He couldn't hear anything from inside, but his eyes were keen enough to catch the man standing closest to Alma whisper something. Whatever he said, it was clearly permission for the woman to open up.

Since when does a shopkeeper take orders from a customer? Longarm wondered. Then Alma was at the door, turning the key and letting him in.

Longarm was all set for Alma's friendly greeting to an old customer; what he got was a look of cool appraisal.

"What can we do for you, today, sir?" she asked over her shoulder as Longarm followed her into the shop, past the racks of Winchester and Henry repeaters. She looked pretty much the way she always did. Her long brown hair was carelessly twisted into a bun that allowed several wispy tendrils to feather her long neck. The years had begun to catch up with Alma. Faint crow's-feet had taken up residence at the corners of her slate-gray eyes, and the laugh lines bracketing her wide, sensual mouth seemed to be a little deeper, but her full figure was just as enticing as ever. Longarm's pulse quickened as he watched her swaying hips quiver beneath the bleached cotton twill of her dress. Her bodice, scooped low and cinched with pink ribbon, seemed about to be overwhelmed by the amount of cleavage it had to contain. As usual, Alma's creamy, round breasts threatened to spill out over the top of her dress, but somehow they didn't, despite the way they jiggled and bounced.

She was a big woman, there was no arguing that point, but you couldn't really call her fat. For one thing, Alma was tall enough—at five feet ten inches—to carry her delightful abundance. For another thing, she was no pear-shaped matronly type. Alma had curves, big, beautiful, shapely curves. She was

8

just right, and the Lord had clearly been in a good mood the day he fashioned her...

But today there was no sparkle in her gray eyes, no mischievous glint of affection as she watched Longarm and waited for him to make his needs known.

"What'll it be, sir?" she repeated impatiently. "I'm quite busy," she added, glancing nervously at the four quiet, stern-looking men.

Longarm had, of course, figured out that these four jaspers were on the wrong side of the law as soon as he'd clapped eyes on them, but this in itself was nothing unusual, even in as civilized and up-to-date a place as Denver. Every second or third man he ran into had run afoul of the law somewhere along the line. Automatically he'd already riffled through the mental list of faces, names, and descriptions that he'd culled from wanted posters and personal experience over the years; these fellows weren't there, that was for sure, and those were the only ones he was really interested in, since they were all wanted on federal cases. Longarm was a United States deputy, not a town constable or county sheriff, and matters of local jurisdiction were none of his damn business.

They were up to no good, that was obvious from the proddy way they were acting, but what was their play?

In the back of Longarm's mind was the worry that he'd inadvertently caught Alma in the middle of some small-time shady deal. If that was the case, he'd just as soon shut his eyes to it, rather than embarrass an old friend who'd found that she had to bend local law a little to keep her business afloat.

So he thought he'd play along with her, and wait and see what might develop...

"I'll take a can of Kent's gun oil," he said, giving Alma a wink just to let her know things were all right.

"I'm sorry," she replied politely, but a mite coldly. "We're all out."

At first Longarm thought he'd heard wrong.

"We sold the last can yesterday," she continued, shrugging. Longarm just stared. "But—"

"Now this here lady's just told you she's sold out of that

9

gun oil, friend," one of the men cut in. He was big, and had
his wide-brimmed hat pulled low, as if to hide his face. The
man's coal-black, Sunday-go-to-meeting suit had something
rust-colored crusting its frayed lapels.

Longarm kept silent. He could feel the other men closing
in behind him. He didn't turn, but kept his eyes on the brown-
ish, crusty stuff on the big man's lapels, thinking about how
much it looked like dried blood.

"Why ain't you answering?" the big man demanded sharply.
He brushed back his suitcoat in order to rest his right hand on
the hard-rubber grips of his revolver.

"Maybe he don't hear too good." One of the others laughed.
Longarm took him in with one quick, sideways glance. He was
of average height, and wore a green corduroy suit, a tan, flat-
topped Stetson set back on his full head of sandy-colored hair,
and two guns. One was in plain sight, strapped around his
waist. The other gave itself away by the telltale bulge it made
riding beneath his coat, just under the jasper's left armpit.

"Are you deaf, mister?" the man demanded. "Do we have
to spell things out for you?"

"Not at all," Longarm replied with a smile. "Reckon I'll
try somewheres else."

"You do that," the man with the shoulder holster said. His
grin was easygoing, but his eyes were cold and hard.

"Try the gunsmiths along Larimer," Alma suggested.

"Thank you, ma'am, I will," Longarm said, and turned to
leave. There was a brief moment of confrontation when the
two men guarding the shop's door refused to budge. Longarm
balanced himself and held his breath, ready for anything.

"Yeah, you try over on Larimer," the big man suddenly
said. "This fellow's going to try over there," he elaborated for
the benefit of his friends.

The guards at the door nodded and relaxed. They looked
away from Longarm as they stepped aside to let him pass.

Longarm made his way out of the shop. He continued walking until he'd reached the end of the row of stores and was
sure that he was out of sight. He was now certain that something
was very wrong inside the gun shop.

The fact that Alma had treated him coolly, despite their long friendship, was only the tipoff. What had convinced him that she needed his help were her remarks concerning the gun oil. Kent's was the only brand Longarm used. Granted, she was allowed to run out of the oil once in a while, but it was the way she *said* she'd run out that had cinched the matter as far as he was concerned.

He extracted his wallet from the pocket of his frock coat, removed his silver deputy's badge from its fold of leather, and pinned it to his lapel. He slid his Colt out of its holster and made his way around the corner of the row of shops to approach the gun store from the rear. Running out of Kent's was one thing, but Alma would *never* sell the last can of his favorite brand to somebody else . . .

Longarm was very cautious as he circled around the end store and began to make his way along the rear alley. There was no telling what he might find, or who he might come across. That dried blood on the big man's lapels was still on his mind.

Alma's store was wedged between the painless dentist and an emporium devoted to the sale of hardware. The deputy crouched down behind several barrels of nails near the hardware store's service entrance. From there he could spy on a buckboard drawn up in Alma's yard. There was a man seated on the driver's bench, cradling a Winchester in the crook of his arm.

As Longarm watched, the back door of the gun shop was kicked open. Out came the two men who had briefly blocked Longarm's exit. Each was carrying a wooden crate filled to the brim with cardboard boxes of rifle and pistol ammunition. The two dumped their booty into the bed of the wagon and then hurried back inside.

Longarm nodded to himself. Things were starting to make sense. This gang was looting Alma to replenish their stocks of ammo and weapons.

Longarm was about to move in against the fellow minding the wagon, when he heard a faint moan. It was coming from behind some crates stacked against the side of the hardware store. Longarm hurried to investigate the sound, staying low to avoid being spotted by the gang's lookout in the buckboard.

11

"P-please . . . I'm h-hurt . . ."

Longarm saw a man's body wedged into the narrow space between the crates and the building. The poor fellow was blood-spattered. He was a small, frail-looking, elderly man, with a thin horseshoe of gray curls encircling his bald dome. He was wearing steel-rimmed spectacles, but one of the thick lenses was cracked.

"Lord, I'm dying," the man groaned. "Get me out," he begged Longarm. "I'm hurting something awful!"

"Quiet now," Longarm cautioned him. "If my guess is right, the fellows who did this to you are still close enough to finish the job." He grabbed hold of the wounded man's shoes and tugged him halfway out, then hauled him the rest of the way free by his bloody leather apron.

"They knifed me, they did," the man gasped, coughing and crying. "The big fellow in the black suit . . . I caught them skulking around Alma's back door . . ."

Longarm crouched down beside the little man, who had begun the day nattily dressed in green wool trousers, a white shirt, and a red tie, as well as that apron. "Are you the owner of this hardware store?" he asked as he examined the wide gash in the man's side.

"I am," the merchant said weakly. He looked up at Longarm through his cracked spectacles, fingering the badge pinned to his lapel. "How bad am I, Deputy?" he asked. "I'm dying, aren't I?"

Longarm frowned. The poor old fellow's shirt was sopping wet with the blood that was seeping from his wound.

The man nodded. "That's what I thought," he mourned. "That big bastard gut-stuck me like it was nothing at all . . ."

"Tell me quick," Longarm whispered, keeping an eye on things in Alma's yard. "How'd it happen, exactly? I'll need to know when I—" Longarm froze in mid-sentence.

"Go on and say it," the dying man coaxed him. "You'll need to know in order to testify against them at their trial for my murder. We both know *I* won't be around to do it," he added bitterly.

"You're going to make it," Longarm lied.

The man's laugh turned into a wince. "Like hell I will. You

12

don't have to beat around the bush concerning my chances. Now listen good, sonny, I haven't got enough time left to repeat myself . . . I arrived early to do some work around the place before it was time to open. I caught those bastards poking around Alma's back door. I asked them what they were up to. Well, the big one, the leader of the bunch, he came up to me real friendly-like. He told me that he and his men were there to make a delivery. I was about to ask him where his load was when he pulled a bowie knife out from underneath his jacket and stabbed me with it. He dragged me back here and put me behind those crates, figuring I was either dead or as good as . . ."

He screwed his eyes shut, as he moaned softly against the pain. "Well, what are you planning, Deputy?"

"I'm going to get you a doctor," Longarm began.

"No!" the man pleaded. "You get those bastards!"

"If I do, you're dead for sure," Longarm warned.

The old man scowled. "I'm dead anyway, and you know it," he said disdainfully. "Anything that hurts this bad has got to be fatal."

Longarm couldn't decide what to do. How could he leave a man to die right here in the middle of Denver, when help was just minutes away? The answer was that he couldn't. He'd fetch a doctor. Those outlaws could be caught later. First he had to try to save this man's life.

"I'm getting you some help—" he began.

Blood-sticky fingers rose up to clutch at Longarm's sleeve. "Listen to me!" the shopkeeper implored, his voice harsh with pain. "You do as I say, sonny! You leave me be and go after those bastards! If they did this to me, what do you think they intend to do to Alma when they're through robbing her? She's seen their faces just like I have . . ."

"You're right," Longarm muttered. He nodded respectfully at the man. "You're a brave one, as brave as they come. I'll try and get this over with quick—"

"Just do it," the shopkeeper said. "Go on, do it!" He waved Longarm off.

The deputy moved back to his place behind the barrels. That same pair of outlaws had just completed their third, heavily laden trip to the buckboard. Longarm watched as they dumped their loads under the gaze of the rifleman minding the wagon, and then began to trudge back to the gun store.

"I'm going now," Longarm whispered. "Rest easy..." He glanced back over his shoulder. The shopkeeper was sitting stone-still where Longarm had propped him. His breathing had stopped and his eyes were wide, unblinking, unseeing.

Longarm swallowed hard. "Rest easy," he repeated to the dead man. Then he glided as quickly and silently as an avenging angel toward the buckboard. He timed his approach to reach the seated guard just as the other two outlaws disappeared back into Alma's shop for another load of stolen goods.

The guard had a scraggly red beard. He was wearing denims and a tan flannel shirt. He wasn't wearing a handgun. Longarm managed to get close enough to snatch the rifle out of the man's grasp before he knew what was happening. The surprised outlaw tried to turn around, but froze when he felt the barrel of Longarm's Colt pressed up against his ear.

"You're making a big mistake, mister," the outlaw snarled. "You're going to be mighty sorry..."

Longarm ignored the man's bluster. He wanted to know what the gang had planned for a getaway in case some of them managed to elude capture. "Quick," he whispered, "where are the horses for the men inside?"

"Big Tom is going to skin you alive—" the outlaw began.

Longarm thumbed back the hammer of his Colt. The oily, metallic double click, close by the outlaw's ear, had the desired effect. "The horses are hitched up in front of a cafe on Colfax. They're just down the block," the outlaw gasped. "Hey, now, mister, you calm down, okay?"

"What's the plan?" Longarm demanded.

"Uh—um—" the outlaw stammered.

"Come on!" Longarm pressed harder with his Colt.

"Ow! Easy, mister!" the outlaw begged. "I can't hardly think with that gun in my ear!"

"You've got ten seconds," Longarm intoned, keeping an eye on the doorway of Alma's shop. Those other two jaspers were due out at any moment.

"The plan was for us to get this wagon loaded and for me to drive it out of town," the outlaw blurted. "Tom and the

14

others would take care of the woman inside, and fetch their mounts. Then we'd all link up at Cutter's Rock, just outside of town. We figured it would attract less attention to have a fellow dressed like me, without pistols, drive the wagon alone, just like any trailhand on his way to a nearby ranch."

"Not bad," Longarm mused. "A haul like this would have kept you in guns and bullets for a year."

"That's what Big Tom figured," the outlaw agreed. "Listen, mister! My pals will be right out. You can't risk firing a shot—"

"Is that why Big Tom stabbed that poor old man?" Longarm growled. "I've got a knife right here in my other hand," he fibbed. "Maybe I ought to slit your throat."

"P-please . . ." the outlaw moaned as rivulets of sweat rolled their way down through his sparse red whiskers. "G-get it over with if you're g-going to k-kill me!"

Longarm sighed. He wanted these men to suffer for their crimes, but he just didn't have the heart to torment a man. He lowered the Colt's hammer and then raised the gun and brought it down hard against the crown of the man's hat. The outlaw's eyes rolled upward as he lost consciousness, toppling sideways. Longarm caught him before he could fall to the ground, and positioned him on the buckboard's bench so that it looked as if he'd dozed off. He leaned the Winchester against the slumped-over figure, and then boosted himself into the bed of the wagon, where he waited to take the other two outlaws by surprise.

The pair came out a few seconds later. Longarm didn't dare peek up over the side of the wagon to get a glimpse of them, but from the way they were huffing and groaning, he knew they both had their hands full with heavy loads.

"Goddammit!" one of them cursed. "We're busting our asses while Bob gets to take a nap!"

"We'll see to it that he does the unloading," his partner muttered. "Don't you worry. We'll make him pay—"

Longarm rose up, his Colt pointed between the two of them. "Speaking of paying up, gents . . ."

The two outlaws exchanged startled glances. They couldn't do very much else since both had their hands full.

"It's that same jasper from inside," one of them said.

"Only now he's wearing a badge," his friend grumbled. "I knew there was something fishy about you, mister," he addressed Longarm. "We never should have let you out of there."

"Reckon not," Longarm smiled. "Now you boys hold on to those boxes and come closer," he ordered.

Both men eyed his Colt. "He can't do nothing with that gun," one of them said nervously. "It'd warn Big Tom if he shot us."

"I'm willing to take that chance," Longarm said cheerfully.

"We could yell," the other outlaw remarked.

"If you do that, I'd have nothing to lose by shooting the both of you," Longarm countered as he hopped down out of the buckboard. "I'm starting to lose patience. Do as I say or I'll blow your fool heads off."

"I don't aim to get killed," said the outlaw who'd threatened to shout. "I'm your prisoner, lawman." He came forward docilely.

"Awww, *shit*," his partner sulked, but he followed suit.

Longarm quickly plucked their revolvers from their holsters, and tossed the guns away. He ordered them both to set down their crates, then herded them over to the rear of the buckboard, where he threaded his handcuffs through the spokes of a wheel and snapped a bracelet on each of the men's wrists, fettering them to the wagon.

Next Longarm checked the condition of the unconscious driver. Satisfied that the outlaw would remain out of action, he began to make his way toward the back door of the gun shop.

"You two stay quiet," Longarm warned the outlaws over his shoulder. "If you boys make noise, then *I* can make noise, with *this*." He waved his Colt at them.

Longarm pressed himself against the side of the building and then slipped inside, crouching low and keeping his gun at the ready. Now the hard part was beginning. He had to take these last two without endangering Alma.

He was in what appeared to be the store's stockroom. Crates and boxes and empty glass display cases were haphazardly scattered about. The room's only light came in through the open doorway. Moving cautiously across the shadowy interior,

Longarm made his way through a curtained doorway into a second room, this one lantern-lit. Here there were machines, and several worktables strewn with partially disassembled rifles and pistols. This was obviously the shop area where Alma repaired her customers' broken firearms.

A curtain was all that separated this room from the front room of the store, where she was being held by Big Tom and his accomplice wearing the green corduroy suit, the man with the easy smile and snake eyes. Longarm edged forward until he could peek through a gap in the curtain.

"What's taking them so long?" Big Tom growled. "I've got a funny feeling..."

"They're probably passing a flask," his green-suited companion remarked disgustedly.

Longarm watched as Tom brushed back his black suit jacket to draw his revolver. The deputy's heart stopped as the outlaw seemed to aim at the curtain.

"You go on back there," Tom ordered the other man, pointing the way with his gun. "Tell them to snap it up."

"You both better git now, while you still can," Alma said scornfully. "Customers are going to start coming in here..."

"I guess we'll take that chance." Tom laughed, nodding mirthfully to the sandy-haired man outfitted in green. "'Sides, woman, maybe I ain't finished taking everything I've got in mind. There's you, for instance," he leered.

"You wouldn't dare touch me!" Alma said. Her tone was haughty, but Longarm saw the way her hands rose fearfully to shield her breasts from Tom's hungry eyes.

The other outlaw had been following the exchange and licking his lips, the way a dog will when it watches its master eating.

Big Tom noticed the man staring, and swore softly. "You git now! Do what I told you!"

The outlaw nodded and drew his own gun as he hurried toward the curtain. "I'll be right back. Don't start without me," he joked.

Longarm stepped away from the doorway and flattened himself against the wall. His plan was to knock out the man in green, then order Tom to give himself up. The outlaw leader still had his gun in his hand, but Longarm was hoping that the fight would go out of him once he knew his men had been taken and he was covered.

The man in green pushed his way through the curtain, his gun at the ready. Longarm let him take a couple of steps into the room before he swiped the barrel of his Colt against the outlaw's ear.

Longarm stepped in quickly and put an arm around the unconscious man's torso as he began to slump, then lowered him gently to the floor, at the same time easing the revolver from the outlaw's nerveless fingers and hiding it behind a crate, where the gunman wouldn't be likely to find it, should he come to. Then he turned his attention to what was going on in the front room. And none too soon.

Big Tom had apparently heard or sensed something, and was now approaching the back room, at the same time bringing his revolver to bear on the curtain.

Standing to one side and poking his Colt through the curtain, Longarm called out, "Federal deputy! Drop your iron, mister!"

The last part of this was drowned out by the report of Big Tom's pistol, as its slug punched a smoking hole through the velvet curtain.

Longarm came all the way through the doorway. He fired twice, crabbing sideways. His first round went high, but the second bullet took Big Tom in the chest. The outlaw staggered backward, but he didn't fall and he didn't drop his gun.

Longarm ducked low as Tom blasted away at him, his slugs going wild, shattering the glass in a display cabinet. Alma, Longarm was glad to see, had the sense to throw herself to the floor as gunfire filled the small shop.

Longarm was about to fire at Tom again when he heard an odd scraping noise coming up behind him. He looked over his shoulder in time to see the man in green crawling through the curtained doorway, reaching beneath his suit jacket and coming up with a small pistol.

The shoulder holster! Longarm reminded himself ruefully as the dazed outlaw rose up on his knees and squeezed off two quick shots from his little gun.

18

Longarm whirled around so fast he lost his balance, landing hard on his butt. Falling was the only thing that saved him; the outlaw's shots went through the space his chest had just occupied.

Longarm fired back twice, his shots punching into the outlaw's belly. The man cried out, dropping his gun to clutch at himself as he fell sideways across the curtained threshold.

In the split second the exchange had taken, Big Tom, his chest oozing blood, had staggered forward to loom over Longarm. The hulking outlaw glared at his adversary as he held his revolver loosely in his blood-sticky right hand.

"I'm going to kill you slow, Deputy," Tom hissed. "I'm going to make you pay."

"Like you killed the old man, Tom?" Longarm demanded harshly.

"Just like that," Tom said, grinning. His teeth were outlined with the bright red blood rising out of his punctured lung. "I'm going to cut you up slow..." His left hand fumbled at the sheathed bowie knife at his belt.

The cagey outlaw meant his action to be a distraction, Longarm realized. It almost worked, too. While the deputy watched that left hand, Tom's revolver swung toward him.

Sprawling back on his elbows, Longarm angled up his Colt and squeezed the trigger.

Big Tom cried out, dropping his drawn knife as Longarm's bullet shattered his collarbone. He was swaying now, like an old tree in a gale, but still he managed to stay on his feet, without dropping his gun.

And Longarm realized with a sinking sensation that he'd fired all five chambers of his own Colt.

Big Tom grinned as he read Longarm's thought by the look in his eyes. The wounded outlaw tried to raise his gun but his right hand would no longer function. Big Tom had to grip his revolver in both of his hands in order to bring it to bear on Longarm.

The lawman knew there was no time to fumble for the derringer tucked away in his vest pocket. Big Tom's gun muzzle was staring him right between the eyes. Longarm watched in horror as the outlaw thumbed back the revolver's hammer.

"Looks like it's going to end up that we killed each other, Deputy," Tom said as he began to squeeze the trigger.

Longarm saw Alma leap up to rush toward the outlaw. "Don't you do it!" she cried out.

"Alma! No!" Longarm roared as Big Tom turned, instinctively swerving his gun toward the charging figure.

Alma's hands were clasped together. She brought them up before her as if to beseech Big Tom for mercy.

Instead there was a *crack!* as if a dried branch had been snapped in two. He saw a tongue of blue flame lick out from between Alma's fingers.

Big Tom's right eye disappeared in a burst of red foam. The outlaw's mouth opened in a silent yawn as he clapped his left hand to his bloody eyesocket. His revolver dipped toward the floor and finally fell from his limp fingers. The cocked gun hit the wooden planking hammer-first, so that it discharged, sending a slug into a corner of the room.

Big Tom never heard his last shot. He died on his feet, his head slumped forward onto his chest, adding fresh blood to his lapels, already stained with the blood of the murdered hardware store owner. As Longarm and Alma watched, the big outlaw fell face-first, landing hard, and lying still.

Longarm got to his feet, brushing himself off. "You had that little peashooter all the while?" he asked Alma as he extracted the spent shells from his Colt.

The woman nodded sheepishly. "It's a .22-caliber single-shot," she said, holding up the puny gun, which appeared to be little more than a thumb's length of blue tubing and a sliver of walnut.

"Where'd you have it stashed?" Longarm asked with real interest as he gave Alma's form-fitting dress the once-over. He slid five fresh rounds into his Colt and reholstered the weapon.

Alma's hands rose up to her deep cleavage. "I've got a little holster that clips on to my, um..." She blushed.

"Alma!" Longarm laughed. "Do you mean to say that your gun is holstered between your—"

"Custis, don't you say it!" she implored, casting a mortified glance toward the people who'd been attracted by the commotion.

Longarm turned his attention away from Alma's obvious charms, toward the crowd of rubberneckers now crowding around the front door. "One of you folks fetch a constable!" he ordered.

"On my way, sir!" a boy called out. He sped off, anxious to do Longarm's bidding, so that he could later brag to his school chums about how he helped a federal deputy foil a holdup.

"I take it you managed to palm that derringer of yours about the time Big Tom here threatened to rape you?" Longarm asked Alma. He mimed the way her hands had flown to her breasts in response to the dead outlaw's leering advances.

Alma nodded. "That's how it happened, Custis. I'm sorry I waited so long. You see, I know a lot about guns, but I've never, ever *killed* anyone."

Now that the shock of the morning's incidents was wearing off, Alma looked perilously close to breaking down. Her gray eyes had grown large and shiny, and she'd begun to shake.

Longarm went quickly to her, folding her within his embrace. "Listen to me," he murmured. "You did exactly the right thing. You only had one shot, and you fired it when it would count the most."

"B-but I never k-killed before!" She began to sob softly against his chest.

"Alma!" Longarm consoled her. "Don't look at it that way! After all, you saved my life!"

"I d-did?" Alma stopped crying long enough to look up at Longarm's face, to see if what he'd said was in earnest. "That's right." She nodded, brightening considerably. "I saved your life." Her eyes grew thoughtful as she stared at Longarm appraisingly.

A pair of uniformed Denver policemen elbowed their way through the crowd to enter the gun shop. "What's happened here, Alma?" one of them asked. Then his gaze fell on Longarm. "Oh, no," the constable sighed. "It's *you*." He shook his head. "Tell me, Deputy, is there anybody alive for me to arrest, or do they all go to the morgue, as usual?"

21

Longarm ignored the cop's sarcasm. "Actually, there's three out back waiting to be booked," he said.

"Go fetch them," the constable told his partner.

"You'll need these," Longarm told the officer, tossing him the keys to his handcuffs as he passed. "This one here went by the name of Big Tom," he explained, nudging the corpse with his boot. "He murdered the old fellow who ran the hardware store next door."

"What!" Alma gasped, turning pale. "Zeke's dead?"

"I'm sorry," Longarm said. "It seems that this fellow Zeke discovered these outlaws snooping around your store. They killed him for it."

The constable groaned in confusion. "Look, Longarm, why don't you just stop by the station and file a report?"

"I'll do that as soon as I can," Longarm replied, looking at his pocket watch. "Right now, I'm late to report to my boss—"

"Oh! Don't leave me alone!" Alma cried out.

"But, Alma—"

"You know," the constable mused aloud as he peered at Big Tom, "this man does look familiar. I think I've seen a wanted poster on him . . ." The constable shook his head. "'Course, it's kind of hard to tell, with his face blown apart like it is."

"Oh, Custis!" Alma once more began to blubber, forcing Longarm to put his arms around her.

"Hey!" Longarm addressed the constable over and around Alma's considerable bulk. "Could you at least get these corpses out of here?"

"All in due time," the cop snapped. "Ah! Here's the stretcher boys now!"

Longarm sighed in relief as the two corpses were heaped on stretchers and carried out of the shop, escorted by the town policeman. "See, Alma?" Longarm soothed, patting the woman on the back. "They're gone."

"Don't leave me! Please don't, Custis . . ."

"All right, Alma . . ." Longarm said, abandoning all hope of getting to work anywhere near on time.

"Here's your cuffs and keys," the second constable an-

22

nounced, reappearing from out of the back room of the shop. "Couple of our own men have your prisoners in tow."

Longarm pocketed his property as Alma clutched at him. "Did you take care of that other—" He hesitated, eyeing the top of Alma's head, which was about at the level of his chin. "—that other situation, out back?"

"Poor Zeke!" Alma wailed.

The constable winced at the noise. "It's done," he nodded.

"Thanks." Longarm sighed gratefully, rolling his eyes as Alma's tears soaked his shirtfront.

The constable winked. "Don't mention it, Longarm. I can see you have your hands full. All right, folks, the show's over," he decreed, chuckling to himself as he shooed away the spectators. "At least the show any decent people would want to watch." He gave Longarm one last, knowing nod before making his own exit, shutting the door to the shop behind him.

Silence filled the store's interior. "At last we're alone," Alma sighed. Her fingers began to work at the buckle of Longarm's gunbelt.

"Alma . . ." Longarm intoned, backing away.

"Oh, no!" Alma implored, wrapping her arms around him. "Custis, don't run away!"

"Alma, I *can't!*" Longarm groaned in her embrace.

She looked at him skeptically.

"Run away, I mean," Longarm elaborated as Alma hugged him tight. "Damn, but you're strong!"

"Even stronger than that," she giggled triumphantly. "I've built up my strength by working in my repair shop," she added. "Come on, I'll show you."

"Aw, Alma," Longarm protested. But her fingers, strengthened by years of turning screwdrivers and sanding gun stocks, had dropped a bit lower, to grab at the front of Longarm's trousers. He'd grown hard despite himself, due to the double armful of warm, wriggling woman pressed against him. Alma had now made full use of that convenient handle which filled the front of Longarm's pants. Through long experience he'd learned that when somebody had you there, it was best to go where you were being led . . .

23

"This is where I do all my repair work," Alma said as she pulled him through the velvet-curtained doorway. "See? Totally private. No windows." She let go of Longarm's crotch and began to work at the knot in the ribbon that held her bodice cinched tight.

"Alma, I'm awfully late," Longarm began.

"Don't worry," Alma reassured him. "It won't take very long." She giggled. "At least, I don't *usually* take long..." Her fingers picked at the knot holding her bodice closed. "Damn this knot," she fretted.

"Alma, you're upset," Longarm mumbled, his resolve weakening as his desire grew. "I know you're grateful to me, but I don't want to take advantage of your—"

"Custis Long!" Alma laughed delightedly. "You silly! Look at me. No man has ever taken advantage of me unless I wanted him to! Besides, Custis," she said, "you owe me!"

Longarm stared at her in puzzlement. "What do you mean, I owe you?"

"Well, Deputy," she teased. "I *did* save your life..." She gave up trying to untie the pink ribbon, and began to tug at it in frustration. "Oh, damn this stupid ribbon to hell!" she cried.

Longarm looked around the shop while he waited bemusedly for Alma to free herself of the dress. There was certainly nothing comfortable or inviting about the room, he decided. There were lathes and heavy-duty vises bolted to many of the worktables; stacks of metal tubing for gun barrels and boxes of wood blocks to be carved into rifle stocks; and tools and metal shavings scattered everywhere.

Alma strode over to where a pair of metal snippers lay beside a box of screws. She ran the snippers across the bands of ribbon.

"Alma?" Longarm began. "Maybe we should go somewhere else. This place is—"

He froze in mid-sentence. Alma heaved a sigh of relief as the severed ribbon gave way, her bodice parted, and her breasts sprang free like a pair of convicts breaking out of prison.

A pair of very large convicts, Longarm thought to himself as he gazed, awestruck. Suddenly the machine shop seemed a very romantic spot, after all.

"Well?" Alma asked, her hands on her hips. "Do you like them?"

Longarm considered the question rhetorical. Her breasts were big, firm, perfectly round, and held proudly, juttingly aloft by the muscle tone Alma had developed through her years of manipulating the tools of the gunsmith's trade.

"Well, I never..." Longarm said, as soon as he got his voice back.

"No, I wouldn't think you ever did," Alma chuckled in agreement. "Here's a nice worktable for us to use," she announced. "I've got some clean dropcloths stacked beneath it. I spread them out before I take a gun apart, so I don't lose any of the parts. Several of them, one on top of another, will make us a nice soft bed."

As she bent to gather up the cloths, Longarm decided that her nipples were like percussion caps. The description seemed apt, considering her occupation and the fact that the mere sight of them made Longarm feel like exploding.

He quickly shed his clothing as Alma spread out the cloths. He checked his pocket watch, a part of his mind still fretting over the lateness of the hour and what would be in store for him when he finally showed up at work.

"Custis, I'm waiting!" Alma scolded mildly, wriggling out of the last of her garments. "You get over here," she demanded. "Right now!"

Longarm turned and began to approach her. "My Lord," he murmured. "You are a handsome woman..."

She caught her breath, her gray eyes widening as her gaze fell to his groin. Absentmindedly she reached out to stroke a nearby length of steel tubing, cut to replace the barrel of a twelve-gauge shotgun. "Now I know where you got your nickname," she whispered in awe.

Her hands latched on to him greedily. Longarm laughed and ran his palms across the satin-smooth skin of her lushly upholstered bottom. Alma began to nibble kisses across his chest, and guided his hand between her legs. Then she clamped her thighs tightly against his exploring fingers.

She moaned, then broke free to hop up on the cushioned

worktable. She sat on the edge, holding wide her arms to beckon Longarm forward.

Her breasts were right at perfect kissing height. Longarm buried his face in her deep, fragrant cleavage.

"Ooohh! Your mustache tickles!" Alma laughed ecstatically as she threw back her head and ran her cool, tickling fingers across Longarm's broad, muscular back.

She was squirming like a puppy having its belly scratched. Longarm found that he could more effectively tease and tongue her swollen nipples by clamping his hands on her buttocks.

Alma was whimpering now. She spread her legs to lock them around Longarm's slim hips, and collapsed back upon the table, her silky, supple belly flexing as she stretched her arms out over her head. Longarm toyed his hardness against the moist, matted fur between her legs before he began to tickle his throbbing tip along her wet crevice. Alma gasped as she reached with grasping fingers to pull him in.

"Dearest, you've got to! Now!" she begged. "If I wait another moment I'm going to die!"

That was what Longarm was waiting to hear; it was his belief that a fellow ought to wait until a female had herself worked up into a proper tizzy before beginning serious business. He slid into her as easily as if she were a honey jar. He let himself sink to the hilt, and then withdrew halfway, setting up a slow rhythm.

Alma began to bray like a mare being mounted by the herd stallion. Her long, pink, finely sculpted legs rose straight up until both limbs were in the high-noon position. They stayed that way while Alma caterwauled her way through an orgasm that shook the rafters and turned the carefully laid-out dropcloths into a sodden, twisted mound of wrinkled fabric.

"That was marvelous!" she whispered as her spasms subsided. Her pretty gray eyes were still squeezed shut with pleasure. She patted Longarm's haunch affectionately. "And you're not even half done, are you, dearest?"

"Not even," Longarm chuckled. "I hope you haven't started something you can't finish, honey."

She laughed delightedly. "Let's ride!"

Clasping her hands across the small of Longarm's back, she

began to undulate her hips in long, easy lopes, to match his stride. Waves of pleasure washed over Longarm as he bucked and ground against her.

"Oh, I'm g-going to d-die, Custis!" she moaned, arching her spine in an attempt to take in every last, delicious bit of the shaft that was so marvelously impaling her. "Oh, you're doing it to me again!"

This time Longarm quickened his rhythm, herding her along into her climax the way a drover urges a steer along a loading chute. His growls of pleasure as he spent himself inside her were drowned out by Alma's wails. She experienced a series of convulsive orgasms that turned her arms and legs to rubber and left her totally vanquished.

After their breathing returned to normal, Longarm slid out of her and then hopped up on the table to stretch out for a few moments of rest before taking his leave. He would have liked to spend the whole day right here, making Alma sing, but duty, in the wrathful form of Billy Vail, was waiting for him to make an appearance.

"Custis?" Alma cooed, darting her tongue into his ear. "May I ask you something?"

Longarm pillowed his head upon her luscious breasts. "Ask away, honey . . ."

"How come a handsome stud like you hasn't yet gotten himself roped in by some lucky lady?" She giggled, her voice still thick with their lovemaking. "It's brazen to ask, I know, but I've been a widow for a while, and I could do with a real man around the house. And this business of mine does right well, I might add. So, Custis, what I was wondering was—"

"Hush now, Alma," Longarm sighed. He'd been worried that something like this would rear up to spoil their fun. He'd known Alma for a long time, and had always been tempted to get to know her better. He'd resisted the temptation out of fear that lovemaking would end up ruining their friendship. "Let's us drop this subject right now, honey . . ."

"Why?" she demanded, sounding just a bit miffed. "Is there something wrong with me, Custis?"

"Alma, there isn't a thing wrong with you," Longarm replied firmly.

"Honest?"

"Alma, you're more woman than any man deserves, and if that isn't the truth, may God strike me dead—"

Longarm was about to say more, but he was cut off by Alma's scream and a grating male voice.

"God may not strike you dead, lawman, but I intend to!"

Longarm caught a glimpse of someone striding in through the darkened doorway that led from the storeroom. Alma was writhing hysterically in an attempt to get enough of the dropcloths bunched together to hide her nudity. By the time an extremely startled Longarm got himself untangled, the intruder had the drop on him.

It was the outlaw dressed in denims and a flannel shirt, the man who'd been guarding the buckboard until Longarm had knocked him out. His hands were cuffed in front of him, and his Winchester was gone, but in its place was a Smith & Wesson .38-caliber revolver.

The outlaw gestured with the gun he held in both of his fettered hands. "I took this off of the constable who was supposed to be taking me to jail," the man smirked. "Except that I knocked him out and got away."

"Leave us alone! Get out of here!" Alma cried. "The town law will track you here!"

"Shut her up," the outlaw said. "Or I will."

Longarm's eyes narrowed. He didn't like blustering thugs who threatened defenseless women. On the other hand, he was bare-ass naked, facing an armed fugitive, and pretty much pinned to the table by the leg Alma had just now thrown across his belly.

"Hush." Longarm soothed the shivering woman. "Settle down." He figured that Alma was more likely to pay attention to his commands than to those of the outlaw.

"That's right, lady," the outlaw sneered. "You'll have plenty to scream about when I start on you."

"She has given you good advice," Longarm told him. "The constables will put two and two together and trail you here." As he spoke, he casually bunched the twisted dropcloths behind his head into a pillow. "If I was you, I'd take advantage of

28

my good luck so far by hightailing it out of Denver." He laced his hands behind his head as he settled back against the soft mound of cloth he'd created.

"I intend to leave town, lawman." The outlaw smiled coldly. "But I have a score to settle—with you, and with her, as long as she's around as an eyewitness."

"Oh, no," Alma whimpered. "Please—"

"I told you to shut up!" the outlaw growled.

"If they catch you, they'll hang you," Longarm warned mildly. As he spoke, he noticed that the outlaw had not yet cocked his pistol. Of course, cocking the stolen gun was not absolutely necessary, since the Denver police force was equipped with double-action sidearms . . .

"They're going to hang me sooner or later," the outlaw said with a shrug. "They'll stretch my neck for my part in murdering that meddling old fool that ran the hardware store next door." Once again the fugitive smiled mirthlessly. "But you know what I figure, lawman? I figure a man can't be hung more than once, no matter how many folks he's killed. Hell, when you think of it that way, it seems like I'm getting a better deal, the more folks I take with me."

Longarm stared at the outlaw. "Know what *I* figure, old son? I figure that I should have cracked your skull when I had the chance. I should have knocked you straight down to hell."

"But you didn't!" The outlaw spat. "And now I'm the one with the gun in his hands."

"Listen to me," Alma cut in. "I've got money hidden here."

"Where?" the outlaw demanded sharply.

"I'll give it to you," Alma said quickly. "All of it. Just let us go—"

"I want that money now!" he shouted.

"Alma, you fetch it for him," Longarm instructed, surreptitiously working his hands deeper into the cloth bunched behind his head. "Listen, you," he addressed the anxious outlaw. "I'll stay still, and she'll get that money for you. All right?"

The outlaw nodded in Alma's direction. "Hurry it up."

She began to blush. "Custis," she whispered, "I'm not dressed."

"Fetch the money, Alma," Longarm repeated patiently.

She began to slide off the table, clutching a dropcloth in front of her.

"Leave that cloth on the table," the fugitive chortled, licking his lips as he eyed Alma's lovely form.

"Custis?" Alma looked miserable.

"Do as the man says." Longarm sighed.

She let go of the cloth and hopped off the table. Longarm watched the outlaw. As he'd hoped, the fugitive was a no-good, dirty murderer, but he was still a red-blooded male.

Alma was just turning her attention to a wall cupboard when she heard the shot. She whirled around in time to see the outlaw's gun falling to the floor as he stared in wonder at the smoking hole in his chest. "How'd you do that?" she demanded of Longarm as the outlaw crumpled dead.

Longarm held up his brass derringer, the one that he usually kept nestled in his right-hand vest pocket, clipped to his watch chain.

"Do you mean to say you had that all the time?" Alma demanded.

"Yes." Longarm smiled. "But not hooked on to any sort of foundation garment. I brought it along to the table after we got undressed, and stashed it next to our heads beneath the drop-cloths. Of course, what with all of our love-tussling, it got moved around a bit. I had to search for it."

"But how did you know to hide it in the first place?" Alma cried out in exasperation.

"Whoa, now, woman. Slow down." Longarm laughed. "I didn't know we were going to have trouble. I just always try to keep a gun handy in situations like this. A fellow's never more vulnerable than when he's turned his attention to a lady's charms."

Alma turned pink. "Speaking of which, I guess we'd better get our clothes on. The town law will be here any moment, I'd wager." She quickly gathered up her things and began to put them on. "But, Custis, you took an awful chance on pulling that derringer. Why, you had to aim and fire, and all the while that outlaw had his gun on you."

Longarm nodded as he hitched up his britches. "That's true,

but don't forget, I've practiced aiming and firing quite a bit. Also, his *gun* may have been on me, but his *eyes* were on you—or, I should say, on your—"

"Well, you just don't *have* to say." Alma smiled wryly. "I still say you took a chance."

"I had to, if I was going to save us." Longarm shrugged. "I had something else in my favor. That jasper hadn't yet cocked his gun. A double-action's trigger-pull takes a certain amount of effort. I was counting on the fact that I'd have an edge against a handcuffed man handling an unfamiliar, stolen weapon." He winked at her. "I guess this time I counted right." He noticed Alma sadly contemplating the bits of pink ribbon that once held her bodice together.

"Custis," she moped. "When I cut it up, I wasn't thinking. How am I ever going to get home with my—my you-know-whats hanging out?"

"Come here." Longarm chuckled. Once she did, he quickly threaded his black string tie through the bodice's eyelets, so that Alma could cinch it closed.

"There now," Longarm teased, as he slipped on his frock coat and set his Stetson on his head. "We've closed the corral gate on that brace of champions—"

"Custis?"

"Yes, Alma?"

"About what I was asking you before . . ." she began bashfully.

"Honey, I've really got to get going," Longarm said, strapping his Colt around his waist.

"I just wanted to say that I withdraw the offer," she said sorrowfully, giving him a hug and a kiss. "You're a fine man, Custis Long, but you're not the man I want to marry."

"Why not?" Longarm laughed, intrigued.

Alma shook her head. "I've been around guns a long time. I love them. At least I love to sell and fix them, but the woman who hitches up with you had best love to hear them being fired!"

Chapter 2

Longarm wrapped things up at the police station and finally managed to get to the Federal Building. The stairways and corridors were jam-packed with paper-toting jaspers who had their hair slicked back shiny enough to give an honest working man eye trouble. Longarm wrinkled up his nose against the stink of their cologne as he made his way toward the big oak door whose gold-leaf lettering read UNITED STATES MARSHAL, FIRST DISTRICT COURT OF COLORADO. Alma's musky woman-scent was still on him, but what the hell, Longarm mused. He'd wear *that* sort of perfume anytime. And so, he reckoned, would any honest man, given half a chance.

Somewhere close by, a clock began to chime. Longarm counted twelve strikes of the gong. It was high noon, and here he was reporting in to Billy Vail. He was three hours late!

"Look on the bright side, old son," Longarm mumbled to himself. "You've probably set a new office record." Taking a deep breath, he hauled open the oak door and stepped inside.

The marshal's pimple-faced clerk looked up at Longarm with awe in his eyes. "Three hours, Mr. Long. Nobody's ever been—" Words failed the clerk as he stared. He had a black smudge of ink on his jackrabbit nose, and a cat's cradle of nasty-looking black rope across his grimy fingers. He was hunched over his half-dismantled typewriting machine.

"Something bust on you, young fellow?" Longarm queried.

The clerk snapped out of his stare, and shook his head impatiently. "No, I'm just putting in a fresh spool of ribbon."

Longarm just nodded. The job looked only slightly more difficult—if a whole lot dirtier—than stripping down the engine of a steam locomotive.

"You keep on with your work, there," he instructed the clerk. "No need to announce me to himself."

"He's awful mad," the clerk warned Longarm as he crossed towards Vail's inner office.

Longarm hesitated, thumbing up his Stetson to scratch at his head. *"How* mad?"

The clerk's rabbit nose began to twitch with mirth. "He's passed through the yelling stage. Passed through it about around ten-thirty this morning. Now he's at the point where he *looks* calm, but there's that low-pitched growl coming out of his throat. Like what you hear when a mean old dog has a bone 'tween its paws, and you try and take it away."

Longarm sighed. "I know that sound. Well, time for me to meet my Maker. I'll just slip in quiet-like. It'll give me half a chance to draw my Colt in case he decides to slap leather just at the sight of me."

"Awww, he wouldn't do that." The clerk sighed, sounding just a mite too wistful for Longarm's taste.

As it turned out, Vail had no need to draw his gun. He already had his big old Walker Colt lying on his desk. The marshal's bald scalp normally had a baby's-ass-pink tinge to it, but today it was flushed an angry red. "You're three hours late, you big son of a bitch," Vail murmured, his voice dangerously cold and calm. "Late, and you're not wearing a tie." The marshal shook his head, eyeing his Walker Colt. "Last time you were late, I said I'd shoot your left ball off if it happened again. Remember me saying that, Long?"

"I can explain this, Billy," Longarm promised. "I was all set to be here on time, but—" He paused. "You probably don't want to hear all this," he suggested hopefully.

Vail picked up the Walker Colt, using it to point toward the morocco-leather chair in front of his mahogany-topped desk. "Sit down," he said. "Explain. Take your best shot at it." Vail's jowls shook with malicious laughter.

Longarm took a seat and quickly launched into an almost complete report of the morning's violent incidents, leaving out any mention of his romantic interlude with Alma.

Vail's anger seemed to drain out of him as he listened to his deputy's story. When Longarm had finished, the chief marshal heaved a sigh and sat back in his chair. "I swear to God, Longarm," he said in an awed tone, "I don't know how one jasper can get into so much mischief before lunch. Experience has taught me that you likely ain't lying, so I won't bother checking out your tale with the Denver P.D."

Longarm started to breathe a sigh of relief, but it was cut short when Vail suddenly leaned forward, pointing a pudgy forefinger at him, and yelled, "But where the hell's your goddamn tie!"

Longarm's hand came up and groped at his collar. "Uh, I had one when I started out this morning, Billy," he explained. "But, uh, Mrs. Wilkerson's dress sort of came undone during the scuffle, so I, uh, had to lend her one so that she could pull herself together."

Vail's eyes narrowed as he contemplated his deputy. "Why is it, Longarm, that the more you tell me, the less I think I really know?"

Longarm started to reply, but Vail waved him off. "Never mind," he said. "I don't aim to compromise your misguided notions of gentlemanly behavior. Anyway, we've no more time to waste on why you were late, since we've already lost the morning. It's a damn shame, too. I wanted you to make the morning train—"

"Aw, hold on, Billy!" Longarm said. "I just got back from a butt-breaking case. I ain't had time to get my laundry done. Shit, I ain't even filed a report yet."

"Your sense of duty warms my heart. You can dictate it to my clerk some other time."

"That's what I always do, anyway," Longarm moped. "Billy, I'll be straight with you. I haven't got the starch left in me to

35

chase after more—" He looked bleakly at Vail. "Well, more *what?*"

"Bank robbers," Vail replied.

"More bank robbers," Longarm scowled. "It ain't fair, Billy. I've been out a *month—*"

"This case is *important.*"

"They're all important," Longarm grumbled.

"The local law requested you specifically," Vail said, a sly look on his face.

"Asked for me?" Longarm said, hating himself for showing any interest.

"Let's see now, where's that file?" Vail began to rummage through the blizzard of papers blanketing his desk.

"Asked for *me*," Longarm repeated with pride. "Well, I guess cream rises to the top—"

"Yeah, and shit floats," Vail added sourly. "I can't find the goddamned file—oh, yeah! It's in the cabinet."

The marshal's bones creaked as he rose from his chair and trudged out from behind his desk, toward the wooden files that lined one side of his office. Longarm, watching him, shook his head.

Vail wasn't more than fifteen years older than Longarm but he was about twenty-five pounds overweight. The marshal was spending too much time draining beer kegs. He was dressed in a baggy gray suit, a wilted white shirt, and a black string tie similiar to the one Longarm had started out wearing this morning. Hanging low beneath Vail's swollen gut was a gunbelt from which dangled the holster for his Walker Colt.

"I forgot that I stuck the reports on this case in the cabinet," Vail was explaining. "The first incidents took place a good two weeks ago."

"A fortnight's a hell of a long time to let a trail cool," Longarm observed.

"Look, Custis, just let me fill you in on this case." Vail pulled the file from a drawer and then returned to his desk. "If you don't want it, I'll assign it to someone else."

"I don't want it."

"You haven't heard those details," Vail said, spreading the file open before him.

"Billy, you mean I can actually turn this down if that's my choice?" Longarm shook his head. "That's not like you."

"Listen to what's happened." Vail eyed his deputy, his voice growing subdued. "You're not going to like what you hear."

Longarm stuck an unlit cheroot between his teeth and leaned back in his chair. He had a thousand questions he wanted to ask, but the years had taught him that Marshal Vail couldn't be rushed into revealing his hand when what he had in mind was playing his cards one by one.

"There's been a series of exceptionally vicious bank robberies in Texas while you've been out on assignment," Vail began. "Clerks or tellers have been coldbloodedly shot dead during each of these holdups, for no reason, as far as we can tell."

"Just pure, cussed meanness," Longarm nodded. "I've come across that kind of shootist before. But why does a federal lawman have to get involved in what seems to be a pretty clearcut local case, even if it's a bloody one? Hell, Billy, if you sent deputies after all the bank robbers in your jurisdiction, you'd need ten times more men than you've got."

"I know that," Vail grumbled. "It'll be a cold day in August when I've got to be told my job, Deputy. *I* don't mosey in to work three hours late! *And* without my tie!" He smashed both of his meaty fists on the top of his desk.

Longarm winced against Vail's verbal onslaught. "Sorry, Billy."

"Well you oughta be!" Vail huffed. "Anyway, the local law always has the right to request our involvement in a case, and after due consideration I agreed to send the man they requested. Which is you. The Texas Rangers are only concerned with cattle rustlers these days, and anyway, after you hear the rest you'll likely agree that the Rangers are the wrong hombres for this particular job."

"Let's have the rest, then." Longarm sighed, doing his best to stifle a yawn. His inability to get to sleep last night was starting to catch up with him. Of course, his involvement with the outlaw gang, and with Alma, hadn't helped matters any . . .

"The first bank to be robbed, and the biggest of them all, has put a five-thousand-dollar reward on the gangleader's head, as a sort of gesture to the family of the murdered teller. As I said, this all took place about two weeks ago. Last week I heard tell that an old friend of yours was getting involved." Vail eyed his deputy. "Fellow name of Deke Tyler."

Longarm shrugged. "Sure, I know Deke. Had the opportunity to work with him on a rustling case maybe seven summers ago, back when he was the marshal of a town in Wyoming Territory. He was a good man to have beside you in a shootout in those days, and I imagine he's the same way now."

"The way I heard it, you saved Deke's life," Vail drawled. "Is that true?"

Longarm busied himself striking a match and puffing his cheroot alight. He didn't like blowing his own horn. There were plenty of jaspers around who were ready and willing to play the braggart. "I just happened to catch a glimpse of some fellow aiming at Deke, and I just happened to be a little faster to fire, that's all." He heard the note of irritation in his voice, but decided he didn't give a damn. "It never makes me proud when I shoot a man, you know what I mean, Billy?"

"I know," Vail said, satisfied. "I wouldn't have a man on my force if he felt otherwise. I only brought it up because it means that Deke owes you a favor, one you might want to collect on before this case is over."

"So far I ain't been persuaded to accept this job," Longarm pointed out. "That is, if you weren't joshing me about my right to turn it down."

"I wasn't," Vail declared. "It's up to you, Custis, but you haven't heard it all."

"What I've heard only convinces me that I'm not needed," Longarm countered. "Deke has built up a reputation as an expert bounty hunter."

"That's a fact," Vail agreed.

"And we both know *why* Deke became a manhunter?" Longarm raised one eyebrow inquisitively as he puffed a perfect, blue-gray smoke ring.

"I've never met the man personally," Vail said, "but I've heard his story." The marshal shivered.

"Then let's not get into the grisly details today," Longarm said quietly.

"But you ought to realize that Deke can bring his quarry back dead or alive, and still collect his bounty," Vail told him.

"So what, Billy?" Longarm glanced up at the banjo clock ticking away behind Billy's desk. If he managed to wrangle his way out of here pretty soon, he could nap for a few hours and wake up early enough this evening for some well-earned recreation along Larimer's saloon strip. "From everything you've told me, these bank robbers deserve to be brought back dead if they resist arrest."

"You say that now," Vail muttered. "And so did I, until I learned the last bit of information."

"Deke will track that son of a bitch murderer and his gang to the ends of the earth, if need be. I'm more convinced than ever that I oughtn't to take this case," Longarm announced. He stood up to take his leave. "Just who is the fugitive, anyway? Do we know his identity?"

"We do," Vail sighed. "We also know that it's not a he, but a *she*."

"A woman?" Longarm blurted, surprised. "Well, now that I think on it, it's happened before. There's Belle Starr, and Kate Bender, to name two who proved that the female of the species is deadlier than the male." He tipped his hat to Vail. "I still don't want it, boss."

"It was a town marshal named Farley who specifically requested you, Longarm," Vail said. "You remember good old Farley, don't you?"

"Sure I do, and so should you, Billy," Longarm admonished. "He helped save your skin when you rode out that way after Wink Turner and his outlaw army."

"Of course I remember him!" Vail said. "It's because I feel I owe Farley that I said you'd help out on tracking down this *alleged* murderess."

Longarm had to laugh. "That's the first time I've ever heard you give an accused criminal the benefit of the doubt, Billy."

"This is the first time I've ever wanted to," Vail replied, so softly that Longarm almost didn't hear him.

"I am sorry that Sarah Township's bank got held up," Longarm shrugged. "I'd always figured that the Starbuck presence would keep most outlaws out of the area. Jessie Starbuck's ranch is one of the biggest in the state." Longarm smiled. "Maybe she and Ki will give Deke Tyler a hand. That settles it! They need me on this case about as much as a buckboard needs an extra wheel. You said I could turn it down, Billy? Well, I am."

"Jessie Starbuck can't help out on this case," Vail said quietly.

Longarm wasn't surprised. "You've met her, Billy. You know how busy she is running that business empire her daddy left." Longarm sighed. "Hell, I don't know how she finds the time to be so darned pretty..." He shook his head. "You shouldn't have told me that Jessie's not around. A chance to visit with her might have gotten me to agree to go to Sarah. Looks like Deke will have to go it alone."

"There's a reason why Jessie can't help," Vail began.

"The answer is no, Billy. *No!*"

"She can't help Deke because she's the woman he's hunting!"

Longarm stared hard into Vail's eyes. "You're telling me that Jessie Starbuck is wanted for bank robbery and murder in the town her own father built?"

Vail nodded. "I'm sorry, Longarm. I know you're sweet on her." He looked helpless. "Farley was one of the eyewitnesses who saw her gun down the bank teller. He managed to arrest her, but she broke out. Now she and her gang are on the loose." He held out the file folder. "They've hit other banks, and killed during each job."

Longarm rubbed his weary eyes. "And now Deke Tyler is on her trail?"

"None other." Vail waved the folder in the air. "She needs help real bad, Longarm. Expert help. What do you say?"

Longarm took the folder. "I say I'd better get a move on if I'm going to make that afternoon train."

★

Chapter 3

Longarm tossed and turned on a lumpy, red plush bench seat near the rear of the Texas & Pacific passenger coach. He felt about a hundred years old. He had the entire two-passenger seat to himself, and it was about half as much room as he needed to stretch out.

Narrow, swaying, stuffy railroad coaches had become Longarm's world. Two days ago he'd left Vail's office, hurried back to his rooming house to fetch his saddlebags and Winchester .44-40, and then rushed over to the stables to collect his riding tack. Vail's harried clerk had met Longarm at the Denver train station with all the papers and vouchers a federal lawman needed to travel on official business with the government picking up the tab.

That was forty-eight hours and several train transfers ago. Now Longarm's army-surplus McClellan saddle and Mexican bridle were safely stowed in the baggage car, and his personal belongings and Winchester were stashed beneath his seat. He was on the last train, and the last leg, of his journey. All he had to do was get through the night. In a few hours they'd be in New Mexico, and then, by tomorrow afternoon, they'd reach Sarah, Texas.

Longarm eyed the now tattered file resting beside him on the dusty crimson plush. He'd read and reread its entire contents during his long journey. It was the damn craziest thing! Page after page of the report made perfect sense until you'd finished the file. Then you were right back where you'd started—totally confused!

Longarm had done his best to put aside his personal feelings about Jessie. He'd done his best to be as objective about this case as he would be about a case where the individuals involved were unknown to him.

But the situation *still* didn't make any sense. Why would Jessie Starbuck become a bank robber? She certainly didn't need the money! The Circle Star ranch was one of the largest in Texas, and steers made up only a small part of the Starbuck fortune. Jessie's father had served with Admiral Perry's fleet when the commodore had opened up Japan with his gunboats, back around 1850. Alex Starbuck had been smart. He'd realized the potential in the Orient, and set about building up an import/export business that he headquartered in San Francisco. With the profits he accrued from bringing silk and jade into the States and exporting machinery to the Orient, Starbuck expanded his holdings to include lumber, minerals, and cattle. Soon, Starbuck enterprises formed a web stretching across America. Starbuck picked himself a peach of a wife named Sarah, and the happy couple had a lovely daughter, whom they named Jessica. Things went fine until an unscrupulous bunch of Prussian businessmen tried to muscle in on Starbuck's business. When money wouldn't work, they tried violence. The first assassination attempt against Alex Starbuck left him unscathed, but killed his wife. Starbuck turned the control of his empire over to his minions, and retired to his cattle ranch, devoting himself to his daughter, and to building the finest cow town in Texas, a town he named Sarah, in memory of his murdered wife. Things had stayed peaceful until a while ago, when the cartel struck again, this time succeeding in killing Alex Starbuck. The cartel thought they'd now have things their own way, but they hadn't reckoned on Alex Starbuck's indomitable spirit being passed down to his only offspring.

Jessica Starbuck took over her father's empire, and it prospered under her shrewd but compassionate rule. Longarm had met the beautiful Jessie when he was sent to hunt down Alex Starbuck's murderers. She proved herself to be a worthy ally in that investigation.

Longarm had worked with Jessie on one other case since that first one, the case where Wink Turner was brought down by Marshal Vail, and a cartel-backed candidate for the United States presidency was stopped cold by Jessie and Longarm. He and Jessie had sort of hit it off during their two adventures together. Longarm supposed that he'd grown sort of sweet on her...

Old son, you just rein in that wandering mind of yours, Longarm scolded himself. *It makes no sense to moon over Jessie, when what you've got to figure out is how to get that pretty neck of hers out of the hangman's noose!*

Once again, Longarm found himself stumped. Jessie was so wealthy that *money* couldn't be the motive for the bank robberies. But why else would anyone rob a bank? And how could she hope to get away with it? Jessie Starbuck was a famous woman in the west. Her likeness had often been printed in the newspapers, in happier times. Longarm guessed that a picture of her would once again make the front pages across the country, this time with the word "Wanted" emblazoned beneath it.

The more Longarm thought about it, the more it gave him a headache. He couldn't even distract himself by perusing the pretty little filly who'd perched herself upon an aisle seat two rows back. The woman looked to be in her twenties, and was dressed in a traveling gown and Paris hat of green velvet. The emerald hue nicely set off her blue eyes and halo of curly red hair. She had a pert, upturned nose dusted with freckles, a sparkling white smile, and a come-hither look in those robin's-egg-blue eyes. Longarm had been able to look her over during a few casual, over-the-shoulder peeks. He wasn't sure when she'd boarded, but if she was still on the train, there wasn't anyplace much between here and Sarah for her to get off.

That was another reason why Longarm, upset over Jessie's troubles, was keeping to his own company. It looked as though the red-haired woman was going to Sarah, and Longarm didn't want anything to keep him from concentrating on business once he got there.

He turned back to the manila folder, placing it on his lap and opening it to the last page. He stared at the writing on it, wishing that he could just crumple the damned sheet of paper into a ball and in that way crush it out of existence. Up until that last page, the reader could hold on to the hope that all that went before it in the report was some terrible mistake, that somebody else had been mistaken for Jessie . . .

But then the reader came to that last page: Marshal Farley's affidavit. Farley was the Starbucks' oldest and closest family friend, and he'd positively fingered Jessie as the gangleader.

Longarm closed the file. He would not reread Farley's damning testimony. Soon enough he could hear the story from the old lawman's mouth.

Out of the corner of his eye he saw a big fellow take the seat opposite him, on the other side of the car's narrow aisle. He paid the newcomer no particular attention beyond noting that he was there; he was tired, and in no mood for conversation. He tipped his Stetson forward over his eyes and shifted his long frame in a vain attempt to make himself a little more comfortable, and it was then that the fellow spoke.

"Reckon they'll let anybody ride in a train these days." The man chuckled. "I pay good money, and they let in riffraff who put their big feet up on the seats . . ."

After a momentary flash of annoyance, Longarm decided to ignore the man's rude comments. There was always somebody with a bee in his bonnet, ready to pick a—

Longarm frowned. There was something familiar about the fellow's voice, that whiskey-soaked baritone . . .

"I'll be damned!" he exclaimed as he jackknifed himself up out of his recumbent position and pushed his Stetson back from his forehead. "Deke Tyler, you old vinegarroon!"

"Custis Long, I was wondering when you'd get around to

recognizing me!" Tyler stuck his big, callused hand across the aisle.

"Lord above!" Longarm grinned as he took Deke's hand and shook it heartily. "You look just as ugly as ever!"

"I was just about to say the same thing about you, Longarm." Tyler shook his head. "But you always were just a little faster on the draw than me."

"'Least you've gotten more honest," Longarm joked.

"Faster on the draw, but slower in the head," Tyler finished with a wink.

"Just shut up for a minute," Longarm said happily. "Let me look at your ugly self . . ."

Deke Tyler had always been a tree-tall, rawboned son of a gun. Back when he'd been Longarm's age, he'd had a flat belly and agile slimness to go with his height. Now that Deke was in his forties, the years showed, and not only in his tanned, lined, leathery face, which resembled the side of a craggy mountain in the Sierra Nevada. He no longer had that catlike grace about him. Now he was more like a lumbering grizzly bear, all swag and swagger and growled warning. It was hard to tell where his stomach left off and his barrel chest began. He was dressed in low-cut canvas trail pants that showed a hint of his belly protruding over his belt buckle, and a well-broken-in, mustard-yellow wool shirt. A brown leather vest and flat-topped, snuff-brown Stetson completed his outfit, while a scarlet handkerchief sagging from his broad neck gave it a touch of color.

There was certainly nothing loud or colorful about Deke's boots or gunbelt. His boots were low-heeled, like Longarm's. They were of cordovan leather, and just now white with trail dust. Deke's holster rode high on his right hip, suspended from a cartridge belt. His revolver was a double-action Colt Lightning, with peachwood grips. It was a smaller gun, of lesser caliber than Longarm's. It looked pretty funny, perched there on Deke's hip, just about dwarfed into resembling a derringer by the girth and height of its owner.

It might look silly, but Longarm knew just how fast Deke could draw that Colt and have it pointed at some jasper. Men

45

who got themselves on the wrong side of Deke usually learned that big doesn't necessarily mean slow.

Longarm looked quickly around the coach, noticing that the red-haired woman was now paying avid attention to both of them. Longarm paid her no mind. What he was looking for was a sign of Deke's gear.

Tyler read his unspoken thought. "I've been riding a couple of cars back. Got on yesterday morning."

Longarm nodded. He knew where Deke was heading, and why, but he didn't have the heart to spoil the pleasure of their reunion just yet. It was seldom that a man got a chance to renew an acquaintance with an old boy from out of the past who was worthy of being called a true friend.

"Hey, Deke, you still carrying Li'l Squirt?"

"Why, sure, Longarm." Tyler thumbed back over his shoulder. "He's riding in my saddlebag, 'neath my seat."

Longarm shook his head, chuckling. Li'l Squirt was a twelve-gauge, double-barreled shotgun, sawed off to a twelve-inch length. A foot-long barrel didn't afford a shooter much accuracy beyond thirty feet, but that was just fine with Deke. The bounty hunter had replaced the weapon's shoulder stock with an over-sized pistol grip so that he could thumb back the hammers and fire the gun with one hand. Li'l Squirt's kick was enough to break most men's wrists, but then Deke Tyler wasn't most men. He kept Li'l Squirt in a specially designed saddle holster when he was on horseback. On foot, he kept it stuck through his cartridge belt, wedged against the small of his back, but within easy reach.

"Hell, Longarm," Deke said expansively. "I'd never go anywhere without Li'l Squirt. I'd sooner give up my Colt. Li'l Squirt actually *saves* lives. Why, nothing persuades some pissant with a price on his head to surrender and come along peaceably like the sight of Li'l Squirt's cold, black eyes staring hungrily at his bellybutton."

"But what about shooting from a distance?" Longarm asked. He knew the answer Deke would give him, but wanted to hear it again, just for the simple pleasure of it, the way a man will want to hear an old song.

"I don't *care* to shoot men from a distance!" Tyler's disdainful reply was uttered in a throaty growl. When he frowned, the lines in his face looked like desert arroyos. "Doesn't strike me as seemly for a man to gun down even the worst son of a bitch from far away. The jasper doesn't even know what hit him, that way." Tyler just about restrained himself from spitting on the passenger coach's worn carpeting. "Now, the Lord above can strike down a man from afar—that I can accept—but it seems a mite presumptuous for us mortals to do that kind of thing. No, sir! No long guns for me, Longarm. Rifles are fine if you're bird hunting, I guess, because the fact that those critters have wings sort of evens things out." Tyler wagged an admonishing finger. "But that's the only time."

Longarm grinned to himself. The old songs sung by the true-blue Westerners were still the best. "Of course, a problem arises when some fellow shoots at *you* from a distance. Ain't that so, Deke?"

"Well now," Tyler grunted, "how other men choose to conduct themselves is no affair of mine."

A quiet spot developed in the conversation. Longarm listened to the clacking of the wheels against the tracks, and guessed that he had to ask the question sooner or later. It was a tough one to ask because of the pain it would bring to Tyler, but it had to be brought up, just out of the interest and concern a man is obliged to show toward a friend. The question Longarm was trying to find a gentle way to ask had nothing to do with Jessie Starbuck...

"Deke?" Longarm began, steeling himself. "I trust that everything is fine with your daughter?"

You had to look closely to see the flicker of anguish in Tyler's narrow amber eyes. Longarm had looked closely. As he watched, Deke Tyler seemed to retreat into himself. Longarm studied the play of emotions on Tyler's face, and thought about the memories old Deke was reliving.

Wyoming Territory had always been a hard, violent part of the country. This was especially true during the years when Deke Tyler had served as the town of Redbone's first marshal. The citizens of that ramshackle Wyoming cow town had chipped in to supply their marshal with a horse. They had put bars on the windows of one of their shacks to serve as their marshal's office and jail. They had bought a sturdy length of rope to hang rustlers. That was just about all the help Deke ever got in his job as the only law for hundreds of miles around.

Still, Deke did his job well. Redbone gradually became known as an unhealthy place to be if you were on the wrong side of the law. By the same token, Deke never once allowed a hanging to take place before the circuit judge could arrive to make the execution legal. He sent a lot of men to prison, and killed a few who decided that they'd rather not go, but he saw to it that the folks thereabouts could raise their cows in peace.

It was during this period in Deke's life that he and Longarm had met. They'd ridden together on a rustling case big enough to interest the federal government. Longarm had shot down an owlhoot who was attempting to bushwhack Deke, and Tyler had promised to repay the favor someday. By the time Longarm was ready to leave Wyoming Territory, he'd been so impressed with Deke that he offered him a job as one of Marshal Billy Vail's deputies. Longarm didn't have the power to hire a man, but he knew that Vail would jump at the chance to get somebody like Deke on the force.

Tyler had thanked Longarm for the offer, but turned it down. Wyoming was his home, and there was a lady he had his eye on. Longarm said that he understood, and the two men parted as friends.

Longarm had managed to maintain sporadic contact with Tyler. Whenever federal business took him that way, he checked up on his old friend. It turned out that Deke had resigned as town marshal in order to marry a woman named Nancy and start a cattle ranch of his own. Before very long the couple had themselves a daughter, whom they named Mary. Things looked good for Deke Tyler. Longarm once or twice caught himself feeling envious. It looked like Tyler was going to end up a wealthy, Wyoming cattle baron.

It had *looked* as though Deke Tyler was going to end up happy.

Little Mary was about twelve years old the day Deke said goodbye to his wife and daughter and started out, along with the rest of the men in the vicinity, on a three-week cattle drive to the nearest railroad depot. When Deke returned from the drive, he found his ranch burnt to the ground. Nancy had been shot dead, her body left for the flies and buzzards.

And Mary, twelve-year-old Mary . . .

Deke had found her huddled in the charred remains of their home, naked, badly beaten. Raped. Many times. Her mind was gone; she was incapable even of speaking.

These things had been done to Deke Tyler's family by a gang of outlaws who'd escaped from the territorial prison. They'd vowed revenge against Tyler for his part in bringing them in; he'd held them in the little Redbone jail until marshals could arrive to take them to Cheyenne for trial.

Well, Longarm now thought as he watched Deke sag against the red plush of the coach seat, *they got their revenge, and likely enjoyed it, at least until Deke caught up with them—one at a time.*

As for Mary, her physical wounds eventually healed, but her mind and soul were another matter . . .

Deke, as well, suffered a cruel transformation. He became a bounty hunter.

As Longarm watched, Tyler seemed to come awake, fighting his way out of his reverie and into the present the way a strong swimmer will defeat a current trying to carry him out to sea.

"You asked about Mary, Custis, and I thank you for your interest," Tyler said politely. "She's pretty much the same. The doctors say that she doesn't talk or laugh." Deke shrugged away his sorrow. "But that means she's not crying either. Right, Custis?"

Longarm just nodded. What could he say? Terrible things had been done to that little girl, things no doctor knew how to mend. A sawbones could put a splint on a broken limb, but how could you heal a broken soul?

"Anyway, Custis, you should see this hospital back East," Tyler said. "I made the trip to make sure about things before I sent Mary there. This place has got trees and gardens and park benches . . . Mary's got a real fine room, and folks who care about her." Tyler's smile faded. "Of course, a place like that mostly caters to rich folks. It's expensive."

"Reckon it would be, Deke," Longarm said. The fees that

sort of sanatorium would command had to be far out of the reach of ordinary folks like Deke Tyler. There was only one way for Deke to earn the kind of money it took to keep his beloved Mary in that private sanatorium back East. A good bounty hunter could make that kind of money. Deke Tyler became the best.

"You know what, Longarm?" Tyler suddenly asked.

Longarm prepared himself, growing attentive and cautious. There was something in Deke's tone, and in the fact that he'd ceased using Longarm's Christian name, that made the deputy think a new topic of conversation was about to come around. *And this time,* Longarm mused wryly, *I'm the one who's going to feel uncomfortable.*

"Well," said Tyler warmly, "you're not answering, but I figure you're listening. During that trip back East to see Mary, I saw another patient in the place. One that you might be interested in hearing about."

"I reckon you aim to *make* me hear it, whether I'm interested or not," Longarm muttered.

"You reckon right, friend." Tyler chuckled. "It seems this patient—a young fellow in his teens, he was—came from a very rich family, a family that gave their male child the best of everything. Now that isn't unusual, because most of the patients there have rich relatives. Anyway, it seems that one day this young prince found himself an ax and chopped his mama and sister into little bitty pieces." Tyler eyed Longarm expectantly, as if he wanted the deputy to comment.

Longarm saw fit to oblige him. "Hell, Deke, I reckon anyone can go as mean loco as a rabid dog on its third day—" He froze, realizing that the sly Tyler had led him into a trap.

"I agree with you, Longarm," Tyler continued quickly. "Ain't it funny how the rich and privileged can often become just as violently crazy as the poor riffraff?"

Longarm opened his mouth to reply, but before he could get a word out, he was cut off by an imperious feminine voice.

"Do you think that's what's happened to Jessica Starbuck, Mr. Tyler?"

Both men twisted around in their seats. It was that red-haired woman dressed in green velvet, the woman who'd been

50

sending Longarm friendly signals ever since he'd noticed her.

"I ask you that, Mr. Tyler, because that's my own personal theory about the Starbuck case." The woman flashed both men a dazzling smile. "Let me introduce myself, gentlemen. My name is Birdy O'Hara, and I'm a newspaper reporter. I work for the *Philadelphia Traveler*."

Longarm noticed that all the while she spoke, her eyes were fastened on the manila folder lying beside him on the bench seat. *Old son,* he thought, *it appears that Miss O'Hara's bedroom eyes are the direct result of what you might be able to tell her about Jessie.*

"May I sit down, Deputy Long?" the freckle-faced redhead asked, quickly picking up the manila folder in order to seat herself next to Longarm. "You see, I already know who you are, just as I know who Mr. Deke Tyler is, and what he does for a living." She placed the folder on her lap, but made no attempt to open it. "I always do my homework, gentlemen. As a woman in what is predominantly a man's business, I find that I have to excel at my job in order to be taken seriously." Once again her smile washed over the both of them. At the same time she casually removed the clutch bag she had tucked under her arm, and laid it on top of the manila folder.

"This was a private conversation, ma'am," Longarm said. "By the way, Miss O'Hara, may I have that folder?"

"Folder?" Her luminous blue eyes grew round with innocence. "I—"

"The one underneath your purse, ma'am," Longarm explained. He held out his hand. "May I have it, please?" He smiled at her.

"Oh! This!" she gasped. "Why, of course, Deputy," she replied sweetly, returning the folder and his smile.

Longarm met her steady, slightly mocking gaze. The message he read in those pretty eyes of hers warned him to stay on his guard. The biggest, meanest bear in the forest could be lured into a leg-hold trap by a whiff of honey. Something told Longarm that this red-haired, freckle-faced lovely was an expert at honey traps.

Meanwhile, Deke Tyler had been busy perusing the female reporter's figure. She had fine, full breasts that strained the brocade front of her high-necked dress. Her garments did little to hide the trimness of her waist, the graceful curves of her hips, and the saucy swell of her pert rump, perched on the edge of the coach seat.

Birdy O'Hara caught the bounty hunter looking, and smiled to herself in satisfaction. "Mr. Tyler," she began, turning her attention toward what appeared to be greener, more promising pastures, "I did some investigating of the young man you mentioned—the rich young ax murderer—"

"May I ask why you investigated that young man?" Longarm interrupted. "And why you were eavesdropping on our conversation a few moments ago, before joining in uninvited?"

"First of all, Deputy Long, I wasn't eavesdropping. You and Mr. Tyler were talking in a public place and I happened to overhear your exchange!"

Longarm noticed that her blue eyes had grown dark with anger. He kept his own face poker-straight, but inwardly he chuckled; Miss O'Hara's temper was on a very short fuse! "That doesn't explain your interest in our business, ma'am."

"My interest is quite proper, Deputy," she sniffed. "I've been covering the Starbuck story since it broke, over two weeks ago. My byline has appeared on the front page of the *Traveler* every day since then. I investigated that young ax murderer for some insights into the Starbuck case. Jessica Starbuck is well known, and her sudden, sordid descent into a life of bloody crime is big news. The sort of news my readers are interested in."

"I'll just bet they are," Longarm muttered just loudly enough for her to hear him.

She flashed another sharp glance at him, and pressed on. "Anyway, gentlemen, my investigations into that young man's past revealed that his mind was warped by laudanum addiction."

Longarm rolled his eyes upward and then turned to gaze out the window at the passing desert landscape, now being painted a myriad of vibrant pastel shades by the westering sun. Laudanum, he knew, was opium extract, and as such, it was far more likely to produce sleep than a murder spree, but the idea most folks had about "dope fiends" was pretty hard to dislodge.

"Miss O'Hara," Tyler was now saying, "are you suggesting that Jessica Starbuck's behavior might be the result of opium addiction?"

The girl brightened. "Exactly, Mr. Tyler."

"Call me Deke, ma'am," the bounty hunter said with a courtly nod.

The girl smiled flirtatiously. "Thank you, Deke. It's so rare that one finds a gentleman here on the frontier."

But bullshit's plenty common, Longarm thought before saying aloud, "Let's just hold up a minute there, young lady. Nobody has proven that Jessica Starbuck is an opium addict or a drunk or anything else. Miss O'Hara, my advice to you is not to go off half-cocked here and start concocting wild theories."

"Deputy, must you be so tedious?" The redhead sighed.

Longarm took a deep breath to control his temper. "All I'm saying," he explained calmly, "is that all of this may well turn out to be a case of mistaken identities."

"Don't be absurd!" Birdy O'Hara's pouty, beestung lips curled in scorn. "There are plenty of eyewitness accounts, as you must know by now."

"She's right, Longarm," Tyler said mildly. "It isn't likely that folks who've known Jessica Starbuck all their lives would make that sort of mistake."

"Of course I'm right," she purred, a half-smile playing at the corners of her mouth. "I'd quite forgotten that people call you Longarm, Deputy. You see, I've done a little background investigation on you, as well."

"And just what have you found out, Miss O'Hara?" Longarm demanded.

"That you are a personal friend of Jessica Starbuck." Her eyes glinted as she said the words "personal friend" in a way that implied a great deal more than casual friendship. "The Justice Department had no business sending out a deputy who has a personal interest in the woman who's being called the Society Bandit."

"There you are!" Longarm scoffed. "You and your newspaper are more interested in cooking up headlines than in digging out the truth!"

"How dare you accuse the *Traveler* of printing lies?" O'Hara demanded. "Why, you don't even read our paper, I'll bet."

"I've got to admit that I don't," Longarm told her.

"And if you *want* us to know the truth," she argued slyly, "you ought to let me see that folder."

"This folder is private," Longarm declared firmly. "And if you're so all-fired anxious for facts, why is it that you'd accuse Miss Starbuck of being a laudanum addict with absolutely no proof to back up your allegations?"

"No proof, eh?" She laughed triumphantly, reaching into her clutch bag for a leatherbound notebook and a pencil. "It just so happens that I do have evidence to back up what I've said." She riffled the pages of her notebook for a moment, and then fixed Longarm with a cold stare. "It's written right here, Deputy, and backed up by the records at my newspaper's offices. On Jessica Starbuck's last trip to San Francisco, she was reported to frequent what polite society terms a fancy house, one that has been subsequently shut down by the authorities. That bawdy house turned out to be the center of the city's illegal opium network!"

Longarm felt his anger rising. He knew the case to which this arrogant young woman was referring. On his last visit to the Starbuck ranch, Jessie had told him all about her adventure in San Francisco. The Prussian cartel had been the real owners of that combination cathouse/opium den. Jessie had set her sights on foiling the villains she'd dubbed "opium rustlers" because the drug they were selling for such huge profits was destroying the lives of innocents . . .

"Jessica Starbuck's father made his initial fortune in the Orient," the girl was saying. "Miss Starbuck is fond of all things Oriental. Why, she even has a half-Japanese, half-American fellow as a bodyguard! Obviously, this fondness for the Far East extends to opium."

"Obviously, you don't know what you're talking about!" Longarm thundered.

"For instance, Deputy?" O'Hara asked, licking the point of her pencil.

"For instance, you only have *part* of the story concerning Jessie's involvement with that San Francisco brothel. She was *infiltrating* it, in order to get evidence against the owners that would stand up in a court of law." Longarm froze. This minx of a reporter was busily scribbling down everything he was saying!

"Well? Go on, Deputy," she said, looking up at him with her pencil poised.

"Just what do you think you're doing?" Longarm demanded.

"I'm jotting down your quotes for the story I intend to file once we reach Sarah," she explained.

"Now you hold on," Longarm growled. "What I've been saying is private-like. It's not for you to print!"

"You poor dear," she said condescendingly. "If you're going to play my game, you'd best learn the rules. You've got to make it clear that what you're telling me is not for publication *before* you impart the information, not after."

Longarm resisted the urge to throttle her. Instead, he savagely bent the manila folder in half and stuffed it into the pocket of his frock coat. He stood up to sidle past the reporter and out into the aisle.

"If you'll all excuse me..." Longarm stomped his way toward the rear of the car, going out onto the open platform.

The sun was just setting, casting purple shadows across the New Mexico desert. The sky was a bar of gold carelessly splashed with india ink. Longarm took deep breaths, letting the cool early-evening breeze take the simmer out of his fury. Out here where the rocks and sand and cacti never changed, a man could gain some perspective...

As the light faded, and that bar of gold that was the sky gradually became immersed in ink, Longarm heard the coach door behind him open and shut. There came the scrape and flare of a match. A cloud of tobacco smoke tickled Longarm's nose before the breeze wafted it away. He didn't turn around, but merely leaned his elbows on the platform railing.

"Hell of a thing when a man like you lets a little trollop

like that reporter get to him," Deke Tyler mused. "Why, she can't be more than twenty-odd years old. A colt like her needs to be taken to the woodshed, not taken seriously."

Longarm chuckled. "I know that, Deke. *She's* not that important, but she does have the power to print some awful lies about Jessie." He turned to face the bounty hunter. "Lies that could tarnish a good woman's reputation."

Tyler studied the glowing ash on his cigar. "Seems to me that you're digging the spurs into your own flanks awful hard over this Jessica Starbuck, son—"

"You say that because you've never met her," Longarm countered.

"That may be." Tyler nodded. He looked hard into Longarm's eyes. "But I *aim* to meet up with her." His voice was quiet but firm. "You know that, son."

"I know that the reward for her capture is five thousand dollars," Longarm replied bitterly. "It's payable whether she's brought in dead or alive, so I guess it's all the same to you."

Tyler's sand-colored eyes flashed fire, the way the desert floor will flash when the noonday sun glares down. "Now I ought to be getting riled at you, Longarm, because I never suffer a fool to speak uncivil-like to me." He took a deep breath, and then let it out slowly. "But I'm not riled, because I know you're not a fool, and you didn't mean what you just said." He nodded once. "I forgive you, Custis, because I know you're upset." That faraway look once again stole over Tyler. "I also know what being upset can do to a man's common sense," he murmured.

"I know you do, Deke," Longarm said plainly. "I apologize for letting my temper do my talking for me. I truly do, old friend."

Tyler winked, punching the deputy's bicep in good fellowship. "Hell with it, right?" He reached into his hip pocket for a battered metal flask, unscrewed the stopper, and handed it over to Longarm. "Have a swig, it'll do you good!"

Longarm helped himself to a long pull of excellent bourbon whiskey while Tyler continued talking.

"You know, Custis, when I returned that day to find my ranch gone and my wife killed, and Mary . . . well, when I found out who'd done that to me and mine, I set out after them with killing on my mind. There were five of those bastards. The first three fought me, so I did end up killing them, but by then my anger had sort of burnt itself out. The last two gave themselves up, and I brought them in alive, to stand trial for what they'd done. Since then I've hunted down a lot of owlhoots, and I do everything I can to bring them back alive. I'd rather see them spend years in a cage. Jail is a lot tougher row to hoe than a quick, clean death."

He took back his flask and took a swig. "Now, Custis, that brings us to the present situation of Jessica Starbuck."

"I'm going to do my damnedest to get to her before you do," Longarm said quickly. "I know you could use that reward money, and I'm sorry about that, but—"

"Hush on that," Tyler said, his tone friendly but laced with warning. "We're not going to talk anymore about my need for money, or why, and that's that. I don't like to tell my troubles to others, Custis. It's not my way. Hell, I've done more crying and complaining to you than I ever have to anybody else, but that's because we go back a long ways." He took another swallow of bourbon, and then stuck his cigar back into the corner of his mouth.

"Then we understand each other," Longarm declared, lighting up a cheroot of his own, and watching the breeze whip the smoke away.

"I've got one last thing to get off my chest," Tyler announced, "and then I'll say good night to you. A bunch of summers ago you saved my life, Custis—"

"Drop that, Deke," Longarm said gruffly, scowling to hide his embarrassment.

"Can't drop it," Tyler stubbornly insisted. "I owe you. Now because I do, I'm going to try extra hard to bring Jessica Starbuck in alive. I promise you that I'll do that, even though from what I've heard, she's quicker to kill than a stepped-on rattler." The bounty hunter briefly clasped Longarm's shoulder, then sidestepped around the deputy to head back to his own seat in a car to the rear of the train.

Longarm stayed outside for a while. He tried to ease his tired brain by concentrating on the wind buffeting him, but it was no use. The thoughts went around and around inside his skull like a half-wild mustang endlessly roaming the perimeter of its corral.

Sighing to himself, Longarm went back inside. He had the car all to himself. Birdy O'Hara had evidently moved forward to another coach. *Well, good riddance,* Longarm told himself.

He settled back into his seat for the night. He was lulled by Deke Tyler's bourbon in his belly and the clacking and swaying of the train, but Longarm slept little. He was anxiously looking forward to getting the facts about this mess from Marshal Farley, and from Ki.

Longarm was wide awake as dawn stole in through the window of his empty, silent coach, filling the interior of the car with a ghostly blue light that gradually brightened into a sunny Texas day. He breakfasted on a stale poor-boy sandwich he bought from the box the conductor carried through the train, washing it down with a gulp of Maryland rye from the bottle he had stashed in his saddlebags. The morning hours crept by endlessly, but eventually it became afternoon.

Longarm was ready and waiting at the coach door as the train chugged its way to a stop alongside the Sarah Township depot. He hopped down, his saddlebags thrown across his shoulder. Crates and barrels on the long, raised platform of the station obstructed Longarm's vision, so that he didn't glimpse Deke Tyler or Birdy O'Hara getting off the train. He was heading toward the baggage car to claim his riding tack when he caught sight of Marshal Farley.

Farley saw him at the same time, and began to wave. He was a big-bellied, thick-necked man dressed in baggy gray pants and a brown flannel shirt. His badge glittered on his broad chest.

As Longarm approached, Farley removed his hat to wipe the sweat from his forehead. He had a bandage wrapped like a turban around his head, making his yellow hair stick up like baled tufts of hay.

Joe Farley was usually a jovial, easygoing fellow, but today the expression on his sunburned face was serious and sad. Longarm's heart began to pound. There was an ominous air

58

about the old town marshal; he looked as if he was getting ready to tell Longarm some especially bad news.

"I guess my telegram didn't reach Marshal Vail in time, Deputy," Farley said as he shook hands with Longarm. "It's good to see you, but I reckon you've made this trip for nothing."

"You mean Jessie's been cleared?" Longarm began hopefully, but Farley's hard edge stopped him cold.

"Nope, I don't mean nothing like that," Farley muttered. "I just mean you're too late to help."

Longarm steeled himself for the worst. "Joe," he whispered, "don't tell me that she's been shot."

"Hell no, Longarm!" Farley paled. "Thank the Lord, we've averted that! She's turning herself in, you see."

"When?" Longarm exclaimed. "And where?"

"In front of my office," Farley replied. He rested his right hand on the battered old Peacemaker holstered on his hip, as he squinted up at the sun. "In about half an hour. Ki is the one who talked her into it. He'll be escorting her in." The old lawman looked doleful. "And then, Longarm, it'll be my sad duty to lock Jessie up!"

Chapter 4

"I've already got one of her bank-robbing gang in jail," Farley told Longarm as they collected his McClellan saddle from the baggage car and began to make their way to the marshal's office. "We got him two weeks ago, nabbed him right at the scene of the bank robbery," Farley boasted.

"Your report says you were there while it was taking place," Longarm observed.

The marshal nodded. "That's how come I've got this bandage on my head."

He led Longarm past the Western Union office, which was located near the cattle holding pens, and down a side street that intersected the town's main thoroughfare. "I reckon you still remember your way around, eh, Longarm?" Farley asked.

Longarm nodded. Sarah was a good-sized town. Its wide, regularly sprinkled Main Street had raised wooden sidewalks and a host of stores, saloons, and cafes. The three-story, brightly painted Cattlemen's Association building was the town's centerpiece. Stretching out in orderly blocks behind the building was the residential area. There, in addition to pleasant homes and colorful gardens framed by white picket fences, were the town church and two schools, a primary and a secondary one.

They reached the combination jail and office, and Farley kicked open the oak door. "Come on in," he invited as he made his way across the office to sit down behind his desk. "You can dump your gear in the corner there."

Longarm did as he was told. He looked around the office. A pair of windows bracketed the front door. A door to the rear, just behind Farley's desk, led to the cells. Along one wall was a rack of rifles and shotguns, all securely locked in place by a length of chain threaded through their trigger guards. On the opposite wall hung a ragtag collection of wanted posters and a duty roster that told which one of Farley's pair of deputies was out patrolling. Several straightbacked chairs stood lined up alongside a paper-littered sideboard beneath the roster.

Longarm took a chair and set it down in front of Farley's desk. He pointed at the door behind the marshal. "Is that where you've got that gang member locked up?" When Farley nodded, Longarm said, "I'll want to talk with that jasper later, but now why don't you fill me in on the events during the robbery?"

"Gladly," Farley said. "Since you're here, Longarm, I hope you can make some sense out of this sorry mess. You know, Alex Starbuck and I go back a long ways. Why, I remember the day he said to me, 'Joe, if anything should happen to me, see that you keep watch over Jessie.' Yep, he said that to me, Longarm. And now I've got to put his little girl behind bars. Why—"

"Marshal?" Longarm chided Farley gently. "You were going to tell me about the robbery?"

"I'm getting to it," Farley grumbled. "I was sitting right here at my desk when some young tyke comes running in with the news that the bank was being robbed. My on-duty deputy was somewhere on patrol—I only keep one man on at a time," Farley elaborated. "Things are usually pretty quiet here in Sarah."

Longarm nodded impatiently, wishing that the rambling marshal would get to the meat of the matter—where and when he saw Jessie.

"Well, Longarm, I had no choice but to rush to that bank all by my lonesome, and that's what I did," Farley declared. "I drew my gun and charged inside. I figured I'd take them by surprise." The marshal paused expectantly. "Is that how you'd have done it, Longarm?"

"Maybe. It depends on the situation," Longarm said. Privately he thought Farley's actions had been pretty dumb. The old boy was lucky that a knock on the head was the worst injury he'd suffered.

"There were five of them in there, Longarm. Three ordinary-looking bandits, a man dressed entirely in black"—Farley sighed—"and Jessie. They were all wearing bandannas across their faces. Jessie was wearing denim pants and a wrangler's jacket." The marshal chuckled fondly. "You know those duds she likes to wear? Tomboy duds." Farley's smile faded. "She was holding her smoking Colt, laughing over the body of the gunned-down teller lying at her feet. That teller's name was Todd Wilson. He's left a widow and four little children."

Longarm was silent and thoughtful. "Two things, Marshal. First of all, you didn't actually see her shoot anyone, and second, you didn't see her face?"

"Plenty of others saw her shoot Todd," Farley replied. "And I did get a look at her face. You see, I rushed in there so fast that I had the drop on those five—for a moment at least. What happened was that seeing Jessie there took me totally by surprise. I was dumbstruck, Longarm. I couldn't bring myself to do anything but stare. Jessie whirled around so fast that her bandanna slipped down. We looked into each other's eyes for a split second, and Longarm, I swear I saw my death in those big green eyes of hers." Farley shuddered. "But before Jessie could shoot me, one of the other outlaws snapped a shot in my direction. I threw myself to the floor and, well . . ." Farley's normally florid face turned an even deeper shade of scarlet. "I guess I threw myself down a mite too hard," he mumbled sheepishly. "'Cause my head hit the corner leg of a desk, and I knocked myself out."

The look of contrition on the marshal's jowly face made Longarm want to laugh. "Don't take it so hard, Joe. You were lucky. They must have thought that shot they sent your way had killed you. I guess they were in too much of a hurry to make sure." Longarm grew serious. "But what you're saying is that you only caught a scant glimpse of this woman."

Farley shook his head. "I appreciate what you're trying to do, Longarm," he said wryly. "I *wish* I was wrong, but I'm not. It was Jessie standing there in that bank. It had to be. That female had Jessie's walk, her mannerisms—hell, I would have recognized her even if her mask had stayed on. I bounced her on my knee when she was little." He glanced at the pocket watch set in a small stand on his desk. "And now I've got to go outside to meet her, bring her in here, and lock her up to stand trial for this bank robbery and murder, and robberies and murders in other towns in the territory."

"I'm coming outside with you," Longarm said as Farley stood up. "You might need some help."

"I am a mite worried about a couple of folks in town," Farley confessed. "Tempers are running pretty hot, you see. Word has gotten around about how Jessie hasn't missed a chance to murder innocent people during each of her bank robberies. Right here in Sarah, there's people who are claiming that Jessie is going to go scot-free because she's rich."

Outside, a small but boisterous mob had formed across the street from the marshal's office. Farley had ordered both of his deputies to report to work today. He now directed his men to keep an eye on the crowd.

Longarm counted twenty people gathered on the raised wooden sidewalk directly across Main Street. In the forefront was a silver-haired, elderly man wearing an expensive blue suit, fancy, hand-tooled Justin boots, and a pearl-gray Stetson. He was comforting a thin, plain-looking woman dressed all in black, who stood weeping into a lace hanky.

"That there is Todd Wilson's widow," Farley quietly informed Longarm. "The man in blue next to her is Bob King, owner of the Lazy K cattle spread. His land abuts the Starbuck ranch. He's about the wealthiest rancher in the territory—after Jessie, of course."

"What's his connection with the murdered teller's widow?" Longarm asked.

"Mr. King has kindly taken over the mortgage payments on her family's home, and he's given her a little something to help support the four children," Farley explained. "Nothing improper about it," he hastened to add. "Old Bob's got a wife of his own, after all. Lots of folks have contributed to the family Todd Wilson left behind. Bob King, being the wealthiest man around, has just contributed more, is all."

"What about those jaspers leaning against the front of that saloon?" Longarm asked, indicating four men wearing union-suit undershirts, dusty overalls, and work shoes.

"Those fellows are Todd Wilson's cousins," Farley muttered. "They're all honest enough, and hold down jobs, but they like to get drunk and raise a ruckus on Saturday nights. Todd was the best of the family, that's all I've got to say—"

"Hey! Marshal Farley!" called out one of the Wilson cousins. He was a tall man with the build of a physical laborer.

"Where is that no-good she-killer?"

"She'll be here, don't you fret none," Farley yelled back. "Just you keep your temper, Walt!" He leaned his head toward Longarm. "That's Walt Wilson," he whispered. "The meanest of them all."

Longarm scrutinized the group. No one was wearing guns, he was glad to see. He shifted his gaze as the men lounging against the wall of the saloon noticed him and began to mutter among themselves.

Longarm saw Deke Tyler appear behind the saloon's bat-wing doors. He had a mug of beer in his hand. He silently toasted Longarm with it, smiled, and faded back into the interior shadows.

"Here she comes!" one of the members of the mob called out excitedly. "Riding down the street like she's proud of what she's done!"

Longarm looked up Main Street. It was Jessie, all right, mounted on a big roan, moving at a walk. Ki rode beside her on a slightly smaller, chestnut-colored horse. Out of the corner of his eye, Longarm saw Birdy O'Hara push her way through the crowd to reach the sobbing Mrs. Wilson. The reporter had that notebook of hers out. Longarm wondered briefly about what sort of angry quotes the wily newspaperwoman was drawing out of the grief-stricken widow.

"Marshal!" a voice from across the street jeered. "You gonna handcuff her, or handle her with kid gloves?"

Bitter laughter rose up from the assembled spectators. Farley shook his head as he exchanged wary glances with Longarm. The town marshal noticed his nervous deputies fingering their revolvers as they watched Jessie approach.

"Leave those guns in their holsters, you fools!" Farley hissed.

The deputies looked doubtful. "But, Marshal," one of them wavered. He was a tall, gaunt man with pockmarked cheeks and a thin, drooping mustache. "She's a murderer—"

"Don't backtalk me, Chuck!" Farley spat. "Do as I say. Both of you move across the street and see to it that none of those folks lose their heads when Jessie reaches us."

Farley turned to Longarm as the pair of deputies moved to follow his orders. "They're good men, but Sarah's a quiet town. They're not used to bank robberies and killings. Chuck, there, was the deputy on patrol the day the robbery took place. He arrived just as Jessie and her gang were making their getaway. I was still lying on the floor, knocked out. Chuck managed to get the drop on the last of the robbers to leave the bank. Jessie and the other three rode away without a backwards glance."

"I'm glad Chuck kept cool-headed enough not to kill that robber." Longarm nodded in satisfaction. "It'll be very interesting to talk to that jasper."

Jessie and Ki reined in their mounts to come to a halt in front of the marshal's office. Her eyes widened at the sight of Longarm. "Custis! Have they dragged *you* into this?" she began. She seemed about to say more, but then, noticing that everyone assembled could hear her, she simply smiled wearily at Longarm, murmuring, "I'm glad you're here."

Longarm smiled up at her. He thought about what Farley had said: *"I'd have recognized her even if her mask had stayed on . . ."* Gazing at Jessie now, he knew what Farley had meant. Once glimpsed, there was no forgetting Jessie Starbuck!

Her eyes were as green as spring grass, and her long, tawny mane of honey-blond hair glinted with a hint of copper beneath the strong Texas sun. She was dressed as Farley had earlier described her, in tight denim jeans and a matching wrangler's jacket. The trail garb, designed for riding, fit her lush figure like a second skin. It did not in the least hide her long legs, her high, full breasts, and her firm, well-rounded backside. Now she sat astride her horse with her pretty head held high, ignoring the taunts of the crowd. Longarm had seen many pretty women in his day, but none was more beautiful than Jessie Starbuck, a true Texas princess, the proud product of the Lone Star State.

"Why, she's still wearing her gun!" somebody yelled. A menacing growl of outrage threaded its way through the mob like a snake.

"Leave it to Marshal Farley!" the deputy named Chuck pleaded. He and his partner scurried across the breadth of the crowd like collie dogs trying to control an unruly flock of sheep. "The marshal will do what's right," the deputy soothed, the sweat rolling down his neck and sticking his blue chambray work shirt to his skeletal back.

"Marshal, I have kept my part of the bargain," Ki said softly, brushing a thick lock of his long, blue-black hair back from his forehead. "I have brought Jessie to you." His dark, almond-shaped eyes scanned the crowd uneasily from his vantage point astride the chestnut gelding.

His eyes were the only part of his face that moved just now. Otherwise his fine-boned, angular features were immobile, unreadable, his wiry body erect and relaxed atop his mount. He turned his gaze back to Farley and said, "Can you keep your part of the bargain, Marshal?"

"Don't fret," Farley grumbled. "I'll keep Jessie safe, now that she's in my custody."

Ki nodded impassively and turned toward Longarm. "Greetings, my friend," he said, presenting the deputy with a rare ghost of a smile. "I wish that we were meeting under more pleasant circumstances."

Ki was dressed in worn, snug-fitting denim jeans, a blousy, cotton-twill pullover shirt, and a loose, many-pocketed, black leather vest. He was hatless, and on his feet he wore a pair of rope-soled, black canvas slippers. He was not wearing a gun, but Longarm knew very well that this did not mean he was defenseless; on the contrary, he was the most capable bare-hands fighter Longarm had ever met, and he was adept with an astonishing array of weaponry, both exotic and common-place.

He had, Longarm knew, been trained as a warrior—a samurai—during his boyhood in Japan, the land of his birth. His father had been an American merchant seaman, his mother a Japanese noblewoman. Both had died when Ki was quite young, and Ki, left without the protection of his parents, had been left to fend for himself, cast out of his mother's family, who had never approved of her marriage to a "barbarian."

He had sought out and apprenticed himself to an aged samurai, Hirata, who saw through the boy's skin to the warrior's spirit beneath, and cultivated that in the young Ki, until he became the most formidable of fighters.

After the death of Hirata, Ki, now a full-fledged samurai, decided that it was time he found a master to serve, since this was the samurai's function in the Japanese feudal system. Naturally, no wealthy Japanese lord could be expected to take a "mongrel" into his service, but Ki remembered his father speaking in admiring tones of Alex Starbuck. From what his father had said, Ki concluded that here indeed was a master worthy of his talent and skill. He stowed away aboard a Starbuck ship and sailed to San Francisco, where he made his way to the Starbuck offices and there pledged his life and abilities to a deeply impressed Alex Starbuck, who took Ki on as his personal servant. After Alex was killed, Ki became his daughter's companion and bodyguard, and her ally in the continuing war against the ruthless Prussian cartel.

"Jessie," Marshal Farley now said, "I'll have to ask you for your gun."

A samurai's oath of allegiance lasts a lifetime, no matter what, Longarm had learned upon his first meeting with Ki. He wondered what was going through Ki's calm mind—and through his unruly, passionate heart—as the samurai sat stoically upon his horse, watching Jessie surrender herself to the law.

The street had grown silent as Jessie slowly unstrapped her Colt from around her narrow waist and handed the gunbelt down to Farley. Jessie's roan whickered nervously at the sudden quiet as she swung her right leg up to rest it across her saddle.

"You'll probably want this as well, Joe." Jessie sighed as she tugged her derringer from the top of her boot. She dropped the tiny pistol into Farley's outstretched hand.

Farley self-consciously cleared his throat. "Jessica Star-buck," he announced in a loud but slightly wavery voice, "I hearby arrest you for bank robbery, and for the murder of Todd Wilson—"

"And for that she's gonna die!" Walt Wilson suddenly screamed in rage from across the street.

Longarm spun around in time to see the four Wilson cousins spring away from the saloon wall, revealing the rifles they'd hidden behind them. Farley's two deputies had stepped up on the sidewalk, turning their backs on the gawking crowd in order to witness Jessie's surrender. Now they were sent sprawling by the attacking Wilsons.

Longarm dashed into the street, maneuvering to intercept the troublemakers before they did Jessie any harm. He drew his Colt as he ran, hating the thought that he might have to shoot a couple of these grief-maddened relatives of a murdered man. The problem was that there were four of them, armed with rifles, and they were just about to jump down from the raised wooden sidewalk. It looked as if Longarm was not going to get a choice in the matter.

"Let's kill that murdering bitch!" Walt Wilson roared. His eyes were red with tears and fury as he took the lead, vaulting over Farley's fallen deputies and into the street. He began to race across, raising his Spencer repeater to his shoulder while zigzagging to elude Longarm and get a clear shot at Jessie, who sat frozen on her horse.

The rest of the Wilson cousins had advanced to the edge of the sidewalk. They'd levered rounds into their rifles and were aiming at Jessie, but before they could fire, a firm voice commanded their attention.

"You boys set those long guns down, right now," Deke Tyler ordered as he stepped out through the saloon doors. He had his Colt Lightning in his right hand, and his pistol-gripped, sawed-off shotgun in his left. "Set those guns down," Tyler repeated solemnly. "'Else Li'l Squirt here is going to eat you for lunch."

The three men looked into Tyler's eyes, and then into the gaping double barrels of the shotgun. "Hell," one of them chuckled nervously, "she'll hang anyway . . ." The three sent their rifles clattering against the wooden sidewalk.

Seeing that Tyler had taken control of the situation, Longarm quickly holstered his Colt. Now that it was one against one, he was reasonably confident he could stop the remaining cousin without seriously hurting him.

"Outta my way!" Wilson wailed in frustration as Longarm crabbed first to one side and then the other, waving his arms above his head to block the man's field of fire. Wilson, to his credit, made no attempt to shoot Longarm. The laborer was not a murderer, but a man who only wanted revenge against the woman he believed had killed his relative.

"Damn you!" Wilson snarled as Longarm closed in. He swung the barrel of his rifle at the deputy's head. Longarm instinctively ducked low, and Wilson, laughing wildly in triumph, quickly sidestepped, brought up his Spencer, and fired at Jessie—

But the laborer had not taken into account Ki's superbly honed reflexes. Seeing that Longarm had failed to stop the man, Ki launched himself from his saddle to tackle Jessie, sweeping her off her horse and out of the bullet's path. He absorbed the impact of their fall with his own body, his resilient muscles cushioning Jessie so that she landed as lightly as a feather.

Meanwhile, Longarm had locked horns with Wilson before he could fire again. Once more the enraged man used his rifle as a club, swinging it wildly, and leaving himself wide open. Longarm stepped in close and drove his right fist into Wilson's gut. The man grunted in pain, letting his rifle dangle from his fingers. Longarm plucked the weapon out of his hands and tossed it away.

The fight went out of Wilson with the loss of his gun. He stood with his head bowed and his hands laced across his bruised belly, looking for all the world like a punished truant squirming beneath a schoolmaster's stern gaze.

"I was wondering if you could handle that lout," Tyler chuckled from across the street, still keeping an eye, and his shotgun, trained on the other three Wilson cousins.

"Thanks for the help, Deke," Longarm said with a grin. His smile disappeared as he regarded his defeated opponent. "You know that you came close to getting yourself and your fool family killed?"

"I just . . . I'm powerful sorry, mister," Wilson blubbered wetly. "But why'd she have to kill Todd?" He wiped his nose on his sleeve. "Todd never hurt nobody. And why'd you mix in, anyway?" he demanded fiercely.

"I mixed in because I'm no 'mister,' I'm a deputy U.S. marshal," Longarm began, but he softened his tone when he saw the fear in the big, weepy jasper's bloodshot eyes. "Aw, don't worry, I ain't going to arrest you," he grumbled. Turning to where Ki stood with Jessie, he called out, "Ki, why don't you take Miss Starbuck into the marshal's office? I'll be in directly."

Ki nodded and, taking Jessie by the arm, led her through the open door of the marshal's office. Longarm watched them go, then picked up Walt Wilson's Spencer out of the dust and tossed it to one of Farley's deputies as he walked over to where Deke Tyler was keeping the remaining three Wilson cousins covered. The other deputy, the one named Chuck, was in the process of ordering an amused Tyler to hand over the prisoners. The rancher, Bob King, had joined the verbal fracas, arguing on behalf of Mrs. Wilson that her relatives be released. To add to the general confusion, Birdy O'Hara was shrilly demanding her right to interview the Wilsons.

"Custis, I got all these turkeys squawking at me," Tyler complained. "I figured to ignore the lot of them until you filled me in on your plans for these rough, tough gunslicks here." He gestured with his shotgun toward the crestfallen cousins.

"We're the local law around here," the deputy named Chuck declared furiously, his mustache twitching. "Those men are under arrest!"

"Just a moment," Bob King cut in. "If these poor fellows are put behind bars, I'll get the best lawyer I can find to defend them." He patted the sniffling Widow Wilson on her bony, black-clad shoulder. "There, there, my dear. Justice will triumph."

"Do I or do I not get a right to hear what these men have to say?" Birdy O'Hara shouted, waving her notebook like a battle flag.

Tyler slid his Colt back into its holster, but kept his sawed-off shotgun at the ready. "Custis," he said, "straighten all this out. I'm getting a headache."

Longarm took his wallet from his coat pocket and displayed his federal badge to the surly town deputies. "My silverware outranks those badges you boys are wearing, so these men are my prisoners until I decide otherwise."

"You've got no jurisdiction in this case," Chuck argued.

"You go ask Marshal Farley how much I've got," Longarm told him. "He called me in on this, so I reckon you'd better have a talk with your boss before you cross me, right?"

"Damn," Chuck sighed. He and his partner trudged off in defeat.

"I demand to know what charges are being filed against these men," Bob King said, his arm still around the widow. "And what right does a bounty hunter have to keep a gun on them, I'd like to know?" he added, eyeing Tyler with obvious distaste.

"If I was you, fellow, I'd save that evil eye for someone else," Tyler warned evenly.

King quickly stepped away from the widow and opened his coat. "I know your reputation, Deke Tyler, but I'm telling you now, in front of all these people, that I'm not wearing a gun!"

The bounty hunter shook his head. "Mr. King, I reckon you're old enough to be my daddy. I ain't in the habit of shooting old geezers, be they rich or poor."

King's gnarled hands contorted into claws. "You'll rue the day you spoke to me that way," he whispered to Tyler. "One word from me and you'll be run out of this town—"

"That's enough!" Longarm said sharply. "I've about run out of patience with the lot of you! Number one, there's a whole passel of charges I could hang on these Wilson boys. For instance, Walt there attacked me, and I figure that these other three were his accomplices. Assaulting a federal law officer is a serious offense—"

"You can charge them as you like, Deputy," King said

smugly. "Making those charges stick is a far different matter."

"Nobody said I was going to charge them," Longarm shot back. "Only that I *could* if I was of a mind to." He took a deep breath. "Which I ain't, as they're not worth the trouble, and I don't want them cluttering up Marshal Farley's jail while Jessie Starbuck is in there."

"Looks like you fellows can go," Tyler announced, lowering the hammers on his little shotgun.

"Can we have our rifles back?" one of the cousins asked shyly.

Longarm shook his head. "'Fraid not. Collect them from Marshal Farley later on. Right now, the four of you just skedaddle on out of here while I'm in a good mood."

They did as they were told, without hesitation, moving off down the street with Birdy O'Hara scampering after them, peppering them with questions. Now that the excitement was over, and Jessie was out of sight inside the marshal's office, the crowd began to disperse.

"Do we have anything else to discuss, Mr. King?" Longarm asked pointedly.

"Not at the moment, Deputy," the rancher said with a thin smile. He turned his attention to the widow of the murdered teller. "Come along, my dear. Some tea, perhaps?" he asked as he led her away.

"Well now," Tyler grinned, wedging his scattergun into its usual carrying position, beneath his gunbelt, at the small of his back. "Guess it's all done. Jessie Starbuck is behind bars, and there ain't nothing left to do but wait for the trial." He started toward the saloon. "Come on, I'll buy you a drink."

"Not right now, Deke," Longarm replied. "I want to talk with Jessie and get a word in with that other prisoner, the one Farley's deputy caught at the scene of the robbery. Thanks again for stepping in to help me back there."

"Hell, it was nothing," Tyler winked. "I still owe you for saving my life. The way I figure it, I didn't do you a favor a while ago, as much as I did those Wilson boys a favor. It looked to me like you were fixing to shoot them up some, am I right?"

Longarm nodded. "Didn't want to do it," he chuckled, "but

73

I didn't see any way out of it until you got the drop on them."

Tyler laughed. "Just call me if you need any more help, like if some stable boy gets riled at you." With that he hitched his thumbs into his gunbelt and made his way back through the swinging doors of the saloon.

Longarm collected the three remaining rifles surrendered by the Wilson cousins and lugged them across the street to Marshal Farley's office. Inside, he found Farley slumped in his chair behind his desk, and a despondent Jessie seated upon the straightbacked chair Longarm had earlier occupied. Ki stood leaning against the sideboard, his arms crossed as he watched over Jessie.

"Longarm," Farley began, "my deputies came in complaining about you."

"Sorry about that," Longarm apologized. He set the rifles down on the floor and hunkered down to examine them. "I didn't mean to tread on their toes."

"Nothing for you to be sorry about," Farley grumbled good-naturedly. "You were within your rights. I set the both of them straight. They won't give you any more backtalk."

"It's like you said, Marshal," Longarm mused absently as he worked the action on one of the guns. "Your deputies are good men, but right now the trouble in Sarah is a mite big for them to handle." He displayed the rifle he'd been examining to Farley. "Look at this Winchester, dammit," he growled. "It's got a broken firing pin. A couple of these others are just as bad. Those dumb jaspers risked their lives attacking Jessie with useless guns!"

Farley shrugged dejectedly. "It's like I told you. Tempers and emotions are running wild around here. Folks aren't using their heads. I haven't seen such an outbreak of lynch-mob fever since the old days, when folks thought every stranger had a running iron hidden in his saddlebags."

Longarm smiled at Jessie. "I guess you've not lost your knack for getting men all riled up."

"Oh, Custis, it's not funny," Jessie said miserably. "The people here have spent their lives trusting the Starbuck name."

Longarm nodded. "And now they feel bitter and betrayed. I understand all that, Jessie." His eyes dropped to the broken rifle in his hands. "I don't suppose you've got an explanation for all this?"

"Only that I didn't do it, Custis, if that's what you want to know." She bit down upon her lower lip, fighting against the tremor in her voice and the tears welling up in her wide green eyes. "I—I know it looks bad for me, but—but—" Her voice faded as she lowered her head into her hands and very softly began to cry.

Longarm put down the rifle and straightened up. He walked across the room to place a gentle hand on Jessie's hunched shoulder. He and the other two men could only exchange help-less glances as her muffled sobs filled the room.

"Damn," Farley growled in exasperated grief. "Damn, damn, *damn!*" He shook his head. "I never thought I'd rue the day I took on the job of being town marshal of Sarah."

"I'm sorry," Jessie managed to gasp. She tugged a hand-kerchief out of the pocket of her jeans and blew her nose. "There, I'm all right now. I will *not* embarrass myself, or any of you, again!" Her eyes gleamed like wet emeralds as she fixed a look of determination upon her tear-streaked face. "Not again," she repeated quietly. "I suppose it's time for me to be locked up?"

Farley shrugged, and then nodded timidly. "I've got no choice in the matter, Jessie."

"You could use your authority as town marshal to release her on bail until the circuit judge arrives," Ki suggested.

Farley shook his head. "I can't rightly do that, considering the seriousness of the crimes she's been accused of," he said, his tone dismal. "Folks would say that she was getting special treatment, and they'd be right." Farley frowned at Ki. "Any-way, letting Jessie wander around free would defeat the whole point of our plan."

"What are you two jaspers jawing about?" Longarm de-manded.

"Perhaps I should explain," Ki broke in. "I'll start from the beginning. Marshal Farley's head injury during the bank holdup kept him bedridden, but he sent his two deputies out to the Circle Star to arrest Jessie—"

"Wait a minute," Longarm interrupted. "Was Jessie at the

75

ranch, with you, on the day of the robbery?"

"Regrettably not," the samurai replied. "It is our misfortune that Jessie chose the previous morning to leave the ranch for a few days to ride the range."

"You mean to say she went out all by herself?" Longarm asked.

"Hey, you!" Jessie scolded the deputy. "Just because I've been arrested doesn't mean I can't talk. The answer to your question is that I most certainly *did* go by myself. I often camp out for a few days all alone. Sometimes I like to be alone! What's wrong with that?"

"Nothing. I give up!" Longarm chuckled. "It's just kind of unusual for a woman to do that sort of thing." He winked at her. "But I always said you were unusual."

Jessie just smiled, but her blush revealed her pleasure at Longarm's compliment. "Ki knew where I was planning to camp, in case I was needed back at the ranch, but—"

"But," Longarm said, "knowing where you are is not the same as being there with you. I was hoping that Ki could supply you with an alibi for the day in question, but then I very much doubt that his testimony would stand up, considering his long relationship with your family." He turned back to Ki. "What happened next?"

"When the deputies demanded that Jessie be turned over to them, I explained that she was not on the immediate premises." He smiled. "I neglected to inform them that I knew exactly *where* she was, and the two deputies, in their excitement and haste, neglected to ask me that particular question."

"They rode back empty-handed," Farley said in disgust. "I rode out there myself, as soon as I was able," he added, gingerly tapping the bandage covering his head.

"By then, a few days had passed," Ki continued. "I had made contact with Jessie, told her as much about this madness as I knew, and suggested that she stay hidden until I was able to get to the bottom of it all."

"That's how things remained for a week or ten days," Farley added. "Ki and I were at a standoff. I threatened to haul him in for obstructing justice, but he convinced me that if I left him alone, he'd figure out a way to clear Jessie." The marshal blushed. "So I left him alone, because I *wanted* Jessie cleared, even though folks in town had begun to talk among themselves about how maybe I was too personally involved to be the law in this case. Anyway, Longarm, that sort of talk can lead to a lynch mob, and I wanted to nip that kind of trouble in the bud. So I wired your boss, Billy Vail, and asked that you be sent. I figured a federal badge would put some scare into a hanging mob." He grinned. "I guess I figured right."

"So far, at least," Longarm muttered. He turned to Ki. "Did you find anything out?" he asked.

"I'm afraid I didn't," the samurai admitted, staring at the floor. "Meanwhile, other bank robberies and murders were being committed, and Jessie was being blamed for them, as well. Marshal Farley warned me that vigilante groups had formed to hunt Jessie down. While she was hiding out, there was always the chance that those bloodthirsty hunters might stumble upon her."

"I told Ki that if he persuaded Jessie to surrender herself to me, I could keep her safe," Farley said. "Her being in my jail would also give her an airtight alibi against any further crimes committed in her name."

"So here I am," Jessie sighed. "And here I'll stay, locked in a cell until the judge arrives."

"When will that be?" Longarm asked.

"Another fortnight," Farley replied, glancing at a wall calendar. "I reckon the county seat will want her, but I can call in enough old favors to keep her here for the time being." He smiled at Jessie. "At least here you'll be more comfortable."

Jessie smiled back at the marshal. "Thank you, Joe. For everything. You've been as fair as could be . . ."

"Aw, shucks, Jessie," Farley murmured. "It's not like I think you're guilty—" He hesitated, staring blankly. "But then again, I saw you in that bank. Saw you with my own eyes!" He groaned in confusion. "Come on, I'll rest easier, and maybe be able to think clearer, once I've got you safely locked away." Farley opened his desk drawer for the ring of keys to the cell block behind his office.

"Before you do that, I'd like to talk to your *other* prisoner," Longarm spoke up.

"It's a waste of time," Farley warned. "I've already grilled him, and he sticks by his story that Jessie is the gangleader."

"I'd still like to try," Longarm said. "That outlaw is the only person who could positively clear Jessie, here and now."

"All right." Farley held up the key ring. "But I'll have to ask you for your gun. I know there are very few men who could get the drop on you, Longarm, and that down-and-out coyote I've got back there isn't one of them, but I still can't take the chance. This town is a powder keg sitting next to a campfire. A jailbreak would be just the sort of spark that would blow things sky-high."

Longarm slid his Colt from its holster, slapping it down on Farley's desk in exchange for the ring of keys. "What's this fellow's name?"

"Calls himself Smitty," Farley replied. "I've never seen him before."

Longarm nodded. "Well then, I guess Smitty and I are going to have a chat." He shrugged off his frock coat and hung it across the back of Jessie's chair. "Whatever you folks hear, just ignore it," he instructed.

Farley's eyes narrowed, but it was Jessie who spoke up. "Custis," she warned, "I won't have a prisoner roughed up on my account! I don't want that sort of help!"

"Nothing like that," Longarm assured her. "Just all of you stay out of the jail, no matter what," he repeated. "Smitty and I can best conduct our business together *in private*."

Chapter 5

Longarm made his way around Farley's desk, opened the door to the cell area, and walked through, shutting it firmly behind him. The jail behind the marshal's office was built like a stable. It was long and narrow, and consisted of three cells in a row. Smitty was in the last cell. Just now the prisoner was standing on his bunk, his ear pressed against the bars of the cell's single window, set high up on the wall. He hadn't heard Longarm enter, which gave the deputy a moment to study up on the man who held the key to this mystery.

The captured outlaw was short and slender. Longarm reckoned that Smitty stood no more than five feet seven inches tall, and couldn't weigh more than one-forty. He was wearing broken-down jeans covered with patches, and a scarlet flannel shirt, its sleeves raggedly torn off at the elbows. A hat that looked as if it had been trampled on in a cattle stampede rested on the pillow at the head of the bunk. The only things the least bit noteworthy about Smitty were his boots, cut from crimson-dyed leather and studded with conchos. Like most cowboys on either side of the law, Smitty had chosen to invest the little money he had in Justin boots, sadly neglecting the rest of himself.

Longarm silently approached the cell. When he reached the door, he jingled the key ring. Smitty's head swiveled around at the sound like that of a dog hearing its master's call. He had thick black hair that fell down his forehead in greasy ringlets, and a bushy beard that hid the bottom half of his face. His bright blue eyes seemed to fill with mirth as he regarded Long-arm.

"What's going on, Deputy?" The little man laughed excitedly, hopping down from his bunk to caper like a monkey in a cage. He had a high, thin voice that rose to a cackle as he spoke rapid-fire. "I heard a shot, but then nothing! Who got killed? Come on, Deputy! Tell me! Did Jessica Starbuck turn herself in?"

Longarm said nothing, but merely waited, amused, until Smitty ran himself out of breath. He used the time to search his memory; *something* about this jailbird struck him as familiar . . .

At last Smitty paused to breathe. He gripped the bars of his cell door. "You're not answering me, Deputy." His eyes looked feverish. "You don't answer me, I don't answer you, get it?"

"Step back from the door," Longarm told him.

"You coming in here?" Smitty asked anxiously, but he did as he was told.

"We're going to have a talk," Longarm explained. He let himself into the cell and then locked it up behind him. "I'd like to know how you knew I was a deputy," Longarm said, slipping the key ring into his pants pocket. "I'd like to know why you seem so familiar to me, Smitty."

"You never saw me before, Deputy," the little man replied nervously. He tried to get away from Longarm, who towered over him, but there was nowhere to go in the tiny cell. He settled for sitting down on the bunk.

Longarm looked around. There was nowhere for him to sit, the only furniture in the cell being the bunk along the back wall. There was an odorous slop bucket in the corner. Since sitting beside Smitty, who also didn't smell that good, lacked appeal, Longarm decided to remain standing.

"I may not know *you*," Longarm told the prisoner, "but you knew I was a deputy marshal as soon as I walked in here, and I'm not wearing my badge. How's that, Smitty?"

The little outlaw shrugged. "I guess that town marshal must have mentioned something about you coming." He brightened. "Yeah, that's it! The old codger with the bandage around his noggin told me."

"Uh-huh," Longarm acknowledged, meanwhile trying to place the familiar-looking man. He stared at Smitty's beard. "How long have you had those whiskers?"

"What, these?" Smitty laughed. "Why, for years, Deputy. What about Jessie Starbuck?" He chattered eagerly. "Is she here? Did she turn herself in or did they catch her?"

"She turned herself in. By the way, Smitty, just how did you come to link up with Jessica Starbuck?"

"I rode in to her ranch some months back," the prisoner explained. "I asked for a job, and was told that they were all filled up on drovers and wranglers. I was leaving when Jessie herself approached me and said that she had another kind of job I might be interested in." He smiled, his teeth shining white against his greasy black beard. "And here I am, Deputy. I guess that job she had in mind didn't turn out too profitable for either of us."

"Oh, I don't know about that," Longarm mused. "*You* sure got the short end of the stick, that I'll admit, but Jessie and the rest of the gang stole a lot of loot from those banks."

"Yeah, well . . ." Smitty frowned. "She's caught now."

"*You're* caught," Longarm corrected him. "Miss Starbuck turned herself in. Things like that can make a big difference in the minds of a judge and jury."

"You don't have to tell me about the law—" Smitty shut up fast, fear flickering in his eyes as he realized his mistake.

"Oh," Longarm remarked, "so you've been accused of crimes before! Where would that be, old son?"

Smitty winked at Longarm. "You're a clever one, aren't you, lawman? All right, so I've been in a little trouble before. What of it? Jessie Starbuck out there is the murderer, not me! Why don't you grill her, Deputy?"

"I'll be getting to her soon enough," Longarm promised the

man. "One thing I'm going to ask her is why she and her gang just rode off and left you." He shook his head sympathetically. "That wasn't very square of them, right?"

"Nope," Smitty replied, his voice tight. His foot began to tap a staccato rhythm against the plank floor of the cell. "Look, I don't want to answer any more questions, all right? A counselor-at-law came around to see me last week, but he's not been back. Where's that counselor, huh?"

Longarm moved closer to the prisoner. "I *do* know you from somewhere," he muttered. Smitty tried to shrink away, but Longarm gripped him by the chin to tilt his head up to the light coming in through the cell's high window.

"Old son, I think it's the beard that's giving me trouble," Longarm decided. "Why don't you shave for me, Smitty?"

"Hey! I don't want to!" Smitty cried out. He tried to pull away, but Longarm's strong fingers gripped his chin whiskers. "Let go. You can't make me shave!"

Longarm released the prisoner's chin in order to grab hold of his shirt front with both hands. He lifted Smitty straight up off his bunk, shaking him out like a dusty saddle blanket. "Friend, I can make you do anything I want," he said impatiently. "Shaving is the least of it!"

"A-all right," the little prisoner implored, his crimson boots dancing madly on thin air. "Just put me d-down!"

Longarm set him down. Smitty suddenly balled his hands into fists and slammed a one-two combination into Longarm's belly. It happened so fast that Longarm didn't have time to block. He simply tightened up his stomach muscles and took what Smitty had to dish out. They weren't bad punches. The little jasper was quick, and knew how to put his shoulders into it. On the other hand, his punches didn't hurt Longarm very much. Smitty was just too small to do a large, fit man any damage.

"You finished, old son?" Longarm asked.

Smitty dropped his hands to his sides. "I would've punched you in the nose if I could've reached it," he moped. He tensed himself, shut his eyes, and waited for Longarm to retaliate.

Longarm patted him on the shoulder. "Next time pick on

somebody your own size." He chuckled. "Reckon I deserved what you gave me," Longarm continued. "I never should've lifted you up like that, but you riled me, and today my patience is running thin. We'll call it all even."

Smitty nodded. "Do I still have to shave?" he asked slyly.

"Yep," Longarm replied. "The only choice you've got is how you want to do it: with a sharp razor, water, and soap, or Indian style."

Smitty shook his head, puzzled. "I don't get it."

Longarm grinned. "The Indians *pluck* their whiskers out, one by one."

Smitty shuddered. "Make it *hot* water, and it's a deal."

One of Farley's deputies brought what was required, and then Longarm was once again left alone with the prisoner inside the cell. It took Smitty a quarter-hour to scrape his cheeks clean. When he was done, he wiped the last traces of soap from his shiny pink face and turned to present himself to Longarm.

"I thought so!" Longarm beamed. "I thought I recognized you." He pondered for a moment. "Leroy Hoggs! I arrested you two or three years ago in Nebraska. You were drawing up fake bills of sale for stolen cattle."

"I knew I was done for as soon as I saw you jingling those keys, Longarm," the prisoner said dully.

"The way I heard it, Leroy, you escaped during your trial," Longarm continued.

"Told them I had to go to the outhouse, and slipped away through a loose board while the guard waited out front. Sometimes being small has its advantages," Hoggs boasted. "I've been on the run ever since."

Longarm nodded. "Are you ready to change your story about how you came to join Jessica Starbuck's gang? We both know there's no way you'd have applied at her ranch for a job."

"I wouldn't know which end of the cow to rope," Hoggs agreed dejectedly. "Look, Longarm, if I tell you the truth, what's in it for me?" He paused. "I'm facing a trial for armed robbery and being an accomplice to murder. You know me, Longarm, I'm no killer!" He laughed nervously. "Sure, I carry a gun and all, but I've never shot anybody!"

"I know that, Hoggs." Longarm shook his head. "But it looks bad for you. I suppose I *could* take you back to Nebraska to stand trial for that business..."

"Yeah, you could do that," Hoggs murmured hopefully.

Longarm smiled. "You'd only get five or six years for that. It'd be a lot better than getting hung, wouldn't it, Leroy?"

"It's a deal, Longarm!" Hoggs said in obvious relief.

"All right, then. Start talking!"

Hoggs was only too glad to begin. "About a year ago I joined up with Seth Weeks's gang. He's got a hideout here in Texas, in a cow town past its glory named Roundpatch. The place is a ghost town now, except for bandits..." Hoggs giggled. "Seth Weeks calls himself the 'outlaw mayor' of Roundpatch. Everybody there answers to him."

Longarm was skeptical. "From what I've heard, Seth Weeks is a pretty tough hombre."

"Sure, he's tough!" Hoggs laughed. "I bet he's killed even more men than you, Longarm!"

"Maybe so," Longarm said evenly. "Reckon that's one contest where I don't mind coming in second. Anyway, what would an hombre like Weeks want with the likes of you, Leroy?"

Hoggs raised himself up to his full height and puffed out his chest. "I'm no use in a scrap, but I'm the best ink artist around. Weeks and his men are tough, but most of them can't read or write their names, let alone draw up a phony bill of sale. Now and again they'd rustle some cattle. Until I joined up with them, they had to take the beef down to Mexico to sell it. With my counterfeit papers, they can drive those cows east to the railway depots. There's always a buyer from Nebraska or Kansas who's willing not to look too close at an altered brand, and providing the paperwork appears to be in order, he's willing to pay top dollar for good cattle."

"That still doesn't explain how you ended up involved in a bank robbery, Leroy," Longarm pointed out.

Hoggs's newly shaven features took on a stubborn expression. "I know a lot more, Deputy. About a lot of things..."

"Then speak up," Longarm demanded.

"I don't think so." Hoggs shook his head. "Not until I get some kind of guarantee," he said craftily. "Yeah, that's it . . ." He moved over to the bunk and squatted down like a mule refusing to budge another inch.

Longarm took two quick steps to loom over him. "You're trying my patience again, Leroy. If I pick you up this time, it'll be by those fancy red boots of yours . . ."

"Hold on, Longarm," Hoggs said, shrinking back against the cell wall. "You can rough me up, that's a fact, but I can take a punch if I have to." He shivered, and then repeated, "If I *have* to. And in this situation, that's what I'll do . . ."

"Leroy, what am I going to do with you?" Longarm sighed, his hands on his hips. He'd only been bluffing about working the little jasper over. Longarm had never in his career as a lawman used force on a man, unless it was to take or keep him in custody. He wasn't about to start beating up prisoners now. "A guarantee, huh?" he asked dourly.

"Look at it from my side, Longarm," Hoggs chattered shrilly. "I know plenty! But once I give you what I know, I can't take it back if you decide to leave me to these Texans who're hankering to see my neck stretched!"

"All right, Leroy." Longarm grimaced, clapping his hands over his ears. "Simmer down! What do you want me to do?"

"Write it down on paper that you'll take me back to Nebraska." Hoggs swung his legs up onto the bunk and stretched out with his hands behind his head. "Yeah, Longarm, write it down on paper." He winked. "Things inked on paper have always suited me mighty fine."

"You'll get your paper, Leroy," Longarm replied. He collected the razor that Hoggs had used to shave with, and then unlocked the cell door. "See you in a while," he said.

"Why don't I wait for you here?" Hoggs remarked caustically.

"Goodbye, Leroy." Longarm chuckled, leaving the cell and then relocking it. He headed down the long, narrow corridor toward the door that led to Farley's front office.

"Deputy?" Hoggs called.

Longarm turned. "What is it?"

"I've got one more request."

Longarm made a fist and shook it at Hoggs. "I've about had all the trouble I'm going to take from you."

"Simmer down," Hoggs blurted uneasily. "This won't cost you anything." He began to blush. "I want you to call me Smitty, not Leroy. I *hate* the name Leroy, always have. I've gotten used to 'Smitty' these last couple of years. Okay?" he finished meekly.

Longarm rolled his eyes toward the ceiling. "See you in a bit, *Smitty*."

Marshal Farley swung around in his swivel chair to confront Longarm as he made his entrance into the office. Like Jessie and Ki, Farley had an expectant look on his face. "What's going on? What's happened?" he demanded.

"Here's the razor," Longarm said. "And your keys, Joe." He handed the items to Farley as he made his way around the desk and into the center of the office. "Not that our prisoner in there is the type to use a straight razor—either on us or himself," he added wryly. "He's not the suicide type."

"Did you get anything out of him?" Farley asked. "What was all that about having him shave?"

"His real name's Leroy Hoggs, and he's wanted for forgery in Nebraska," Longarm began. "I'll fill you in on all of that later, Marshal. I had him shave because I thought he looked familiar, but I had to get those whiskers off his face to be sure."

"Did he say anything that might help Jessie's situation?" Ki asked.

"He started to tell me some things, but I had to make a deal with him before he'd promise to tell us what we really want to know," Longarm replied.

"What sort of deal?" Farley asked suspiciously.

Longarm looked uneasy. "It's kind of a long story, Joe, with an ending you're not going to like." He patted Farley on the shoulder. "Just trust me for now. And give me a pen, some ink, and a sheet of paper."

Farley was mystified. "Hell of a time to write a letter, is all I've got to say," he mumbled as he began to rummage through his desk for the needed objects.

"I'm not writing a letter." Longarm smiled. "I'm drawing

up an agreement between Hoggs and myself. He wanted certain points between us written down on paper."

Farley handed him a bottle of ink and a pen. "You'll find paper stacked there on the sideboard. I don't know what you promised that man," he warned, "but I hope you know you've got no authority to make a deal with *my* prisoner."

"Oh, I know that," Longarm assured him, "and you know it, but old Leroy doesn't. He's mighty comfortable with things spelled out on paper, all nice and proper, because he's always been able to make money by doing the spelling."

"But everything he's ever written has been a forgery," Farley pointed out. "Bills of sale not worth the paper they were printed on..."

Longarm just nodded, his grin stretching wide. He pulled a chair over to the sideboard and quickly jotted down the promises he'd made to Hoggs. He was feeling very optimistic about being able to clear Jessie in just a little while. Once Hoggs confessed everything he knew, the real bank robbers would be identified. At the most, the robbers would be apprehended; at the least, Jessie would be safely out of it.

At that point, Longarm figured he could cajole Farley into handing Leroy Hoggs over to him. After all, Hoggs had not even made it through the first of the series of bank robberies, and he was about to supply Farley with information that could well lead to the marshal's having a whole jail full of *real* desperadoes to bring to court when the circuit judge arrived. Hoggs was not about to go scot-free. Longarm would see that the petty crook paid his debt to society in a Nebraska prison.

He set down his pen and waved the sheet of paper in the air to dry the ink. It looked as though everyone would be happy, including himself. To tell the truth, he felt obligated to keep his word to Hoggs, who deserved a small break in exchange for bringing about the capture of some bigger fish, and saving Jessie Starbuck from the gallows!

Longarm got to his feet. "It's a fine feeling when a thorny-looking case suddenly turns out to be any easy one to solve." He chuckled.

"Custis, do you really think it's going to be all right?" Jessie asked hopefully. "I can't believe this nightmare is almost over."

Longarm winked at her. With his drawn-up agreement in hand, he made his way around Farley's desk and through the door to the jail. As he approached Hoggs's cell, he saw that the prisoner was once again standing on his bunk in order to press his ear to the barred window. *What could Hoggs be listening to now?* Longarm wondered.

"Leroy? I mean, Smitty?" Longarm called.

Hoggs spun around. "It's Longarm!" he said loudly.

"What the hell?" Longarm gaped. He heard wood splintering, and a woman's surprised yelp coming in through the jailhouse windows. Hoggs had been talking with someone outside in the alley that ran alongside the jail!

"Ki!" Longarm shouted at the top of his lungs. *"Check the alley!"*

He let the sheet of paper flutter to the floor as he sprinted back along the corridor and wrenched open the door to Farley's office. The marshal was on his feet, his Peacemaker in his hand, and Ki was just stepping out the front entrance. As Longarm watched, Ki streaked past one of the front windows to careen around the corner of the building and into the alley.

Farley was pale with alarm. "Is it a jailbreak?"

"Don't know," Longarm snapped as he snatched his Colt off the marshal's desktop and threw himself back into the jail corridor.

Longarm's greatest worry was not that somebody was trying to free Hoggs, but to kill him. The little man wasn't worth spit to the bank-robbing gang, but if he spilled what he knew to the law, he could cause those bank robbers some trouble...

Hoggs was still standing on his bunk, craning his neck to see what was going on outside his window. His bright blue eyes grew big and round at the sight of Longarm's Colt.

"Hey now, Deputy!" Hoggs raised his hands over his head. "Don't shoot!"

"Get down on the floor, you damn fool!" Longarm shouted.

"Huh?" Hoggs stared back, confused.

"Get down!" Longarm roared. He raised his Colt to cover the cell window in case a sniper appeared to ambush the prisoner.

Hoggs misinterpreted Longarm's intent. "Don't shoot me!"

he squeaked, flopping to the floor and then crawling underneath his bunk.

"Ki!" Longarm called out, hoping the samurai could hear him through the windows of the cell block. "What's going on? Are you all right?"

Ki's voice came back loud and clear from the alley. "There is no danger, Longarm! I have the intruder in hand! Meet me back in the office!"

"C-can I get up?" Hoggs asked.

Longarm nodded, holstering his Colt. "I'll be back to see you in a minute!"

He returned to Farley's office in time to see Ki reappear in the front doorway with a kicking, squalling Birdy O'Hara tucked under his arm. "I should have known," Longarm muttered.

"Tell this lout to put me down!" the woman howled.

"Who is that?" Jessie demanded in consternation.

"Her name's Birdy O'Hara, and she's a so-called journalist from back East." Longarm sighed as Ki set the livid lady reporter on her feet.

"I found her lying sprawled in a clutter of wooden crates," the samurai explained. "Evidently she had stacked them up into a makeshift ladder in order to reach the prisoner's cell window."

"The question is why," Longarm mused.

"I wanted to interview the outlaw who rode with *her*," Birdy O'Hara sputtered, pointing at Jessie. "What's wrong with that?" She brushed the dust from her green velvet skirt.

"You could have asked us for permission," Longarm said.

"Permission?" Birdy laughed, brushing back her thick, red, curly hair. "I don't need your permission to do my job, Deputy Long." She smiled wickedly. "Or should I call you Longarm, as Mr. Hoggs does?"

Longarm's eyes narrowed. "Just how long were you out there?"

"Long enough to hear your entire conversation with Mr. Hoggs," O'Hara announced with a toss of her head. "Long enough to hear about Seth Weeks, and the outlaw town of Roundpatch—"

"Confound it!" Farley exploded. "I don't even know about this! What's going on around here?"

"Let me explain it to you," the blue-eyed, freckle-faced reporter answered sweetly. "Because you won't get any information out of Longarm, I can attest to that! Your prisoner just confessed to Deputy Long that Seth Weeks and Jessie Starbuck are in league—"

"He did not say that!" Longarm growled. "He said that he's one of Seth Weeks's men, all right, but Jessie's not yet been mentioned."

"Well, perhaps I am reading between the lines a bit," O'Hara confessed demurely. "I suppose we'll have to wait until we get to Roundpatch before Miss Starbuck can be positively linked with the notorious outlaw."

"What do you mean, 'until *we* get to Roundpatch'?" Longarm asked.

"I've never in my life laid eyes on Seth Weeks!" Jessie said.

"That's *your* story, sweetie." O'Hara smiled. She produced her notebook and pencil from her skirt pocket and jotted down Jessie's remark. "But then you *would* say that, wouldn't you, sweetie?"

Jessie got to her feet. "How would you like to have your rooster-red hair torn out by the roots, *sweetie?*" she asked, her tone icy cold.

Birdy shook her head sadly. "You are a violent one, aren't you, Miss Starbuck? Marshal, shouldn't she be locked up?"

"How dare you?" Jessie huffed. She began to advance upon the reporter.

"Hold on now," Longarm soothed, stepping between the two women. "A cat fight between you two is the last thing we need."

"Marshal, I demand that Jessie Starbuck be put behind bars, in the name of public safety!" O'Hara declared hotly. "Then we'll discuss our departure for Roundpatch."

"There's that 'we' again," Longarm groaned.

"Don't you be telling me my job, Miss O'Hara," Farley grumbled. "And as far as going to Roundpatch is concerned, you can just forget it."

"Now see here, Marshal Farley—" Birdy paused to lick the point of her pencil. "Is that F-A-R-L-E-Y?"

Farley sighed. "There's no way you can be allowed to go

to Roundpatch. It's no place for a woman, especially a pretty little thing like you. They'd eat you up alive in Roundpatch. Why, *I* don't even go there."

"You mean to say that you let dangerous outlaws roam free?" Birdy asked incredulously.

"Roundpatch is out of my jurisdiction," Farley said. "Up until the bank robbery, Seth Weeks's gang has stayed clear of Sarah Township." He nodded toward Jessie. "Mostly because of the Starbuck presence hereabouts," he added.

"I see." Birdy smiled thinly. "Well, I warn you all that I fully intend to accompany you on your excursion to Roundpatch to bring Seth Weeks to justice. That is the only way I can be sure you won't attempt to whitewash Jessica Starbuck's part in all of this!"

"Now I'm losing my temper, little miss," Farley fumed. "Nobody has ever accused me of being a crooked lawman before, and I don't cotton to it now."

"You've got a choice," Birdy said flatly. "Take me with you when you go after Seth Weeks, or I write it up the way I just told it!"

"Get out of my office," Farley said thickly.

"First I want to see Jessie locked up!" the reporter demanded.

"Get out of here before I lock *you* up!" Farley roared.

"You're going to read about this, Marshal," Birdy warned. "That is, *if* you can read!" She turned on her heel and flounced toward the door. She pulled it open, stared outside, and then looked back in with a nasty smile. "I think I'd rather be outside with all of *them*, than in here with you poor people." She giggled.

"What are you talking about?" Longarm said as he crossed to one of the office's front windows.

"Good luck, Miss Starbuck." The reporter leered. She hurried out, calling over her shoulder, "You're going to need it!"

Longarm swore softly as he gazed out the window. "It's a lynch mob. There's the Wilson cousins, the widow, and that rancher, Bob King. And a whole bunch of others, including some hard-looking men wearing revolvers."

"That'd be some of Bob's drovers," Farley said as he peered

out the other window. "I was worried about that. They must have been in town, and old Bob's gathered them up to back this dumb play of his."

"Hey, Deputy Long!" Walt Wilson shouted from across the street. "We're here for those rifles you took off of us!"

"We got something for Jessie Starbuck too!" another of the cousins yelled, brandishing a coil of rope.

"Where in tarnation are those deputies of mine when I need them?" Farley sighed. He turned to Longarm and the others. "Look, I'm going to try to talk some sense into that mob. Longarm, the keys to the cells are still on my desk. I think you'd better lock Jessie up."

"Oh, no," Jessie breathed.

"It's for your own safety, Jessie, honey," Farley said quickly. "Go on now, do as I say. Longarm, lock her up!" With that, he checked the load in his revolver, reholstered the weapon, and stepped outside.

"Stay out of this, Marshal Farley," Bob King shouted. The rancher stepped down into the street, brushing back his coattails as he did so, to reveal a gunbelt.

Farley shook his head. "I see you found yourself a pistol, Bob. But aren't we both just a mite too old for a showdown?"

"We've got no quarrel with you, Marshal!" the widow Wilson called out in a voice that was raw and harsh from crying. "We only want to see justice done to that woman who killed my poor husband!"

Farley held out his hands. "I'll tell you how to do what's right! Wait for the judge to get here, so that Miss Starbuck can have a proper, legal trial!" As he spoke, he looked up and down the street for a sign of his two deputies.

"We've already tried and convicted her, Farley," Bob King replied loudly. "And now we're going to hang her. It's no good looking for your men, Marshal. A couple of my boys have taken care of them."

"King, my deputies had better be all right," Farley seethed. "If they're not, I'm going to lock you up!"

"Your deputies aren't hurt!" King shouted back. "Nobody's going to be hurt, except for the one who deserves to be!"

Roaring its approval, the mob surged forward into the street.

The rope-bearing Wilson cousins and the defiant rancher were in the lead.

"Halt!" Farley thundered. "Halt, I say!" He drew his Peacemaker and fired once, into the air.

Longarm, Jessie, and Ki watched the proceedings from inside the office. "That's bad," Longarm said. "In a tense situation like this one, the first shot fired quickly leads to the second."

"It's Bob King," Jessie stormed. "That sanctimonious old coyote is only pretending to be interested in law and order. He's been agitating things ever since this trouble of mine began. For years he's wanted the Starbuck land that adjoins his property, and now he thinks he's going to get the opportunity to grab it for his own!"

"Reckon so." Longarm nodded sourly. "Reckon there's all kinds of scavengers lurking around, figuring to wrangle a sweet deal out of your troubles."

Farley's gunshot had caused the lynch mob to falter. "Put that gun away, Marshal, while you still can," Bob King said ominously.

"I'm telling you citizens to disperse!" Farley called out. "I'm warning you not to come any closer!"

King, his eyes fixed on Farley, raised his hand to wave the mob forward. He himself took one tentative step, and then another. "You won't shoot, Farley. Admit it," the rancher intoned. "We elected you town marshal . . ."

"I'm warning all of you!" Farley yelled, his voice trembling with emotion. "Stay away from this jail!"

"He's bluffing," Bob King told the mob. "Come on!" The Wilson cousins plodded forward like obedient beasts of burden.

Farley raised his Peacemaker, gripped it with both hands, and took trembling aim. "I'll kill the first man who reaches the middle of the street!"

"You wouldn't dare!" King declared, his aged face flushed with anger.

"Stay away from my jail," Farley said hoarsely. He thumbed back the hammer of his gun.

"That's it," Longarm stated flatly. "Farley's painted himself into a corner, and he's going to need help to get out of it." He took Jessie by the arm and began to lead her toward the cells. "You will be safer in a cell," he reassured her.

"Custis, listen to me!" Jessie insisted, digging in her heels. "You can't lock me up!"

"This is no time to argue," Longarm said gruffly. "Farley needs help, and the quicker I get you in a cell, the quicker I can get out there."

"No!" Jessie said, pulling away from him. "Listen for a minute!"

"All right," Longarm said impatiently. "Say what's on your mind."

"Custis, you don't know these people like I do," Jessie began. "They're true-blue Texans, through and through, and once a Texan sets his mind on a course of action, he's as stubborn as a Gila monster chewing on a jawful of boot leather."

"Jessie, you're just stalling." Longarm glanced worriedly out the window.

"Dammit, Custis, I'm not! Those people are set on hanging me, and unless you and Farley are prepared to shoot them down, that's just what they're going to do! We both know you can't kill people just because they've lost their senses. That means they'll overrun you, and lynch me."

"Just what are you suggesting?" Longarm asked.

Jessie took a deep breath, then said, "I'm going to make a run for it."

"No way," Longarm cut her off. "I'm locking you up." He grabbed hold of her by the back of the collar and began to steer her toward the cells.

"But, Custis!" Jessie argued wildly. "I'm useless in jail! And you won't be able to clear me if you're forced to remain here, guarding me from a lynch mob night and day."

Jessie was writhing and twisting in Longarm's grasp like a roped wild mustang. "Complain all you want," Longarm scolded her. "I'm doing this for your own good." He winced as her boot caught his shins.

"Longarm," Ki put in, "perhaps Jessie is right." He moved to intercede in the struggle.

"Stay out of this!" Longarm warned him. "This is official business!"

Ki hesitated, thinking furiously. He wanted to help Jessie, but Longarm was a federal law officer.

Jessie decided the question for him. "Ki! Help me!" she begged.

That was all Ki needed to hear. "Sorry, my friend," he said, his voice tinged with true regret as he moved in against the astounded lawman.

Longarm released Jessie and turned to meet the attack. *First I'm trying to put Jessie behind bars, and now I'm boxing it out with Ki,* he thought wildly. *This really is a bad dream...*

He thought briefly of drawing his Colt, but there was no way Longarm could use a gun on a friend. That meant mixing it up with Ki in a barehanded brawl, and while Longarm knew how to use his fists, he'd seen Ki in action a few times...

Still, Longarm tried to do his best. It just wasn't good enough. Ki was a flurry of arms and legs. He never actually struck Longarm, but the next thing the deputy knew, he was flat on his back, staring up at the ceiling. His gun was somewhere on the floor across the room. Jessie loomed into his field of vision.

"Custis, whatever happens," she murmured tenderly, "don't hate me. I swear to you I'm innocent."

She blew him one quick kiss, and then she was hightailing it out the door, with Ki on her heels.

Longarm shook himself out of his stupor and began to scramble across the floor on all fours to retrieve his gun. He heard Farley yell, "Jessie, halt!" and Bob King roar, "She's getting away!"

Longarm grabbed his gun, got to his feet, and started for the door. "Confound that hellion," he swore, his temper boiling over. "I'm going to tan her hide—"

"No!" Farley yelled. "Hold it!" This time his voice was close to a scream.

As Longarm reached the door, he heard a shot.

Oh, no, he thought as he lurched out onto the sidewalk. All his anger toward Jessie was gone, wiped away by that single, awful gun blast.

Chapter 6

"Sorry, my friend," Ki had told Longarm as he moved against the lawman to free Jessie. And the samurai had meant it. *How shameful to use force against a friend!* he thought.

Ki knew that Longarm was quick enough to draw his gun, but he had no fear of being shot. Longarm was too honorable a man to shoot him.

Longarm's hands never strayed toward his gun, but rose up in fists instead. The look of righteous determination in the deputy's eyes was an inspiring thing to see, Ki thought.

Longarm struck first, with a hard left jab to Ki's chin. As his left fist hurtled toward Ki, the samurai's right forearm rose up in a circular motion to deflect the punch to the outside. Ki stepped back, keeping his right hand on Longarm's extended left wrist. The deputy countered with a short right to Ki's solar plexus. The samurai blocked that punch with his left forearm in the same manner. Now he had both of Longarm's wrists in his strong fingers, and he used the deputy's own momentum to tip him forward, off balance. As Longarm literally hovered on the toes of his boots, Ki snatched the deputy's Colt from its holster and tossed it behind him. Longarm, meanwhile, had overcompensated for his loss of balance by rocking back onto his heels. Ki used the deputy's backward momentum to his advantage by quickly stepping to one side and performing a *yoko-qeri-kekomi,* or side foot-thrust to the back of Longarm's knee. Longarm's leg buckled. His arms windmilled wildly as he began to topple backwards. He hit the floor on his back, hard enough to knock the wind out of himself.

Ki had guided Longarm's fall to make certain the deputy did not strike the back of his head against the floor. The entire clash had taken only an instant, for Ki's fluid series of movements resembled a dance more than fisticuffs. He'd nodded politely to Longarm, and then hopped over the prone deputy and headed toward the door.

"Custis, whatever happens, don't hate me," Jessie had implored Longarm, offering him a kiss. Then she'd run out the door.

Ki was right with her as they slipped past the surprised Farley. Ki and Jessie's eyes—her emerald ones, and his almond-shaped brown ones—locked together for a fraction of a second. Jessie clasped his hand in her own. "See you," she whispered, and then she began to run down the very alley in which the samurai had discovered the reporter.

"Jessie, stop!" Farley shouted.

Bob King thundered, "She's getting away!"

Ki watched Jessie run, then turned to face the street, preparing himself to repel all those who would try to pursue the one woman he cherished above all others on earth. He heard a shot—

And wondered if the bullet had pierced his heart, so great was the pain he felt inside.

Longarm burst out of Farley's office in time to see the town marshal still pointing his smoking Peacemaker across the street. The marshal had shot one of Bob King's gunslinging drovers.

"What happened?" Longarm asked, standing by Farley's side, his own gun at the ready.

"I warned him," Farley loudly told everyone present. "You all heard me."

The cowboy was still on his feet, holding his revolver, but

he began to sway as he stared down in shock at the bloody hole Farley had put into his side. As he slumped to the ground, his pistol falling from his suddenly limp fingers, his buddies on either side grabbed his arms to prop him up. The wounded drover's boots trailed in the dust as the cowboys hurried him off toward a doctor.

"He was aiming to shoot Jessie in the back," Farley continued. "I did warn him to stop."

"You had no right to shoot my man!" Bob King said furiously. "He was trying to stop an escaped fugitive!"

"Stopping fugitives is *our* job," Longarm pointed out. "If you folks hadn't gathered to string her up, Jessie wouldn't have run. If you'd see fit to disperse, we can begin the business of catching her."

"Boss?" one of King's men called uncertainly. He and the other drovers looked to the rancher to decide what to do. They were tough men, but they hadn't counted on a shooting, expecting Farley to back down instead. The town marshal had stood his ground, however, and now Longarm had joined him.

"We could still go right through you, and through that slant-eyed bastard who thinks he can block us out of the alley," King taunted Farley. "Now that Jessie has run, she's fair game."

"If I have to, I'll shoot again," Farley announced.

"And I'll back his play," Longarm added.

"Here come my deputies," Farley breathed in relief.

Chuck and his partner had their guns out. They were herding along two of King's men, who had their arms up.

"These two bums got the drop on us, Marshal," Chuck apologized, chewing on the fringe of his drooping mustache. "We'd still be prisoners if it hadn't been for Mr. Deke Tyler. He discovered us in back of the saloon, and kept these two covered until we could pick up our guns."

Farley nodded. "Let them go. Bob King!" he called. "You take your men and get out of town while the getting's good."

Now that there were four lawmen, the rancher backed down. "You've won this round, Farley. Enjoy your job while you still have it. And remember what I said. Now that Jessica Starbuck has escaped, she's fair game to be brought down by any honest citizen!"

The Wilson cousins had been standing by quietly this entire time, content to let an important man like Bob King argue their case. Since it now appeared that King was giving in, Walt Wilson spoke up.

"Come on!" he told his three relatives. "She went down that alley. Maybe she's still in there. All of us together can take that damned Chinaman!"

Ki smiled inwardly as the four men rushed him. He'd been hoping that someone would dare try to pass him; he'd been gentle with Longarm, but he felt no warmth or kindness toward these lumbering oafs.

Walt Wilson was the first to reach Ki. The samurai met the man's attack with a full-force roundhouse kick that caught Wilson on the bridge of his nose. Blood spurted from the big man's nostrils and mouth as he fell to the ground.

The remaining three closed in around Ki like a pack of snarling dogs. One of the cousins used the thick coil of rope he was carrying to slash at Ki. The samurai protected his face with a series of blocks, but the rough hemp tore the skin from his forearms, making him bleed.

"We got him!" The rope-swinging man chuckled. "Get around behind him. Use your knives!" he instructed his cousins.

Longarm began to move toward the melee to lend Ki a hand. The samurai had put Walt Wilson out of it for the duration, but Ki still looked to be in bad trouble. That fellow with the rope had done him some damage, and now the two Wilson cousins behind him had drawn wicked-looking skinning knives from the pockets of their overalls.

"Stay out of this, Longarm," Ki commanded, noticing the lawman's concern.

One of the men behind Ki rushed in, his knife held like a lance before him. Ki glanced over his shoulder and then hopped forward a step to put himself out of reach of that outstretched blade. He bent forward at the waist, executing an *ushiro-geri-kekomi,* or backward foot-thrust. His heel sank into the knife-wielding man's belly up to the ankle. Ki's attacker let his blade fall forgotten as he clutched at himself and crab-walked to the sidelines, wailing that he was ruptured.

The man with the rope, realizing that the tide was turning

against him, warned his remaining cousin away from Ki. "Get after Jessie Starbuck, while I hold this Chinaman—"

The man dashed by Ki, slashing at him with his knife as he passed. Ki was able to avoid injury as he grabbed the man's wrist, but the samurai's fingers had grown slippery with his own blood, and the man was able to pull free.

"That's it!" the man with the rope shouted in triumph. "Get after her and cut her good!" He moved to prevent Ki from running after his cousin.

But Ki had no intention of physically pursuing the man. He dropped back several paces, into a crouching stance, then hurled himself forward, leaping high into the air a good eighteen inches above the six-foot-tall, rope-brandishing man in his path. At the same time that he was performing his leap, Ki reached into one of the pockets of his leather vest to extract a *shuriken* throwing star. The weapon looked like the wheel of a spur, except that the shuriken was three inches across and forged of high-grade steel. Each of its six points was razor-sharp.

At the apex of his leap, Ki snapped his wrist to send the *shuriken* humming after the man running down the alley. He had not aimed at the man's back, for killing was not Ki's intent...

The disc whirred through the air like a metallic dragonfly. As it closed the distance between itself and its wildly fleeing target, it began to drop in elevation. The Wilson cousin screamed in pain as the star embedded itself in the back of his ankle, just above the top of his low-cut work shoe. The star's sharp edges sliced through the Achilles tendon, spilling the man to the ground.

The rope-bearing cousin looked over his shoulder at what had been done to his relative, then gazed awestruck at Ki. "I—I give up, all right?"

"You will not chase Jessie." Ki did not say it like a question.

"I w-won't, honest!" the man promised earnestly, dropping the coil of rope. "S-see?" He held his arms wide in supplication.

Ki turned his back and walked out of the alley. He would spare this remaining man, for there could be no honor in striking him. The samurai had looked deep into the man's eyes and seen that his spirit had been broken. That was an injury far more telling than any he had inflicted upon the other three. Ki took deep breaths to relax himself as he left the alley. He did not fear an attack from behind, because he knew that the remaining Wilson would never again dare to confront him.

Most of the lynch mob had scattered when Farley shot the drover. With Bob King and his men gone, Farley had been free to watch the fight in the alley. The town marshal now stood with his hands on his hips as Ki approached.

"Longarm filled me in on what happened in my office," Farley said sternly. He scrutinized Ki's bloodied arms. "Do you need to see a doctor, or do you want to go straight to jail?"

"Hold on now," Longarm said. "I don't see any need to lock Ki up."

"Excuse me, friend Longarm," Ki interrupted. "But of course I must be locked up." He bowed to Farley. "I have broken the law by aiding in the escape of a fugitive."

"I'm glad to see you're willing to lock *somebody* up!" Birdy O'Hara said dryly, appearing from out of the general store next door to Farley's office.

"Oh, no," Longarm groaned. "Are you back again?"

"I never left," the girl announced staunchly. "I witnessed this entire sorry mess."

"Talk about your bad pennies," Deke Tyler observed, stepping out of the doorway of a feed-and-grain store on the other side of the alley.

"Not only did you break the law, Ki," Farley was lecturing the samurai, "but you also broke your promise to me. We had a deal. You were going to have Jessie surrender herself to me for safekeeping!"

"I beg to differ, Marshal," Ki politely said. "I broke no promise to you. Jessie did indeed surrender herself into your custody. Then she escaped. And you must admit, Marshal Farley, you could not have kept your part of the bargain—"

"Now hold on, you!" Farley seethed. "I was doing my damnedest to protect Jessie. Why, I even shot a man over her."

"You did an honorable job," Ki agreed, "but if Jessie had remained in your office, the lynch mob would have overrun you. It was Jessie's escape that confused things, diffusing the determination of the mob."

"Are you going to listen to this all day, or are you going to lock him up?" Birdy O'Hara demanded. "It's plain as day that he's Jessie Starbuck's accomplice."

"He's going to jail, miss, don't you worry," Farley said. "Ki, you sure you don't need medical attention?"

The samurai grinned wolfishly. "I am fine. Have the doctor see to the Wilson cousins."

"He also ought to be charged with assault against those Wilson men," Birdy O'Hara broke in. "They were within their rights to make a citizen's arrest. Jessie is a wanted fugitive—"

"Oh, shut up." Longarm sighed. "Now let's all cool down," he said loudly. "Farley, maybe you don't have to arrest Ki, because maybe Jessie isn't wanted. Or at least maybe she won't be, after we talk to Leroy Hoggs."

"That's right," Farley said, brightening. "You did mention that Hoggs had some light to shed on this case. Well, then. Let's go talk to him."

"I demand to be present!" Birdy O'Hara announced.

"Absolutely." Longarm scowled. "Freedom of the press and all. Besides, I can't wait to see the look on your face when Leroy clears Jessie."

"Mind if I come along?" Deke Tyler asked.

"Not at all, Mr. Tyler," Farley said. "By the way, I'm beholden to you for freeing my deputies."

Tyler shrugged. "I would have stood by you and Custis right here, except that a man in my position has got to be careful. A lynch mob is a tricky thing. I suspected it would come to shooting, you see. I've got no badge to hide behind if some geezer with a short memory suddenly decides I was a mite too lax with my gun during that sort of incident."

"I understand, Mr. Tyler," Farley said. "You used good judgment. I was the only one with the authority to use my gun. I only wonder how long this job is going to remain mine," he added, under his breath.

Longarm, Farley, Ki, Birdy O'Hara, and Deke Tyler all crowded through the marshal's office and into the cell block's narrow corridor. Leroy Hoggs chuckled when he saw them coming.

"Quite a party," the little man said. "And all to see me, huh?" He winked at Longarm. "I heard the ruckus out there. So Jessie got away from you."

"Leroy—I mean *Smitty,*—just tell them what you told me," Longarm instructed.

Hoggs looked away. "I don't know what you're talking about, Deputy."

"What do you mean?" Longarm asked, perplexed. Out of the corner of his eye he saw Birdy O'Hara smiling and nodding to herself as she scribbled something in her notebook. "You were going to explain how you ended up at the bank after joining Seth Weeks's gang."

"I don't know any Seth Weeks," Smitty said stubbornly. "Jessie Starbuck recruited me for the robbery, at her ranch!"

"Smitty—I mean *Leroy*—" Longarm growled, "Miss O'Hara *heard* you implicate Seth Weeks."

"Just a moment, Deputy," the girl interrupted. "I was eavesdropping outside the jail when I heard those comments. I had no way of watching what was going on inside this cell. You're twice the size of this little man, Deputy Long. Perhaps you coerced him into making those statements."

"Yeah, that's it, Miss O'Hara," Hoggs agreed eagerly. "That's how it happened! You write it up that he coerced me." Hoggs sneered at Longarm. "He made me shave, too."

"Miss O'Hara, did you have something to do with changing his testimony?" Longarm asked the female reporter. "Why did you do it? Just to make a better story for your paper?"

She ignored his accusations. "You were looking forward to seeing my face." She laughed jubilantly. "But I'm having a fine time watching yours, you poor, sweet, silly man." She waved a mocking goodbye as she took her exit, saying, "I've got to file my story all about Jessica Starbuck's jailbreak."

"She's going to put me on the front page," Hoggs bragged, watching her go. "Pretty, ain't she?"

"Shut up, Leroy," Longarm said. "'Else I'm liable to come in there and 'coerce' you some more."

Leroy shut up.

"Jessie is out there all alone, Longarm," Ki mused softly.

"No gun, no horse, no friends, hunted by an entire state for a crime she did not commit."

"May not have committed," Farley corrected the samurai. "Don't forget, I myself was an eyewitness to the bank robbery in Sarah."

"It just doesn't make sense," Longarm complained.

"That's something we can all agree on," Farley said. "Come along, Ki, I'm locking you up in the first of these three cells." He led the samurai away, saying, "Jessie's gotten herself in deeper than ever, I'm afraid. That minx of a reporter called it true. The fact that Jessie hadn't yet been locked up is a technicality. Jessie Starbuck has pulled a jailbreak!"

The sheet of paper upon which Longarm had drawn up the proposed agreement between himself and Leroy Hoggs still lay on the floor where it had been dropped. Longarm stared down at the paper. He had been so optimistic when he'd first written it up! Now the crisp white sheet was wrinkled and smudged, tattooed with the black heel marks of those who had entered the cell block so hopefully, only to hear Hoggs recant his testimony.

The sheet of paper looked bad, Longarm mused. About as bad as Jessie's future.

Longarm looked up to meet Deke Tyler's sympathetic gaze. Tyler shrugged.

"Sorry it's turned out this way," the bounty hunter said quietly. "But it looks as if I've got a job to do here in Texas, after all."

★

Chapter 7

Jessie spent a dreadful six hours hiding out in the crawlspace
beneath the town's barbershop. Years ago, when Sarah Township was nothing more than a few buildings hastily thrown up
along a narrow, muddy Main Street, Jessie's father had rolled
up his sleeves to help old Mr. Brewer erect his barbershop.
Jessie had been a mere child then, but she remembered how
the elderly barber had demanded that the crawlspace be built
in case, as he'd put it, "those danged Mexican soldiers come
back to reclaim what they've lost." The crawlspace had a false
front that camouflaged it. Mr. Brewer had long since passed
away, and the barber who took his place had repainted the shop
and installed a new chair, but she doubted that he'd ever discovered the crawlspace.

But she knew about it, because Sarah was her town; it even
carried her mother's name. How horrible it was to feel so alone
in the middle of one's home!

Six hours spent curled in the dark while the mobs outside
howled for her blood; Jessie had felt like a fox in its lair,
wincing as the noise of the hounds grew ever louder. The
crawlspace was dirty, and stank of rodents. Once or twice

during her ordeal, Jessie thought she'd heard the skittering of tiny claws.

But she had steadfastly refused to think about the horrors sharing this dark, dank space with her. She'd reminded herself that she was all alone, with no one to count on but herself. Ki was more than likely in jail, and Longarm—

No, she couldn't bring herself to think about Longarm just now. What must he think of her, Jessie wondered? She'd sworn to him that she was innocent, but how could he believe her after what he'd seen? She'd begged him to believe her even as Ki was attacking him; she'd begged for his trust even as she was running away . . .

No! She had to block those thoughts from her mind if she was to endure her time in this dark and suffocating place. She cried to herself a little bit, and slept off and on. Gradually the sounds made by her hunters faded away, and the glimmer of light visible through a crack in the false front dimmed to dark. From somewhere so close to her face that it almost made Jessie scream, a cricket began to chirp.

It was nightfall. Jessie could breathe a little easier. Like all fugitives, she belonged to the night, and could take comfort in shadows that would hide her from curious eyes. Now was the time to make her escape.

She cautiously pushed aside the false front and crawled out from beneath the barber shop. The shop was closed for the evening, and the side street it was located on was empty. It was suppertime, Jessie could tell, both from the last lavender glow of the dying sun on the western horizon and from the growling of her empty stomach.

Well, food would have to wait. She had no money to buy herself something to eat, and in any event, who in town would sell it to her without shouting for help?

She hurried down the street, formulating a plan as she went. She needed three things: money, a gun, and a horse. A horse would afford her the mobility she would need to reach her ranch and get herself some money and weapons. The law would certainly be waiting for her at the Starbuck residence, but she'd cross that bridge when she came to it; right now she needed transportation home.

Her own horse was out of the question. By now the big roan was more than likely secured in the town marshal's stables. Trying to snatch an already saddled horse hitched up somewhere on Main Street was too risky. That sort of escapade would be just the invitation some hothead needed to put a bullet in her back.

The town's livery stable was only a few blocks away. She could stick to back alleys for most of the journey, only having to cross a public street at the very end. If her luck—such as it was—held out, and she could reach the stable while the boy who tended the place at night was still out fetching his supper, she could take a horse, saddle it, and hightail it out of town.

There were a lot of *if*s to the proposition, Jessie thought sourly, but the strategy was the best she could come up with at the moment. Hanging around town would only bring about her capture, and who was to say that those who might trap her would bother to turn her over to Marshal Farley?

Jessie was under no illusions. She was not fighting for her freedom any longer. She was fighting for her life.

So be it, Jessie thought as she faded back into the darkness of an alleyway. *I guess it's time to add the crime of horse theft to my already sullied name.*

It took an agonizing quarter of an hour for her to slink her way from doorway to doorway. Finally she reached the last alley, and she ran its length as if it were a gauntlet. A scrawny dog, nosing in a pile of garbage behind a café, looked up impassively as she scurried past. The dog woofed once, but softly, as if its eyes, glowing green in the semidarkness, could see that she was a fellow scavenger, and hence nothing to fear...

At the mouth of the alley, Jessie hesitated. The stable was now in sight, but to reach it she had to cross this wide-open, moonlit expanse. There was a saloon nearby, which made this a far busier thoroughfare than the sleepy sidestreet where the barbershop was located.

Jessie pressed herself against the side of a building and waited. Her ears picked up the tinkle of the saloon's piano, the laughter of men, and the sound of feet trudging by. Jessie waited patiently, but the footsteps never completely faded away.

A portion of the alley behind her was suddenly flooded with light. She was exposed!

Jessie froze, her heart in her mouth. She instinctively reached for the Colt that was no longer strapped about her waist...

"I see you!" a man's voice snarled. "Get out of there, or I'll kill you! Out, I said!"

Jessie shut her eyes, trying to stifle the scream of terror rising in her throat. The musical sound of a bottle shattering filled the alley. She heard a loud yelp, and then the scrawny dog she'd seen earlier ran past her, whining, its tail tucked between its legs.

Jessie heard a harsh, satisfied burst of laughter, and then a wet, slopping sound. A rancid odor of garbage reached her nose. The light thinned to a wedge, and then totally disappeared as a door thudded shut.

Then and there, something eased inside of Jessie. She had almost, but not quite panicked. Now she vowed to herself not to come that close to hysteria again. She was a Starbuck, and she'd been in worse scrapes than this before. She'd gotten herself out of those, and she would get herself out of this one.

Feeling almost lightheaded with her new-found bravado, Jessie stuck her head out into the street and looked both ways. There wasn't a soul in sight except for that mangy mongrel, just now twisting around to lick at its haunch where that bottle had hit.

"Keep an eye out for me, fella," Jessie murmured as she took her first tentative steps out of the alley.

The mongrel, its attention caught by her soft words, dipped its head in her direction and gave a timid wag of its tail. It watched Jessie dash across the street and then rose, keeping its distance as it trotted after her.

Jessie sighed in relief as she reached the relative safety of the stable and darted around to the side of the building. She would use the side door, and not open the main doors until she had a horse saddled and ready.

There was little chance of her being seen at this point, Jessie knew. This side of the stable was out of sight of the street. There was a small corral here where the horses could take some exercise, as well as a watering trough and several bales of hay.

110

The water in the trough looked like molten silver in the moonlight. The tangy smell of horseflesh filled the air. To Jessie it was a welcome scent, compared to the trash-littered alleyway.

She sidled along the corral fence, peering in the semidarkness to make out the narrow outline of the door in the wide, weathered expanse of the building. She found it finally, and was fiddling with its latch when the hay bales arranged alongside the door suddenly exploded with movement.

Jessie gasped, bringing up her arms to protect her head from the tumbling bales. Something clawlike whipped out to grasp her ankle. Her leg was pulled out from under her and she fell sideways to the ground.

"Well, lookit wha' I caught . . ." a man slurred.

Jessie twisted around onto her back. The Stetson-topped silhouette of a drover loomed up from behind the tumbled bales of hay. Jessie squinted, trying to make out her assailant in the darkness. She used her free leg to drive short, powerful kicks at her attacker, the way Ki had taught her. Her boot heel stabbed into something soft. She heard a startled grunt of pain, a muffled oath, and then she was free!

She quickly got to her feet, but her antagonist was just as spry. "Let me be," she hissed in warning, like a disturbed rattler, but the man only laughed.

"You shut up! Don't give me orders!" He shoved her roughly against the side of the stable.

"I'll scream," Jessie began, trying to break away from him.

"No you won't," the man jeered. He pressed his body against hers, his mouth slobbering against her cheek. "I know who you are, Miss Starbuck. My boss, Bob King, would pay me quite a bonus to bring you to him . . ."

Jessie cringed against the drover's advances. "You're drunk," she accused. "Get away from me, you reek of whiskey!" She gagged as his fetid breath fanned her face.

"What if I am?" The drover pinned her against the wall. "You can't be so high and mighty anymore, Miss Starbuck. You're just an outlaw bitch who ain't fit to be with decent folks. Smarten up! You be nice to me and I'll protect you from the law."

Jessie struggled to get free. She tried to get hold of his gun.

"Don't do that," he snarled, slapping down her hands. "I'll hurt you, bitch!"

Jessie lowered her arms to her sides. Drunk as he was, he was big and strong. He had the advantage while she was trapped against the wall. Jessie was afraid of taking the offensive, lest he make good on his threat to do her serious harm.

"Tha's right." He chuckled approvingly as she stood docile before him. "You like me, dontcha, Miss Starbuck? You prob'ly never had a *real* man, sittin' in that fine house of yours, ain't that right? All the *real* men couldn't say boo to a rich woman like you, but you ain't so high and mighty anymore." His fingers began to grope at the buttons of her blouse. "I'm goin' to do you *good*, Miss Starbuck!"

With all her strength, she jammed her knee up into his groin. The drover doubled over, retching in pain, but as Jessie tried to run, he caught her left wrist to keep her from escaping.

As the drover pulled her back, Jessie went with the momentum. She twisted around to face the drover, forming an *ippon-ken*, or "one-knuckle" fist. According to Ki's instruction, she did her best to drive her fist into the drover's eye.

It had seemed an easy maneuver when she'd practiced it with Ki, but now it was dark, and her opponent, experienced in the art of street brawling, was bobbing and swaying. Or maybe he was just too drunk to stand still. In any event, Jessie missed his eye, painfully ramming her knuckle against his forehead. The strike might have stung the drover, but that was all. He muttered something unintelligible, hauling her closer by her arm, like a fish on a line.

Jessie kicked out at his kneecap. The drover grunted in pain, releasing her arm, at the same time raising his open hand to slap her.

Jessie formed a *yonhon-nukite*, or "spear hand," and thrust her stiffened fingers like a blade at the drover's face. She managed to catch his lip, drawing blood. The drover, meanwhile, was wildly slapping at her. It was a silent battle, except for their huffs of breath. Neither wanted to alert others—Jessie because she feared capture, the drover because he didn't want to lose his chance to take his pleasure with the fine Starbuck

112

woman. His reflexes were slowed by drink, but he was too tough for Jessie to seriously hurt him. That meant it was only a matter of time before one of his wild swings connected. When it did, Jessie would be finished.

Finally the inevitable happened. The drover managed to land a slap. It was only a glancing blow, but it caused Jessie to see stars. She reeled backwards, the back of her head slamming against the stable wall. Her knees sagged, but she managed to stay on her feet.

"Got you, bitch," the drover spat. Jessie's fingers formed claws. She was too hurt and exhausted to think. She only knew that she would resist. Let this bastard kill her if he could. She'd gouge out his eyes...

A low, constant growling, awful to hear, came from somewhere very near. Both Jessie and the drover paused, stunned and surprised by the sound, to look in the direction of the noise.

Something—an animal—was perched on one of the upended bales of hay. *It's that mongrel dog!* Jessie realized.

The scrawny mutt stood with its four spindly legs spread upon the haybale as if poised for a leap. Its mangy fur bristled thickly, and its head hung low between its narrow shoulders as it showed its teeth to the drover.

The dog was small, but it was close by, and its snarl was frightening in the darkness. The drover momentarily forgot about Jessie. He drew his gun.

Jessie formed her hands into a double fist and brought them down with all her might on the drover's wrist. His gun fell to the ground. He tried to backhand her, and the dog chose that instant to attack.

The animal literally hurled itself against the drover, snapping its jaws at his face. The drover managed to get his hands around the dog's throat. He held it at arm's length while it writhed and twisted in his grip. The dog's growls turned to howls as the drover squeezed the life out of it.

Meanwhile, Jessie had snatched up the man's fallen revolver. As the drover threw the limp body of the dog against the hay bale, she gripped the gun by its barrel and brought its butt end down upon the crown of the drover's Stetson.

The drover groaned and crumpled to his knees. Jessie hit him again. He fell sideways and lay still.

Jessie went to the dog. It was lying on its side with its neck broken, lifeless except for its paper-thin rib cage, heaving like a bellows, and its eyes, which followed Jessie's every move.

"You saved my life, fellow," Jessie whispered. "You're a good dog."

The animal made no sound; it was incapable of sound, but its brown eyes seemed pleased. Jessie stroked its head, and its tongue, dry and velvety soft, lapped out to touch her fingers.

She was wondering what she could possibly do for the animal when, mercifully, it died. Jessie stroked its fur one final time.

Behind her, the drover began to moan loudly. Jessie stood up, the revolver in her hand. For one brief moment of white-hot fury, she saw herself cocking the gun and killing this bastard . . .

She shook herself, getting hold of her emotions. *My God,* she thought, *I'm starting to think just like the bloodthirsty murderess I've been accused of being!*

The drover had been drunk. Now he was lying at her feet with a battered skull, perhaps seriously injured. She could not coldbloodedly murder a helpless man, no matter how horribly he'd behaved.

Suddenly he started shouting, "Help! Help!"

"What's going on in there?" somebody yelled from the street. "Who's in that yard?"

No time to get a horse now, Jessie thought, backing away from the stirring body on the ground. She turned on her heel and began to run, the drover's pistol still clutched in her hand.

"It's Jessie Starbuck!" she heard the drover call out in a shaky voice. "She jumped me from behind. Took my gun!"

The side street upon which Jessie found herself was narrow and dark. She ran blindly, knowing only that she had to put distance between herself and the shouts that were coming from the stables. Somebody began to fire a gun. "Jessie Starbuck! Jessie Starbuck is here!" a man yelled between the shots.

A lantern was thrust from the second-floor window of a

building Jessie was passing, and a woman leaned out to stare down at her. "Here she is!" the woman shrieked. "She's over this way!"

Jessie put her head down and ran. She careened around the corner of the block, to find herself on an avenue that paralleled the town's main street. Here were the rooming houses and cheap eateries that catered to working drovers and wranglers between jobs.

There was nobody on the street just now. Jessie spied a large, canvas-topped freightwagon slowly rolling down the block, in a direction that was taking it out of town.

Behind her she could hear the shouts of the pursuing mob. Jessie began to sprint toward the wagon, catching up with it and tossing her stolen pistol inside. She grasped the raised tailgate with both hands and hoisted herself up and over the edge, to sprawl safely inside.

She'd landed soundlessly on what appeared to be a stack of folded blankets. The driver had not heard her. He was still sitting on the bench seat of the wagon, with his back to her. Jessie shuffled around to peek cautiously over the tailgate.

The crowd chasing her was just turning the corner onto the street. "Where'd she go, dammit?" a man holding aloft a lantern complained in frustration.

"There! A wagon!" somebody else yelled out, a pistol in his hand. From where Jessie was sitting, it looked as if he were aiming right between her eyes.

"Forget that," the man with the lantern said. "That's just Barney the drummer's wagon. She ain't with Barney, that's for sure."

Barney the drummer, so that's who I'm hitching a ride with, Jessie mused as she watched the steadily shrinking crowd from her hiding place. She glanced back over her shoulder at the driver. *No wonder he didn't hear me,* she thought to herself. *Old Barney is pretty deaf . . .*

Nobody knew his last name, or how old he was, except that he had to be at least seventy, what with his nut-brown face, as wrinkled as the hills of the Texas Panhandle. Barney's bony skull was totally bald, except for a fringe of snowy white, wispy hair, and his pale blue, watery eyes were as rheumy as a newborn colt's.

Before cow towns had sprouted all over the West, wagons like Barney's were a common sight, Jessie knew. The drummers had been the immediate descendants of the richly laden trade caravans that left Eastern outposts like St. Louis, to travel the Santa Fe Trail during the first part of the century. The caravans journeyed to Mexico, where baubles were exchanged for furs and precious metals. Later, as ranchers began to settle the unpeopled territories, the drummers crisscrossed the vast, open spaces, selling everything from pots and pans to ribbons and bows.

The majority of drummers had gone the way of the percussion-cap firearm and the Pony Express. Most folks found it more to their liking to do their shopping in town. But there were still a few holdouts like Barney, making a thin living by stocking up with goods, and then carting the stuff to those few ranchers who were just too far away to make the journey easily for themselves.

Old Barney had stopped by the Starbuck spread more than once, so Jessie knew that the geezer made more from charitable handouts than from actual sales. Nobody minded. Old Barney was one of the last of his kind. Soon his profession would go the way of the buffalo.

Jessie hid her stolen pistol beneath a bolt of gingham. The next town was a small settlement named Sageville, several days away at the rate this wagon was traveling. Barney was such a fixture in the territory that it was unlikely anybody would pay him any mind. He'd discover her sooner or later, of course, but Jessie had always been kind to him. She expected he'd treat her politely.

As for his being afraid of her—well, Jessie couldn't be positive, but knowing how deaf old Barney was, and knowing how much time he spent alone, out on the trail, there was a good chance he didn't even know she was wanted by the law!

Jessie wrapped herself in one of the blankets. As hungry as she was, she didn't dare search the clutter inside the wagon for something to eat. She was afraid Barney would hear her rummaging around. Right now she didn't have the energy to deal with him. Besides, she was as tired as she was hungry; the day's events had fully exhausted her.

Sighing, Jessie curled up like a cat in the gently rocking wagon. Within seconds she was sound asleep.

★

Chapter 8

Longarm ate supper by himself, in a small café on Main Street, and then returned to Farley's office, hoping to persuade the marshal to release Ki. Longarm had tried to get the samurai freed that afternoon, but Farley was adamant about keeping Ki in jail, at least until he had a chance to discuss the situation with the mayor, later in the day.

Farley, who was seated behind his desk, scowled as Longarm entered his office. "Have you heard the latest?"

"I'm not sure I want to," Longarm replied.

"You'll hear it anyway," Farley said. "Why should I have to suffer alone? Jessie was sighted down at the other end of town, by the stables. She jumped a drover who was too drunk to defend himself, knocked him out, and took his gun. She hasn't been seen since."

"When did all this happen?" Longarm asked.

"About an hour ago." The marshal tapped the sheet of paper on his desk. "I've written it up and added it to the record. It's just one more black mark against her, I'm sorry to say."

Longarm shrugged. "We haven't heard her side of it yet. Who knows if that drover was right, or even telling the truth?"

Farley nodded in admiration. "You're loyal to your friends, I'll say that for you, Longarm."

"As long as we're on that subject," Longarm continued, "did you get a chance to discuss Ki's situation with the mayor?"

"I did." Farley looked down at his ample belly. "Before I fill you in, I want you to know that I feel just as loyal as you do toward Jessie and Ki. Hell, maybe I'm even closer to them than you, because I've known them so long."

Longarm smiled. "We don't have to argue that point, Marshal. And you don't have to convince me of your fondness towards Jessie."

"All right then," Farley sighed. "Here's the way the mayor and I see it. If I let Ki out of jail, everybody in town will accuse me of favoritism. My effectiveness as marshal will be zero. Right now I'm just holding on to my job by a hair. The mayor has warned me that if there's another slip-up, he'll have to ask for my resignation." Farley looked pained. "I've been town marshal of Sarah for close to fifteen years. I don't want to lose my job."

"I understand that," Longarm replied. "But surely you know that no useful purpose is being served by keeping Ki in jail?"

"Sure, I know that," Farley grumbled. "He's no criminal, if that's what you mean. I talked things over with him earlier today. I asked him if he'd give me his word not to escape, and you know what he said?"

Longarm chuckled. "Let me guess. He said something along the lines of, '*Honorable* Marshal, I cannot *dishonor* myself by pledging to remain in your *honorable* jail, while Jessie is wandering alone. It would not be *honorable* . . .'" Longarm paused. "How was that?"

Farley permitted himself a weary smile. "Not bad, except that Ki used the word 'honorable' a few more times . . ." He shook his head. "I'm not kidding myself, Longarm. I know that trying to keep Ki in that cell against his will isn't going to be easy." He pointed toward the samurai's weapon-laden vest, draped over the back of a chair. "I took away his bag of tricks. You know he's got coiled ropes and little knives and all kinds of things in that garment of his?"

"I know," Longarm said.

"Reckon not having it will slow him down some?" Farley asked hopefully.

"I doubt it." Longarm grew thoughtful. "Did you strip-search him?"

"What?" Farley asked, startled. "Why, no!" he blurted. He glared suspiciously. "You trying to scare me, Longarm? Why would I want to strip-search the man, for God's sake?"

"Because if you didn't, Ki most likely has something hidden about his person that'll allow him to pick the lock. It could be a pin in his hair, or sewn into his jeans, for instance."

"Go on," Farley scoffed. "He couldn't do that with a little old pin—could he?"

Longarm nodded. "*I* could. I've seen *Jessie* pick a padlock with a hairpin, and she told me that Ki taught her how."

"Oh, damn," Farley worried. "What am I gonna do? How am I gonna get Ki to allow himself to be strip-searched? I've only got two deputies."

Longarm shrugged. "You could call in the army."

"That's not funny. I've got a real problem on my hands!" Farley moaned. "Longarm, I don't suppose you'd do it for me?"

"I won't, and I can't." Longarm laughed. "Don't forget, Marshal, Ki has already mopped the floor with me. I'm handy enough with my fists, and I know a few down-home, West-by-God-Virginia rasslin' moves, but I'm no match for Ki without my Colt. And I won't use that against a friend," he added.

"I know that," Farley said. "And Ki knows that, as well. So there he sits, biding his time."

"You've got a real problem," Longarm sympathized.

"What I've got is a bundle of dynamite with a fuse burning away," Farley corrected him. "I might just as well hand in my badge."

"Come on now, Farley," Longarm said. "It's not as bad as all that. Put out that fuse by letting Ki go."

"Don't you see, Longarm?" Farley demanded in exasperation. "Either way, I'm finished. If I let him free, I'll be accused of favoritism. If he escapes, I'll be branded an incompetent." He sagged in his chair. "The town will complain to the mayor, and to save himself, he'll sacrifice me."

"There *is* one other way," Longarm began.

Farley raised an eyebrow. "I'm listening," he muttered dejectedly.

"Bail," Longarm said.

"Bail?" Farley mused, perking up. "Bail . . . Dammit, Longarm, that's not a bad idea!" Suddenly he frowned. "But who'll do it? I mean, Jessie sure as hell ain't going to ride in to pay the ticket."

"I'll do it," Longarm volunteered.

"Why would you pay it?"

"For the same reason I've been trying all day to get you to release him," Longarm said patiently. "Number one, he's a friend. Number two, he's useless sitting in jail. If he's released, he can help us find Jessie. You've got to admit that nobody is better able to track Jessie than Ki."

"Why would he agree to track her?" Farley asked.

"For the same reason he agreed to bring her in. Right now she's in danger of being picked off by every hothead in the state."

"So I set the bail, and you pay it," Farley theorized aloud. "Simple as that. If anybody questions me about it, I can show them the law, and point out that a federal deputy marshal paid the ticket. I'll be off the hook." Farley grinned in relief. "Longarm, you're one brilliant son-of-a-bitch!"

Longarm chuckled. "You're half right, anyway."

"When do you want to do this?" Farley asked. "The sooner the better, as far as I'm concerned," he added anxiously. "It'd be just my luck for him to break out before I get the bail papers drawn up."

Longarm reached into his pocket. "How's right now?"

"Perfect!" Farley beamed. He cocked his head to one side and stared up at the ceiling. "That'll be—um—three hundred dollars!"

Longarm gaped. "Did I hear you right?"

Farley nodded. "You did."

"Three hundred dollars? Marshal, what the hell kind of bail is *that?*" Longarm shook his head. "I want to get Ki out of jail, not buy him!"

"It's got to be a lot of money," Farley argued. "You saw

your reaction when I told you the sum? Well, that's the kind of reaction I want from everybody else. Nobody can accuse me of bending the rules in Ki's favor when I tell them that I set his bail ticket at three hundred dollars."

"It's too much, Farley," Longarm said flatly.

"It's not too much, and this ain't a flea market," the marshal shot back hotly. "It's what it is."

"Where am I going to get that much money?" Longarm complained.

"Wire Billy Vail to send it to you," Farley suggested. "After all, you'll get the money back, provided Ki shows up for his trial, two weeks from now."

"It'll take me a couple of days," Longarm warned.

"So be it."

"What about that bundle of dynamite about to explode in your cell block?" Longarm reminded the marshal.

"Good point." Farley pursed his lips shrewdly. "I want you to go back there and tell Ki what's happening. Try to get him to sit still. Fill him in on your plan. Let him know that he's due to be sprung."

Longarm stood up. "All right." He sighed. "I'll tell Ki now, and send my wire to Denver first thing tomorrow morning, when the Western Union office opens."

"Good enough," Farley said, exchanging his ring of keys for Longarm's Colt. "I'm going to put up notices on the bulletin boards at city hall and the newspaper office, stating that bail has been set. I want everybody in town to know what's going on. Rumors are what lynch mobs feed on."

Longarm walked around Farley's desk and opened the door to enter the jail area. Ki was in the first of the three cells. He was seated on the floor, with his legs crossed and his hands lightly resting on his thighs. His eyes were closed, and he was breathing slowly and regularly.

"He's been like that for hours," Leroy Hoggs complained from his cell down the line. "He don't talk, he don't move— it gives me the willies, it does!"

"I'm not talking to you, Leroy," Longarm growled.

At the sound of Longarm's voice, Ki's eyes opened slowly. "Hello, my friend," he said.

"Let's talk in private," Longarm began. He fitted the key into the lock, but then hesitated. He still had his derringer, but a gun was useless if you weren't prepared to use it. "I'm coming into your cell, Ki, but before I do, I want you to give me your word that you won't try to use this opportunity to escape. Is it a deal?"

Ki nodded once. "I swear. I would not take advantage of your good nature twice in one day, my friend."

"You'd trust a Chinaman?" Leroy Hoggs demanded, aghast.

"We're not speaking, Leroy," Longarm repeated. He unlocked Ki's cell and went in and sat down on the bunk. As the samurai rose to his feet, Longarm motioned him to sit beside him so that they could conduct their conversation in private.

Before Longarm could get a word out, Ki whispered, "I promise I will appear for my trial, so that you do not forfeit my three-hundred-dollar bail."

Longarm stared at him. "Now how do you know all that?"

"I heard you and Marshal Farley discussing the matter."

Longarm looked beyond the cell, to the thick oak door that led to Farley's office, a good fifteen feet away. That door had been closed, and he and Farley had not been shouting. Longarm looked back at Ki skeptically.

The samurai shrugged. "You asked me and I told you. The important thing is that I understand the need for patience on my part. Despite what Marshal Farley might think, I am fond of him, and have no wish to see him lose his job because of a certain tendency I have toward rashness of action."

"I appreciate that," Longarm replied. "Now then, you know it's going to take me a few days to raise the money. Is there any chance you can tell me where Jessie might be?"

Ki looked into Longarm's eyes. "My friend, you are the one person I would tell, if I knew. You are the only man I would trust to protect Jessie while I sit here"—his lip curled in distaste—"in this flimsy cricket's cage." He sighed. "But I do not know her whereabouts."

Longarm frowned. "I believe you. You don't lie." He shook his head, feeling defeated and disappointed. "Ki?" he asked. "Do you think she's guilty?"

"I do not," Ki stated firmly.

"Farley positively places her at the bank robbery," Longarm reminded him.

"And Farley is an honorable man who has great love for Jessie," Ki added. "I understand all that. And yet, despite such a positive identification, I still maintain that she is innocent. This is all far more complicated than it may seem."

Either she did it or she didn't," Longarm countered. "That's the nub of the situation."

Ki was silent for a moment, then he said, "This afternoon, before she escaped, she swore to you that she was innocent, remember?"

Longarm nodded, and Ki went on, "You have been a lawman for many years. In that time you've dealt with many criminals and doubtless been told many lies. You are not a slow-witted man, and I imagine you've developed a certain feeling for the truth, am I right?"

Longarm shrugged slightly, then nodded again.

"Then look into your heart," Ki said earnestly. "Consider your feelings for Jessie. They are no secret to me."

"Such as they are, they're my feelings and I reckon there ain't a lot I can do about 'em," Longarm said. "And even though you're such a mysterious cuss, I think I can see a glimmering of your feelings for Jessie, and I'm pure sorry if mine cause you grief."

A brief flicker of sadness passed across Ki's features, but then it passes as quickly as it had appeared, and he said, "My feelings are those of a man, but my pledge is the pledge of a samurai. I bear you no ill will. No such oath binds you. Look within yourself, Longarm, and you will no longer feel uncertain. You will be able to concentrate upon rescuing her from this misfortune."

Longarm nodded and rose to his feet. As he left the cell and locked the door after him, he told Ki, "I'll start working on getting your bail first thing in the morning."

"I understand," Ki replied. "And when I am free, the two of us shall work together to rescue *our* Jessie."

Just before leaving the cell block, Longarm glanced back

at Ki. The samurai had resumed his position upon the floor. His eyes were closed, his legs were crossed, and his hands were resting lightly upon his thighs.

The sound of Ki's deep, rhythmic breathing was in Longarm's ears as he shut the oaken door behind him.

Longarm supposed that he should head back to his hotel room and go to bed, so he could be up at dawn. Sarah was a cattle town, and ranchers needed to know stock prices back East at the earliest opportunity. That meant receiving a wire, so the town's Western Union office likely opened at the first glimmer of the sun. At this time of year, the sky began to lighten around six. Longarm wanted to be first in line to command the key operator's attention.

But he just didn't feel like sleeping, despite his exhaustion. Lord, it had been a long and eventful day!

Longarm strolled along the gaslit Main Street. It was a sultry evening and people were out and around, having late suppers in the cafés, or shopping the several stores that had evening hours. Sarah was a good-sized town, a place where a stranger could get lost. As Longarm walked the street, he found himself feeling like some sort of spirit or ghost—a creature that was invisible to everyone else, a being that could see and hear, but that was all . . .

Old son, it comes from spending most of your life traveling from here to there, Longarm told himself. *You're in a different town every week or so, and the people who you meet either want your help or are out to kill you.*

By chance, his stroll ended up in front of the Union Saloon, the biggest watering hole in the town. Longarm had been in there on previous trips to Sarah. He knew they served a man an honest drink for a fair price. He decided to have a few to wash away his depression. Longarm knew what was getting him down. It was being here in Sarah, Jessie's home town, without having Jessie around. Damn, every little thing about this place brought back a different memory of time he'd spent with her.

The Union was a cavernous place, brightly lit by gas lamps. Gaming tables took up half the room, with tables for drinking taking up the other half. Leading up to the second floor was a wide, red-carpeted staircase. If a man had an "itch" and the desire and hard cash to get it scratched, one of the saloon's "hostesses" would escort him upstairs.

Longarm made his way toward the fifty-foot-long, polished mahogany bar. The saloon's several bartenders were all busy serving their thirsty patrons. They drew mugs of draft from built-in taps decorated with ornate metal spigots, or poured shots from the extensive display of bottles on the backbar, beneath a wide, gleaming mirror.

Longarm put his foot up on the brass rail of the bar and waited for it to be his turn to be served. Off in one corner of the room a banjo player was plucking out a jangly but cheerful melody, and if that wasn't enough, there was the steady buzz of the crowd to keep a man company and take his mind off of his troubles.

And if *that* wasn't enough, there were those sweet-smelling hostesses, and those big, soft beds upstairs.

But tonight Longarm would settle for the banjo music, the company of the saloon's jumble of patrons, and a good drink. He reckoned that he was just an old-fashioned sort of cuss, but he'd never gotten used to the idea of *paying* a lady for her favors...

"What'll it be?" asked the bartender, a beefy, balding fellow wearing a white shirt, a black shoestring tie, and a dark brown, leather apron. As he spoke, his eyes looked somewhere past Longarm, searching out his next customer.

"I'll have a double shot of Maryland rye, and a draft to put out the fire," Longarm said.

The bartender smiled slightly in acknowledgement of Longarm's remark, and hurried to get the drinks. He returned with the glasses, took Longarm's money, slapped down his change, and disappeared to wait on the next man.

So much for friendly conversation, Longarm thought dourly. He reckoned that if a fellow longed to jaw with the Union's bartenders, he'd do best to get thirsty at an off-hour!

He knocked back half of the healthy slug of rye the bartender had poured him, and followed it up with a foamy sip of beer. As he drank, he gazed into the mirror behind the bar, letting himself be entertained by the constantly changing kaleidoscope of colorful activity.

One table of four drovers caught his attention. *If looks could kill,* Longarm mused. Those four men were burning holes into his back with their eyes!

He studied their reflections in the mirror. Two of the men he recognized as some of the drovers who'd been backing Bob King's play in front of the marshal's office that afternoon. The other two men were unfamiliar to him, but Longarm surmised that they also worked for King.

Longarm knew that a true-blue cowboy was a hard-working son of a gun who didn't have much money to spend on whiskey or fancy duds. These men of King's were drinking up a storm, and they had real slick boots on their feet, fine Stetsons on their heads, and double-action Colts in their holsters.

Longarm reckoned that King used these particular men as regulators rather than as drovers. That was not unusual. Some cattle barons took the descriptive moniker literally, recruiting a small army of gunslicks who pretended to be drovers, but earned their expensive keep by punching people, not cows...

The four drovers stood up. Longarm's hope that they were leaving was dashed when they didn't bother to sweep their change off the table. Two of the men drifted casually toward the staircase. The pair he didn't recognize made their way to the bar, where they bracketed Longarm.

"Well, if it isn't Deputy Long," the man on his left said. "Can we buy you a drink, Deputy?"

Longarm gestured toward the glasses in front of him. "I've got a drink, boys."

"Maybe Farley already bought him his liquor," the man on Longarm's right suggested. He tipped back his Stetson with its fancy, braided leather hatband.

"That's probably it," the man on the left nodded. He reached into the pocket of his pearl-buttoned, gray silk shirt for a cigar, and stuck it between his teeth. "Old Farley was probably grateful to the deputy here for saving his ass."

Longarm made no comment, but merely continued to sip his beer. He left his rye untouched. Something told him he was going to need all his wits about him before the evening was through.

"How about it?" the man in the silk shirt quizzed him. "You did save his ass this afternoon, you know."

Longarm glanced toward the staircase, where the two drover-gunslicks were loitering halfway up. *Good vantage point to pick me off in a shootout,* he observed.

"I don't know about me saving Marshal Farley," Longarm said. "He did pretty well against that jasper who drew on Jessie Starbuck."

"Hell!" spat the man wearing the fancy Stetson. "Duke would have shot that lump of shit's head off if he'd been paying attention. Farley bushwhacked Duke, is what happened!"

Longarm shrugged. "But Duke got shot and Farley didn't," he said brightly. "Guess that's what counts, eh, boys?"

"What counts is having the law on your side," the man in the gray silk shirt observed, chewing on his unlit cigar. "Take Jessie Starbuck, for instance . . ."

Yep, there's going to be trouble, Longarm thought. "You boys watch your step now," he said softly.

"A rich bitch like Jessie Starbuck can use her money to twist the law around to suit her own ends," the gunslick in the silk shirt continued, ignoring Longarm's warning. "She just snaps her fingers and the law shoots down an honest fellow like Duke in order to cover her jailbreak." The man shook his head. "What is this world coming to?" He sighed mournfully.

"A man can't even walk the streets at night safely," the man in the leather-braided Stetson declared. "Why, that Starbuck bitch jumped me from behind a few hours ago."

Longarm glanced at the man with renewed interest. "You're the one, huh?"

"Damn right I am, Deputy!" The gunslick glowered darkly. "I'd been doing some drinking, so I was a little slow, lucky for her! She hit me with a rock or something, and stole my gun!"

Longarm looked at the gleaming ivory grips filling the man's holster. "It didn't take you long to buy that nice, expensive replacement," he said.

"Mr. King pays us good." The man grinned, showing jagged teeth. "You get my drift, dontcha, Deputy?"

Longarm nodded. "You boys work for King as shootists. I understand that. I also understand that King is hungry for some Starbuck land adjacent to his own property."

"What of it?" the man in the silk shirt demanded, chomping furiously on his cigar.

Longarm turned in his direction. "For one thing, it makes your partner's accusations a little shaky, wouldn't you say? Your boss was probably right pleased to hear about another crime to pin on Jessie. Did he give your partner that fancy gun as a token of his appreciation?"

"That's just the kind of bullshit that Farley handed me," the mean wearing the Stetson sneered. "I go to him to report a crime, like a citizen ought to, and he insults me by suggesting that I was lying about Jessie Starbuck attacking me! I expected *that* old goat to have been bought off by that rich bitch, but not a federal lawman."

"You better shut up," Longarm said evenly.

"Two kinds of law, that's what we've got in Sarah," the fellow wearing the Stetson continued. "One for ordinary folks, and one for rich bitches."

"I don't allow anyone to say that I can be bought," Longarm growled.

"Hell, maybe she didn't give Deputy Long any *money,*" the man in the gray silk shirt drawled. "Maybe she gave him something else."

Longarm sipped at his mug of draft. *Keep cool,* he commanded himself, then said, "Listen to me, you two. Do yourselves a favor by collecting those two jaspers on the staircase and walking out of here while you still can."

"You know, I think my partner's right," the man wearing the Stetson chattered nervously. His right hand began to hover above the ivory grips of his pistol. "I think she did buy Longarm with a piece of her pretty little tail. After she knocked me out, she started to fiddle with the buttons on my pants—"

Longarm, gazing into the mirror behind the bar, watched the man in the gray silk shirt give an almost imperceptible nod to the men on the staircase.

"Know what?" the man wearing the Stetson hissed at Longarm. "I think that rich bitch sucked on my pecker—"

He was drawing his ivory-gripped revolver as Longarm smashed his beer mug across his face. The jasper went down screaming as the glass shattered on impact, turning his face to a bloody pulp.

The men on the staircase had their guns out as Longarm jammed his left elbow into the solar plexus of the man wearing the gray silk shirt. The blow staggered the gunslick, knocking the cigar out of his mouth. Longarm whipped the man around to shield himself from the guns of the men firing from the staircase.

The gunslick's silk shirt was ruined as the rounds meant for Longarm punched into him. Longarm let him slump to the floor as he crabbed sideways, drawing his Colt and firing three shots.

One of the shootists on the staircase was spun around by Longarm's .44-caliber slugs. He tumbled down the steps, hitting the foot of the staircase and lying still. Longarm's other shots thwacked off the thick banister behind which the remaining gunslick was hiding.

Out of the corner of his eye, Longarm saw the bleeding man he'd smashed in the face rising to his knees. The man was sputtering something unintelligible out of his ruined mouth as he aimed his ivory-gripped pistol in Longarm's direction.

The man on the staircase was bobbing up for his second try. Longarm snapped a shot his way to slow the gunslick down, then spun around in a crouch to fire his fifth and final shot at the man on the floor.

The slug struck the bleeding man in the throat. He dropped his ivory-gripped pistol to clutch at his neck. His head lolled as he sank backwards to the floor, the back of his skull making a loud cracking sound as it struck the planking.

Longarm doubted that the gunslick had felt the damage done to his skullbone. From the way he'd fallen, Longarm was pretty sure the man had died before his head hit the floor.

As dead as I'm going to be, Longarm thought as he watched the one remaining man on the staircase take careful aim. The Colt in Longarm's right hand was empty, and there was no time to go digging for the derringer in his vest pocket. He caught sight of the banjo player, pale as a ghost, staring horrified in his direction.

"Jessie, goodbye," Longarm murmured under his breath as the man on the staircase squeezed his trigger.

Then the man's aim went wild as three shots in rapid succession slammed into his body, making him dance like a marionette with jerked strings. The man's revolver clattered down the red-carpeted staircase, and then his body followed, as if those puppet strings had been cut. As the gunslick's lead-riddled corpse sprawled across the body of the man Longarm had already shot, the deputy twisted around to see who had saved his life.

Deke Tyler stood just inside the batwing doors of the saloon. The blued, slender barrel of his Colt Lightning was still smoking. Tyler stared grimly at the man he'd killed. His craggy features softened as he turned his gaze to Longarm and holstered his weapon.

"You all right?" he asked. His whiskey-soaked voice echoed loudly in the tomb-quiet saloon.

Longarm nodded. He took out his wallet, opened it to display his silver badge, and showed it to the cowering bystanders who'd begun to crawl out from underneath the saloon's tables.

"I'm a deputy U.S. marshal," he announced. "Somebody fetch Marshal Farley!"

"Who were these low-lifes?" Tyler was asking.

Longarm scowled as he reloaded his Colt. "Regulator types who worked for Bob King."

Tyler scrutinized the features of the man in the gray silk shirt. "Now that you mention it, I recognize this one. He's one of the pair who were holding Farley's deputies captive." Tyler glanced at the man who'd been wearing the fancy Stetson. "That one looks like the second of the pair, but I'm not sure. You messed his face up some."

"Seemed like the right thing to do, at the time." Longarm lit up a cheroot.

"Deputy Long?"

Longarm turned to confront Chuck, the town deputy with the drooping mustache. "Farley's home in bed, I take it?" Longarm asked.

"Don't rightly know where the boss is, but he's off duty, that's for certain," the deputy allowed. He glanced at the carnage, uttering a long, low whistle. "Looks like Judgement Day itself has come to Sarah Township." He stared blankly at Longarm. "What happened here?"

"These four gunslicks who work for Bob King got it in their heads that they could earn a bonus by taking me out of the picture." Longarm pointed at the staircase. "Two of them were up there, and one on either side of me at the bar."

"You got them *all*, Longarm?" Chuck asked, amazed.

"They're dead, ain't they?" Longarm replied, winking at Tyler.

"Two of them were the jaspers who got the drop on me and my partner this afternoon," Chuck said. "The town won't miss them, and that's a fact. Seeing as how you're a federal lawman and were attacked by these thugs, it looks pretty cut and dried. Don't reckon you'd want to press charges against their employer, Mr. King?" the deputy asked hopefully.

"I'd like to, but I can't," Longarm explained. "We've got no evidence that King put them up to it. Actually, he probably didn't. If these jokers had been able to kill me, they would have ended up in a federal prison. Bob King would have known that."

"And they didn't, is that it, Longarm?" Chuck asked.

"Probably didn't think it through all that far," Longarm remarked. "They saw me, got their bright idea, and made their move. They were most likely already daydreaming about taking the credit for my demise."

Chuck nodded. "Reckon that's so. I'll have them carted out of here. You'll stop by later tonight to file a report?"

"I'll stop by to do that tomorrow," Longarm replied firmly.

"Good enough." Chuck made a face at the bloody remains of the man with the fancy Stetson. "First he ran into Jessie Starbuck, and then you. Reckon it wasn't his night."

"Reckon not," Longarm agreed softly.

"Come on, I'll buy you a drink," Tyler offered Longarm as Chuck took his leave.

"You got your flask with you?"

"I do."

133

"Then I'll tell you what," Longarm said. "We'll go outside and have our drink in peace." He indicated the gawking patrons of the saloon. "We'll get no privacy in here. They'll be pointing and staring and whispering behind our backs all night."

The two men left the Union Saloon and strolled several blocks up Main Street, to an unoccupied bench in front of a general store. A gas lamp lit the spot agreeably. Tyler hauled out his scratched and battered flask, took a long pull, and handed it to Longarm.

"Cigar?" Longarm offered.

Tyler nodded. "Don't mind if I do."

They smoked and drank in silence for several minutes, letting the sultry night breeze and the sound of the moths batting against the glowing gas street lamp wipe away the stink of gunsmoke and the screams of dying men. Longarm went over it again and again in his mind, but he couldn't see how the outcome might have been different. Those four gunslicks had meant to kill him, and so it was kill or be killed, as simple as that.

"Thanks for keeping me out of it," Tyler suddenly said.

Longarm shrugged. "I remembered what you'd told Farley this afternoon, about your not having a badge to hide behind. Figured it would all work out neater if it got written up that a federal law officer had done all the shooting."

Tyler thought about it. "There were witnesses . . ."

"Most of them had their heads down, what with all the lead flying around the room. I wouldn't worry about it." Longarm smiled. "By the way, thanks for saving my life."

"Hah!" Tyler laughed, slapping his knee. "I wondered when you'd get around to mentioning that. Anytime, old friend, anytime."

"Reckon we're all even now," Longarm observed.

"Eh?" Tyler began, but then he nodded. "Oh, you mean because once you saved me, and now I've saved you. Yep, reckon we are even. And maybe that's a good thing."

Longarm eyed the bounty hunter. "How so?"

Tyler exhaled. "I'm setting out to track Jessie Starbuck down tomorrow." He took a folded map out of the inside pocket of his leather vest, and spread it out on the bench between them.

"This here's Sarah." He tapped a smudge on the parchment. "And this here dot," he continued, obliterating the spot in question with his thick, blunt forefinger, "is a hole-in-the-wall cow town called Sageville. I figure to follow the trail in that direction, to see what I can see."

"You think Jessie went to Sageville?" Longarm asked doubtfully.

"I've got to start somewhere, and the town next to this one is as good a place as any," Tyler reasoned. "Besides, that outlaw ghost town, Roundpatch, is halfway between the two, and about a day's ride to the east. If Sageville doesn't pan out, I'll head back that way and see what Roundpatch's outlaw mayor, Seth Weeks, can tell me."

"You leaving first thing in the morning?"

"Nope. I got a few things to do before I go." Tyler ticked his errands off on his fingers. "I've got to rent a horse, buy some supplies, and see somebody at the town bank, to make sure that the five-thousand-dollar reward is still being offered."

Longarm shook his head. "You may not get out of town until nightfall."

"You could be right."

Both men grew awkward as an uneasy silence developed between them. Longarm listened to the bench creak as he shifted around, uncrossing and recrossing his legs. Along Main Street, traffic had thinned out as the few shops and cafés that had been open locked their doors for the night.

"Well, it's getting late," Tyler announced, puffing on his cigar. He folded up his map and tucked it away.

"Deke?" Longarm began. "If I don't see you tomorrow, I, um, I—"

"Oh, shut up." Tyler chuckled. "I don't expect you to wish me luck, if that's what you were fumbling to say."

"I know how badly you need the reward," Longarm began.

"We weren't going to talk about that anymore," Tyler reminded him sharply. His tone grew gentle. "I promised you I'd do everything I could to take Jessie alive, and I meant it." The bounty hunter stood up to rest his hand on the pistol grips of the sawed-off shotgun wedged into his gunbelt.

"Thanks for the help. And the drink," Longarm said.

Tyler nodded. "Thanks for the stogie. Good night, Custis."

Longarm watched the bounty hunter saunter away. Most likely Tyler was staying in the same hotel, but Longarm let him go off by himself. The deputy wanted a few moments to think things through, all by his lonesome.

He doubted that Jessie had gone back to her ranch. Farley had a third, temporary deputy posted there to arrest her if she tried something so obvious. He didn't have much confidence in Tyler's Sageville idea, either. Jessie would surely be recognized in a one-horse settlement like Sageville.

That left Roundpatch. It wasn't much to go on, but right now it was the only idea Longarm had.

But first things first, Longarm reminded himself. Tomorrow morning he'd send his wire to Billy Vail, requesting Ki's bail money. Then the two of them could decide what to do next.

Longarm stood up and stretched, then meandered his way back to his hotel. As he walked, he gazed up at the starry sky.

Jessie, he thought, *wherever you are tonight, I hope you're sleeping safe and sound.*

★

Chapter 9

Jessie woke up abruptly, gnawing on the back of her hand to keep from screaming. She'd been having a horrid nightmare, one in which she'd been cornered all over again by that drover. The dog had been there, but this time the animal had been a wolf, and was against her. Jessie could still see in her mind's eye the menacing beast's long, curved, glistening fangs...

She shook herself to banish the ghoulish image. *Where am I?* She wondered briefly, and then it all came back to her.

She was in Barney the drummer's covered wagon. Back in Sarah, she'd managed to hoist herself inside just as the wagon was pulling out of town. The lurching movements of the vehicle had lulled her to sleep. She realized with a start that the wagon was no longer moving.

Alarmed, she turned to peek out over the wagon's raised tailgate, only to find it lowered. Barney was nowhere in sight, but the marvelous smells of brewed coffee and fried bacon told her that the drummer could not be far off.

Well, I can't stay wrapped in these blankets forever, Jessie decided. *Barney obviously discovered me, but was kind enough to let me sleep. I'd better go talk to him.*

There was no getting out of the wagon over the lowered tailgate, which had a fold-down leg, allowing it to double as a table. Right now its surface was littered with dirty mixing bowls, a slab of bacon, and opened burlap sacks of coffee, flour, sugar, and salt. Jessie crawled on all fours toward the front of the wagon, maneuvering over and around Barney's motley assortment of goods: pots and pans, bolts of cloth, jars of candy and preserves, chests of drawers filled with pencils, fishing hooks, buttons, ribbons, thread, string, and a host of other small items. A large paperboard eye chart was affixed to one of the covered wagon's roof ribs, along with a dozen pairs of wire-rimmed spectacles with lenses of various strengths. Jessie discovered a chest filled with cutlery, tin plates, mugs, and a box of assorted books and periodicals. Buried beneath those containers were other boxes and chests, into which she could not poke her insatiably curious nose.

By the time she'd reached the front portion of the wagon, Jessie felt as if she'd fought her way across the floor of the biggest and best stocked general store in Sarah Township. One final obstacle stood in her path. It was a large crate marked WIGS. Jessie peeked inside the box. It was filled with hairpieces! At first she was stumped as to why in the world Barney thought he could sell wigs, but then she remembered that an epidemic of scarlet fever had swept the state a decade ago. Poor old Barney must have thought he'd be able to make a killing selling the wigs to the unfortunates who'd lost their own hair to the disease . . .

She scooted up on top of the box of wigs, and from that vantage point she was able to climb out onto the bench seat of the wagon. She saw Barney sitting hunched beside a crackling campfire. It was still dark outside, but the starry sky was beginning to brighten with the first gray glimmerings of dawn.

I've been asleep a long while, Jessie scolded herself. She glanced around nervously, wondering just where on the trail they'd stopped for the night. *Barney could have summoned the law while I've been snoring away.*

Briefly she considered retrieving from its hiding place the gun she'd taken from the drover who'd attacked her. But that was silly, she realized. If somebody wanted to capture her, he would have taken her while she slept. Besides, there was nobody around for Barney to alert.

The old drummer heard her stepping down from the wagon. He turned, scratching at his bald, leathery brown scalp as he squinted at her with his rheumy blue eyes.

"Well now, Dora! It's about time you rose!" He presented Jessie with a toothless grin. "I kept yer breakfast nice and warm," he continued. "Buckwheat flapjacks and bacon cooked crisp! Just the way you like it!"

Jessie sat down across from the old codger, careful to keep the fire between them. She eyed him warily. "Barney, do you know who I am?" she asked softly.

"'Course I do, Dora!" He dug into the breast pocket of his workshirt for a plug of chewing tobacco. "And I know how you always like to sleep, so I didn't wake you. Now come on and eat yer breakfast." He gestured toward a covered pan nested in the glowing embers.

Jessie had no idea what was going on, but she wasn't about to turn down a meal, not when her stomach was growling. She ate ravenously, much to Barney's amusement.

"You always did have an appetite, Dora." He chuckled, pouring her a tin mug full of coffee. "It's good yer gettin' it down so fast, 'cause we've got a ways to go today, and the sun's almost up."

Jessie sipped at her coffee. "You mean to Sageville?"

"Nope, won't make Sageville till tomorrow. Today we've got to stop at a couple of ranches."

Jessie grew worried. This close to Sarah, she would surely be recognized by any ranchers she met along the way. "Um, Barney, maybe I'll just stay inside the wagon when you make your calls—"

"Don't be talkin' nonsense, Dora!" Barney paused to spit tobacco juice into the fire. "'Course you can't stay in the wagon. The folks will want to see you again, after all these years! You'll help me sell my goods, just like you used to."

Jessie stared into her coffee. What was going on was clear enough. Old Barney was senile. He'd discovered Jessie curled up asleep in the back of his wagon, and he took her for someone named Dora. Jessie was willing to humor the old codger. For one thing, it made life between them a lot simpler as long as she was hitching a ride. The problem was that the ranchers they'd be calling upon would not be senile. How was Jessie going to convince *them* that she was this Dora?

She decided to try to find out who Dora was. "That was a fine breakfast you made for me, Uncle Barney," she said.

"Uncle!" the drummer exclaimed. "Who you callin' Uncle, girl?"

"I—I meant Papa," Jessie quickly corrected herself.

"Papa?" Barney stared at her. "Have you lost yer senses, girl?"

Jessie gave up. Dora—assuming she had actually ever existed—was obviously not Barney's niece or daughter. She listened as Barney fumed about females being crazy critters. Then suddenly she had an idea.

"Barney," she said, "whatever happened to that likeness of me that I used to have?"

The ancient drummer grinned. " 'Tweren't yers, it was *mine,"* he chortled. "I still got that picture stuffed 'tween the leaves of my Bible, in my possibles sack."

"Your sack!" Jessie echoed enthusiastically. "Where's your sack?"

"Cut it out, Dora," Barney said. "You know where it is."

"Barney!" Jessie shouted, her temper now becoming frayed. "Where's the sack?"

The drummer flinched. "No need to yell, Dora. It's hangin' up behind the wagon seat, just like always."

Jessie hurried back to the wagon. She was anxious to see what this Dora looked like. Perhaps there would be more information about the woman along with her likeness. She climbed up onto the bench seat and felt around behind it for Barney's possibles sack. The leather satchel was hanging just where he'd said it would be. Jessie reentered the wagon. She found a candle in a holder, along with a box of matches. She lit the candle and rummaged around in Barney's sack until she found the Bible.

"Don't you be yellin' at me!" the drummer suddenly complained. "Come on out here and wash these pots, dammit!"

"Hush, Barney," Jessie murmured absently. She held the

tattered, faded daguerreotype up to the flickering flame of the candle. The image was blurred, but Jessie could indeed make out the three-quarter-length likeness of a woman. There wasn't much she could tell about this person named Dora, besides that she was well past middle age and had long hair, gone either white or gray. Jessie squinted at the image. It was hard to tell, but she thought Dora was wearing spectacles.

Spectacles, Jessie mused, shifting her gaze from the daguerreotype to the paperboard eye chart and the collection of spectacles for sale. She had an idea. It was daring, but if she could make it work, her problem of being recognized would be solved for the time being!

The drummer was furiously chewing his tobacco and muttering oathes to himself when Jessie stuck her head out of the wagon.

"Listen, Barney," she instructed. "Don't you come into the wagon until I call you."

"We got to get movin'!" the drummer countered.

Jessie took a deep breath to gain control of her temper. It was exasperating talking to the old fellow, but she was, after all, taking advantage of him. "Barney?" she called sweetly. "Dora wants to take a bath."

"Hell, girl," he snorted in disdain. "Can't take no bath in a wagon!"

Jessie smiled to herself. *I guess he's not as senile as I thought.* "Well, Barney, I've got to take care of some . . . *womanly* matters. So don't you come in here!"

"Oh, all right," Barney moped. "What am I supposed to do while I'm awaitin' on you, eh?"

"Well, you could make yourself useful by washing those dirty pots," Jessie suggested. "And you could water the mule team."

Barney spit into the fire. "I always get the short end of the stick!" he groused. Jessie watched him gather up the breakfast things and trudge off toward a nearby stream. Then she disappeared inside the wagon and set to work.

She propped up the largest of Barney's mirrors and wedged the daguerreotype into the upper right-hand corner of the looking glass's gilded frame. Then she began to gather together the

141

items she'd need to bring about her transformation from Jessie Starbuck into the Dora of Barney's photograph.

First she required cosmetics. She found most of what she needed in a cabinet that Barney had set aside for those products so eagerly purchased by the wives of the ranchers he visited. There were lip rouge and powder of the proper shades, and what Barney didn't stock, Jessie thought she could mix up on her own, utilizing talcum powder and the colored leads from some of the pencils in the tinker's odds-and-ends chest.

It took Jessie a little less than an hour to age herself thirty years. The soft lead came in handy to create the illusion of lines and wrinkles in her flawless skin. Satisfied with the results, she next turned her attention to her hair.

She pinned up her own copper-blond tresses, and then opened up the crate of wigs that Barney had never been able to peddle. There were, of course, no gray hairpieces, but she did find one shoulder-length, ash-blond wig...

Her eyes fell upon a bottle of black ink. She uncapped it and dipped a lock of the wig into the solution.

No, too dark, she thought, gazing at the results. She rummaged around in Barney's wide-ranging stock until she came upon some chalk. She ground the chalk up in a mortar and pestle, and mixed the white dust with some of the black ink and a few splashes of water. The resulting mixture turned a sample of the wig just the right shade of gray.

"Father Time himself couldn't have done a better job!" Jessie laughed out loud. She was beginning to enjoy her playful efforts at masquerade; busying herself with these various tasks was allowing her to forget about her problems for a little while.

She quickly daubed the rest of the wig with the graying solution, then set it outside to dry in the morning breeze.

Clothes were next on the agenda. She needed something dowdy and plain. Fortunately, dowdy and plain dresses were the only kind Barney stocked. She selected one that was high-necked, long-sleeved, and dark blue. The spinsterish gown did a far more effective, if still less than adequate, job of hiding her figure than did her skintight denims.

By the time she'd put on the dress, stashing her own clothes beside the stolen revolver, the wig had dried. She fit it upon her head, brushed it into order, and was delighted with the results. Still, she needed one last touch.

She moved to the display of wire-rimmed spectacles, consulting the eye chart to select the pair with the weakest lenses. All she really had to do was keep the spectacles perched on the tip of her nose. That way they would add to her disguise, and she could peek over them in order to see clearly.

With the spectacles in place, she checked herself in the mirror. She did not look exactly like Dora, of course, but more like her own grandmother. Still, if any of the ranchers they called upon remembered Dora, they would most likely assume that this elderly, gray-haired, bespectacled female had to be the woman in question.

"Girl? Girl! I finished them pots, and the mules is ready!" Jessie heard Barney calling.

She peeked outside. He was at the rear of the wagon, fiddling with the tailgate. Jessie climbed down from the wagon's front and called to him.

Barney stopped what he was doing and came trudging around the side of the wagon. "What do you want now?" he was muttering, but he stopped abruptly to stare at the transformed Jessie. The old drummer rapidly blinked his weak eyes; his knees buckled slightly, and he began to sway on his feet.

Jessie grew alarmed. Had her disguise been too successful? Had she gone from fueling a dotty old man's reveries to becoming a frightening ghost from out of his past?

But the spell that had come over Barney faded, even as his toothless smile grew. "Dora," he whispered, more to himself than to the woman standing before him. "Dora, I done everything. Now we can leave."

Chapter 10

Longarm was up with the morning sun, but he still found a long line of bleary-eyed, cigar-smoking cattlemen in front of him at the Western Union office. The ranchers were all waiting for the telegraph office's opening. When the designated hour rolled around, they managed to monopolize the harried clerk until eight o'clock. Then trouble on the wire left cattlemen and lawman alike cooling their heels until close to nine.

Longarm briefly considered flashing his badge to get priority service, but he discarded the idea. For one thing, requesting bail money for a friend was not exactly official business, even if Longarm did rationalize the request by claiming that he needed Ki to help him track a wanted fugitive. There was another reason he didn't want to draw unwarranted attention to himself. Several of the cattlemen waiting at the telegraph office had given him wary looks. It occurred to Longarm that their fellow rancher, Bob King, had probably already circulated *his* version of the events that took place in the Union Saloon last night. It didn't take much imagination for Longarm to surmise what King had told his cronies, namely that one of his drovers had reported a complaint against Jessie Starbuck, an argument had ensued, and Longarm had shot down four of King's men in cold blood.

So Longarm kept a low profile by waiting his turn, just like any citizen. An hour one way or the other wasn't going to make much difference, he decided. Billy Vail still wouldn't be able to get the money wired back to him for another twenty-four hours at the least.

At last it was Longarm's turn. He'd already jotted down the body of his message on the yellow paper Western Union supplied for that purpose. He thrust the sheet of foolscap at the young clerk behind the counter. "This is urgent business; it's got to go out at once," he began.

The clerk held up one hand to silence him. "Be right with you, sir," he muttered, and promptly disappeared from view below the countertop.

Longarm peered over the edge to see the clerk remove his leather visor before squirming to reach the rack of wet-cell batteries beneath the table that held his sending set. Longarm watched the kid fiddle with the tangle of wires and then worm his way out from beneath the table and stand up.

"I thought it might have been a loose connection at this end," the clerk announced to no one in particular. "But it ain't."

"Something's wrong, I take it?" Longarm said with a sigh.

The clerk tapped his key experimentally a few times. "She's dead," he announced flatly. "I guess we still have trouble on the line."

Longarm nodded. "How long to fix it?"

The clerk looked apologetic. "I can't really say." He shrugged. "I don't do the fixing."

"I know that, son," Longarm growled from between clenched teeth. "I asked how long?"

"W-well, then, sir," the clerk stammered. He'd suddenly realized that he'd been left all alone with the very fellow who just last night had shot down four of the toughest regulators Bob King could find to hire. "Y-you see, how long it'll stay broken depends on where on the line the trouble is . . ." He trailed off helplessly.

Longarm glanced at the pendulum clock on the office wall.

146

He shook his head. It was already ten o'clock in the morning. "Reckon I'll wait here for a bit, just in case the trouble clears."

The clerk was obviously not thrilled about that, but he smiled gamely. "Would you like some coffee, Mister—" He glanced at the signature on the yellow sheet. "I mean *Deputy* Long?"

"Nope," Longarm grunted. "What I want is to send a telegram."

The clerk nodded, looking miserable. "Mind if I get a cup of coffee?"

"Nope."

"I'm going to get it now, okay?" the clerk said soothingly, moving with exaggerated slowness.

Longarm had to grin. "Relax, son. The Justice Department would dock my pay if I shot a Western Union clerk."

The key operator stared for a moment, but then smiled back in relief. "Deputy, you can trust me to do my job. I'll send your wire out as soon as the line's clear, I promise."

Longarm winked at the clerk. "Thank you. This ought to cover the charges." He flipped the operator some coins. "Keep the change for your trouble," he added. "If you want to find me for any reason, I'll be at Marshal Farley's office."

He walked out and strolled toward Main Street, detouring at a café along the way for a quick breakfast of steak and eggs. It was just eleven by his pocket watch as he entered the marshal's office.

"Longarm!" Farley exclaimed, rising up from behind his paper-strewn desk. "I've had my deputy out searching for you all morning!"

"Relax, Marshal," Longarm said. He lit up his after-breakfast cheroot, his most longed for smoke of the day. "I told Chuck that I'd be in today to fill out a report on last night's shootings."

"I'm not talking about that," Farley said.

"Well, I've been at the damned telegraph office since six this morning," Longarm said. "Don't worry, the wire to Billy Vail requesting Ki's bail money will be sent as soon as possible—"

"Will you keep quiet for one second, Longarm?" Farley

demanded. "The reason I've had my man out searching for you is to tell you that you're too late!"

Longarm stared, puzzled. "Too late for what, Marshal?"

"To bail Ki out!" Farley declared. "Somebody beat you to it."

Longarm pushed past Farley and into the cell block. The cell's open door swung gently in the breeze that followed Longarm in. The cell was empty!

"Who?" Longarm demanded as he made his way back into Farley's office. "Who would have bailed Ki out, except for me?"

"That little redhead of a reporter," Farley replied. "Birdy O'Hara, that's who!"

Ki was quite surprised to find that his second day in jail was to begin with an early-morning visitor, especially when the visitor was not Longarm, but the female journalist the samurai had yesterday apprehended in the alley outside the cell block.

"Somebody to see you," Farley announced as he showed Birdy O'Hara in. "Unless, of course, you don't want to talk to her?" the marshal strongly suggested.

"On the contrary," Ki replied. "I am curious as to why Miss O'Hara is here."

"Longarm ain't going to like this," Farley grumbled, scratching at the bandage on his head as he left the cell block.

Today the young reporter was wearing a sky-blue and daisy-yellow cotton-print dress that brought out the robin's-egg hue of her big, bright eyes. She seemed to be gloating as she surveyed Ki through the bars of his cell.

"My, my." She chuckled. "The zoo is getting crowded, isn't it?"

"Hey, Miss O'Hara!" Leroy Hoggs called from his cell two doors down. "You want to interview *me* some more?"

"Not today," she answered, paying no attention to the would-be bank robber.

"Then what does bring you here?" Ki asked.

"As usual, nothing but my own grim determination," Birdy replied with a scowl. "Farley tried to refuse me admittance, but I pointed out to him—"

"You should not do that," Ki interrupted her.

"Huh? Not do what?"

"Frown and scowl and pout," he said. "You are far too young and attractive to be so world-weary."

"What? Why, how dare you!" she demanded in annoyance. "Keep your impertinent remarks to yourself!" She began nervously to twist a tendril of her red hair around on her fingers.

"But see how pretty you look when you blush," Ki observed. "You need to hear more compliments."

"Oh, I've had my share of sweet talk. More than my share," she said disgustedly. "Now just listen to me," she commanded, regaining her businesslike posture. "As I said, Farley tried to keep me away, but I pointed out to him that he'd posted public notices announcing the amount of your bail. That means any interested party can pay it." She smiled sweetly. "So here I am."

"You would pay my bail?" Ki asked sharply. "Now it is my turn to grow flustered. Why would you do this thing?"

"Not out of the goodness of my heart, and that's for sure!" she shot back.

"That motive never entered my mind," Ki said wryly.

"Then let's get down to business. I'm willing to make a deal with you. I pay your bail right now, this very moment, and in exchange, you take me with you on your search for Jessie Starbuck."

"No," Ki said.

"But Deputy Long won't take me. That bounty hunter, Deke Tyler, turned me down. You're my last hope!"

"Then you are out of hope, because I will not take you along with me," Ki repeated.

"Deke Tyler is going to Sageville," Birdy said slyly. "If he finds Jessie there, she is as good as dead!"

Ki kept silent.

"Is that what you want?" the girl demanded. "For Jessie Starbuck to be brought back tied across the saddle of Tyler's packhorse? That's how he'll do it," the reporter insisted. "Jessie's worth five thousand dollars to him, alive or dead. You know what a wildcat Jessie is! She'll be a lot easier for him to handle dead!"

"That will not happen," Ki swore. "I will prevent it."

"How, by sitting in that cell?" she asked, and then laughed scornfully.

"Longarm will bail me out—" Ki began.

"Don't count on it, sweetie." Birdy chuckled. "Three hundred dollars is a lot of money for a saddle-worn deputy marshal to raise. And even if his Denver office does decide to advance him the money, it could take days to arrive. Days!" She paused. "It'll only take a moment for Deke Tyler to point that shotgun of his at Jessie and blow a big, bloody hole in her."

Ki was at the cell door in a flash, his splayed fingers reaching through the bars for her throat. Alarmed, Birdy stumbled backwards, barely getting out of his reach.

"You are indeed fortunate that a locked cell door stands between us," Ki told her softly.

"Calm down," she soothed him. "I'm sorry if I went too far, but I'm only trying to help you. It'll be Tyler who kills her, not me."

"Be careful what you say," Ki told her.

"I will," Birdy promised quickly. "We'll be friends, you'll see. Now how about it?" She tapped her purse. "I've got a bank draft for the three hundred dollars right here. I stopped off at the town bank to get it, on my way to Farley's office. My newspaper arranged for me to have a credit line here in Sarah to cover my expenses. You could be out of jail and on your way to rescue Jessie in a matter of minutes."

Ki began to shake his head. "I cannot take you."

"Then you'll rot here in this cell," she warned him. "You've got to accept my deal, because—" She smiled triumphantly. "Because you owe it to the oath of allegiance you swore to protect Jessie Starbuck!"

Ki's broad shoulders sagged in defeat. This vixen was speaking the truth. "I agree to your terms," he said.

"Don't take it too hard, sweetie," the girl said. "You're not the first. But I want you to *swear* to take me wherever you go in pursuit of Jessie," she cautioned. "I've asked around town about you, and I know you won't break your word." She chuckled. "Not even to me," she added softly.

Ki looked at her curiously. "I told you that I agree to your terms. Accordingly, I have already given you my word, and will not break it."

Now it was Birdy O'Hara's turn to appear momentarily subdued. "I'll, um, pay the marshal," she said, flustered. "He'll give you back your horse. Now listen, Ki. I've already arranged for a mount to be rented to me at the livery stables—"

"Can you ride?" Ki cut her off.

"As well as any man!" she said archly. "All I have to do is return to my hotel room, change into riding clothes, and grab a bag I took the liberty of packing beforehand." She winked at him smugly.

"Very well, I will meet you at the livery stable," Ki said. "We will ride to the Starbuck ranch for supplies and weapons that I will need."

"Fine." She nodded. "I'll pay the marshal right now!" She started for the door that led out of the cell block, but then hesitated to look back at the samurai. "You really *will* meet me at the stable, won't you?"

Ki nodded gruffly, and Birdy O'Hara beamed. "Marshal Farley!" she called loudly. "I've got something for you, Marshal!"

Chapter 11

"I don't believe this! I don't goddamned believe it!"

Longarm sat slumped in Farley's office, with his hat tipped over his eyes and his boots up on the marshal's desk. "Yesterday at this time everything was under control! Jessie was turning herself in, that damned Leroy Hoggs was going to cooperate. I mean"—he thumbed back his Stetson to glare at Farley—*"everything was under control!"*

"Get your feet off my desk," Farley grumbled, but without much real conviction. "My head hurts," he added, gingerly readjusting the bandage wound around his skull.

"It's that reporter," Longarm sulked. "She's managed to outfox us at every turn."

"What do you mean, *us?*" Farley asked. "I'm happy. I've got three hundred dollars worth of bail money in my safe, and a very slippery fellow out of my jail."

"That's right!" Longarm growled. "Thanks a lot, old friend!"

"Don't take that tone with me, son," Farley shot back. "What was I supposed to do? Tell that little minx 'No, thanks, I'm waiting on somebody *else* to pay my prisoner's bail'?" The marshal snorted disdainfully. "Get your feet off my desk, I told you."

"But I'm the one who gave you the idea about setting Ki's bail," Longarm reminded him, at the same time leaving his boots right where they were.

"Hey," Farley said with a shrug, "ideas are free. They're floating in the air for anyone to catch."

"I'll remember that next time," Longarm remarked dryly. "All you can catch is flies..."

"I'll ignore that last remark," Farley said generously. "You're just taking it out on me 'cause you're screwing up this case." He grimaced as Longarm's boots squeaked across his desktop. "Dammit! You're scratching the finish!"

"The only finish this desk ever had was dust," Longarm muttered. "Lord, I'd like to get my hands on that Birdy O'Hara. First she turns Leroy Hoggs against me, and then she steals Ki. I'd like to—" Longarm stopped to stare at Farley. "First Hoggs, and then Ki." He chuckled, snapping his fingers. "I do believe I have an idea."

Farley stared dully. "What is it?"

"Why don't you just snatch it out of the air the next time it buzzes by," Longarm said, winking. He got to his feet and maneuvered around the marshal's desk and toward the cell area.

"Hey, where are you going?" Farley demanded.

"To see Leroy," Longarm called over his shoulder.

"Wait a minute! You leave your gun! Hoggs is still my prisoner, and this is still my jail—"

But Longarm was already through the doorway and on his way down the narrow corridor toward the last cell. As he walked he rearranged his features, wiping away his smile and replacing it with a glum expression.

Little Leroy Hoggs looked up eagerly, but was disappointed when he saw who it was. "Oh, it's you, Deputy. I was hoping that it was that lady reporter..."

"She's gone, Leroy."

"Huh?" Hoggs looked perplexed.

"Left town, with Ki," Longarm elaborated. "What made you think she'd come back to bother with you?"

Hoggs just shrugged, turning away from the bars of his cell. "I dunno. I just thought that—" He blushed. "Nothing..."

Longarm nodded knowingly. "You thought she'd bail *you*

out like she did Ki. Sorry, Leroy. She played you for a sucker."

"What do you mean, she played me for a sucker?" Hoggs asked suspiciously. He cocked his head to one side as he noticed Longarm's hangdog expression. "And what's wrong with you? Did you eat something that disagrees with you?"

"Hell, no, Leroy! I'm worried on your account. It all fits together with how Birdy O'Hara played you for a sucker. Think about it!" Longarm shook his head. "Here I was, all ready to cut you a fine deal. I had it all written down that I'd haul your ass back to Nebraska to do a few years of easy time in exchange for helping me out with this case." He sighed. "I was even going to call you Smitty. But what happens? That pretty little hellcat sweet-talks you for a few moments and you toss away the whole thing. And for what? To get your name in the newspapers, and to make *her* look good with her bosses back East."

"Oh, I dunno," Hoggs said meaningfully. "Maybe I got something more out of it than that."

"You did, old son. You surely did," Longarm agreed. "You earned yourself the right to hang!"

"What?" Hoggs squeaked. "Come on now, Deputy! I didn't commit no hanging offense! You know I didn't!" He pointed a wavering finger at Longarm. "You can't let me hang. Why, it's illegal, goddammit!"

"Leroy, my hands are tied," Longarm sighed. "Why do you think I look so worried? You know about the ruckus that occurred yesterday afternoon? The whole town was all set to string up Jessie Starbuck."

"So?" Hoggs demanded.

"So, Leroy, Jessie's gone. But *you're* still here."

Hoggs paled. "Me?" he whispered. "Why'd they want to hang me? I ain't killed nobody, not ever in my life!"

"I know that," Longarm assured him. "But you know how crazy riled up a lynch mob can get. Worse than a pack of rabid wolves! They're hankering to hang somebody, and you'll do in a pinch. After all, Leroy," Longarm reminded the anguished man, "you *were* a member of the bank-robbing gang."

Hoggs clutched the bars of his cell and groaned desperately, "You've got to protect me! You and Farley protected Jessie! You've got to do the same for me!"

"We would if we could, Leroy," Longarm said apologetically. "But we won't be here."

"Where you going?" Hoggs cried out in despair.

"Farley and I have to go after Jessie," Longarm explained. "We'll leave behind one deputy to mind the store." Longarm looked wistful. "But I'm afraid one deputy won't amount to much when that mob comes screaming for your blood."

Hoggs nodded. "Listen, I'm ready to make that deal we talked about!"

"Sorry, Leroy," Longarm said. "That deal was good when Jessie was still here to benefit from it. Now that I've got to chase her, you'll have to do better."

"What do you want?" Hoggs pleaded. "Just tell me. I'm—"

Longarm held up his hand. "Quiet!" he hissed. "Did you hear that?"

"W-what?" Hoggs whimpered.

Longarm drew his Colt. "I think there's somebody lurking in the alley outside your cell," he whispered.

"Oh, God!" Leroy moaned. "Longarm! I've got a *real* deal for you! You'll probably be heading toward Roundpatch, right?"

"I was thinking on it," Longarm said. "Yep, Leroy. Farley and I might mosey along in that direction."

"Then you take me with you, and I'll lead you right there!" Hoggs coaxed.

"You've got to do better than that." Longarm shook his head. "We know how to get there on our own."

"Sure, you can *get* there, Longarm," Hoggs said. "But unless you and the marshal bring along an army, Seth Weeks's sentries will cut you down before you even *sight* the town." The little prisoner puffed up his chest. "I know where those sentries are hidden. If you do get challenged, I know the passwords." He paused hopefully. "I sure could save you gents a lot of trouble."

"Maybe we *will* take you along with us," Longarm mused. "I'll discuss it with Farley." His eyes narrowed. "But before I do, I want you to come clean about Jessie Starbuck!"

"I'll tell you everything I know, Longarm. I swear it!" Hoggs said devoutly. "But not until we're safely out of town."

"Leroy," Longarm said warningly. "You're in no position to dicker terms."

Hoggs stubbornly shook his head. "You said it yourself, Longarm. I've already been played for a sucker. It ain't going to happen again," he vowed. "You get me away from these lynch mobs, and I'll talk. But not until! From now on, I'm playing the cards I've got one at a time."

Longarm considered the situation briefly. He couldn't very well argue with Hoggs's assertion unless he wanted to contradict himself. Besides, this time around, Longarm had promised the little jasper nothing in return for his cooperation beyond a rescue from a mythical lynch mob. Now that Jessie was on the run, nothing much could be gained by insisting that Hoggs clear her. Who'd believe the word of a criminal who'd already changed his story twice? No, Longarm thought. The only way to get to the bottom of all this was to capture the rest of the gang. Roundpatch was as good a place as any to start the search, and if Hoggs had told the truth about those hidden sentries, having somebody who could get the posse through the gauntlet was essential.

"All right, Leroy. I'll talk it over with Farley." Longarm headed for the marshal's office. "If I was you, I'd stay away from the window," he advised over his shoulder. "They might dispense with the necktie party and decide to shoot you."

Hoggs nodded. "I'll hide under the bunk! You think that'll be all right, Deputy?" he asked anxiously.

"Good idea, Leroy." Longarm made a supreme effort, and was able to keep from grinning until he'd reentered Farley's office.

"I heard, I heard," Farley grumbled, waving aside Longarm's summary of the conversation before it could begin. "I kept the door open a crack so I could listen in."

"Well? What do you think?" Longarm asked.

Farley made a face. "Do we really have to go to Roundpatch?" he began. "I mean, I ain't afraid or nothing, but it's kind of like Seth Weeks and I have a deal. He and his outlaws leave Sarah alone, and I leave Roundpatch alone. Know what I mean?"

"Yep, but Weeks broke the deal first," Longarm said.

"How so?" Farley asked.

"I think he robbed your bank and killed that teller," Longarm replied. "Come on, Farley, you know Jessie! If she was going to set about becoming a bank robber, she'd never throw in with a lowlife like Seth Weeks!"

"You're saying Weeks framed Jessie somehow?" Farley pondered the theory. "That fits in with little Leroy in there claiming to be a member of Weeks's gang, but what about the woman I saw in the bank? That was Jessie, I tell you!"

Longarm sighed. "Let's eat this here apple one bite at a time. All I know is that Weeks is the only lead we have."

Farley nodded sadly. "Roundpatch, here we come."

Longarm rubbed his hands together gleefully. "At least we'll be doing something!"

"But we can't leave for another day or so," Farley interjected.

"What?" Longarm groaned. "The outlaws we're after could scatter at any time. We can't afford to wait another day!"

Farley cradled his bandaged noggin. "You do what you want, Deputy. But the way my head hurts, I can't handle that sort of ride and live to tell about it. I need another day's rest, at the least."

"Then I'll go alone," Longarm said. "Just me and Hoggs. You and a deputy or two can follow us later."

"You can go when you want, but Hoggs travels with me," Farley corrected him. "He's my prisoner, and if he gets freed, it'll be under my supervision."

Longarm rolled his eyes in exasperation.

"Relax," Farley muttered. "Seth Weeks has been the outlaw mayor of Roundpatch for a long time; he'll stick around for another few days."

"And what about Jessie?" Longarm asked hotly.

Farley glowered. "I *care*. But it won't help her if I have a relapse. Be reasonable, Longarm. It's already close to one o'clock in the afternoon. By the time we got ourselves supplied, and arranged for my deputies to come along, it'd be close to dark."

Longarm slammed his fist down on Farley's desk. "Another goddamned day of doing nothing!" he shouted.

Farley winced. "It'll be *two* days if you don't get out of here! You're giving me the goddamnedest headache!"

The afternoon sun hovered above the western horizon, glowing fiery red. Ki and Birdy O'Hara cast long, purple shadows as they rode across a wide, grassy plain dotted with small herds of cattle.

Birdy slowed her mount and looked around. Some brown, desolate-looking hills shimmered in the distance. They were about the only feature of the landscape, except for the cows and a far-off grove of trees, to break up the vast, gently swelling ocean of green grass.

"How long until we reach Starbuck land?" she called to Ki, who'd reined in his horse.

The samurai smiled. "We have been on it now for the last two hours."

The reporter's normally wide eyes grew even rounder. "I must say, I'm impressed." She rubbed her saddle-weary, denim-clad backside. "Then we must be almost there?" she asked plaintively.

"Just through that grove of trees," Ki replied, pointing. "You've been doing fine so far," he added encouragingly. "Do all women from the East ride as well as you?"

"Only the ones who receive riding lessons," she said with a tight smile.

"Then you come from a wealthy family?" Ki asked.

She shook her head. "We were dirt poor. A, uh, *friend* paid for my lessons. But that was several years after I left home. The ranch house is through that grove of trees, you say?"

Ki wanted to ask more, but he was quite aware that the girl wished to change the subject. Still, he had had a glimpse of something that lay beneath the woman's brusque, brash exterior.

We are all the sum of our experiences, he thought. *If this woman behaves badly, it is because she has been treated badly herself. The tragedy is that she perpetuates her own unhappiness through her callous and arrogant treatment of others.*

As he gazed at Birdy O'Hara out of the corner of his eye, he was struck by her beauty, but he was also aware that such exquisiteness, like that of a fine sword, is blended inextricably with the very thing that makes it deadly . . .

"When we get to the ranch, you can rest," Ki said. "Come on!" He kneed his chestnut gelding, the same horse upon which he'd ridden into town yesterday, into a steady lope.

Birdy O'Hara watched him ride off. She sighed to herself and coaxed her own mount, a gray mare, in the same direction. The reporter winced as her tender bottom thudded against the saddle. In truth, while she had received the benefit of riding lessons, it had been quite a while since she'd put them into actual practice. Well, she thought, at least she'd brought along the proper clothes for an extended time on the trail. In addition to her snug-fitting jeans, she wore a black silk blouse and a dark green corduroy hacking jacket. Her wide-brimmed Stetson shielded her fair, freckled skin from the strong sun. Her boots were low-heeled so that she could as easily walk as ride.

She couldn't believe her eyes when she caught her first glimpse of the Starbuck house. It looked more like a storybook castle, as far as she was concerned. The big house was built of stone, with the main, middle section three stories tall. One-story wings jutted out to either side. Nearby were storage sheds, stables, and a bunkhouse for the hands. Trees were plentiful, lending a cool touch of greenness to the area.

As the duo rode up to the veranda of the house, a young wrangler hurried over to see to their horses. He greeted Ki deferentially, while trying his adolescent best not to gawk as Birdy O'Hara swung her shapely leg out of her stirrup and dismounted.

Ki noticed the boy's rather inappropriate behavior, but chose not to remark upon it. He would have been more worried about the young fellow if he had *not* stared!

"We will be riding out in an hour or so, Pete," Ki instructed. "Please fill some canteens for us, and ask Cook to pack two sets of saddlebags with supplies."

"Yessir," the young wrangler replied. "Sir? Is there any news about Miss Jessie?"

Ki shook his head. "None, Pete."

"We're all of us—the hands, I mean—" The young cowboy looked down at his scuffed boots in embarrassment. "We're all of us rootin' for her to come out of this mess all right."

"Thank you, Pete," Ki quietly replied.

"Sir?" the wrangler called as Ki and Birdy started toward the front door. The young hand paused to glance uncertainly at the reporter, but then shrugged and continued on, "There's a fella inside, has himself a badge. Says that Marshal Farley hired him on to watch things here in case Miss Jessie shows up." The baby-faced wrangler sneered. "Lucky for him she ain't showed up, is what all of us hands say. Anyhow, sir, I thought you'd want to know."

Ki nodded.

"For whom was that show of loyalty put on?" Birdy demanded as Ki led her into the front hallway.

"It was not a show," Ki said mildly. "The hands are loyal to Jessie because she treats them well. Just as people dislike you because you mistreat them," he added.

"Don't you lecture me, mister!" She looked around as they entered the main room of the house. "My, my," she taunted. "What a rich daddy's money won't buy!"

Though this part of the house was three stories tall, there were only two floors. The second-floor bedrooms opened out to a corridor, one side of which was a railed balcony that overlooked a huge combination dining and living area. The dark-stained roof rafters formed a cathedral ceiling that soared high above the massive slate fireplace. Comfortable furniture and colorful scatter rugs were arranged about the polished wood floors. Off to one side, on a raised area all its own, stood a handsome mahogany dining room set.

"It is true that Jessie inherited this fine house, and a wide-ranging business empire from her father," Ki said. "But under Jessie's control, the family fortune has prospered."

"I guess we *should* give her credit for not destroying in a matter of a few years what it took her father a lifetime to build," Birdy spat sarcastically.

"Jessie has been successful, but not because of the wealth that her father handed down to her," Ki replied. "She has been successful because her father passed on to her a far more valuable inheritance: a positive outlook with which to tackle the obstacles placed in her path—"

161

"Spare me your sermon," the girl sneered as she fingered a bronze statuette displayed on an end table near a sofa. "Save it for those hayseeds you've got working this place, probably for slave wages. One thing will be interesting, seeing how Jessie's 'positive outlook' is going to deal with an 'obstacle' like the gallows."

"Miss O'Hara," Ki began as he advanced upon her. "Do you know what you need?"

"Don't you do anything you don't want to read about in the papers!" The redhead warned. She anxiously backpedaled across the room, toward a brace of curtained bay windows, trying to put as much furniture between herself and Ki as possible.

"Hey, you!" a man suddenly called from the doorway of the big room. "You stop your shenanigans, and right now!"

Ki calmly turned his attention to the newcomer. The man was burly and dressed in twill pants, a red flannel shirt, and a light-colored Stetson, bleached by long years of wear beneath the Texas sun. He wore black high-heeled boots, and a pistol was strapped around his waist. A glittering star was pinned to his shirt pocket.

"You all right, Miss?" the man asked Birdy O'Hara.

"I am *now*." She sighed in relief. She had only an inkling of what Ki had intended to do to her, but something in his eyes had told her that her saddle-sore backside would have been the worse for it!

"I do not know you, friend," Ki said. "I assume you are the temporary deputy that Marshal Farley has hired?"

"I'll ask the questions here," the man said gruffly. "Now then." He thumbed back his Stetson. "The last I heard from the marshal, you were a prisoner. How do you come to be out?"

"I bailed him out," Birdy O'Hara announced. "He belongs to me, Deputy!"

"The first part of what she has said is true," Ki added, meanwhile glaring at the reporter, who was obviously quite enjoying vexing him, now that she thought she was safe on the far side of the room.

"You got anything to prove what you're saying?" the deputy

demanded. "Otherwise, how am I supposed to know you're not a fugitive, like the woman who owns this here spread?"

Ki nodded. "That is a reasonable question." He reached into the back pocket of his jeans for a folded sheet of paper and held it out to the approaching deputy. "This is a document from the marshal, vouching for what we have said."

The man took the form from Ki and quickly read it. "This seems to be in order," he muttered, "but I can't know for sure if it's the straight goods." He shook his head, smiling at the seemingly unarmed Oriental. "Reckon you'll have to ride back to town with me so that we can check all this out."

Ki shook his head. "I understand that you are new at your job, and wish to make a good impression upon Marshal Farley," he began politely, not wanting more trouble with the law.

"Quit your jawing and get ready to ride," the deputy cut him off brusquely.

"Please listen," Ki insisted. "I do not have the time for this—"

"You're coming with me," the deputy growled. "I'm starting to lose my temper!"

"Ki, maybe you should go," Birdy O'Hara suddenly said, worried now. "He's a lot bigger than you." She'd seen Ki in action yesterday, but that had been against a few no-account louts. This deputy looked far more capable than those cloddish Wilson cousins.

"Listen to the lady, little man," the deputy warned, prodding Ki with his thick, blunt forefinger. "You're coming back to town with me, whether you like it or not!" His finger jabbed Ki's chest to emphasize each word.

Ki's left hand flew out to capture the deputy's right wrist between his thumb and forefinger. The startled deputy tried to pull his hand free, but was unable to budge it an inch.

"What the hell?" The deputy stared dumbfounded at his suspended wrist. Ki appeared to be only lightly grasping it between his two fingers, and yet . . .

The deputy jerked his arm with all of his might. His neck muscles corded with the effort. Sweat began to glisten, and then dribble down his face. "What is this, a trick?" he gasped.

163

"Leggo!" He brought up his left hand to try to pull his wrist free, but Ki's sinewy fingers had somehow transmuted themselves into immovable steel.

The panicked lawman gave up his efforts. His left hand dropped down and stretched around behind his back to grope for the pistol on his right hip.

Ki let him clear the revolver from its holster before he used his right hand to bat it out of the man's grasp. "No guns," he said quietly as the Smith & Wesson .45 seemed to sprout wings and fly across the room.

The deputy tried to knee him in the groin. Ki blocked the attempt with his own upraised knee, and then clamped the rest of his left hand's fingers around the man's wrist. The samurai began to *squeeze*. Hard.

The deputy's already twisted features abruptly paled. His mouth gaped wide as he howled in pain.

Ki kept up the relentless pressure, driving the big man down to his knees. "When I let go of you, I want you to leave this house and stay out of my way. Do you understand?"

The deputy nodded soundlessly, wincing as his agony continued. Ki released him and stepped away.

The deputy slowly got to his feet. He eyed the general area where his pistol had fallen.

"Leave your gun where it is," Ki instructed. "With your gun hand bruised, your ability to aim would almost certainly be impaired. You would miss, and I would be obliged to kill you. Besides, I am only asking you to leave the house, not the ranch. You may retrieve your pistol after we have left."

The deputy cradled his injured wrist in his other hand. His face purple with humiliation, he sidled past Birdy O'Hara, unable to look her in the eye as he stalked out of the room.

She looked at Ki with admiration. "You and I are a lot alike," she said, her blue eyes shining.

Ki seemed amuse. "How so?"

"Well, if I want something, I take it," she declared fiercely. "Like you, I don't let anything stand in my way."

"You think that is an admirable quality?" the samurai inquired.

"I do!" the woman said staunchly, her hands on her shapely

164

hips. "Are you trying to say you don't consider it an admirable quality?" she demanded skeptically. "Just a little while ago you were raving on and on about Jessie Starbuck's determination—"

"Quiet," Ki ordered. "Determination is an admirable quality only if one's goals are admirable."

"You're a very moral person, I'm sure," she snapped back. "But you should be grateful that you've never had to make *hard* choices!"

"You presume so much." Ki chuckled, shaking his head. "You imagine that everyone else has had things so much easier than you have."

"Most have! Because of their luck. When folks have a head start on you in life, you've got to make up for your disadvantage any way you can." The reporter stopped. She was flushed with emotion. "Oh, never mind," she murmured.

Ki let the conversation drop, in acknowledgement of her embarrassment. "I thank you for your concern on my behalf," he said as he approached her.

"What do you mean?"

"When that deputy was confronting me, you seemed worried that I might be hurt."

"Oh, that!" Birdy sniffed. "Well, I was just concerned about my investment. I've got three hundred dollars tied up in you, mister. I didn't want my money—"

Ki cut her off by taking her in his arms and kissing her. He momentarily enjoyed the feel of her lips against his, and her soft breasts, beneath her black silk blouse, pressed against his chest. Her musky female scent, intensified by their long ride during the warm afternoon, dizzied him, strengthening his desire. Then she was twisting free of his embrace.

"How—" She paused to gasp for breath. "How dare you!" She brought back her hand as if to slap his face, but then thought better of it, remembering what had happened to that deputy . . . "What right did you have to—"

"According to your rules," Ki said, "it is an admirable quality to take what one wants." He pointed to the staircase that led up to the second floor. "The last door on your right at the top of the stairs is a guest room. You may rest there while

I make some final arrangements for our journey. Sleep while you can. We ride through the night."

He turned on his heel and strode out of the room. Birdy O'Hara watched him go. When she was all alone, she brought her fingers up to her mouth, savoring the taste of him still on her lips.

And she smiled.

★

Chapter 12

Sageville wasn't much. The cow town had one narrow, muddy street, and only a few weatherbeaten wood-frame buildings to call its own. The town existed pretty much as a layover stop for cowboys passing through, and as a mail drop for the ranches in the surrounding area. Sageville's few private residences were inhabited by families who'd realized that they had too many kids and too few cows to make it as ranchers. The center of town was a combination general store, saloon, café, and post office run by the mayor. His stock of goods was, of necessity, limited. Old Barney regularly brought his wagon through the settlement in hopes of enticing the few housewives in town to part with their pennies for some bauble they couldn't get locally.

Sageville could hardly compete with even one of Sarah Township's shoddier back alleyways, but to Jessie, the rough-hewn settlement looked like paradise. Disguised as Dora, she'd spent the last day and night more or less alone with Barney, and his constant blathering was driving her out of her mind!

She'd always been fond of the codger, but she'd never before had to remain in his presence for more than a few moments. Traveling for hours at a time along dusty trails in his plodding, mule-drawn wagon was a whole different experience. Listening to Barney while trying to concentrate on her own troubles was a torture Jessie had not counted upon having to endure.

Her only respite had come during their infrequent detours to ranches along the way, when Barney had focused his attention on his potential customers. His sales patter continued non-stop as he hauled out crates and cartons of merchandise for the edification and entertainment of the homesteaders. These folks didn't have much money to spend, but they also didn't see many new people. They didn't buy, but they did offer their guests home-cooked meals and a place to wash.

Jessie needn't have worried about anyone questioning the presence of "Dora." Either they didn't remember that Dora hadn't been around the last time Barney had made his meandering circuit, or, in the traditional manner of prairie folk, they were too polite to stick their noses into another individual's business.

Barney pulled his wagon up in front of a splintery, paint-blistered watering trough to let his mules drink their fill. The spry old geezer hopped down from the driver's bench and paused to stretch his creaking bones. He waved to a few curious passersby shuffling through the mud as they made their way down Sageville's main—and only—drag.

"Come on, Dora," Barney scolded. "That there's Hutch's store." He produced his plug of tobacco from out of the pocket of his workshirt, and spat out a mouthful of sludge in exchange for a fresh chew.

His toothless gums working on the stiff tobacco gave Jessie a chance to talk. "Barney, you're not planning to set up your display of wares right here, in front of the town's general store?"

"Why, sure," Barney said, grinning. "Old Hutch, he don't mind. He makes enough off of these folks the other three hundred sixty-four days of the year. He enjoys seeing me as much as any Sageville citizen!"

Jessie shrugged. Who was she to tell the drummer his business? She fiddled with her gray wig to make sure it was on

168

straight, lowered her spectacles down to the tip of her nose so that she could see what she was doing, and climbed down from the wagon.

She tried hard not to make too much of a face as her boots made a squishing, sucking sound in the mud. "Barney? Won't the stuff get awfully dirty?" she asked.

"Dora, I'm commencin' to think you're gettin' *senile*," Barney fumed. "Always askin' to take a bath in the wagon, and now forgettin' how we peddle the goods. Don't you 'member, girl? We lay out a tarp and put the merchandise out on top of it."

As Jessie nodded dutifully, a large, fat man dressed in a black velvet suit left the general store to approach their wagon. The man's sparse, dark hair was worn slicked back, and he had three days' worth of beard on his jowly cheeks.

"Howdy, Hutch," Barney greeted the man. "Dora, you 'member hizzonor, the mayor of Sageville, and proprietor of—"

"Howdy, Dora," Hutch interrupted, not bothering to give Jessie a second glance. "Barney," Hutch continued, "this ain't the best morning for you to be doing this. I've got a lot of mail at my place waitin' to be picked up. You being here attracts people to town, and I don't want folks coming in right now."

"But Hutch," Barney replied, his tone deferential. "I'm here already. Even if I don't put out my goods, folks will still come by to ask to see what I've got." He shrugged. "I can't ride out of town and then come back."

Hutch's chubby, scowling features relaxed into a smile. "Suppose you can't, old-timer." He chuckled, patting Barney's bony shoulder. "All right, then. I guess I'll have to make the best of the situation." He sighed uneasily. "I just wish that mail had been picked up. I never know when that stagecoach is going to be coming through."

"You reckon the mail is luring outlaws?" Barney asked.

"Six times a year, a coach comes through here on its way to Sarah," Hutch replied. "Right now I got two months' worth of letters sitting in three canvas sacks beneath my counter. With no bank in town, a lot of those envelopes contain folks' money being sent to banks at points east."

"Keep yer voice down," Barney hissed, looking around warily.

Hutch locked eyes with Jessie, and then silently shook his head. "Barney," he began patiently, "it's no secret. If I *kept* it a secret, folks wouldn't know to bring in their mail."

Barney nodded shrewdly.

"Dora, I'll have my clerk come out to give you and Barney a hand unloading," Hutch said.

"Much obliged," Jessie replied, adjusting the timbre of her voice to sound as old as she looked.

"My pleasure, ma'am," the fat town mayor said, as respectful in his manner as any decent sort would be to an older woman. "Barney here has talked a lot about you over the years," he added, before heading back to his store.

Jessie stared after the man, dying to know more about herself. But of course she couldn't ask! She turned her attention to Barney, who was busy lowering the tailgate of their wagon.

"I don't see any law around," Jessie remarked as she helped the old man settle the tailgate's single supporting leg in the mud. "Is Hutch the town constable as well as the mayor?"

"Nah, he wears a lot of hats, but that ain't one of them. Jody, his clerk, is the constable. He's a skinny young fella. Used to be a cowboy till he fell off his horse and busted up his back. He healed up, more or less, but he can't walk too good, or do much heavy work. Hutch there gave Jody a clerking job and saw to it that the poor hombre got the town constable's job as well, so as to earn hisself a few extra dollars a month. Jody can't shoot or fight worth a lick, what with his injury, but Sageville is a quiet place. There ain't enough cows to interest a rustler, and no bank to rob. Usually, Sageville is beneath the notice of outlaws."

"Except for six times a year, when the mail piles up," Jessie muttered. "Like now."

"Eh?" Barney glanced at her sharply. "What? You don't have to fret about that. I'll protect you."

Jessie grinned. "Thank you, Barney."

"Shucks," the old drummer clucked, blushing clear to the top of his bald, wrinkled scalp. "I'll never let nothin' happen to you, Dora."

170

A frail, freckle-faced man in ill-fitting clothes hobbled out of the general store and began to lurch across the street toward them. Jessie noticed a metal rod rising up out of the open collar of the man's flannel shirt. The poor fellow's chin rested upon a curved pad atop the metal rod.

"Act like you don't notice nothin'," Barney hissed urgently. "Old Jody got nursed back to health by the lady who runs the boardinghouse in town. They ain't got no doctor here. The lady and the town blacksmith put their heads together and come up with that there steel brace Jody's got to wear if'n he wants to walk."

"And he's supposed to be able to help us unload?" Jessie whispered back.

"You watch and see, Dora." Barney chuckled in admiration. "Jody don't let his troubles stop him from doin' what he sets out to do."

"Barney, ma'am," the unfortunate man greeted them, holding out his hand.

When it was Jessie's turn, she shook with Jody. His long, thin fingers felt parchment-dry, as dusty as bones found along a Texas Panhandle trail.

"Let's do it," Jody said.

The wagon took over an hour to unload. Jessie and Barney handed the lighter things to the disabled Jody, who was incapable of climbing up into the wagon. Most of the items he had to drop onto the spread tarp, as his back brace kept him from bending or stooping. Accordingly, Barney and Jessie handed over only unbreakable goods. Jody struggled to do his part, but Barney breathed a sigh of relief when he could decently thank the man for helping, and get rid of him.

"And he's the town law?" Jessie shook her head, once Jody was out of earshot. "He doesn't even wear a gun or a badge."

"Like I said, they gave him the job to help him out," Barney huffed, wiping the sweat from his bald dome with a big yellow bandanna. "He couldn't draw and aim a gun, so what's the use of wearin' it? As for the badge, well, that caused some trouble. Jody is a proud sort. You saw how hard he worked. Nasty fellas had a way of jokin' when he wore his star. 'Course, Jody had to challenge them, and luckily they always backed down.

Who'd fight a cripple like him? Anyway, it was causin' too much of a ruckus, so Hutch talked him into keeping that there star pinned to the inside of his lapel . . ."

The day passed quickly. Jessie found herself enjoying her duties as a vendor. She'd always considered herself a shrewd negotiator in the varied businesses she'd inherited from her father, but some of the Sageville women she found herself dealing with put her to shame! After a particularly lengthy give-and-take between herself and a young girl anxious to own a few yards of cotton cloth and a dozen buttons, "Dora" felt as proud over the coins she'd wrested out of the deal as Jessie Starbuck had once felt after winning timber rights to a thousand acres of forest.

She and Barney went for dinner at Hutch's general store. Initially, Jessie had been concerned about the old drummer leaving his goods unguarded, but Barney put her fears to rest.

"Folks here is poor but honest," he confided to her as they counted up the day's take. "Glory be, Dora! We took in close to five dollars!" Barney crowed. He winked at a smiling Jody standing behind the store's counter. "She always could outsell me."

"I shouldn't of let you stay," Hutch grumbled from his rocking chair, but he smiled to show that he was kidding when Jessie looked his way. "Bet you ain't never made that much money in one day in your entire life?" he demanded of her.

"Haw! And that's a fact," Barney guffawed.

"I never worked harder for a profit," Jessie said truthfully, and wisely let the matter go at that.

"I see you finished your stew, Miss Dora," Jody said. "We got plenty. And I baked up all this sourdough bread."

He laughed as Jessie hurried for a second helping. "No disrespect intended, ma'am," he hastened to say, "but I swear, you eat like a healthy woman about one-third your age!"

"She always did!" Barney laughed happily, beaming at her.

Jody glanced from his stew caldron to the wall clock above the potbellied stove. "Guess that coach ain't gonna make it through here today."

"Nope, guess not," Hutch said sadly. "Hell of a time to be stuck with all this mail."

"I got me a pistol right here," Jody confided, patting a lump beneath his baggy coat. "Nobody's touchin' those mail sacks beneath this counter while I'm around."

"Now you listen to me," Hutch said sternly. "We have any trouble, I want you to hand those bags over, easy as you please! Got that?"

"I'm town constable," Jody sulked.

"You just do as I tell you," Hutch said. "'Cause I'm the damned mayor!" When Jody didn't reply, Hutch growled, "Don't get insolent on me, boy!"

"Come on now," Barney laughed anxiously. "Let's not spoil a good time! I'm buyin' a round of beers for everyone!" he quickly added.

Jody and Hutch exchanged fond grins of apology. "Ain't nothin' gonna happen nohow," the crippled constable said.

"Reckon you're right," Hutch mused worriedly. But his eyes strayed to a small poster tacked up on a bulletin board in one corner of his emporium.

Jessie hadn't noticed the handbill amid the store's clutter, but now that she saw it, she couldn't tear away her stricken gaze.

Jody, misunderstanding the meaning of Jessie's upset, quickly comforted her. "Don't worry, Miss Dora. She ain't been seen in these parts."

"Fellow passing through last week dropped that wanted flyer off," Hutch elaborated. "The bank in Sarah put up the reward."

Jessie could only nod. She had no voice. She stared at the line drawing of the woman, and at the legend inscribed beneath it:

!!!WANTED!!!
JESSICA STARBUCK
MURDER AND BANK ROBBERY

An awkward silence filled the room. Jessie, noticing the bowl of stew on her lap, set it aside, her appetite vanished.

"You heard the man," Hutch said to Jody. "He said he was going to buy us all a round. When Barney offers to buy, you've got to move quick, lest he change his mind!"

"Right!" Jody exclaimed all too brightly, hobbling to the beer keg. He was in the process of drawing them all mugs of the amber brew, when the door to the store suddenly opened.

They watched as two men wearing canvas dusters sauntered in. They had the creased, sun-bronzed skin of drovers, but one of the pair had ghastly white scars ringing his neck. Both moved with menacing grace. They wore their guns butt-forward, with their creaking leather holsters angled across their flat bellies. As they laid eyes on Jessie, they touched the brims of their Stetsons.

"Howdy, ma'am," the scarred man whispered hoarsely. As he spoke, his partner's hard eyes scanned the layout of the store.

Jody seemed to be put somewhat at ease by the newcomers' show of manners toward Jessie. "What can we do for you gents?" he asked officiously.

The two men gave the clerk a quick once-over, their gaze lingering on the steel brace jutting out from beneath his shirt. Then they grinned, the way mean, junkyard dogs do when something helpless falls on their side of the fence.

"What can you do for us?" the man who'd greeted Jessie continued, in what was more of a wheeze than a voice. "Well, for starters, how about some of that stew?"

"Comin' up!" Jody went to the shelf, where he slowly and awkwardly reached up for a pair of bowls.

The two newcomers exchanged amused glances as they watched Jody move. "Make sure it don't go cold on us there, Speedy," the man wheezed. His laughter sounded like the hiss of a snake.

Jessie, watching Jody's back, saw the disabled man flinch at the insult. *Don't respond*, she thought desperately. *Jody, don't give them an excuse to—*

"Jody, you give these two fellows a beer on the house," Hutch suddenly decreed from his rocking chair, like a king on his throne. "We always like to welcome a stranger passing through town with a free beer." He chuckled. "What brings you boys to Sageville?"

"We're drovers on our way to a job," the man wearing the necklace of scars whispered in reply.

Hutch nodded. "Always wanted to be a cowboy myself." He patted his big belly. "But I drank too much of that there brew you're about to sample to ever find me a horse capable of carrying me."

Everybody laughed. Jessie gazed at the mayor with new admiration. He was purposely making fun of himself to divert the newcomers' attention away from Jody's disability. The idea was to allow the thin-skinned, proud town constable a few moments to cool off. Like Jessie, Hutch must have become obsessed with the thought of the gun the disabled man had cached beneath the folds of his scarecrow coat. Right now that gun's existence was not to their advantage; it was a ticking bomb, threatening to destroy them all if Jody dared to pull it against these dangerous newcomers.

She wondered if Hutch knew—as she did—that these two were lying about being drovers. She expected that the fat mayor had come to that conclusion by the sick look in his eyes as the laughter in the room died away.

The two men began to eat their stew standing up. Jessie and the others watched them uneasily. The air of camaraderie that had earlier existed was now a mere memory. There was no more easy conversation, but only an awkward silence, and the sounds of the two newcomers eating.

Jessie's every instinct told her that there was going to be bad trouble. Neither Hutch nor Barney was wearing a gun. That was just as well, she thought. No gun at all was better than a weapon in the hands of someone who didn't know how to use it. She thought of the revolver she had hidden in Barney's wagon. If only she could get to it! A woman using a gun with her skill would certainly draw more attention to her than Jessie wanted, and might give her away, but she couldn't worry about that now. Lives were in the balance. Her old woman's disguise would probably protect her if trouble broke out, but Hutch and Barney were goners if these two newcomers were able to goad

175

Jody into a suicidal attempt at defending his honor.

The crippled constable was in the process of limping around the counter toward the two men, carrying their beers. "Tell you what, Speedy," the man who spoke in a whisper told him. "Seeing as how those drafts are free, we'll trade them for some whiskey."

Jody stared at them in disbelief. "The mayor didn't offer you no whiskey—"

"Quiet, Speedy," the scarred newcomer hissed between spoonfuls of stew. "I don't want you to argue," he whispered. "I just want you to do it."

For one awful second, Jessie thought that Jody was going to toss the beer into the man's face.

"These gents can have the whiskey instead of the beer, Jody," Hutch said, but this time his tone was strangely weary. It was the voice of a man who saw the future and was coming to realize that there was little he could do to change the course of those inevitable events.

As Jody went for the whiskey, Hutch continued, "I want to make everything as easy as possible. Do you gents catch my drift?" He smiled nervously. "No fuss necessary."

The fellow with the damaged voice nodded as he set down his empty bowl. "That's a square deal."

"What we came for, mostly," the other man said, speaking for the first time, "is to mail us a letter." He winked at Hutch in his rocking chair. "We'd heard that this was the mail drop for the area."

Hutch stopped rocking. "It is," he said evenly.

"But you fellows just missed the pickup," Jody said shrilly.

"I hope not, Speedy," the other man said in his hoarse wheeze, not even deigning to look in Jody's direction. "Because if we did, we'd be mighty upset."

"You didn't miss it, gents," Hutch hurriedly cut in. "Jody?" He laughed. "You must be mistaken."

Jody stared into Hutch's eyes for a moment. "Yes," he said dully. "I'm mistaken."

"Here's the letter," the scarred man with the damaged voice grunted.

Jody held out his hand for it. "Give it to me and I'll put it away."

The man snatched back his arm. "Well, no, Speedy," he whispered. "I'm a worrisome sort. I've got to *see* you put the letter into the mail sack." He tossed the envelope onto Jody's counter. "Go ahead, and let me see you put it in the sack," he repeated.

Jessie actually saw Jody's right hand begin to inch toward his coat. It looked as if the bomb was about to explode.

"Jody," Hutch said calmly, "you just do what this gent tells you."

Jody stared at the two men. The look in his eyes was one part defiance and one part pleading. "I'm the town constable," he murmured. "I take my job seriously. You can trust me to put this letter with the rest—later!"

The scarred man grinned. "Nope. I want you to do it now, *Constable* Speedy."

Jody stood still and defiant.

"Maybe you can't handle it, you being locked up in that steel brace," the man wheezed disdainfully.

"Jody! Damn it!" Hutch thundered. His outburst seemed to startle everyone in the room with the exception of the two newcomers. "Just get away from the counter!" He softened his tone as he addressed the two men. "You gents go right around back there and put that letter in the mail sack yourselves, if you like. It's right underneath the counter."

Barney, who'd been strangely quiet through the last few minutes, suddenly spoke up. "I notice you got a little throat problem there, sonny," he said to the wheezing newcomer.

The man scowled at the drummer. "Is that what you notice, old man?" he croaked.

"Sore throat?" Barney asked.

The man's hand rose to finger his scarred neck. "Are you looking for trouble, you old geezer?"

"Not a-tall, sonny," Barney replied. "I jes' asked 'cause I got me some fine cough remedy in my wagon."

"Cough remedy?" The man shook his head in disgust.

"Fine, twelve-year-old, aged-in-oak, sour-mash cough

syrup," Barney said lovingly. "I could go fetch it. My wagon's just yonder, across the road."

"Reckon not," the man wheezed. "You just set right where you are."

"Barney?" Jessie spoke up, doing her best to put the lilt of old age into her voice. "Why don't I fetch these nice young men that sour mash?"

"You, Dora?" Barney shook his head. "Y-you don't know where it is," he stuttered. "I got to go!" He began to rise from his chair.

"Set down," hissed the man with the scarred neck, his right hand instinctively dropping to his gun butt.

"I swear," Jessie trilled. "The older Barney gets— Don't you remember, Barney? *I* put the sour mash away!"

"Old!" Barney sputtered. "Who you calling old, girl?"

"Surely you boys won't mind if I fetch the sour mash?" Jessie asked, peering at them over her spectacles. "Why, one of you could come with me."

The two men exchanged glances. "Why not?" the scarred man said. "All right, grandma, you can go." He turned to his partner. "You go with her."

Jessie nodded sweetly and made a show of rising laboriously from her chair. She had no idea what Barney's plan had been. Most likely to try to fetch help, she guessed. That wouldn't have worked, of course. At this hour of the evening, most of the transients who'd come through Sageville had already left town. There was nobody in the small settlement who was capable of standing up to these two.

She headed slowly toward the door, walking with an old woman's careful gait, so as to increase the two outlaws' sense of confidence. That they were outlaws, she no longer doubted. The only thing that puzzled Jessie was why they were beating around the bush. Clearly they had come to steal the mail. Why didn't they just take it and leave? It almost seemed as if they were stalling for time.

Perhaps they simply lacked the nerve to make their move. If so, that was to Jessie's advantage. Her plan was simple. Once she was in the wagon, she'd hand her escort a keg of something, just to occupy him while she retrieved her gun.

She'd knock the man out, hurry back to the store, and get the drop on the fellow with the scars around his neck. Jessie had long since concluded that those scars were the result of a close brush with the hangman.

As Jessie reached the door she began to feel more optimistic about things. It might even be possible for her to pull this off without revealing her true identity! She could claim the gun belonged to Barney. The drummer wouldn't know what she was talking about, but she could wink at Hutch, point out that Barney had a tendency to forget a lot of things these days, and leave it at that. Everyone would be so relieved that they'd be glad to let the matter drop. Hutch and Jody would take the two men prisoner, and that would be that.

It all hinged on Jessie's ability to do the job without firing a shot. That an old woman could use the advantage of surprise to knock out one man and get the drop on another was plausible. That she could outshoot a pair of gunslicks was something quite different.

As Jessie reached for the doorknob, it began to turn. "Hold it," the man behind her ordered, gripping her by the shoulder. Her spirits plummeted as she watched him draw his gun.

The door opened. Jessie turned back to see who it was—

She gasped. Yes, these two *were* waiting for someone!

Jessie stared, dumbstruck, into her own face! She took in the large green eyes, the copper-tinted blond tresses, the snug-fitting denims, the double-action Colt held steadily in the right hand. She suddenly felt dizzy.

"Jessica Starbuck!" Hutch breathed. "Lord have mercy! Don't kill us, Miss Starbuck! We'll do whatever you say!"

"Dora! Come over here by me," Barney called out.

"You do that, old woman," Jessie's double said.

My God, Jessie thought, *she even has my voice!*

The man with the rope-scarred neck drew his gun. "What took you so long, Jessie? he complained in his whispery voice. "We couldn't have stalled much longer."

"We had to make sure the town was as wide open as it seemed," Jessie's double replied as she entered the store. She stared at the gunslick standing in front of her. "Where were you going with that old biddy?" she demanded.

"Uh . . ." the outlaw fumbled, glancing beseechingly at his neck-scarred partner.

"He was just going with that old woman to fetch some sour mash out of the wagon across the way," the man whispered.

"I told you two sorry bastards to watch this place, and that's what I meant for you to do!" the woman spat.

"Easy, Jessie," said a man pushing in behind the imposter. The newcomer was dressed entirely in black, from his boots to his gunbelt and hat. The nickel-plated Smith & Wesson he held lightly balanced in his left hand had grips of shiny ebony.

"Don't you tell me to be easy on these two," fumed Jessie's twin. "I've had enough of them disobeying me!" She glared at the man with the damaged voice. "Especially you, Dusty. Those souvenirs the hangman left around your neck turn my stomach!"

"Jessie!" the man in black snapped, his light amber eyes flashing fire. He was tall and quite handsome, with thick, coal-black hair. "Let's just get on with this," he finished coolly.

"Jessie Starbuck!" Hutch mourned. "I didn't believe what they were saying about you, but now that I see it with my own eyes—"

Oh, Hutch! Look closely! the real Jessie silently implored. She was helpless to say anything. If she revealed her true identity, who knew what these outlaws might do?

"How could you have killed all those innocent men?" Hutch demanded, well aware that he was treading on dangerous ground, but somehow mesmerized by the woman standing before him. "How could you have done it, Jessie?"

Hutch, it's not me! Jessie railed in frustration. *Don't be fooled!*

And yet she knew that Hutch and Barney and Jody would be fooled. The woman pretending to be her was an excellent but imperfect copy; she was different from Jessie in a thousand little ways.

Little ways . . . that was exactly how most people would be taken in, Jessie realized dismally. The imposter's skin tone, teeth, and height, the shape of her hands and eyes, were all slightly different from Jessie's, but who on earth besides herself could be expected to notice such minimal differences? Perhaps

180

if she ripped off her disguise and stood side by side with this imposter, the men in the room would realize that they were being duped. But Jessie did not dare remove the makeup and wig that had transformed her into Dora. She had to pretend to be someone else while this woman committed atrocities in her name!

But why? Jessie wondered. *Who would want to do this to me?*

Meanwhile, the imposter had crossed the room to stand before the seated mayor of Sageville. "You want to know how I killed those nobodies?" she said, smirking, pressing her Colt against Hutch's forehead. "You really want to see how I did it?" She thumbed back the hammer of her gun.

"Please," Hutch whispered. "P-please . . ."

"Oh, don't!" the real Jessie cried out, drawing her double's attention.

"Well," the phony Jessie sneered, taking her revolver away from Hutch's head. "If it isn't the old hag who caused all the trouble in the first place . . ."

"Let's take the mail and get out of here," rasped the outlaw with the damaged throat.

"Shut up, Dusty." The imposter sounded both bored and annoyed.

The man in black, meanwhile, was staring at the real Jessie, who quickly dropped her eyes to the ground. "Don't hurt us, we're harmless," she begged, careful to maintain Dora's aged tremor in her voice. *And don't look so closely at me,* she added silently. The man in black was muttering to himself as he scrutinized her. He began to approach, angling his head to get a better look.

My God, he's going to see through my disguise, Jessie thought. *But how? Why should he, of all people, recognize me?*

"I'm telling you," Dusty wheezed. "Even a hick town like this can be trouble if you stretch out a job."

The man in black paused. "Yes, you're right." He gave Jessie one last look. "It's just that . . ." He shook his head. "Never mind, let's get on with it!"

"Is it true that this cripple is the only law they've got?" the double asked, pointing her Colt at Jody.

"That's Constable Speedy," Dusty hissed in laughter. "Watch out, he might come gimpin' after you, Jessie . . ."

The woman laughed. Jody, pale and trembling, stared down at his clenched fists.

"The mail sacks are behind the counter," Hutch said quickly. "Take 'em and leave!"

"Fetch us out them sacks, Constable," Dusty whispered harshly.

Jody laboriously bent to the task. An exclamation of pain escaped his lips as he tugged at the heavy canvas sacks.

"Faster, Constable Speedy," Jessie's impersonator commanded. Once again she pressed her Colt against Hutch's temple. "How's this? I count to five. If they're not out in front of us, the fat mayor gets his head blown off."

Jody rolled his anguished eyes as he strained at his burden. "D-don't do that! I'm trying . . ."

"Then I'll count another five, before I shoot that old man there," the imposter continued. "Five more, and the old woman gets hers."

Moaning in agony, the constable struggled to budge the sacks. "Don't shoot him, I'm getting it!"

"One, two," the imposter counted. "Three, four—"

"Stop this!" Jessie cried, instinctively directing her appeal toward the man in black. Somehow she felt that he just might listen to her. "Jody can't move those bags," she said, petrified that the woman night shoot Hutch at any moment. "I'll do it. Jody can't. He's a cripple."

Jody bowed his head and began to weep.

"I'm so sorry," Jessie whispered. "I didn't mean to . . ."

"Dusty, get those sacks," the man in black muttered. "Let's get out of here."

Jessie gazed at the man. Was she imagining things, or was that a trace of shame she saw in his amber eyes?

"Right!" the imposter said. "I'll kill them all right now."

"No! Not this time!" The man in black glanced at the real Jessie. "Not that old woman, not any of them."

"But I'm *supposed* to!"

Jessie watched, aghast, as the woman mimicking her sulked

182

and whined like a child. It looked as if they were goners, after all . . .

"I said not this time!" the man in black snarled. He took a quick, menacing step toward her.

Jessie held her breath, waiting for her double—who was, after all, the leader—to shoot this insubordinate gang member.

"All right," the imposter whimpered, quickly holstering her gun.

Jessie couldn't believe what she was seeing. The imposter was clearly afraid of this man. Why, her entire manner had changed! The fierce, bloodthirsty tigress had become a meek kitten!

She's not the gangleader, Jessie realized. *They all answer to the man in black!*

"I got all there is," Dusty rasped. He had two sets of the saddlebag-like mail sacks yoked over his shoulders.

"Mount up," the man in black ordered him, then turned to the other outlaws. "The rest of you bring these folks outside. We'll keep an eye on them while we ride off. For all we know, they could haul out shotguns and blast us, once our backs are turned."

"I am so sorry," the real Jessie whispered to Jody as they were rounded up and herded out of the general store under the watchful eyes and guns of the outlaws.

"Nothing to be sorry about, Dora," Jody muttered, not looking at her. "You didn't say nothin' that ain't true."

"Jody, listen—" She reached out to comfort him.

"Don't touch me!" he snapped, squirming to avoid her touch. "This cripple don't need no pity!"

They stepped out into the balmy evening. The man in black grabbed Jessie's arm, pulling her to one side.

"What do you want with me?" she asked in her old woman's quaver, doing her best to hide her face from his prying eyes.

"What's your name?" he demanded gruffly.

"Dora. Please don't hurt me!" Jessie figured that pretending to be petrified fit her disguise. In reality, she was curious about this outlaw who'd saved all of their lives.

"That's my Dora!" Barney cried out, ignoring the commands of the other outlaws to stay where he was.

The man in black regarded the old drummer. "This woman has been with you a long time, I take it?"

"Oh, yes, years! Ain't that right, Hutch?"

"Barney's always talked about his Dora," Hutch volunteered.

The man in black pursed his lips, nodding slowly. "Very well, *Dora*. If only I had the time . . ." He left his declaration—or threat—unfinished. "Go stand with the others," he ordered, releasing her.

Jessie couldn't move fast enough to do as she was told. Curiosity was all well and good, but as the saying went, it could kill the cat! She did not doubt that the man in black had been on the verge of recognizing her. Only his need for haste, the obscuring shadows of the night, and the confusing remarks of Barney and Hutch had kept the outlaw from seeing through her disguise.

Who is this man who knows me so well? Jessie wondered. *And why did he spare us?*

A fifth outlaw had stayed outside to watch the horses of the four who'd entered the general store. "Everything quiet?" the man in black asked this lookout as the gang mounted up.

The lookout chuckled. "I've seen livelier cemeteries."

Jessie looked around. She believed that the outlaw was telling the truth. With the exception of Hutch's store, there was not one lighted window along Sageville's solitary street.

"Let's ride," the man in black said. The gang members were wheeling around their horses when Jody made the move he'd been contemplating for the last hour.

It happened too fast. Jessie could only watch, the despair rising up to engulf her as the valiant, foolhardy constable reached for the gun beneath his coat.

"Stop!" Jody roared. "You hold it! All of you! I'm the law!" He lurched toward the startled outlaws, fumbling for his weapon.

It was the hellcat pretending to be Jessie who was first to draw. Laughing, she twisted around in her saddle, leveled her Colt, and shot Jody in the chest.

His eyes went wide with astonishment as the pistol he'd barely managed to draw fell from his thin fingers. The impact of the slug knocked him backwards. He fell hard on his butt, but the steel brace encasing his body prevented his upper torso from slumping to the ground. He sat there, balanced on the brace, with blood streaming down his front, his skinny arms and legs waving feebly.

The imposter's raucous laughter spilled into the night like the cawing of a crow. "Look at him!" she howled with awful hilarity. "He's a turtle! A turtle turned over on his shell!"

Jessie lunged for Jody's fallen gun. Her double fired again. The bullet sent the pistol spinning out of Jessie's reach.

"Shouldn't of done that, old woman," the pretender sneered. "I'm going to kill you."

"Dusty," the man in black said with a scowl, "didn't you search that man for a gun?"

The outlaw shrugged. "Hell, he was a cripple!"

"That cripple almost put an end to our plans," the man in black replied coolly.

Jessie, meanwhile, was staring into the muzzle of her double's gun. "You know my reputation," the imposter drawled. "If I were you, I'd start begging for my life."

"If you were—?" Jessie just shook her head. "Go to hell," she spat, steeling herself for the bullet's impact.

Before the imposter could fire, the man in black sidestepped his mount against hers, throwing off her aim. An instant later, he'd snatched the Colt from her hand.

"What are you doing?" Jessie's double demanded in disbelief. At that moment a lantern appeared in a window across the street.

"Hutch?" a voice called out timorously. "Who's shooting out there?"

"Dusty, you and the others get her out of here," the man in black commanded. "Quick, before somebody comes!"

"But what about *them?*" the imposter argued, her voice trembling with hatred. "You can't let them live, not after they defied me!"

The man in black regarded her sourly. "Go on!" he snapped. "Before you're captured!"

"Come on, Jessie!" Dusty rasped, looking around anxiously. "Let's beat it!" He and the rest of the gang rode off, with the bogus Jessie in tow.

The man in black had remained behind. His horse danced in place as he stared at Jessie for a long moment, a slow smile stretching across his handsome face.

"That was suicidal, Dora." He chuckled. "You came close to killing yourself."

Jessie could only nod. Her throat had gone as dry as death as she stared at the imposter's Colt which he still held in his hand.

Staring at her, the man in black pointed the Colt into the air and fired three shots. Jessie would always remember the impassive look on his face as it was illuminated briefly by the blue flashes of fire erupting from the Colt's muzzle. Then the man touched the brim of his black Stetson, wheeled his horse around, and was gone. The sound of his mount's hooves gradually faded into the darkness.

"What's goin' on?" Barney asked in a daze. "What jes' happened?"

Jessie gazed into the evening's darkness, her mind a jumble of conflicting thoughts. The man in black had again spared them. This time he'd pretended to kill them in order to fool the rest of the gang.

Why? Jessie wondered. *Why did he do it? Did he know? Did he realize that I'm really Jessie Starbuck? That would have explained his remark about committing suicide: If my double had shot me, it* would *have been like Jessie killing herself.*

Jody's anguished moans brought Jessie back to the present. Hutch was kneeling down beside his wounded friend, gently helping him to stretch out on the ground.

"Get this damned brace off me, Hutch," Jody gasped. "At least I can die like a normal man..." Bright blood began to bubble up out of his mouth. Hutch lifted his head to keep Jody from choking on it. "Oh, damn, Hutch," the constable moaned. "They took the mail. I'm sorry."

"You did real fine, Jody!" Hutch told him. "Yes, you did, Constable. You upheld the law as good as any man ever did!"

"Hutch, let's get him to a doctor," Jessie said urgently.

"We don't have a doctor." Hutch stared down at Jody for a moment, then slowly got to his feet. "He's got no need for one now, anyway." He sighed. "Jody's dead."

"Oh . . ." Jessie felt the tears coming. "Oh, Hutch . . ."

"I know, Dora, I know." Hutch wiped his sleeve across his wet eyes. "I wish to hell those outlaws had searched him, found his damn gun, and took it off him!" he spat furiously. "I knew he was gonna go for it sooner or later, I just knew it! Damn that Jessie Starbuck for this," he swore. "Damn her to hell!"

"Yes," Jessie said, nodding numbly. "Damn her to hell."

★

Chapter 13

"Ki, please!" Birdy O'Hara begged the samurai. "The sun's going down. We've ridden all last night, and right through today! Please, let's rest for a while!"

Ki twisted around in his saddle to regard the weary reporter. "Yes, I suppose we should rest the horses."

"Oh, *you!*" Birdy shrieked fiercely. "You woke me up at midnight last night, told me we were leaving, and we haven't stopped since!" She stared at the samurai. "At least I got a few hours of rest in that guest room you directed me to, but you haven't slept at all, have you?"

Ki shrugged. "There was much to do at the ranch before we could depart."

"Just like a man to pretend that he's engaged in important matters all the time," the girl sniffed, her blue eyes flashing fire. "Just *what*, I might ask, was so important?"

"I had to see to my weapons," Ki replied.

"And what else?" she demanded.

"And check our supplies, and see that our horses were up to the journey."

"And?" she insisted. "Well, go on. I'm waiting."

Ki sadly shook his head. "And I had to meditate, to gain an extra measure of serenity and in that way shield myself from your exceedingly shrewish ways!"

Her entire body clenched with anger. "Fine," she said through tightly compressed lips, nodding her head so hard that her Stetson fell off and her tousled red curls bobbed and waved in the breeze. "You go ahead and insult me." She rolled her eyes heavenward. "I should have left you in jail."

"If you had," Ki was quick to point out, "you wouldn't be here." He turned his horse, dipped down from his saddle to retrieve her hat, and handed it to her in one fluid motion.

"And just where *is* here?" she shot back, looking around at the terrain. "We rode into these hills hours ago! Since then it's been nothing but sticky heat and bugs and—" She flinched as a pair of warblers took off from a nearby stand of brush.

"I see that you are tired," Ki noted. "Perhaps I've been too hard on you."

"Perhaps," she admitted, biting her lower lip to hold back her tears.

"Come," Ki said softly. "Just a few moments more, and we'll be at a pleasant campsite." He indicated the girl's gray mare as it pawed the sandstone beneath its hooves and tossed its massive, snorting head. "You see?" the samurai asked. "Even your horse knows that water is near. She wants to go there."

"Where?" the reporter asked, studying her mount's peculiar behavior. "I don't understand—"

"You do not understand because you do not smell what the horses and I can smell. The scent of sweet water is in the air. It is not far off."

"You can *smell* water?" she scoffed. "I don't believe it!"

"It is true," Ki assured her. He smiled faintly. "But not for you, if you do not believe it."

"What?" she stared, then covered her mouth to hide her giggle. "You're crazy," she murmured.

"And you are very young, very innocent, when you laugh," Ki said softly.

"Hmmm." Birdy swiftly regained her composure. "Well, I

190

still don't believe that tall tale you just handed me about smelling water—"

"In your coat pocket," Ki interrupted her, closing his eyes. "Wrapped in waxed paper. A square of chocolate . . ."

O'Hara could only gape at the samurai, awestruck. "Well, I'll be a . . ." She laughed delightedly, reaching into the side pocket of her corduroy hacking jacket for the chocolate Ki had smelled. "Do you want some?" she grinned.

"No." Ki's almond eyes were bright as he shook his head. "I will not take the candy. The kiss I took from you yesterday was sweet enough."

Birdy O'Hara could not hide her blush. "Come along, mister," she scolded him nervously. "Let's get to that water. You need to cool off!"

They rode single file through scrubby clumps of post oak and blackjack. Grasshoppers, churned up by the day's warmth, hurled themselves across the horses' path. The insects sounded like crumpled balls of paper as they bounced off of the rocks.

"Can anybody learn that trick?" Birdy asked.

"Anybody can if they will train themselves," Ki replied. "It is a matter of honing one's senses. The scents of the world, like its sights, are ever-present. It is only a matter of perceiving them."

"Well, I never met anybody who could do it," she called back as they rode. "Have you?"

"Yes, in my homeland," Ki answered. "Here in America I have known Indians who could catch the scent of water, or game, or braves from other tribes. I have met only one white man with the ability." Ki chuckled to himself. "But he smokes too much." The samurai tapped the side of his nose. "Tobacco dulls a keen sense of smell and taste."

She looked over her shoulder. "You're talking about Longarm, I bet." When Ki nodded, she continued, "I knew you were. *Longarm!*" She frowned. "I'll bet the two of you are friends."

"We are," Ki said.

"How *could* you be?" she asked, mystified. "I thought the sacred Miss Jessica Starbuck was the most important thing in your life? Longarm would steal her away from you if he got the chance."

The trail before them widened enough for Ki to draw up alongside her. "Longarm and I are friends," Ki explained evenly. "His relationship with Jessie is not my business or yours, and we shall not discuss it."

"But he's such a dunce!" Birdy chortled wickedly. "I've outsmarted him at every turn!"

Ki regarded his traveling companion wryly. "Do not be smug," he warned. "You think you have beaten Longarm, but all you have done is to take advantage of the fact that he had rules of conduct, and you do not!"

"Is that so?" she replied hotly. "Rules! Rules are for— for—" She shrugged. "Crybabies!" When Ki did not reply, the reporter eyed him slyly. "I'll bet Longarm and Jessie are lovers."

"Enough," Ki snapped. He kneed his chestnut gelding into a trot and rode on ahead, effectively cutting off their conversation.

Birdy O'Hara stared at the proud, quiet samurai's slender, ramrod-straight back. Her full, pouty lower lip began to tremble. She was on the verge of calling out an apology when she shook her head, getting control of her emotions.

"Rules are for crybabies," she softly reminded herself. That was twice she'd been able to make the samurai lose his composure: once at the jail, and once just now. Both times it had come about by bringing Jessie Starbuck into the conversation. Interesting, she thought. She would have to keep that in mind.

The reporter clucked her mount into a trot in order to catch up. If her hands had not been busy holding the reins, she would have hauled out her correspondent's pad and pencil and made a few pertinent notes . . .

The campsite turned out to be everything that Ki had promised it would be. Soil, washed down from the surrounding cliffs of sandstone, had given rise to dense groves of hickory. There was brush everywhere to fuel their fire. The water that Ki had promised was nothing less than a bubbling brook of pure, sweet liquid slithering out into a shallow pool from between two granite boulders.

The samurai unsaddled and watered their horses, and then put braided leather hobbles on the forelegs of the animals before setting them grazing on the tender shoots of grass springing up beneath a leafy hickory tree. Next he spread out the ground tarps and bedrolls, and built their campfire. He directed Birdy to gather up enough wood to last them through the night, and while she wandered the immediate area, the samurai checked over his weapons, so hastily gathered from the armory at the Circle Star ranch the night before.

Ki's bow was designed in the traditional Japanese manner. It was five feet long, and appeared to most people ridiculously lopsided, with its seemingly asymmetrical bends and curves. Ki, who was an expert archer, knew that his "crooked" bow could send an arrow straight and true into a target three hundred yards away.

Ki wiped down the unstrung bow with a soft cloth, checked the string to see if it was frayed, and then, satisfied that his weapon was in perfect condition, slipped it back into the special boot strapped to his saddle. Next, Ki examined his arrows. His leather quiver, called an *ebira,* rode on his hip. The *ebira* held twenty-four arrows, bundled together according to type. Ki now removed his stock of arrows and laid them out upon a blanket to examine them.

The average length of the shafts was three feet. The arrowhead on each varied according to the arrow's intended function. Not all of Ki's projectiles were meant for killing. Several, for instance, were tipped with a crescent-shaped wafer of steel. In Ki's homeland, this type of shaft was known as the "cleaver." It was used to sever a rope, slice through the harness binding together a team of horses, cut down an enemy's battle flag, and so on. Others of the samurai's assortment of arrows had far grimmer purposes. Some were tipped with corkscrew-like points to inflict maximum damage upon their flesh-and-blood targets. Another, called the "willow leaf" from its shape, had as its purpose the deep penetration of an enemy.

Satisfied that the shafts and fletching of his arrows were all in proper condition, and that their heads were all honed razor-sharp, Ki slid the projectiles back into his quiver and turned his attention to his close-quarters weapons.

In addition to his *shuriken* throwing blades and stars, Ki had with him an assortment of *nage teppo*. These were egg-sized grenades developed in centuries past by the *ninja* of the samurai's homeland. Each *nage teppo* was dyed a different color. The red ones created a smokescreen. The white ones erupted into flame. The yellow ones exploded in a flash of light that was harmless but temporarily blinding. The green ones exploded with the destructive power of a stick of dynamite.

Ki had brought along one final close-combat weapon, a *nunchaku*. This was a surprisingly effective device, simple in design and versatile in application. It consisted of two sticks of dense hickory, each a little over a foot long and octagonal in cross-section. They were connected to each other by a short, stout length of horsehair passed through one end of each stick. One stick could be used to whip the other around on its horsehair tether with lightning speed and bone-shattering power, or the sticks could be brought together like pincers to subdue or choke an opponent. Ki kept the weapon in a long, narrow pocket sewn into the inside of his well-worn black leather vest.

Birdy O'Hara was just returning with her second armload of wood. She set it down by the fire and had started to head out for more when Ki called her back.

"We have enough to last us," the samurai said. The sun was now just a faint glow in the west, and the moon had yet to rise. The campsite, surrounded as it was by tall rock outcroppings, had become a pool of darkness. "Twilight is the time when many predators begin their nightly roaming," Ki explained. "I would rather you stayed close by until daybreak."

"Predators, huh?" Birdy O'Hara looked around her and shuddered. "The only such creatures *I* know how to handle are the ones who lounge around the cafés back in Philadelphia. You couldn't get rid of me tonight if you tried!"

The reporter fed wood into the fire until she had it crackling merrily. Ki broke out their cookware and prepared a supper. As they ate, the moon rose and the stars came out. Finally the samurai set down his tin plate and leaned back on his elbows to gaze at the incredible profusion of stars visible in the Texas night.

Birdy sipped at her coffee, watching him. "May I ask you something?"

The samurai looked at her and nodded.

"Does Jessie Starbuck pay you? I mean, a salary or wage or something, for being her bodyguard?"

Ki shook his head. "I do not work for Jessie, as you seem to think I do. I am a samurai, a professional warrior. In my homeland, a samurai is considered incomplete until he finds a great lord to serve. The Japanese term such an incomplete samurai is *ronin*. It means 'wave man'—a man blown here and there, like the waves of the ocean."

Birdy nodded. "And Jessie is this great lord you found for yourself?"

"No. The lord I serve is Alex Starbuck."

"Jessie's father. But he's dead!"

"The oath of allegiance I swore does not end with my lord's death," Ki elaborated. "It lives on for as long as his descendants wish my services."

"But you take your orders from Jessie, right?" she demanded.

"A samurai does not take orders. He merely fulfills the obligations of his oath of allegiance—"

"I swear!" she cut him off. "I'm a writer, but I'm no match for you when it comes to bending words around!"

Ki shrugged. "Just because you do not understand does not mean it is complicated."

"Damn," the girl grumbled. "Answer one question straight. What do you do for money? I mean, you're poor, aren't you? You're as dirt-poor as Jessie Starbuck is filthy rich!"

Ki answered simply, "I have what I need."

"But not much more, isn't that right?" she challenged him. "You own the shirt on your back, and those nasty little toys you were polishing up before, but what else? Even your horse carries the Circle Star brand!"

"I have what I need," Ki repeated.

"But you must have saved Jessie Starbuck's life a thousand times, just as you did yesterday, in Sarah! Doesn't it gall you that she has all the money, while you—" She paused, her eyes

195

growing hard as they filled with amused contempt. "You've only got what you need."

Ki did not lose his temper in response to her insult. He wanted to make her understand. For some reason, he felt that she *could* understand, if only she would allow herself to let down her defenses.

"I have known many rich men," the samurai began, his soft voice clear in the still night. "Some I have respected, some I have not. If I had so chosen, I could have pursued their path and become wealthy, for the hunt after wealth is just like any pursuit of prey, and hunting is what a samurai does best."

Watching his profile in the flickering firelight, Birdy caught a glimpse of his feral smile, and shivered. "So why didn't you?" she whispered. "Aren't there things—luxuries—that you desire?"

"I desire no luxuries." Ki looked up at the sky. "What luxuries do I need? A few hours ago we were gifted with a most magnificent sunset. Now we have the stars in the sky."

"And what good are they to us?" O'Hara asked scornfully.

"They are the luxuries that matter," Ki declared firmly. "They are diamonds scattered across the black velvet that is the sky."

"And worth about as much as your bad poetry," Birdy laughed. "No thanks, mister! I'll take *real* diamonds and fine shoes and clothes, and all that money can buy! Wealth is what lasts, mister! It lasts until we're dead, and what happens after that doesn't concern me in the least!"

"You are very wrong," Ki said.

"And I think you're very stupid!" Birdy spat. "You think you're so logical, so down to earth, but you're not!" Her voice began to rise, along with her temper. "You're nothing but a damned romantic! I've met your kind before." She shook her head. "All of you spout the same kind of nonsense, all about love and honor and so on. Well, let me tell you from personal experience, those fine attributes you worship don't stand the test of time. They never have, and they never will!"

"It is up to us to make them last," Ki said. "We are responsible for preserving what we care about."

196

"You, maybe, but not me!" she said. "Money's what I care about. Your values don't mean a thing to me. I'm glad they don't exist!"

Ki, watching her by firelight, saw silvery rivulets run down her cheeks. "If you do not care, why are you crying?" he asked softly.

"Oh, go polish your arrows," she sobbed, getting to her feet. She hurled her tin cup into the fire and stamped off into the surrounding shadows.

The samurai shook his head in pity as she disappeared. *All the money in the world could not buy back what that woman has lost.* He would allow her a few minutes to regain her composure, then he would go after her. Ki appreciated her desire for solitude just now, but all the same, it was dangerous for her to be out alone.

The trees were black silhouettes against the starry, moonlit sky. Birdy O'Hara, not knowing where she was going, but feeling the need to be alone, headed for the grove. If she spent another moment with that insufferable, taciturn, Oriental moralist, she was going to go insane! How dare he lecture her? Did he think she was a little girl he could take in with his fairy tales?

"Damn him!" she cursed softly. "Damn his simpleminded philosophical prattle. Does he think I'm going to play by his rules?" she asked herself out loud. "Well, I'm not! He's just a—a—"

O'Hara paused in frustration, unable to think of just what she considered Ki to be, beyond handsome and honest . . .

Irritably she pushed aside the low-hanging bough of a tree, and stepped into the grove. She hesitated for a moment; the thick, leafy canopy overhead filtered out the stars and moonlight. It was quite dark in this little forest.

"Come off it, O'Hara!" she scolded herself. "Are you now afraid of the dark, as well as going soft in the head?"

Like kerosene poured on a fire, the thought acted to fuel her fury. She squared her shoulders, ducked her head, and pushed on into the woods, not stopping until she'd reached a small clearing.

197

The clearing was vaguely oval-shaped, and about twenty feet across at its widest point. Here moonlight fell, turning the scattered stones into ghostly pearls, and making the gills and toadstools shine silver among the fallen logs and tree stumps.

Birdy looked about, satisfied that she'd gone far enough. The campfire was no longer visible. She was not worried about becoming lost. She had a good sense of direction, and in any event the grove was not all that large. If she headed back anywhere close to the general direction from which she'd come, she'd spot the glow of the fire soon enough...

She turned her attention back to the clearing, wondering what had caused it. Perhaps it was the Texas version of a fairy ring, she thought wryly. Her Irish grandmother had long ago told her about tiny clearings in the forest where the elves or leprechauns or whatever held their dances...

She giggled. "Well, you can ask Ki," she muttered aloud. "He probably believes in fairies."

That Ki was open and vulnerable in his honesty was *his* look-out, Birdy told herself. There were no rules to the game of life except for the one that went, 'Look out for number one.' She was going places. She'd started with less than nothing and fought her way this far with nothing but her brains and her looks as weapons. She was going to go further, until someday the Starbucks of this world would be forced to treat her as an equal, if not to look up to her as their better!

A person didn't succeed by worrying about his fellow man, despite what Ki might say. A person didn't win by playing according to the rules, despite what the samurai and Longarm believed. If Ki wanted to ignore reality, that was his business. She would not be responsible.

She sat down on a fallen log and picked at the stems of grass between her feet. *Then why do I feel responsible for him?* she asked herself. *Jessica Starbuck is the one I'm after. There's no need for Ki to get in my way.* But she knew he would, invariably, get in her way, and that meant that Birdy O'Hara would have to sacrifice *him* if she wanted to succeed.

A nearby rustling caught her attention. She peered around, trying to distinguish from what direction the rustling was coming, and to see what was causing it. The trees were all still.

They ringed the moonlit clearing like the palisade of a frontier fort.

She was about to chalk up the noise to her imagination when it began again, this time very much closer. The reporter looked around wildly. *There!* Was that a shadow she'd glimpsed, slinking between the trees?

The first faint itch of panic began to crawl up her spine. She felt her breathing quicken and her scalp tighten. The moon chose just that instant to slip behind a cloud. Birdy sat frozen upon the log as the silvery moonlight dimmed, plunging the clearing into murky darkness.

She stood up and took several floundering steps before she tripped over a stone and fell flat on her face. Where was the moon? If only she could see! Perhaps if she called for help, Ki would hear her?

Ki! Of course! She grew furious with herself for not figuring it out. Ki was making that noise! It *had* to be him! He was trying to frighten her, make her call out, and in that way prove that she needed help.

"Ki, you stop this, right now!" she demanded, rising to her knees. "Do you hear me?"

The rustling sound increased. She heard the sound of branches snapping, and then relative silence, marred only by the sound of rhythmic breathing.

"Damn you, Ki!" she cried out. "I'm not frightened, I'm angry! Now stop it!" Furious, her hands skimmed the ground until her fingers curled around a stone. *You expect me to cry for mercy,* she thought savagely. She listened hard to ascertain the general area from which the heavy breathing sound was coming, and then hurled the rock as hard as she could in that direction. "You satisfied?" She laughed. "I've never begged in my—"

A hideous puling noise split the darkness; it was like the combined caterwauling of a hundred tomcats. Birdy, still on her knees and now paralyzed with fear, listened to the sound, and to the pistonlike thudding of her own heart. She had no idea what might make a noise like that.

The roaring, screeching noise came again, a cross between the sound of a locomotive's steam whistle and the tearing of a piece of heavy cloth. All thoughts of Ki had temporarily vanished from Birdy's mind. Whatever was making that noise was not human!

The moon came out from behind the cloud. The beams slanted down to illuminate the scene with spectral light. Birdy stared at the creature standing stock-still at the far end of the clearing.

At first she thought it was a wolf, but then she realized numbly that no wolf could be that big. The nightmarish cater-wauling began again, as the animal began to slink toward her.

It's a cat, she thought. *A cougar, and it's coming for me!*

She tried to scream, but her throat had gone dry. No sound escaped but a strangled wheeze of terror.

The cougar padded closer. She scooped up a double handful of stones and pebbles and hurled them at the beast. Some of the barrage struck the big cat's broad head and tawny shoulders. It turned aside, screeching defiance and showing its fangs, never taking its yellow eyes off her.

"*Ki!*" the reporter heard herself sobbing. The cougar darted to within a few yards of her, then veered away.

"Quiet."

She glanced behind her. The samurai had stepped into the clearing. The puma was now screaming its challenge to the newcomer.

"On your feet," Ki ordered her, moving to her side and helping her up. He kept his eyes glued to the big cat, which had retreated several paces at his approach. "Do you know the way back to camp?" he asked the nearly hysterical woman.

"Y-yes . . ." Her teeth were chattering so much that it was almost impossible for her to speak.

"Then go. Now."

She eyed the cougar, then shook her head. "I c-can't," she whined, terror-stricken.

"Listen to me," Ki said calmly, keeping his gaze on the animal. "Walk very slowly. Do not run."

"It'll chase me!"

"No, it won't chase you," Ki said. She noticed with shock that he was smiling slightly, and suddenly she didn't know which frightened her more, the animal's snarling visage or Ki's predatory smile. At that moment she realized that Ki had in some uncanny way merged his spirit with that of the animal; hunter and hunted had become as one being...

Birdy tried to take a step, but she found her feet rooted to the earth. The puma was now constantly snarling. It was evidently a male, for the air was filled with the suffocating stench of its musk, with which it had sprayed the ground as part of its combat ritual.

"First one step, and then another," Ki was coaxing her. "Soon you will be in sight of the light and warmth of the fire. You will be safe there. Now go on. Slow, steady steps..."

She walked toward the edge of the clearing, concentrating on Ki's voice to help block out her awareness of the cougar. The line of trees that marked the border of the clearing was coming closer. She was almost there. If only she could control her instincts! Every nerve in her body was screaming at her to run!

"Slow, steady steps, Birdy," Ki chanted rhythmically, his voice a lifeline that kept her from drowning in panic. "He will not chase you. He and I are both the same. For us, the fight comes first. The fight is everything."

Birdy managed to hold out until she'd put some trees between herself and the clearing. Then her nerve broke and she began to run like a deer for the campsite. The big cat had not even glanced at her as she departed. The cougar's yellow eyes had remained locked with Ki's.

For the cougar, the fight was everything.

Ki calmed himself, regulating his breathing to gain control of his nervous system. The cat lacked his intelligence, but nature had compensated the beast by allowing it to have use of its senses on both the physical and spiritual planes. The cougar could see, smell, and hear him, but it could also perceive his state of mind.

You cannot win, the samurai's spirit told the cougar.

The cat was over eight feet long, from its nose to the tip of its constantly curling tail. It was now laughing at Ki. The yowling came from deep within its low-slung belly as it drew back its black lips to expose its teeth. It prowled its side of the clearing in a continuous "S" pattern, weaving a step closer to the samurai at each turn.

So be it, Ki thought. A fight was inevitable. As a samurai he had been trained in the art of *ninpō inubue,* the ancient *ninja* technique of charming an adversary's fierce guard dogs. But for the technique to work, the watch dogs—or cats, birds, monkeys, or whatever—had to be previously tamed. The animal had to call at least one human its master.

I call no creature my master, the cougar's proud voice told Ki. It was very still now, its great yellow eyes intent upon the man standing his ground in this natural arena. Its massive jaws yawned wide to emit a steam-boiler hiss. Its long, lithe body was held close to the ground, as if preparing to spring. Its tail twitched from side to side like a metronome.

The big cat screamed its challenge across the clearing. *Who will die?* it asked the samurai.

Ki slowly reached into the pockets of his leather vest for weapons. He had not brought his bow, for he had not known that Birdy was in danger when he'd left the campsite. He had waited a few minutes to allow her some solitude, and then set off in search of her. He had followed her trail of broken branches to this clearing. It was then that he'd heard the woman's hysterical whispers for help, then that the shifting breeze had brought him the predator's scent. There had been no time to fetch his bow and regain the clearing before the cougar took its prize . . .

In his right hand Ki held a *shuriken* shaped like a short, double-ended dagger, and in his left he held a *nage teppo.* The blue-white moonlight turned the shiny, four-inch blade into a glistening steel icicle.

The cougar laughed. *One puny tooth against my fangs and claws? You should have left me the female! I will have her anyway!*

Ki knew that his only chance to kill the cougar was to strike a vital area with his blade. The big cat's broad skull was too thick for an accurately hurled dagger to pierce the brain. That meant a heart strike.

Ki could not hope to reach the cat's heart with a hurled blade. That meant he would actually have to *shove* the glittering blade home; somehow he would have to get close enough to execute a spear-hand strike, sinking his arm up to the elbow in the cougar's body. The dartlike *shuriken* would make the initial incision through the cougar's tawny hide. The rest would be up to Ki.

The cougar flattened its tiny ears against its massive skull. Its breath began to whuff from its throat.

The *nage teppo* grenade Ki held in his left hand was yellow; it would explode on impact in a harmless flash of brilliant light. The clearing was far too small for Ki to use any of his destructive grenades. The blinding bomb would have to do. Ki knew the effect this particular grenade had on human eyes; how it might affect the cougar was anyone's guess. His plan was a simple one. Once the cat had committed itself to an attack, Ki would hurl the bomb to the ground between them. He would shield his own eyes and hope that the brilliant flash of light would serve to temporarily blind and confuse the cougar. Ki would then rush in to thrust the *shuriken* deep into the animal, just behind its bony shoulder blades. He hoped he could do the deed before the sightless cougar's claws and fangs could wreak their havoc. Ki had no illusions about the puma's strength. The animal could take off his arm with the most casual swipe of one of its paws.

The big cat began to stalk toward Ki. As the distance between them lessened, the cougar increased its pace. Ki brought up his left hand in order to fling the egg-sized grenade to earth. The *nage teppo* had a hard but brittle shell When that shell cracked open and the chemical compound inside it was exposed to the air, the explosion of light took place.

The cougar's scream filled the night as it sprang toward Ki. The samurai threw the grenade to the ground, and brought his forearm up to shield his face against the explosion—

But nothing happened!

The *nage teppo* bomb had landed on a soft mound of grass and rotting wood. The impact had not been enough to shatter its shell.

Ki threw himself to one side as the lunging cougar reached for him with its outstretched claws. He somersaulted on the grass, but the agile cat stayed right with him. Ki scrabbled on his back like a crab, trying to gain a little maneuvering space. The cougar swiped at his leg. The samurai twisted away, but not before the cat's claws gouged a furrow down his calf.

Grunting in pain, Ki hurled his *shuriken* at the cougar's head, desperately trying to deflect the enraged animal's attack.

The blade took the cat in its right eye. Screeching in fury, the cougar pawed the dangling steel from its bloodied eye socket and circled warily, looking for an opening against this prey that had turned out to be so worthy.

Ki, still on the ground, had not had time to reach for another grenade. In any event, the cougar was now much too close, and far too focused upon its adversary to be affected by that kind of distraction. Ki had half hoped that his taking the cougar's eyes would spoil its taste for a fight, but that was not to be. The big cat was committed to the death, it was now clear.

Ki saluted his opponent even as he reached for another *shuriken*. *Both of us have been bloodied,* he directed his thoughts toward the cat. *Now we shall see which one of us—if either—shall live . . .*

The cougar darted toward him. Ki brought up his right arm to throw his blade. His sole strategy was indeed a bleak one. Ki would attempt to take the cougar's remaining eye. Then he would draw another *shuriken* and try for its heart. By then, of course, the cougar would be upon him, and it would need no eyes to tear the samurai open.

Ki braced himself to withstand the impact of the puma's three hundred pounds of tooth and talon and steely muscle. The samurai was fully prepared to die, but he wanted to live just long enough to blind the cat completely. That it intended to pursue Birdy O'Hara after finishing with him was obvious to Ki.

As the cat rushed in, Ki let fly his blade. The cougar reared up on its hind legs and batted the *shuriken* aside. It pounced forward, boxing at Ki with its front claws. The samurai contorted and twisted to get out of the way, but his wounded leg was weak and slow. Shouting in rage, Ki kicked with all his strength at the cougar's bleeding eye socket. His foot struck home. Bawling in pain, the cat pulled back. Ki, close to being an animal now himself, sprang to his feet in a semi-crouch, yet another daggerlike *shuriken* finding its way to his hand.

The samurai threw back his head and roared his own battle cry to the screeching cougar. This time the two hunting creatures charged at the same time; cougar and man were within striking distance of each other when a third being burst into the moonlit clearing.

Screaming at the top of her lungs, Birdy O'Hara came to a sliding halt, her boots shuffling for traction on the grass made slick by the newly spilled blood of man and beast. She held something tightly gripped in her two hands as she called to the snarling cougar.

"Here! Damn you!" the reporter shouted. "Come get me, you bastard! I'm the one you want!"

The cat twisted around in midair and went for Birdy. "Oh, sweet Jesus!" the girl wailed, at the same time bringing up her hands and extending them toward the big cat, barely ten feet away.

Ki saw a tiny tongue of blue flame lick out from between her fingers, and heard what sounded like a string of firecrackers exploding. He watched as Birdy rapidly squeezed off six shots point-blank at the attacking cat.

The cougar dug in its heels, yowling in pain as it was peppered by the rounds. Its paws swiped, and its jaw snapped at thin air, the way a dog will when pestered by flies. All of her shots had struck it, but Ki could tell from the sound of the weapon that it was a low-caliber gun. Her pistol was suited to shooting a human attacker, but it did not possess the stopping power to bring down big game like the enraged cougar.

The puma's back was toward the samurai. Ki hurled himself through the air, landing on his knees scant inches from the panting cougar's heaving sides. The cat was already curving around upon itself to lock its massive jaws into Ki's body, to sink its fangs deep into this creature that had already caused it so much misery.

The *kiai*, the "shout of spirit" from which Ki had long ago taken his name, came from deep within the samurai's belly. It was as if for an instant he had become imbued with the roaring

205

cougar's essence. Every ounce of Ki's strength was focused into his right arm as he drove the point of the *shuriken* into the cougar. The puma hissed and spat in consternation as its bristling hide split and the samurai's spearlike arm sank deep into its steaming innards.

Hot blood splurted onto Ki's contorted features. From somewhere that sounded far away he heard Birdy screaming. Her high-pitched wail blended into the puling scream of the cougar as Ki's blade found its heart. The samurai felt hot liquid bubbling up to his elbow from out of the punctured organ. He tried to pull his arm free of the writhing cougar's sinewy body, frightened that the big cat's death throes would tear his limb from its socket.

The cougar was bucking like a bronco. Its hind legs scrambled to disembowel the man seemingly wedded to it. To avoid those slashing hind claws, Ki threw himself up upon the cougar's back, literally riding the cat for a split second as it charged forward.

Then the rampaging cougar's forelegs crumpled. The big cat's broad snout ploughed a furrow in the dirt. Ki, whose attention had been focused upon freeing his arm, was unprepared for the sudden stop. He found himself spinning through the air over the puma's sagging head. Since Ki's arm was still embedded inside the roaring cat, his body rotated through the air on the pivot of his shoulder socket; it was as if the cougar had flipped him over its shoulder.

The samurai slammed down hard against the ground. The impact finally ripped his arm free of the cougar's gaping, bloody side.

While Ki lay there exhausted and bleeding, the wind knocked out of him, the dying cougar's kicking hind legs managed to wheelbarrow its front half forward for another few inches. Then the cat collapsed onto its side. Its frenzied, roaring head twisted around to gnaw and chew at the hole in its side. Then its head suddenly fell limp; its snarls ceased. The cougar's tail whipped down against the dirt one final time before lying still. The big cat was dead.

The clearing was instantly silent. All Ki could hear was his own hoarse exhalations and Birdy O'Hara's muffled sobbing.

206

He lay on his back and stared up at the starry, moonlit night sky, breathing deeply to slow his racing heart. The sweet, coppery smell of spilled blood filled his nostrils. Some of it was his, but most of it belonged to the cougar.

A fine battle, my fellow warrior, the samurai told the hovering *kami,* the departed spirit of the dead cougar.

You fought well, the cat-spirit replied. *I salute you. The female is yours!*

Grinning in acknowledgement of the concession, Ki watched the cat-spirit slink past the moon on its journey heavenward—or was that merely a wisp of cloud?

No matter, Ki thought, reaching out behind him. The dead cougar was close enough for him to stroke its soft, blood-encrusted fur.

Which was just what he did, until the darkness settling down all around him carried him away into unconsciousness.

Chapter 14

Ki was in a bath house, a place of aged wood, tinkling wind chimes, green plants, and dancing motes of lantern light on the crystal-clear surface of the pool in which he floated. The sweet smell of burning incense filled the air. And there was another tantalizingly sweet aroma, that of perfume, for the samurai was not alone in the bath house.

A skilled geisha was ministering to his every desire. Her smooth hands glided over his body; her deft fingers soothed and comforted the warrior's aches and pains.

The geisha poured steaming sake into a thimble-sized porcelain cup. She carefully raised the hot liquor to the samurai's lips, and then—

The geisha, suddenly, inexplicably grew clumsy. The hot sake spilled down the samurai's chin!

Ki woke up, grumbling.

"Take it easy," Birdy O'Hara said. "Sorry, I spilled some of this coffee on you." She set down the tin cup, and awkwardly brushed away the spilled coffee from Ki's chin with her fingertips.

"So much for dreams," Ki sighed.

"What?" Birdy asked.

"Nothing." Ki looked around. He was undressed, and more

or less floating on his back in the shallow brook near the campsite. Birdy had built up the smoldering logs into a bonfire, obviously to protect them against any further animal intruders. "How did I get here?" Ki asked.

"I dragged you, how do you think?" the reporter snapped back. She was kneeling beside Ki, leaning precariously in an attempt to stay dry while she washed clean the wound which the cougar had inflicted upon Ki's leg. "I tried to get one of the horses over to the clearing, but they weren't interested in getting near a cougar, even if it was dead. Finally I fetched a blanket, spread it out, rolled you onto it, and hauled you here that way. It was easier than I thought it would be; the wool sort of glided over the grass."

"You must be exhausted," Ki said quietly. "You could have waited until I woke up."

She shook her head. "I didn't want these claw wounds festering. I figured the best chance you'd have against infection was to get you to the brook and wash these gouges clean." She glanced worriedly at Ki. "Does it hurt?"

"No. The cold water feels good."

She nodded. As she worked, her rolled-up sleeves flopped down into the water. "Oh, damn! This is silk, too!" She eyed Ki, then shrugged and began to unbutton her blouse. "Don't you go getting any ideas, mister!" she warned.

"I am not responsible for my ideas," Ki gently pointed out. "Only my actions."

"I liked you better when you were asleep," Birdy remarked sourly, shrugging off her garment and carefully laying it aside.

Ki, feasting his eyes, replied, "And I like you better like this." The flickering light and shadow cast by the roaring flames only made her partial nudity more alluring. The fire's heat had brought a flush to her face, a sheen of moisture that plastered damp tendrils of her red hair to the nape of her neck. Ki gazed in appreciation at the strong, graceful curve of her delicate back, at her fine round breasts swaying from side to side as she knelt across his thighs. She had the lightest scattering of freckles across her chest, and pink nipples that resembled the first sweet strawberries of summer...

Ki watched her straining rump as she leaned across his lap.

The taut denim fit her every delicious curve as if it had been painted on. Droplets of perspiration rolled down her spine's deep furrow to pool where the waistband of her jeans gaped. Ki glimpsed a teasing hint of the beginning swell of her buttocks whenever she leaned especially far forward.

"You seem very calm, considering that you are half undressed and I am totally nude," Ki observed.

"I've been undressed with men a good deal of my life," she muttered. "And I've seen what you've got before."

"Oh, really?"

"Well, more or less," she admitted. She winked at Ki. "Mostly *less...*"

Her own audacity seemed to fluster her. Her budding nipples began to stiffen, swelling the way a strawberry will ripen to sweetness as the long, hot days of summer progress.

Something of Ki's was swelling as well. Helpless, the samurai colored with embarrassment as he watched the tip of his member poke up out of the water.

The girl saw it, blinked, and began to giggle.

Ki smiled at her and said, "What a delightful sound. That's the first time I've heard you laugh like that."

Now it was Birdy's turn to blush. "Well, it is pretty funny-looking, sticking up out of the water like a turtle coming up for air," she said in an attempt to justify her unaccustomedly vulnerable response.

"Not all *that* funny, I sincerely hope," Ki replied as his member stiffened even further and its head reared up yet more.

Birdy took a few deep breaths to regain her composure. "There," she said at last, "I think your leg has stopped bleeding."

"I think the blood has gone somewhere else," Ki said, staring down at his lengthening organ.

Birdy couldn't help herself; she started giggling again.

Ki smiled. "Please fetch my saddlebags. In them is a small leather pouch containing clean bandages, and a salve that will help the wound to heal."

Birdy did as she was asked. She watched as Ki smeared on the salve and then bandaged his wounded calf.

"What was that stuff?" she asked, wrinkling her freckled nose. "It smells like the devil!"

Ki chuckled. "The odor will soon fade. The salve is a mixture of many different sorts of mosses and barks. It is quite effective as a healing agent."

She was skeptical. "It smelled like mud to me." She leaned back on her elbows, languidly letting the warmth of the fire bathe her bare torso.

"Are you going to continue to torture me, or are you going to get dressed?" Ki teased.

Birdy smiled at him. "Actually I was going to take a bath, as soon as you got your rear out of that brook!"

Ki nodded. "Then I will give you some privacy." He stood up, taking careful, experimental steps until he was satisfied that his leg was sound. He repacked his medical kit and then went to stand by the fire to dry off his wet body.

The girl watched him out of the corner of her eye. His smooth skin seemed as tawny as the cougar's; his muscles were not the bulging sort that O'Hara was accustomed to seeing on strong men. Instead, they seemed wiry and slender. If she did not know better, she would have said that the samurai was too thin to be so strong. Her blue eyes, despite her will, strayed to the samurai's corded thighs and hard round buttocks.

Ki, perhaps sensing her eyes upon him, suddenly turned to transfix her with his dark and level gaze. Birdy felt her heart begin to quicken its pace. She felt hot and cold at once, both anxious and calm.

"I will leave you—" Ki began.

"No!" Birdy blurted, but then gained control of herself. "I mean you don't have to . . . I mean it's up to you . . . I mean I certainly don't mind . . . I'm—"

Ki cut her off. "Birdy, I want to thank you."

"F-for what?" She tried her best to keep her eyes from wandering away from Ki's face to the rest of him. It was difficult.

"For returning to the clearing," Ki said. "For risking your life to save me. Did you have that little pistol hidden in your purse?"

The reporter nodded. "It's a .32-caliber revolver. I bought it just before coming out West on this assignment." She shrugged again, the action of her shoulders making her bare breasts

212

bounce. "I guess I imagined protecting myself against bandits or something." She smiled. "I never thought I'd have to use it to go big-game hunting!"

Ki approached to kneel beside her. "But you saved my life. You risked yourself! You behaved in a totally unselfish manner!"

"Keep your insults to yourself," the reporter cracked. "You can read whatever you want into it, but as far as I was concerned, all I was doing was protecting my investment."

The samurai reached out to stroke her cheek. "I do not believe that, Birdy..."

"Believe what you want!" She kicked off her boots, then stood up to unbutton her jeans. "It made perfect sense for me to get you out of that scrape! I acted totally out of self-interest. What was I going to do out here in the wilderness all by myself if you'd been killed?" she demanded. "How was I going to recoup my three hundred dollars if that cougar had torn you apart? How would I find Jessie Starbuck and continue my series of articles?" Her face was twisted into an ugly grimace, and her blue eyes were glinting in the firelight as she harangued Ki. "I didn't care about you! I don't care about anybody."

Ki jumped up to grab hold of her bare shoulders and shake her. "Why won't you admit that for one brief instant you did care about somebody?" he shouted.

"Don't shout at me!" Birdy cried, pulling away.

Ki bowed his head shamefully. "I apologize. I try not to lose control of my emotions. I try, but—" His voice trailed off. "You say that you are my enemy, and it must be so, for you consistently breach my defenses." He turned away. "Perhaps it would be better if I did leave the camp until you have finished bathing."

Birdy watched him walk toward where his clothes lay folded. The touch of his fingers still burned on her shoulders. *My God, we're so alike*, she thought. *If only I dared to reach out to him! But I won't, I can't!*

"Ki!" she heard herself call out.

The samurai turned to regard her silently.

"Before, in the clearing," she whispered. "After it was all over, and you were lying exhausted beside the dead cougar. I

213

saw you reach out to stroke that animal's fur! It looked to me as if you felt affection toward that creature!"

The samurai nodded. "Love and hate are not so different, Birdy. The underlying passion is the same for both. There is a point in battle where the heat of combat is identical to the spark of lovemaking."

"Do you really believe that?" she asked. "That what goes on between two opponents in a fight is like—?" She was unable to finish her query. Instead she peeled off her jeans to stand naked before the samurai. Her legs were long and perfectly shaped; her thighs and hips looked as if they had been painstakingly sculpted from pink marble.

But unlike marble, Ki knew that this woman's form would be warm and soft...

Birdy stood hunched and trembling, her bravado gone as she fought hard against her tears. "If enemies can love," she whispered, "if you could love the cougar, could you love me?"

Ki simply held out his arms. The girl sobbed once, like someone diving into a deep pool, knowing that there was no turning back. Then she ran to him.

Ki swept her up in his arms, his palms supporting her rounded buttocks as she locked her legs around his waist and began to devour him with kisses.

"Oh, I've wanted you so much!" She laughed, then shook her head as if she were astonished at her own passion. "I can't believe it, but I do want you..." she repeated giddily.

Ki carried her over to where their bedrolls were spread. He laid her down gently, and then stretched out alongside her, to begin nibbling upon her sweet nipples.

Birdy tensed immediately. Ki saw that her eyes were wide with fear. The samurai paused, wondering what was wrong.

"You have told the truth, Birdy?" he coaxed. "You have been with a man before?"

She nodded once. "Please," she whispered hoarsely, "don't mind me. Just go on—"

Slowly, gently, as if she were some wild creature easily spooked, Ki bent his head to the woman's trembling bosom. Her twin globes were weighty beneath his touch, redolent with the musky fragrance of her arousal. He skated his tongue around and around each aureole, his eyes on her face all the while. As he carefully took first one and then the other of her swollen nipples between his teeth, her eyes closed and her own pink tongue slid out from between her lips. She squirmed and groaned beneath Ki's caresses. Her fingers danced down the hard, rippled expanse of his stomach muscles to the steely curve of him, jutting out like a mighty sword.

A crimson flush had spread from her breasts down her soft belly. It was a flush of abandon that reached even to the moist juncture of her thighs, beneath her honey-beaded, ruddy fur.

Ki chuckled, a humorous thought occurring to him. "What? What is it?" Birdy demanded instantly, her body grown taut, her voice edged with tension.

"Relax," Ki soothed. "I was only thinking that with your tousled red curls, your freckles, and your pale skin glowing so pink, you remind me of a ripe fruit—"

She began to nibble kisses across his muscular chest. Her soft lips and velvety tongue licked and sucked at his sensitive nipples. "Maybe I'm a juicy red apple?" she cooed.

"Perhaps," Ki murmured. His fingers slid down between her legs. "But whatever the sort, you are bursting with juice. It seems to be seeping from you already. We must not waste a single drop."

He pulled away from her and swung around, kissing his way down to her warm center. His tongue parted her glistening folds and began to lap up the sweetness coating her the way a morning's dew will coat spring grass.

Birdy cried out in ecstasy. She raised her legs straight up into the air, while her bottom ground itself against the rough wool of the blankets. She reached down to run her fingers through Ki's damp hair.

"God," she crooned. "Oh, that feels so good . . ." Her back arched, and her body began to spasm as low, animallike grunts of pleasure escaped her lips. At that moment she pulled away from Ki. Her fingers in his hair became claws, wrenching him away from her throbbing sex.

"No," she sobbed, turning her back to him and curling up

215

into a fetal position. "I can't . . . I never could . . . I thought that it might be different with you. I wanted you so much, but it can never be different for me!"

Ki, rocking on his heels, reached out to stroke her quivering haunch, pale and white in the moonlight. As he listened to the sound of her muffled crying, the samurai made a decision. It was very difficult for him to pry into another's personal affairs, but this woman was crying out to be rescued from the hellish experience she'd created for herself.

Once again he swept her up in his arms, but this time more as if she were a child than a sexual partner. He held her tight, let her cry herself out, and when the last of her tears had run their course down his sloping shoulder, he rested his chin on top of her head and murmured, "Tell me . . ."

"It's not you," Birdy said between gasps for breath. "Honest it isn't. Sex has been bad for me, always. It's because—" She hesitated. "How can I tell you!" she exclaimed, sitting up and wiping her red eyes with a corner of the blanket. "I'm so ashamed."

Ki smiled at her, then shrugged. "Perhaps you can start at the beginning?"

"The beginning!" she spat. "The beginning was a slum in Philadelphia, filled with too many kids crying themselves to sleep at night because they didn't get enough to eat. The beginning was a father who pissed away every dime he made on liquor, and then figured that the way to quiet his brood was to lay open their backsides with his belt buckle!"

Ki was beginning to understand. "I am sorry, Birdy."

She snorted with grim amusement, at the same time drawing up her knees to her chest and wrapping her arms about herself, as if she were trying to make herself as small as possible. "You're sorry, eh? That's what my mother used to say. 'I'm sorry for the way he beats you, daughter, but he *is* your father.'" She shook her head. "I was thirteen the last time he took his belt to me. I was lying on the mattress in the attic, lying on my belly because my hindquarters were on fire from the backs of my knees on up to my waist, when I decided to run away. I left that night. If they heard me leave, they didn't try to stop me."

"Where did you go?" Ki asked. "To an orphanage?"

"Don't be absurd!" she rasped. "They just would have sent me back to that hole of a home. No, I decided to make my own living. On the streets." Her forehead sank down upon her knees. "I was big for my age... big the way a girl can be... I became a whore! I gave men their pleasure in doorways and alleys! The police were happy to let me operate, as long as I gave them some of the money I earned. Pretty soon I had enough to afford an apartment and fine clothes. The caliber of my clientele improved, but not much else changed."

"Your job on the newspaper, those riding lessons, how did you come by them?" Ki asked softly.

"Barter, my friend." Birdy laughed bitterly. "Favors given for favors received. I learned *that* lesson from the very start of my independence, when that first bastard came up to me beneath the streetlamp and told me what he wanted, and what he'd pay. He called it lovemaking, but I wasn't fooled. I'd been vulnerable once, but I'd never be again! Sex, to me, was a way to get what I wanted—no more, no less. I couldn't afford to be emotional about who I gave my favors to, any more than I could afford to throw away money!" She paused. "You wouldn't happen to have a bottle in those saddlebags of yours, would you?" she asked hopefully.

"No, I'm sorry."

Birdy sighed. "God," she said, her voice shaky. "I could *use* a drink."

"So you gained your education, your sophistication, even your journalist's position, by giving your favors to influential clients?"

"Yep." She chuckled. "It was easy. The men were glad to do it. The hypocrites could pretend they weren't paying for their pleasure, merely helping out a charming young lady in distress." She spat into the darkness. "But I used my head, as well as the slit between my legs. I worked hard on the newspaper, built up a reputation. Then I quit whoring!"

"You weren't fired?"

"Nope. You see, I called my publisher's bluff. He threatened to fire me when I didn't do what he wanted, but I knew that I could always get another job, because I'd become an asset to the paper. All those etiquette lessons other men had bought for me finally paid off. I became a society darling! For a while I even covered a beat in Europe. I became the toast of the Continent: the brash young American lady journalist, with the sharp tongue and sharper pen." She nodded enthusiastically. "Don't you see? I'd won!" she crowed. "I beat them all. I got what I wanted and it didn't cost me a thing!"

"I think it cost you far too much," Ki replied softly, gazing at her. She was smiling, but too hard. To Ki, she looked like a little girl gamely whistling in the dark in a desperate attempt to hold back her fears.

"So maybe I can't *feel* anything," she began to sniffle. "But so what? If you *feel*, you put yourself in a position to be hurt. If you go out on a limb for anybody else, you're nothing but a sucker—"

"And yet you risked your life to help me defeat the cougar," he pointed out.

Birdy colored with embarrassment. "I already explained that to you," she snarled. "I did it for *me!* For business! There was nothing else behind it." She dropped her eyes from Ki's steady gaze.

"Yes, very well," the samurai said evenly. "But whatever the motive, you saved my life. Now I intend to save yours. Lie back," he instructed. When the reporter stared at him in astonishment, Ki said, "It is strictly business, Miss O'Hara. A debt paid. A transaction completed." He smiled coolly. "As you so nicely put it, 'favors given for favors received.'"

Her blue eyes shot daggers at him. "Of all the insufferably insolent, conceited men I've ever known—" She ran out of breath. "And if I refuse? Do you intend to rape me?" she demanded hotly and, to Ki's mind, just a trifle encouragingly . . .

"No." He smiled. "Not rape you. But why would you refuse, Birdy?" He winked at her. "Are you afraid?"

With a squeak of indignation, she threw herself back upon the blankets. "Well, I'm waiting," she cooed, albeit through clenched teeth.

Ki shook his head. "I had it easier getting inside the cougar," he muttered beneath his breath.

"I heard that," she announced.

"Consider it off the record." Ki chuckled, and then he began again, running his fingers through her red tresses as he kissed her nose and cheeks. "You told me before that you wanted me. Is that still true?"

"Well..."

"Don't lie, O'Hara," he quickly cautioned.

"Yes..."

Ki nodded in satisfaction. "That is all you are required to do." His mouth expertly worked its way down her neck, breasts, and belly, until once again he lowered his head between her spread legs, to nip and lick her tender inner thighs. "How fiercely you tremble," the samurai teased her. "Just as proudly as the cougar in the clearing. You are a wildcat, O'Hara, an Irish wildcat, right to the core." His tongue darted and curled, prying apart her sensitive inner folds. "But this time I shall conquer you, my wildcat."

Birdy moaned with passion, even as she tried to pull away. But this time Ki had taken precautions. He had her twitching buttocks firmly in his grasp.

Her hips bobbed as Ki's expert tongue lapped at her. At the same time he swung his own body around so that she could reach his groin with her fingers if she so desired.

Realizing that she couldn't pull away, Birdy surrendered to the flood of sensations washing over her. Her fingers skittered along Ki's loins like the legs of a spider, until she'd reached the throbbing tip of his erection. Her nails tickled and scratched at him, forcing a husky moan of pleasure from the samurai.

Suddenly she began pulling at him. "Come inside me. Now!" she whimpered pleadingly. "Oh, please...now!"

Ki's supple body jackknifed around. He supported himself above her on his strong arms, then slowly slid into her, as easily and perfectly as a warrior's blade slides into its custom-made sheath.

She threw back her head and arched her back. Her lovely legs clamped themselves around Ki's waist. An unintelligible series of noises escaped her lips, as if merely having Ki fill her up were sensation enough, and almost too intense to bear.

She laughed delightedly as Ki showered her face, neck, and breasts with kisses. Her fingers kneaded the corded muscles of his thighs and buttocks. Her nails became the cougar's claws, scratching deliciously along the samurai's strong back.

Then her eyes flew open abruptly, as if she were awakening from a deep trance. She began to shake her head from side to side. *"I can't! I can't—"*

"Stop it," Ki ordered, almost unable to bear the anger and despair he saw in those bright blue orbs. "The past no longer exists." He began to ride her hard, forcing undulations out of her soft, warm belly and a sheen of sweat to rise on her quivering breasts.

"No, no, please—" But despite her protestations, she began to respond. Her wet center rose up to engulf Ki's marble-hard shaft, even as she shook her head in denial. "No, no, please—oh, *please!*"

Ki angled himself to rub the length of his jutting horn against the most sensitive area of her sex. He sawed back and forth, up and down, easily exerting control to dejay his own building orgasm.

Birdy began to moan. Her hips pounded against the blankets. As Ki cupped her rump, lifting her clear of the scratchy, sodden wool, she squirmed and bucked against him.

"I'm coming!" she gasped in awestruck wonder. Her jaws snapped shut with an audible click. The next instant her mouth gaped wide as she let loose with a wailing howl that seemed to echo off the distant hills. Ki roared with delighted laughter as her warm juices flowed out of her.

And then he just roared, as his own climax gushed forth.

Birdy was giggling like a loon, her limbs still twitching involuntarily. "S-so *that's* what it's supposed to feel like," she murmured, her eyes screwed shut.

Ki chuckled. He rose up on his elbows to softly blow her matted hair off her sweaty forehead.

Birdy smiled. She was still so paralyzed with delicious pleasure that she could do little more. "Is this going to subside, or am I going to be all blood and no bones for the rest of my life?" she asked tremblingly.

"Regrettably, it will subside," Ki told her.

"Then we'd better do it again!"

Ki pretended to groan. "I *knew* I had it easier when I was up against the cougar."

"My handsome cougar-killer," Birdy drawled. She burrowed into his chest, sucked at his nipple for a moment, and then began to snore softly.

Ki gently disentangled himself from her embrace, and lay back and laced his hands behind his head to stare up at the starry night sky. Beside him, Birdy continued to purr contentedly in her sleep.

It was still early in the night, but Ki felt rather pleased with himself. He had done a good day's work; not many samurai could boast of having impaled two wildcats in one day!

Birdy O'Hara awoke to find herself alone in the bedroll. She sat up quickly, gripped by panic. Her first thought was that Ki had deserted her. She didn't need to see the samurai's gear, and to hear their horses huffing nearby, to scold herself for thinking such foolishness.

A few moments later he reentered their camp. She saw by the light of the dying fire's embers that he was wearing only his denim jeans. The samurai had cut the trouser leg shredded by the cougar off at the knee, leaving his bandaged calf exposed.

"Go back to sleep, it is only midnight," he told her. O'Hara found that she could not meet his gaze. "Where'd you go?"

"Back to the clearing, to collect my *shuriken,*" Ki explained.

O'Hara nodded. Why did she feel so awkward? The happiness she'd known only a few short hours ago seemed dreamlike. "Ki? About before—"

"Go back to sleep, Birdy," the samurai said, settling down beside her. "We have a long ride tomorrow."

"Where are we going?" the reporter asked, resting her head on his shoulder.

"To find Jessie," Ki murmured, stroking her head. "Isn't that the reason you bailed me out of jail?" he teased.

"Don't be mean," she pouted. "Now I hope we *never* find her." She sighed.

"Ah, but I must find Jessie," Ki told her firmly. "You know

that, my wildcat," he added, softening his tone. "Tomorrow we'll ride to Roundpatch."

"Roundpatch!" she echoed, sitting up. "But, Ki—"

"Hush," the samurai interrupted. "I know Jessie. She will want to get to the bottom of this mess. Roundpatch is where she'll go."

"It's so dangerous there. Those outlaws—" Her eyes suddenly grew wet. "Damn," she muttered, as Ki embraced her.

"There is a risk," the samurai admitted. "Birdy, I am sorry, but I thought you understood that there would be danger if you accompanied me." He hugged her. "I promise to do my best to protect you."

"It's not *me* that I'm worried about," she whispered.

"What, then?"

"Never mind that, Ki," she began, her tone urgent. "About before, I—um, I—" She groaned. "I don't know how to say this—"

"You sound sorry that it happened."

"No!" she said quickly. "Of course I'm not!" She kissed his cheek. "It's just that—well, before it happened, maybe I couldn't feel pleasure, but at least I couldn't feel pain. Now . . ." She shrugged, as the tears rolled down her cheeks.

Chuckling, Ki shook his head. "Go to sleep, O'Hara."

"Whatever happens, our loving each other tonight won't change what I have to do," she warned him. "I've got a job, and I will fulfill my obligations."

Ki nodded. "You will write what you must about Jessie in your newspaper."

Birdy sniffled wetly, wiping her eyes. "You don't understand, but you *will*," she replied wistfully.

"Go to sleep!" Ki commanded, leaning back and closing his eyes.

"What happened between us tonight *won't* change my actions!" she insisted.

The samurai, his eyes still closed, laughed. "It already has, wildcat. It already has."

★

Chapter 15

Early the next morning, Barney the drummer climbed up onto the bench seat of his big covered wagon, and took hold of the reins. Jessie, still disguised as Dora, took her place beside him. Neither one had felt much like sleeping during the night, so they'd begun to repack their goods while it was still dark. Now, as dawn broke, the sky as pink as a baby's bottom and laced through with ribbons of gold and blue, they were ready to leave.

Hutch, the mayor of Sageville, appeared in the doorway of his general store to wave them off. The fat man had shaved this morning, but he looked sunken and tired, and altogether worse than he had the day before.

"I liked him better when he was grubby and happy," Jessie murmured.

The drummer shrugged. "Jody bein' killed hit Hutch real hard. Him and Jody used to jaw the day away. Hutch is gonna be mighty lonesome now."

Barney clucked at his mules. The wagon lurched once or twice until the team found its stride, and then the big wagon began to lumber out of town.

Jessie looked back over her shoulder, watching until Hutch and his emporium had disappeared around the bend. The birds had long since joined together in their rowdy morning chorus. A cool breeze promised to mitigate the day's warmth.

"Not a bad day for a funeral," Barney observed.

"They're all bad when it comes to putting somebody in the ground," Jessie said.

Barney nodded. "Some truth to that, girl. But it's better to plant them on a nice day than on a rainy one. On a rainy, dark, and dank morning, watchin' somebody get buried is about too much for a soul to bear. You feel like you died yourself. On a sunny day it's still a sad occasion, but the light of the sun kinda reminds a soul that as bad as it all seems, the Good Lord must know what he's doing."

Jessie was charmed. "That's very profound."

Barney glanced at her, puzzled.

Jessie shrugged. "It doesn't matter. When did you think that up?"

"I didn't." Now Barney looked worried. "*You* did. You told me that years ago, Dora. Afore you went away. Dontcha 'member?"

"Well! I guess I forgot," Jessie said, smiling.

Barney offered her a toothless grin. "I reckon we're both gettin' old, Dora, girl."

They wended their way along the trail for several hours. The birds had quieted so that the only sounds left to listen to were the squeaks and rattles of the wagon, and the plodding hooves of the mule team.

Barney suddenly halted the wagon. "I gotta get something," he told Jessie.

She watched as the drummer crawled back into the canvas-covered portion of the wagon, and began to rummage around. "What are you looking for?" she asked.

"You'll see." He began to whistle "The Battle Hymn of the Republic."

Minutes passed. Barney's goodnatured whistling faded, to be replaced by muttered oaths as he tossed things around inside the wagon. "Where is it?" he swore. "Damn! Where'd I put it?"

Jessie held her breath, worried that whatever the old man was searching for, it would lead him to her hidden clothes and that revolver. "Barney? If you gave me an idea of what it was you were looking for, maybe I could help. I might have seen it!"

"You didn't see this, Dora, 'cause I've kep' it hid for years and years. Aha!" he exclaimed. "I found it!"

He burrowed his way through the interior mess of the wagon to appear once more beside Jessie. In his hands was a long, curved scabbard. "This here's my sword!" he announced, drawing the glinting saber and waving it in the air.

Jessie was quite impressed. It was a beautiful blade, honed to a fine edge, its entire length polished to a mirror finish, its filigreed hilt and finger guard wound with gold braid.

"Where'd you buy it, Barney?" she asked.

"*Buy* it?" the old drummer snorted. "Why, girl, this here was issued to me!"

"You were in the Civil War?"

"*In* it? Why girl, I helped run that sucker!" Barney nodded vigorously. "Yes, Ulysses Simpson Grant hisself gave me this pigsticker!"

"You *know* Mr. Grant?" Jessie demanded dubiously.

"A man like Grant don't give swords to strangers, girl," Barney explained patiently. "Sure I knew him! I served on his staff. Ulysses and me was as close as two peas in a pod. I was in charge of his whiskey supply."

Jessie stared at him over her spectacles. "What do you mean?"

"I was the one who carried his case filled with bottles of whiskey," he elaborated.

"That's hardly running the war, Barney."

"Well, Grant ran the war, that I'll admit, Dora," the old man said, and then puffed up his chest. "But *whiskey* was what ran Grant! Without me, nothin' would've happened!"

Jessie groaned. "Should I be *believing* this?"

"Sure, if you want my opinion," Barney mumbled. "I've kep' this here saber hid all these years 'cause there's a lot of folks who get riled when they see a remembrance of the old days."

"I'd think a lot of folks would like their chance at one of General Grant's staff members," she agreed dryly. "By the way, Barney, what was your rank?"

The drummer muttered something under his breath.

"Did you say 'second loo,' as in 'second lieutenant'?" Jessie pressed.

"Nope. I said, 'Hey you!'" Barney told her. "That's what he always called me, 'cept for the time he gave me this sword," he insisted stubbornly.

Jessie decided to let the matter rest. "Why'd you dig it up after all these years?"

Barney colored. "Well, Dora, we're comin' mighty close to Roundpatch on this leg of our trek. This is outlaw territory. It belongs to Seth Weeks, the bandit leader. Any lowlifes ridin' the trail do it under Seth Weeks's protection. In exchange, they pay him a piece of their ill-gotten gains."

"Have you ever had trouble with them before?" Jessie asked.

"No, but . . ." Barney frowned. "Usually they poke through my stuff, take a few things, and let me pass. That's if they bother me at all. They know I don't have no money, and I don't sell no guns or ammunition."

"So why are you worried?"

Barney affectionately stroked Jessie's gray tresses, obviously unaware that it was one of his own wigs that he was touching. "Seein' poor old crippled Jody get shot by bandits last night has me spooked, I reckon. I just want to be ready in case of trouble. You got to 'member, I ain't never had you along with me in outlaw territory."

Jessie nodded. She was feeling distinctly uneasy. As always, she was ready to take her chances in any situation, but it would be unfair to jeopardize Barney.

She was worried about that hidden handgun. If the outlaws did stop them, and searched the wagon, would they blame Barney if they discovered the revolver?

Not likely, Jessie decided. For one thing, it was only a single handgun, with a mere six rounds in it. That was hardly a weapons shipment! For another thing, the gun was well hidden, along with her clothing, under a bolt of gingham. She very much doubted that outlaws would have the patience to paw through a lot of "women's stuff" like bolts of fabric.

At least that was what Jessie hoped would happen. She wasn't about to throw that gun away, after last night. She was going to need a pistol the next time she ran into that woman who was ruining her good name! As for the man in black, Jessie would see. She hadn't forgotten the way he'd managed to save their lives.

The day wore on. The wagon rolled through scrubby territory unfit for cattle. This part of Texas wasn't much good for anything except hiding out. All around them were sandstone cliffs, gnarled trees, and weeds. Now and again a cawing crow would shatter the stillness as it swooped across the blindingly blue sky. Grasshoppers scratched away in the undergrowth, while buzzing yellowjackets nosed at rabbit dung and the squashed berries dangling from prickly bushes.

Jessie's mood had begun to match the desolation of the landscape. What nerve she had, thinking that she might catch up to that imposter! Why, the woman had an entire gang to back her up. What did Jessie have? One gun, six bullets, and an old man armed with a sword . . .

Where was Ki, she wondered. And Longarm? Surely they must be on her trail. But no, they couldn't be, for she'd left no trail for them to follow. They might be looking for her, but Texas was a big place. Jessie Starbuck had disappeared with the advent of "Dora."

But, of course, she hadn't disappeared! Jessie Starbuck had last been seen the night before, in Sageville, when she'd brutally murdered the town constable. She could just imagine Longarm's and Ki's response to such news. And if they happened to lay eyes on that imposter, would they be fooled? Marshal Farley had been, and he couldn't be blamed, Jessie had to admit. The woman pretending to be her impersonated her very well. Very well indeed . . . To possess Jessie's looks was one thing, but her mannerisms too? That was impossible! No way to pass that off as coincidence! The imposter had to have been carefully trained. Like an actress, she would have had to rehearse for her role.

The imposter was pretending to be the gangleader, Jessie reminded herself, but it was the man in black who was really in charge . . .

Jessie waved away a pesky fly buzzing at her head. The sweat was rolling down her face. Heavy makeup and a thick wig were not the things to wear on a hot, sunny Texas afternoon, she decided sadly. How she longed to cast aside this disguise! Her spectacles had begun to give her a headache, which was only compounded by the heat. Besides, the wire frames were irritating the backs of her ears and the bridge of her nose.

Barney, noticing her discomfort, offered her the canteen. "Why don't you take a nap inside?" he suggested. "It's a mite cooler in there, I reckon."

"Maybe I will," Jessie said, thinking that she'd be able to remove her wig for a little while. She crawled back into the canvas-covered portion of the wagon and stripped off her spectacles and the heavy wig. It wasn't all that much cooler inside, but at least the canvas cut the sun's glare. The semidarkness was like a balm to her aching eyes. She set aside the spectacles and her wig, and settled back on the pile of blankets. She was asleep in seconds.

"—got nothin', I told ya!"

Jessie awoke. It was Barney's voice she was hearing. Who was he talking to? she wondered. And why had he sounded so frightened?

She crawled to the front of the wagon, and peered out, past Barney. They'd reached higher ground while she slept. The land was now greener, with thick trees all along the trail, which threaded its way through a maze of granite boulders. Jessie shifted her attention to the semicircle of six riders blocking their path.

"Come on now, Barney," one of the riders said. He was a skinny owlhoot, dressed like a peacock in tight red trousers, a grimy blue shirt, and an emerald green frock coat. Instead of a hat, he covered his head with a knotted yellow bandanna. Shoulder-length strands of reddish hair stuck out from underneath the snug-fitting scarf. "You know how it works. You

228

pass through here, and we stop you to do our shopping, right, boys?" He grinned at his companions.

"But I ain't got nothin' you boys would be interested in, this trip," Barney pleaded. "Nothin' at all in there!" he loudly repeated.

He thinks I'm still asleep, and he's trying to wake me up, Jessie realized. She quickly donned her wig and spectacles and made her way out to take her place beside Barney.

"Well, what do you know?" the skinny gangleader laughed. "Old Barney's gotten himself a piece!"

As the outlaws laughed, Jessie, watching the sullen old man, saw him glance down at the sheathed saber lying beneath their feet. "Don't do it," she whispered to him. "They've got the guns, Barney."

"Don't like them callin' you names, girl," he muttered.

"And you said you didn't have nothin' back there, Barney!" the skinny bandit snickered, setting his buddies off on another peal of laughter.

"Why don't you boys do your searchin' and let me pass?" Barney said quietly. "You know I ain't got a gun or bullet to my name, and no liquor. You want shirts or pants, or maybe a cookset or a—"

"Shut up, Barney," the ringleader said pleasantly. "I'll tell you what I want, when I want it." He smiled, showing a mouthful of broken green teeth.

"I jes' like to cooperate," Barney enthused. "You know that about me, mister—"

"I said shut up, Barney." The skinny fellow's dark eyes had gone cold. Now, despite his garish get-up, his stringy hair, and that absurd yellow bandanna on his head, he no longer looked like a clown. Now he looked like what he truly was: a killer.

Jessie felt the menace radiating from the man, as did Barney. The tinker grew very quiet. "Whatever you want, mister," he whispered meekly, "jes' don't hurt nobody."

The leader nodded in satisfaction. He glanced at his men. "Two of you ride around back of the wagon and check what he's got in there."

Jessie kept her eyes downcast as the two men walked their horses past her.

"Hey, you got a nice pair for an old lady," one of the outlaws chuckled.

"She ain't *that* old," his buddy said.

Jessie could smell the stink of these two from where she sat. Their clothes were torn and soiled, and they had grime ground into the folds and seams of their trail-weathered skin. Lord! She wanted to cringe as she felt their hungry eyes upon her, but she didn't dare! That sort of reaction belonged to a younger woman, a woman they might want to rape...

But she didn't even want to *think* about that! She was an old woman, beneath their notice—she hoped! If only the high-necked, long-sleeved, dark blue dress she was wearing did not fit so snugly across her breasts. It had been the most concealing garment in Barney's limited stock, but the cut of the dress was tailored for an older woman, not a youngish female with Jessie's sort of figure. Right now, as the outlaws all gazed at her, she felt as if the spinsterish garment had suddenly gone transparent.

Judging from the sounds of the two outlaws searching the wagon, they were much too distracted to discover the gun. The men were chuckling to themselves about the women they'd had in their lives—getting themselves all hot and bothered, Jessie realized grimly.

No sense kidding yourself about their intentions any longer, Jessie thought. She glanced at Barney. He would try to save her, and he would be killed by these bandits.

All right, she thought. *As soon as those two bastards clear out of the wagon, I'll pretend to be sick and slip inside before anybody can order me to stop. Once I get the gun, maybe I can get the drop on them...*

But she knew it was unlikely that any of these hardcases would be intimidated by a woman holding a gun on them. Somebody would draw on her, and she would be forced to kill him. After that, maybe, if she was lucky, the others would be cowed. She had only six shots, she reminded herself. And there were six outlaws. If it came down to a full-scale shootout, she didn't have a shot to waste!

Behind her, Jessie heard the outlaw pair quit the wagon and remount their horses. The two riders were coming up alongside her as Jessie groaned loudly, "I—I feel faint! Got to lie down!"

She was starting to crawl into the wagon's interior when she saw the skinny leader nod to the outlaws next to the driver's area of the wagon. A strong arm whipped out to grab her around her waist.

The outlaw pulled her off the bench seat, and laid her belly-down across his saddle. Jessie kicked and squirmed, but the outlaw held her fast with a firm hand pressed into the small of her back. She was carried that way, away from the wagon—and the gun—to the rest of the gang.

"Hey." The man carrying her laughed. "She feels right solid for an old one!"

"Told ya she ain't that old." His partner grinned, reaching out to smack Jessie's rump.

"Let her be!" Barney shouted, his voice trembling with rage.

"Just hold on now, Barney." The skinny leader laughed. He brushed back his bright green frock coat to reveal his gun, worn butt-forward in a cross-draw rig strapped high on his left hip. "You sit and behave yourself, old man, else I'll shoot you dead, right here and now."

"She's an old woman," Barney pleaded. "Mister, you don't want—"

"Barney—" The leader's voice had a dangerous edge to it. "I think we've been too lax with you all these years. You know this territory belongs to Seth Weeks, don't you?"

The old drummer nodded unhappily.

"And that means anything that passes through it belongs to Seth or his agents—which is us. Right, Barney?"

"Oh, mister," Barney pleaded. "She's old—"

The outlaw who'd snatched Jessie set her down by some felled trees off to one side of the trail. He and his buddy dismounted and stood on either side of her to keep her from running.

"You're right, Barney, she is old," the outlaw leader said, his eyes locked on Jessie's form. "But she ain't too bad for her age . . ."

"Not bad at all," another of the outlaws said with a leer.

Jessie looked at him and then turned away. The man's greasy, matted beard was wet with drool.

"You know, Barney, none of us have had a woman for

months," the outlaw leader was telling the distraught drummer. "Beggars can't be choosers, right, old man?" He nodded permission to the rest of the men, who quickly dismounted to form a circle around Jessie.

"Don't do this!" Barney wailed.

"Tell you what, Barney." The man wearing the yellow bandanna laughed. "You stay real quiet and behave yourself, and we'll give her back to you after we're done. She'll be a little worse for wear, but she'll be alive."

"P-please!" Barney begged.

"But if you make a fuss, we'll kill her when we're done," the leader cut him off. He swung himself out of his saddle, already working at the buttons of his red trousers as he approached Jessie. "Dead or alive, Barney, that's up to you. But first we're going to have her, and that's a fact!"

Jessie dodged and feinted, trying to break free. The outlaws who encircled her were laughing as they stretched out their arms to block her from running. Slowly they closed in, taunting her, inviting her to take off her dress, warning her that they were going to rip it off if she didn't.

If only she had a knife, or even her derringer, Jessie thought wildly. She could probably kill one of them, anyway, if she had such a weapon. Or at least she could kill herself before these dirty animals had a chance to touch her!

"She moves real good for an old one!" one of the outlaws smirked.

"Once we get her clothes off, she won't look half bad!"

"You boys just remember that I go first," the skinny outlaw who was their leader announced.

One of the men leaped forward to pin Jessie's arms behind her back. Jessie stomped down upon his instep with the heel of her boot, the way Ki had taught her.

The outlaw howled in pain and loosened his grip enough for Jessie to break free, but not before the man's jagged fingernails had hooked the material of her dress, tearing it open at the neck and for an inch down the front, so that now Jessie's shoulder was bare.

The rest of the men whooped in excitement. One of them grabbed Jessie and threw her to the ground.

"I'm first!" the leader growled.

Like wolves in a pack, the men dropped back as their leader approached. The outlaw pulled off his yellow bandanna and stuffed it into his side pocket. He was bald except for that fringe of stringy hair bristling out from just above his ears. His mouth was watering as he stood above Jessie. "You behave yourself now, old woman," he warned.

"Shouldn't somebody be watching the old man?" one of the outlaws wondered aloud.

"You can watch what you want." The leader chuckled. "As for me, I'm gonna watch *her!*"

The outlaws laughed, giddy with excitement as their leader unhitched his gunbelt and tossed it to the ground. Jessie eyed it desperately, but it was well out of her reach.

The eager faces of the gang were riveted on Jessie as she kicked out at the outlaw leader's shins. "I'm warning you!" she spat, feeling like a fool as she peered at him through the distorting lenses of her spectacles. "You stay away from me!"

"Now you listen to me, old girl. Me and my boys are gonna have you, there's no two ways about it!" The outlaw's features darkened with rage. "You be nice, or else we'll bust you up some, understand?" He drew back his boot and kicked lazily at Jessie for emphasis.

"I'm gonna kill you!" Barney screamed in fury. The outlaws whirled around in surprise. While they'd been watching Jessie, Barney had taken the opportunity to draw his saber and climb down from the wagon. Now he was charging toward them, his glinting blade held at the ready, high over his head.

"Stop that old bastard!" the outlaw leader shouted.

"You hold it, Barney!" one of the gang members ordered, stepping into the drummer's path. "Give me that sword or I'll—"

Barney swung the saber full force, catching the outlaw's neck and cleanly lopping off his head.

"Oh, Jesus!" somebody hissed. The bandits stood frozen, some of them staring at their fellow outlaw's head as it rolled like a melon on the ground, the eyes still blinking and the mouth still forming soundless words. Two of the outlaws threw themselves to one side to avoid being sprayed with the gouts of blood shooting up like a geyser from the tottering, headless body. As they watched, the body stumbled forward two paces before slamming to the ground.

Barney, meanwhile, had never stopped running. His bloodied saber was now raised to strike at the outlaw leader.

The man stretched out his left hand imploringly as he crabbed toward his gunbelt lying on the ground.

Barney swung his sword. The outlaw screamed as the outstretched fingers of his left hand were hacked off. The severed digits left crimson trails as they flew through the air to pelt the rest of the gang, who were just now coming to their senses. Their leader was doubling over, bawling in agony as he clutched his maimed hand to his chest.

Jessie had crawled to reach the wailing outlaw's holster. She drew his gun, a double-action Colt.

"Drop that!" the outlaw closest to her shouted, spinning around and drawing his own gun. "Old woman, don't act loco—"

Jessie shot him between the eyes. The dead man's finger jerked the trigger of his gun, the round kicking up a spout of dirt just inches from Jessie. She twisted around to empty her pistol at the remaining bandits.

The three men gathered up their crying leader and ran for their horses. Jessie hadn't been able to hit even one of them! She couldn't understand it until she realized that she'd been trying to aim while she was wearing those dumb spectacles! The distorting lenses had thrown off her shooting. The one man she'd managed to kill had been too close to miss.

The trio slung their leader across a saddle and wheeled around their horses to make for cover. As they rode, one of them twisted around in his stirrups to empty his revolver at Barney's mule team. One of the animals brayed as it shook its suddenly bloodied head. As Barney watched, his mule's eyes glazed. The slain beast slumped against its panicked, bucking companion.

Jessie looked around, her stomach doing flipflops. The scene looked as gory as any battlefield in history. The humming flies had already discovered the severed head of the outlaw. His body, still leaking blood, had turned the ground it was lying upon into a bog. The man Jessie had shot was lying nearby, and the severed fingers of the outlaw leader were strewn about like fat white worms.

"Kilt a mule," Barney mused distractedly, his saber trailing on the ground. "Why'd they want to kill the mules?"

"To keep us from leaving," Jessie replied. "They'll be back, Barney."

"What's that, General?" Barney asked loudly. "Yessir, General!" The old drummer stiffened to attention and saluted thin air.

"Oh, no," Jessie muttered wearily. "Barney!" she called. "Snap out of it! Those outlaws are coming back! We've got to prepare ourselves!"

Barney nodded at her, then turned to address his surviving mule. "Corporal! Sound the alarm!"

Jessie shook her head. She set about gathering up the fallen outlaws' weapons. The gun she held was empty, and as luck would have it, the outlaw leader's gunbelt was smooth; the man evidently kept his spare cartridges on his person. She dropped the useless Colt and checked the gun of the man she'd shot. There were four rounds in his Smith & Wesson and another half-dozen jammed into the stitched loops of his belt. The headless body's gunbelt held a fully loaded Peacemaker. There were no cartridge loops on the man's belt.

Jessie held the two guns and extra bullets in her hands. Between the pair of weapons were sixteen rounds. As a backup, she had the revolver hidden in the wagon. That was another six shots. She nodded to herself. Now that she had weapons, and the outlaws' numbers had been thinned out, things didn't look so bad.

Thanks to Barney, she reminded herself. If it hadn't been for his courage, Jessie would have suffered a hideous fate. She wanted to thank him, but right now, expressing her gratitude would be futile. The old fellow was at the moment unable to hear anything she might say. His eyes were blank, and his voice had taken on that faraway tone which seemed to signal his intermittent lapses into senility.

It had happened last night, after Barney had unwillingly witnessed the Sageville robbery and murder, and it was happening now, after Barney had killed one outlaw and severely wounded another. It was stress that pushed the old drummer over the brink, Jessie guessed; he avoided unpleasantness in the present by escaping into the past.

Well, that was bad. It meant that Jessie could not rely on Barney's help during the next attack. She'd briefly considered giving him one of the guns, but now quickly decided against it. There was no way of knowing if Barney could shoot, and who knew what he might do with a firearm in his present condition?

Don't worry, Barney, you did your part, Jessie thought fondly as she watched the old man talking to his imaginary soldiers. *You saved my life, and now I'm going to protect you.*

She hefted her pistols. It had been Barney's valiant attack that had secured them for her.

Jessie glanced about nervously. The four outlaws could be anywhere. Once the leader got his hand bandaged, and borrowed an extra gun from his friends, he'd be leading the attack. Jessie had looked deep into the eyes of that bastard; she knew he was not about to let the old folks who had decimated his gang and ruined his left hand escape unharmed!

"Barney!" she called urgently. "Unhitch your mule. We've got to get some cover."

"General, let's circle around to cut off them damned rebels!" Barney crowed. "For the glory of the Union, let's burn down the town!"

Jessie seethed in frustration. There was no time to waste! An idea born of desperation occurred to her. "Sir! Excuse me, sir," she said, saluting the peddler.

"Eh? What's that, soldier?" He lurched about to face her. Barney's rheumy blue eyes were unfocused as he gazed past Jessie to view a cavorting parade of phantoms out of the past.

"Sir, I have an urgent message from General Grant!" Jessie began.

"Grant?" Barney echoed, brandishing his sword. "What's he want, soldier?"

Jessie pressed on, hoping that couching what she had to say in military terms would help to penetrate the fog in Barney's mind. "General Grant has ordered us to dig in for an extended campaign."

Barney nodded. "All right, soldier. Hop to it!" He pointed to his mule. "I'll gather up the cavalry mounts and—and—" he faltered, seeming to grow confused.

"And we'll hide behind those rocks," Jessie quickly finished for him, indicating a jumble of boulders beside the wagon.

"Right! You heard my orders, soldier!" Barney decreed.

"Fetch the mule!" Jessie begged. She started for the wagon to get canteens and food to take with them to the rocks.

Barney suddenly dropped his saber to the ground. "D-Dora?" he called out weakly.

Jessie heaved a great sigh of relief. At least she could talk to him when he thought she was Dora! "Barney! Get the mule and get behind those rocks!"

The old drummer began to shuffle off to do as he was told, and then paused. "Dora, they didn't hurt you none, did they?"

Jessie dropped what she was doing and went to him. She gave him a hug and said, "I'm fine, thanks to you."

Barney colored. "Shucks, I wouldn't let nothin' happen to you, girl, you oughta know that." He seemed an exceedingly frail old man as he said, "Reckon I'd better get that mule."

Jessie hurried to the wagon. She laid her three pistols and loose ammo on a couple of blankets, then rummaged around for whatever else she thought might be of use. Finally, her arms filled with the blankets, guns, and provisions, she left the wagon and circled around to where Barney had hidden himself and his mule.

The old fellow lunged at her with his saber as she approached the boulders. "Careful there, soldier," he warned. "I almost mistook you for a rebel!"

Jessie just rolled her eyes. "Let me through, sir."

Barney nodded. As Jessie settled down beside him, he asked, "When's General Grant sending us some reinforcements?"

Jessie, placing her pistols before her, had to laugh. "That's a good question, sir."

★
Chapter 16

Longarm rode at the head of the small posse on its way to Roundpatch. Along with him were Marshal Farley, his two deputies, and Farley's prisoner, Leroy Hoggs, who'd been demanding loudly that he be referred to as Smitty ever since they'd left Sarah Township at dawn. The diminutive, would-be bank robber's wrists were securely cuffed in front of him.

Longarm was keeping an eye on Farley as well as the prisoner. The marshal's noggin was still wrapped in a bandage. Farley seemed to be keeping up all right, but he also seemed a trifle more subdued than usual.

The posse crossed a wide pasture and then stopped to check their maps and get their bearings. They were trying to make up for lost time by taking a shortcut to the last leg of the trail that led to Roundpatch.

"How you doing?" Longarm asked Farley as they dismounted.

"Like I told you already, my cracked skull ain't pestering me half as much as your nagging."

239

"Come on, Marshal," Longarm said with a scowl. "You yourself admitted you couldn't sit around doing nothing any longer."

Farley grinned, resting his hand on the butt of the Peacemaker that dangled on his hip beneath his big belly. "I'm all right. It would do me good to get out of this sun for a minute, that's all."

The two lawmen headed for the dappled shade cast by a large oak tree. Farley leaned against the rough bark and removed his hat. The bandage around his head was sweat-stained, and his normally ruddy complexion had deepened to a far more angry scarlet.

"Ah, it feels good to rest my eyes." The marshal sighed in relief.

Longarm nodded. "Sit down and we'll take a look at the map."

Farley did as he was told, sliding down the length of the tree trunk until he was resting on his haunches. He dug the map out of his shirt pocket and unfolded it between himself and Longarm.

"This here's the break in the hills I was telling you about," Farley said, tapping the parchment. "Once we travel through that pass, we'll be close to Roundpatch. That's when 'Smitty' there can start earning his *deal*." He spat the last word, leaning his head back against the oak bark and closing his eyes. "You know, Longarm, I ain't never in my career made a deal with a prisoner. It surely does gall me to have to start now."

"You're not doing it for Leroy Hoggs. You're doing it for Jessie," Longarm admonished him gently. "And for me. Hoggs came along purely to escape the lynch mob I told him about. He doesn't know I'm asking this."

"Let me see if I got it straight. I drop the bank-robbing charges and you take him back to Nebraska to stand for some phony paper he wrote?"

Longarm nodded. "That's it. It's the deal I offered Hoggs the day before yesterday. He thinks he's lost it. The offer is an ace I'd like to be able to play to get him to come clean once and for all about Jessie's involvement in all this."

"Well, let me chew on it awhile."

"You've been chewing on it since dawn."

"Oh, damn," the marshal muttered. "All right then. It's up to you, Custis. If you want to, you can make your—your *deal* with Hoggs."

"Marshal?" the deputy named Chuck called out. "We got company!"

"Huh? What's going on?" Farley complained, groaning and puffing as he got to his feet.

Longarm had already reached the deputy's side. He gazed at the line of black shapes moving across the prairie. "Riders," he called. "I count close to a dozen of them. Coming this way, and fast."

Farley joined the two men. "They're not outlaws," he murmured. "They're coming from the direction of Sarah, not Roundpatch."

"Sweet Jesus," Hoggs babbled. "Do you think it's that lynch mob come after me?" The deputy guarding the nervous bandit rested a precautionary hand on the back of Hoggs's collar.

Longarm and Farley exchanged a glance. "Looks like your fairy tale about a lynch mob just came true," the town marshal said dryly. He stared at the rapidly approaching riders. "That's Bob King, the rancher that gave us so much trouble the other day. He's got a passel of his regulators riding with him."

"Oh, shit." Longarm sighed. "That's just what we need. A bunch of amateurs."

"You boys mount up!" Farley ordered.

"We going to make a run for it, boss?" Chuck asked.

"Not hardly," Farley snorted. "What have we got to run for? We're the goddamned law! I just want us to be at eye level with those owlhoots coming our way. You two boys remember that you're sworn deputies, and conduct yourselves accordingly. Sit tall in the saddle! Stick out your chests and show your badges!"

Longarm grinned. "Good thinking, Marshal." He removed his own silver badge from his wallet and pinned it to the lapel of his frock coat. "A show of authority is what's called for here." He winked at the stricken-looking Leroy Hoggs. "Don't sweat it, Smitty. For once, the law is going to protect you from honest citizens, and not the other way around!"

"You hope," Farley whispered to the federal lawman out of the side of his mouth. "Old Bob's got us outnumbered three to one. We've got to bluff him, make him forget that if his men covered us and then hung Leroy from this tree, chances are that public opinion back in Sarah would let him get away with it, scot-free!"

Longarm chewed his bottom lip. "But not if anybody wearing a badge gets hurt," he ruminated. "Yep, that's the card we've got to play. Bob King gets Leroy over our dead bodies!"

"Gee, if he killed us, it would sure teach him a lesson," Farley said sarcastically.

"He won't kill us," Longarm said.

"If he *does,* I'm going to be mighty riled at you, Longarm," Farley warned. "All right, men! Here they come. Don't nobody go for a gun until I do, *if* I do!"

Bob King held up his arm to slow his men as they reached the posse waiting beneath the oak tree. The wealthy, silver-haired cattle baron looked more like a banker than a rancher in his fine blue suit, fancy boots, and pearl-gray Stetson. But there was nothing bankerlike about the shiny Colt riding in the expensive glove-leather holster King had strapped around his waist.

"Marshal Farley," King said, nodding stiffly. "I guess you know why my men and I have overtaken you?"

Farley shook his head. "Why don't you spell it out for me, Bob? Me and *Federal Deputy Marshal Long, here.*"

King cleared his throat. "Don't try and impress me, Joe Farley! I helped get you that badge you're wearing, and I can help you lose it! This time I've got you outnumbered and outfoxed."

Farley sighed wearily. "What do you want, Bob?"

King pointed a finger at Hoggs. "I want justice done!"

"Can you be a little more specific?" Longarm asked.

King glowered. "I want that prisoner of yours. I intend to hang him from that oak tree behind you. Is that 'specific' enough for you, Deputy?"

"Can't have him," Longarm said. "Now if you boys will excuse us, we've got lawman's business to attend to."

242

"I will not excuse you!" King thundered. "Today justice will be done!"

"Full of wrath, just like Moses," Longarm said.

"That's exactly right," King countered. "An eye for an eye, Marshal Long. A citizen of Sarah Township was killed in that bank holdup."

"Granted, but Leroy here didn't kill anybody," Longarm said. "He's leading us to the person who *did* do the shooting."

"Jessica Starbuck?" King asked.

"Maybe."

"Maybe?" King laughed, his voice dripping with scorn. "I *know* where you stand concerning Jessie Starbuck."

"And I know your stake in the matter, King," Longarm growled, getting angry. "You're not fooling anybody with this law-and-order stuff. You don't give two shits about the poor jasper who caught a bullet in that holdup. All you want is Starbuck land. You figure Jessie's conviction will help you get it cheap. You're afraid this prisoner might lead us to the truth, which could clear her. Admit it, King. It's not justice that's got you acting like a horse with a burr under its blanket, it's greed!"

King sat trembling with rage upon his horse. "Has your tirade ended?"

"King," Longarm said, "if you don't get your ass out of here, you'll find out that my 'tirade' hasn't even begun."

The elderly rancher smiled. "That's what it comes down to, doesn't it, Long? Force. I've got you outnumbered. Don't make me kill you."

"You can *try* to kill me, but if you succeed, which I kind of doubt," Longarm said, "you'll stand for murder."

King licked his lips nervously, glancing at Farley and his two deputies. "Not if there are no witnesses left alive who might testify against me."

Longarm looked gleeful. "So much for law and order, eh, King? Then let's get down to brass tacks. You start something here, and I'll finish it, as far as *you're* concerned. I may die, but the first shot I fire will take your fool head clean off your shoulders."

King looked back at his men. "You heard him threaten me."

"That wasn't a threat, Bob," Farley interrupted. "That was a promise."

King, smiling dourly, reached out behind him. One of his men handed him a coiled rope. One end of it had already been tied into a hanging noose.

"Oh, no," Leroy Hoggs whined in fear. "Please, no . . ."

King kneed his mount into a slow walk toward the quaking prisoner. "Never try to bluff a businessman," he told Farley.

Longarm angled his horse to block King. "It wasn't a bluff. I'm not going to let you hang him, and if your men start shooting, I'll kill you."

"What do you want us to do, Mr. King?" one of the rancher's gunslicks called out.

"Keep your eyes on Long!" the rancher ordered. "If he tries to stop me, kill him!"

"First man who reaches for his gun, *I'll* kill," Farley announced, drawing his Peacemaker.

The scene grew quiet, except for the soft huffing and whickering of the horses, and the creaking of saddle leather as nervous men fidgeted in confrontation.

"I'm coming through, Long," King warned.

Longarm shook his head. "Not likely."

"You've got to protect me!" Leroy Hoggs blurted out. "I'm your prisoner," he beseeched the lawmen standing between him and the lynching crew. "I don't deserve to hang!"

"Your judgment day has come!" King announced loudly, brandishing his rope. "Prepare to meet your Maker!"

Squealing in fear, the handcuffed prisoner reached into his clothes and then extended his chained wrists toward King. There was a fire-cracker report, and a puff of smoke. As Longarm turned around in the saddle to stare at Hoggs in consternation, King clutched at his shoulder and fell off his horse.

"Stay away, all of you!" Hoggs called shrilly, waving the derringer about. "I've got another shot!"

"Don't shoot him!" Longarm ordered as Farley's deputies drew their guns. "We need him alive."

"I'm getting out of here!" Hoggs announced. He wheeled his horse around and hightailed it away at a flat-out run.

Some of King's drovers began to give chase, on impulse. Longarm quickly sidestepped his horse across their paths. He had his .44 in his hand.

"Nobody move," he warned. "Nobody reach for a gun, or I'll start shooting."

The drovers reined in their mounts. They appeared confused as they watched Bob King, writhing in pain on the ground, and the steely-eyed federal marshal blocking their path.

"What should we do?" one of the drovers asked uncertainly.

"We know about Long's reputation," another man replied. "And Mr. King there could be dying. I don't reckon it makes sense for us to risk our lives if'n our employer ain't gonna be around to appreciate it." He looked at Longarm. "In other words, Deputy, we're out of this, all right?"

Longarm nodded, but he kept his Colt in his hand, just in case.

Farley, meanwhile, was kneeling beside Bob King. "Your boss ain't dying," the town marshal informed the drovers. "But I reckon he's now got more important things on his mind than lynching two-bit crooks. He caught a bullet in the shoulder, but that ain't the worst of it. That fall off of his horse likely broke some of his ribs."

"You've got to help me!" The elderly rancher winced in pain as Farley tentatively prodded his side. "Get me back to town, to a doctor!"

"Farley, you know how to tape him up?" Longarm asked. When the marshal nodded, he continued, "Then here's what we ought to do, I'll go after Hoggs, and continue on with him in tow to Roundpatch. You get King patched up, more or less, and then send him back with one of his men. King? Can you hear me?" Longarm asked loudly.

"Yeah, I can hear you," the rancher gasped.

"Your grandstand play was jackass dumb, King. It's caused me a lot of needless trouble. I could press federal charges against you, but I won't, on one condition.

"Anything, Long," King moaned. "God, I hurt!" he cried out. "Get me home, to a doctor!"

"I want ten of your men to ride as temporary deputies with Farley. They'll take their orders from him. One man can escort you home after your side's been taped up and your bullet wound bandaged. Is it a deal?"

"Yes!" King groaned. "Now bandage me up!"

Longarm grinned at Farley. "Reckon a twelve-man posse will allow you to ride into Roundpatch unchallenged, sentries or no. I'll do my best to soften the place up, with Leroy's help."

"You be careful going after him," Farley warned Longarm. "He's no killer, but right now he's scared out of his mind. He might try something foolish."

"Reckon so," Longarm replied disgustedly.

"Guess you know that you can't take Leroy to Nebraska now," Farley said. "He's going to have to stand trial here in Sarah, for shooting King."

Longarm nodded. "Poor Leroy. Where the hell did he get that derringer, I wonder?"

Farley shrugged. "All I know is he was clean when I first locked him up."

"Well, I sure didn't give it to him," Longarm replied. He glanced at a pale, sweating Bob King. "Do me a favor, Farley, when you tape him up, make it tight!"

Farley winked. "Don't fret, I've got a feeling that before I'm finished with Mr. King, he's going to rue the day he decided to become a vigilante!"

"See you in Roundpatch." Longarm turned his horse and set out after the escaped fugitive. He rode hard, but warily. Leroy Hoggs wasn't very tough, and he *was* handcuffed, but he had at least one round in that mystery derringer of his. Longarm had managed to catch a glimpse of it before Hoggs had made his escape. The little pistol was similar to the double-barreled derringer resting in his own vest pocket.

Even a jackrabbit will turn and fight when it's cornered, Longarm thought. *And right now Leroy Hoggs is one rabbit with a .44-caliber bite!*

Chapter 17

Ki crouched behind a wide, tablelike slab of blue-gray slate. He laid his bow across the flat rock as he scrutinized a distant stand of trees. Then he motioned behind him for Birdy O'Hara to catch up.

"There's another sentry in that grove," the samurai whispered.

Birdy marveled. "How do you do it?" she wondered. "First the one behind that boulder, and now this man." She gazed at the still grove. "I don't see a thing."

"Look harder. Between those two tall pecans. Do you see his rifle's barrel slanting out?"

"My God." Birdy chuckled. "Yep, and I would have thought that was just a branch—if I'd seen it at all."

The samurai shrugged. "I know there are sentries about, it's just a matter of *where*. There could be more of them before we reach the relative safety of Roundpatch's town limits." He frowned. "Infiltration requires skill, Birdy. You really should have stayed behind, with our horses."

"Oh, sure," the reporter said sarcastically. "I didn't come this far to quit when I was within spitting distance of Roundpatch. We've been through all this. You need me, mister! If you want to clear Jessie, you're going to need a witness to substantiate what you find out."

"I understand that." Ki frowned. "But you're risking your life."

Birdy's blue eyes rolled heavenward. "Brother! You sleep with a man and he wants to adopt you! First of all, Ki, if anything happens to you, I'm as good as dead, in any event! How do you expect a greenhorn female like me, stuck out here in the middle of outlaw territory, to get home all by her lonesome?"

Ki smiled. "Your logic is impeccable."

"Everything about me is impeccable," Birdy replied smugly. Her eyes widened as Ki selected an arrow from the quiver on his hip, and notched it into his bowstring. "You going to kill that sentry?"

"I think we can get around him if we are quiet," Ki said.

"You're not going to kill this one either?"

"I will doubtless have to kill many men before this day is over," the samurai said. "I would rather not begin until it is absolutely necessary."

Birdy looked disappointed. "I wanted to see you work your bow," she pouted.

Ki shook his head. "Sometimes I do not know about you, O'Hara." He pointed over her shoulder. "That way. It will get us closer to the town, and allow us to keep these rocks between ourselves and the man in the trees."

They silently made their way past the grove. Ki kept an eye out for guards, and at the same time shepherded Birdy away from loose stones or twigs in their path. The slightest noise could give them away to their hidden enemies.

They stuck to the rocks for long as possible, gradually climbing upward until they crested a hill. Ki urged Birdy to move quickly down the incline until they reached a shallow depression. Then he told her to stretch out beside him, and together they peered over the depression's lip.

About three hundred yards down the slope of the hill, the terrain leveled. Achingly brilliant splashes of sunlight reflected off a stream that twisted like a silvery serpent through a good-sized collection of buildings in various stages of disrepair. Here and there, bridges constructed of raw timber spanned the stream. Ki pointed to a stable and a corral filled with horses.

"So that's Roundpatch," Birdy murmured. "It's bigger than I thought it would be."

"And there are enough horses in that stable to make me think Seth Weeks has an outlaw population to match the town's size," Ki replied. He pointed to a three-story structure that had smoke curling from its stovepipe chimney.

"There's a sign above the door," Birdy said, squinting, "but I can't make it out."

"I can, barely," Ki replied. "It reads 'Town Hall.'" He nodded. "I believe that is where we will find Seth Weeks."

"Because of the smoke?"

"Partly," Ki said. "And partly because of those saddled horses hitched up in front of the hall. But mostly because Seth Weeks calls himself Roundpatch's mayor."

Birdy nodded. "And where else would a mayor hole up but the town hall? So what now? Do we just waltz down there?"

"Possibly," Ki mused. "It is unlikely that there are any more sentries between us and the town." He gestured toward a mottled brown and green pasture beyond the buildings. "That is where they used to graze their steers, back when Roundpatch was a cow town. That prickly grass is too tough for anything but yesteryear's longhorns. A posse on horseback would have to come from that direction."

"No wonder we only ran into two sentries," Birdy said.

"Right," Ki replied. "Weeks has nothing to fear from the direction we came." He smiled. "At least, that is what he thinks."

"Come on." Birdy chuckled. "Let's go meet the mayor."

Ki unstrapped his quiver and laid it alongside his bow. "I'm leaving these weapons here. Any fighting down below will be at close quarters. If we should become separated, meet me back here, all right?"

Birdy nodded and gave him a quick peck on the cheek. "Let's do it!" she said.

They scampered from rock to bush, fallen tree trunk to groundswell, until they reached the foot of the hill. From there they would have no cover until they reached the protection of the town's outlying buildings.

"I'll go first," Ki said. "If there's anybody watching, I should draw their fire. If anything should happen to me, you run back up the hill and make your way to the horses. Do you remember where they are?"

"Sure," Birdy replied. "But how do I get past those two sentries?"

"If there's gunfire, they'll come running to see what's going on," Ki explained. "They'll think somebody has intruded from across the pasture. You'll be able to get by them if you are careful. Once you get to the horses, ride east until you come up against these hills. Then ride around them in either direction—it doesn't matter which—until you come to the main trail. Follow the trail down until you find yourself on the far side of that pasture. Wait there. Longarm and a posse will soon be coming."

"Nothing's going to happen to you," Birdy said dully.

"I like a woman with confidence," Ki replied. "Do you have your gun?"

"Loaded and ready." The reporter held up her small revolver.

"When you see me reach that blue building on the far side of the stream, you come. Got it?" He waited for her nod, and then set off in a fast, zigzagging trot toward the building.

The samurai kept his eyes peeled for any sign of movement or the telltale glint of sun off a gun barrel. Then he was splashing through the shallow stream, and then he was pressing himself against the blue, splintery wall. He watched as Birdy quickly made her way to his side.

"What now?" she gasped.

Ki smiled. "We wait until you catch your breath, and then we work our way to the town hall. Just in case," he told her, "you keep your gun ready, but whatever you do, don't fire unless you absolutely must."

"I know that!" Birdy replied tartly. "I'm not an idiot."

"Sorry," Ki said. "I'm used to doing this kind of thing alone."

Birdy nodded. Her expression softened. "Me too. It's nice not to be alone, at least for a little while."

They flitted like ghosts from building to building, working their way down the deserted streets toward the town hall.

"Where is everybody?" Birdy whispered.

"Inside, out of the hot sun. Eating, drinking, sleeping." Ki shrugged. "Don't forget, this is not really a town. There are no stores, for example. It's an outlaw-inhabited ghost town, more like a camp than a settlement."

They were now in a dark, narrow alley two doors away from the front entrance of the town hall. Ki motioned to Birdy to hang back in the shadows. "I'll make sure the coast is clear," he whispered, and then disappeared around the corner of a saddler's shop that was now vacant.

Birdy stood just inside the mouth of the alley. She waited as the seconds ticked by, wondering if something had happened to Ki. She was on the verge of setting out to look for him when she heard footsteps behind her.

She turned around in relief, then froze. The man staring at her was not Ki.

"Well, what do we have here?" the man drawled.

"Stay away!" she hissed, bringing up her revolver. But the man only laughed, reaching out to pluck it from her grasp before she quite knew what had happened.

She backed away until she found herself pressed up against the building's side. "If you know what's good for you, you'll stay away!" she whispered harshly.

"Oh, I know what's good for me, all right, little lady." The man smirked. He still held her gun pointed down at the ground. "I don't know what you're doing here, but I'm sure glad I found you."

Ki suddenly appeared behind the outlaw. He slammed the edge of his palm against the man's neck. The outlaw's eyes rolled up and his knees buckled. As luck would have it, he reflexively squeezed the trigger of Birdy's pistol as he fell.

"Oh, shit," Birdy groaned as the revolver's report echoed cannonlike in the quiet town. Instantly the air was filled with the alarmed shouts of men.

"Run for that hill," Ki ordered her. "Wait for me where I left the bow!"

"I'm not leaving you," Birdy said as she bent to pick up her gun.

"Go!" Ki cried as he watched the mouth of the alley. A man appeared there, silhouetted by the sun. There was a gun in his hand. Ki's arm whipped out and a *shuriken* glinted briefly in the sun as it whirled toward the outlaw. The man grunted and doubled over, clutching at his belly.

"Will you go?" Ki begged. "Our chance to confront Seth Weeks is gone! If we see him, it will be as his prisoners!"

"All right," Birdy told Ki as he watched the alley's entrance. The samurai heard her running off, and breathed a sigh of relief.

He reached into his vest for a yellow *nage teppo*. Glancing at it, Ki realized that it was the same one he had tossed at the cougar. *This time you had better work,* he thought.

He pressed himself against the side of the building. Outlaws, peering into the shadowy corridor, were approaching from the street, their guns at the ready.

Ki waited until they'd entered the alley, and then hurled the grenade, squeezing shut his own eyes as he did so. He heard a loud pop, the sound like that of a paper sack filled with air being ruptured. The world flashed red behind his tightly clenched eyelids.

Ki opened his eyes. The moaning outlaws were staggering against each other like the blinded men they were.

Ki dashed past the sightless outlaws. The blinding effect was only temporary. He had scant minutes to make good his escape.

He rounded the mouth of the alleyway and darted down the street. A sudden movement caught his eye, but he did not have time to reach before a rifle butt hammered the side of his head. He saw another flash of light, this one a quite private fireworks display, and felt his legs go rubbery, spilling him into the dust.

The samurai shook himself, raising himself up on his hands and knees. He glanced around. A great many grim-faced men had him surrounded. Most of them were holding guns pointed his way.

"What the hell is a Chinaman doing here?" somebody remarked.

"Beats me, but I think we ought to kill him," somebody else replied.

"Before you do that, your boss might want to see me," Ki said. His own voice sounded thick in his ears, and the whole side of his head was throbbing with pain.

"Yeah, I guess we ought to check with Seth," a gruff voice announced. "Two of you take him upstairs."

Ki felt a boot tip sharply prodding his ribs. "Stop that," he muttered.

"On your feet, Chink!" a raspy voice wheezed.

"This Chinaman's still out on his feet!" one of the outlaws laughed as he took up a position on Ki's left.

"Let's march, quickee-quickee, Wong!" the raspy voice taunted from Ki's right.

Ki glanced curiously at its owner, and at the angry scars ringing the man's neck.

The neck-scarred man shoved his gun into the small of Ki's back. "I said quick!" he hissed.

Ki let the two men steer him toward the town hall. The samurai's *nunchaku* was tucked into its pocket on the inside of his vest, but Ki knew that sooner or later these oafs would think to strip him of his weapon-packed garment.

"Feel funny," Ki gasped. "Going to throw up—" He bent at the waist, pretending to gag as he laced his arms across his belly. His two guards jumped back hastily. After a second, Ki straightened up. "Feel better," he nodded.

"Then let's go," the man with the damaged voice wheezed, his gun resuming its position in Ki's back.

The samurai walked on, a faint smile playing across his stern features. The *nunchaku* was no longer in his vest; it was nicely tucked up the billowing sleeve of his loose-fitting shirt.

The first-floor interior of the town hall was a cavernous, littered space lit by gaping window frames that had long ago lost their glass. At one time, pews for town meetings had probably filled the first floor, but the pews had gone the way of the glass and the town meetings.

Ki was led to the staircase. Both outlaws gestured with their guns as he began to plod up the squeaking steps toward the second-floor landing.

"Keep going, all the way to the third floor," the neck-scarred outlaw whispered. "Then down the corridor."

Ki did as he was told, feeling those pistol barrels trained on his spine. A closed door marked KNOCK FIRST confronted him.

"Hold it," the outlaw whispered, drawing up alongside Ki. He knocked and then turned the knob, swinging the door open.

Ki stared into the room. Behind a desk sat an incredibly obese man. He was shirtless, wearing tentlike overalls, the straps of which seemed embedded in the yellowish blubber of his hulking shoulders. The light streaming in from the open windows behind the man made his flesh shimmer like sealskin.

The samurai was instantly reminded of the *sumo yokozuna* of his homeland, the mountainlike wrestlers who slammed against each other in strictly ritualized grappling combat.

Two other men, obviously the giant's bodyguards, lounged in chairs along one wall of the office. They were playing cards.

The fat man stood up. Ki estimated his weight at four hundred pounds. The man had a pencil-thin mustache, and flat black eyes that gazed at Ki with eerie, reptilian indifference.

"What you got there, Dusty?" the fat man asked in a thin, high-pitched voice. As he spoke, he reached into a straw basket on his desk. His pudgy fingers came up with an egg.

The outlaw with the scarred throat shrugged and then whispered, "Caught him snooping around, Seth. He killed Sledge with some kind of throwing knife. Thought you might want to talk to him."

Seth Weeks nodded. He punctured the egg with a nail lying on his desk, and then began to noisily suck out the contents.

"You know who I am?" the fat man asked between slurps.

"Yes," Ki said.

Seth Weeks nodded again. Those lizard eyes of his blinked several times. "Why are you here?"

Ki stood silent.

"Sam?" the outlaw leader called.

One of the outlaws along the wall put his cards facedown on the floor. "Yeah, Seth?"

"Take your knife and slit one of this Chinaman's eyes."

"Sure, Seth." The outlaw stood up, sliding a bowie knife from its sheath hanging on his gunbelt.

"I'm here to find Jessie Starbuck," Ki said quickly.

"Never mind, Sam," Seth Weeks said around his egg. Sam sat down, put away his knife, and picked up his cards. "More of this Jessie Starbuck shit," Weeks muttered. He threw the empty eggshell out the window, and reached into the basket for another one. "I'll tell you, I'm sorry that I ever got involved with this whole shitty plan." The nail made a slight crunching sound as it pierced the new egg. Weeks pressed it to his lips and began to suck.

The outlaws flanking Ki waited patiently. The samurai did the same. Weeks finished his egg and sent the empty shell out the window.

"Hey!" the outlaw leader yelled down to the street. "One of you fetch Lang!" He turned back to Dusty. "Lang might want to talk to this Chinaman. Take him downstairs and wait."

Dusty fingered the scars around his throat. It seemed to be a nervous habit. "What after that?" he wheezed.

Seth Weeks reached for another egg. "Then you can kill him."

"Let's go," Dusty rasped, jamming his gun into Ki's side.

The pair of outlaws steered him out into the corridor and down the stairs. Ki waited until they were halfway down the last flight, since he didn't want Seth Weeks or his bodyguards to hear anything. Then he let his *nunchaku* slide out of his shirtsleeve and into his palm. The two outlaws were behind him, coming down single-file because of the narrowness of the steps. Ki pivoted and smiled up at the two men.

Dusty, his gun at the ready, stared down at him blankly. "What's going—"

Ki brought his right arm around as if he were trying to chop at Dusty's neck. He held one of the *nunchaku*'s hardwood sticks, and whipped the other half of the weapon against the outlaw's ear.

Dusty's gun went flying. The *nunchaku*'s impact had sent the outlaw staggering against the wall. He bounced off it, then fell against the banister, cracking through the rickety railing to fall six feet to the wooden floor below.

The man behind Dusty had been trying to get a shot at Ki, but Dusty, flailing about on the narrow staircase, had frustrated his aim. Now the outlaw could sight down on the samurai, but before he could fire, Ki used his whirling weapon to knock the revolver out of the man's hand. The outlaw turned to run back up the stairs. Ki looped the *nunchaku*'s horsehair braid around the man's ankle, gripped the weapon in both hands, and pulled. The outlaw's feet flew out from under him and he fell face forward. His head snapped back violently as his chin struck one of the stairs, and he lay still.

Ki stared at the man. There was something odd about the angle of the unconscious man's neck. The samurai checked for a pulse, but couldn't find one. The outlaw was dead. The fall had broken his neck.

Ki glanced at the outlaw named Dusty. The man was unconscious but still alive. The breath was rattling out of his scarred throat.

Ki turned and headed for the town hall's doorway. He stopped short as a man dressed entirely in black blocked the exit.

The man looked at Ki and smiled. "I've been waiting a long time for this," he said. "Don't run away so quickly, samurai."

The man stepped into the town hall. Ki glanced past him, but there was nobody else. The man had come alone. Ki could have run, but something told him this encounter was of great importance.

The man was wearing a gun, but he didn't reach for it. Instead, he glanced at Ki's *nunchaku* and then knelt to draw something from his black boot.

Ki stared. The man had produced a *nunchaku* of his own, and an exquisite one, at that! Each eighteen-inch length was tightly wrapped in black leather. Instead of a horsehair braid, the two handles were linked together by a short length of silvery chain.

"You are Lang?" Ki asked.

"Yes, Ki," the man in black replied. He set his black leather *nunchaku* whirling in front of him in a figure-eight pattern. "Fight or die, samurai," he said, and began to advance upon Ki.

Ki tucked one end of his own weapon beneath his right armpit and began to shuffle toward his opponent, balancing the weight of his body on his rear foot.

"The *neko-ashi-dachi*," the man in black said, pronouncing the Japanese words accurately. "The cat's-foot stance, one used effectively before a foot-strike, like so!"

He hopped forward to begin a double roundhouse kick. He swung his left leg up toward Ki's face, brought it down, pivoted on it, then repeated the foot-strike with his right leg. The entire attack lasted a mere second or two, and yet Ki managed to avoid both kicks. All during his attack, the man in black had sustained the whirling of his *nunchaku*. He now swung it hard toward Ki's torso, hoping to shatter the samurai's ribs.

Ki bent his knees and sprang into a backflip. As Lang's *nunchaku* stretched toward him, the samurai tightened his armpit-grip on his own weapon, and then snapped his right wrist forward. At the proper moment he relaxed his shoulder muscles, allowing the *nunchaku* to slip out of his armpit. The extra force generated by the armpit-hold intensified the speed at which Ki's weapon traveled. It wound itself around Lang's *nunchaku* the way a bullwhip's thong wraps around its target. Ki caught the end of his weapon as it whirled back toward him, and pulled with all of his might. Lang's weapon was torn from his grasp. Ki let the momentum of the technique carry his own *nunchaku* over his shoulder. He released his grip, allowing both weapons to fly across the room.

Lang stared at him. Ki smiled. "I am having too much fun to end this prematurely," the samurai said.

Lang's amber eyes sparkled. "I know just how you feel, my old friend..."

He charged, his limbs a flurry of movement. Ki blocked and struck back with lethal speed. The room filled with their harsh grunts of exertion and the slap of wrist against forearm, and then foot striking wrist...

Ki went into the *gedan-barai*, or low stance. He thrust out toward Lang's face with a one-knuckle fist. Lang blocked it and tried to hook Ki's forearm, meaning to haul the samurai into his countering palm-heel strike. Ki dodged the palm-heel, sank even lower into a "horse" stance, and twisted his torso to ram his elbow into Lang's unguarded solar plexus. Lang deflected Ki's elbow with a *kakuto-uke,* or "fishtail" block, then repeated his palm-heel strike.

They were toe-to-toe now. Their shadows upon the wall merged into one as they performed their deadly dance. Ki was aware that Seth Weeks and his bodyguards were upstairs, and that Roundpatch was inhabited by half a hundred outlaws, but he no longer cared.

Lang jammed his boot behind Ki's knee, hoping to shove the samurai off balance. Ki let him think the technique was working, then used Lang's attack to his own advantage, driving his rigid fingers into Lang's belly.

Lang groaned. His guard dropped. Ki danced sideways and delivered a hard, one-knuckle strike to the spot just behind Lang's ear.

The man in black dropped like a stone.

Ki rested his hands on his hips and looked down at Lang's unconscious form. "I am sorry it is over, my friend! Such an excellent battle!"

The samurai hurried to retrieve his *nunchaku.* His eyes lingered on Lang's awesome leather-and-silver weapon. "I shall take yours as well, my friend. As a trophy."

As Ki headed for the door, he glanced again at Lang. He was sorry that the man had been knocked out. Ki was anxious to know how Lang had come upon his considerable combat skills.

Above Ki's head, the ceiling creaked. *Seth Weeks reaching for another egg,* he thought wryly. "We will discuss your training another time, Lang," Ki murmured. "I would also like to know how you knew who I was."

With that, the samurai left the town hall. Across the street, perhaps a dozen of Seth Weeks's men were lounging about beneath a wooden awning.

One of the outlaws was in the process of drinking from a bottle of whiskey when he spotted Ki. The man choked, coughed, pointed a finger across the street, and yelled, "Hey!"

Ki dashed toward the alleyway where he'd been discovered. Hearing the sound of revolvers clearing leather, Ki reached into his vest for a red *nage teppo.* He tossed the grenade over his shoulder. The *nage teppo*—a smoke bomb—erupted in a thick black cloud that hung like a curtain between the samurai and the outlaw's guns.

Ki sprinted down the alley and headed out of Roundpatch the way he'd come. He crossed the stream, zigzagged across the open expanse of ground, and then ran up the hill. He found Birdy O'Hara waiting for him in their agreed-upon spot. Ki slid down beside her, smiling as she drew her revolver.

"You won't need that!" He laughed. "It has caused us enough trouble for one day!"

"You sound happy," Birdy said, her voice strangely flat.

"I am exhilarated! I had a splendid battle!"

"And you got away."

Ki regarded her. "You don't sound very pleased about that." He turned his back to gather up his bow and quiver.

"I'm sorry," Birdy said.

"For what?" Ki began to turn around.

She brought her gun down upon the back of Ki's head. The samurai fell forward, then began to push himself up—

O'Hara hit him again. Ki passed out.

"So very sorry..." she repeated, and then rose to trudge down the hill toward Roundpatch.

★

Chapter 18

Jessie and Barney spent several fitful hours waiting for the outlaws to renew their attack. The day wore on. For most of the afternoon Barney was content to lovingly polish his saber. Jessie had pinned together her torn dress. At around four o'clock, her nerves were put to the test when the old drummer began to shout orders to an imaginary cavalry troop.

"Hush, Barney," she pleaded. She tried not to look at the flyblown horror that was the outlaw's severed head and bloody body.

"It's hot," the old man complained. His misery had evidently brought him out of his senile spell. "These rocks are makin' my bones ache, and those dead men are starting to stink! Can't we rest in the wagon?"

"I'm sorry, Barney." Jessie glanced up at the bright blue sky. "I'm feeling a bit sunstruck myself, but we'd be sitting ducks in the wagon. I should have thought to bring along a canvas tarp. We could have rigged a lean-to for shade."

"I'll get it now," the drummer began.

"No!" Jessie said. "It's too dangerous." She stared out at

261

the surrounding trees. "It's been a long while since we fought them off."

"Maybe they left," Barney suggested hopefully.

Jessie smiled. "I wish that were true, but I don't think so."

"What do *you* know, Dora?" Barney said, scowling. "I say they're gone. We beat 'em real good, you and me, girl."

"I *feel* that they're still here."

"Hush, old woman!" Barney ordered her. "Who served with General Grant, me or you? And what are you doin' with them pistols? You don't know nothin' about pistols. Give 'em here!"

He reached for the revolvers and Jessie pulled them out of the old man's reach, saying, "Barney! Stop it!"

Barney jumped to his feet. "How dare you talk to an officer like that, soldier?" he demanded.

"Oh, Barney . . ."

"I'll have you court-martialed—"

Whatever else Barney might have been about to say was drowned out by the sound of a shot and the spanging noise of a round ricocheting off a nearby rock.

Jessie grabbed the loose cloth of Barney's shirt and pulled him down. "Keep your head down," she told him. "And watch behind you. They might try to circle us."

Barney eyed her curiously, but did as he was told. Jessie pegged a couple of shots toward the muzzle flashes she'd glimpsed. She didn't expect to hit anything, she just wanted to keep them excited and shooting. After all, they had to run out of ammunition sometime . . .

The outlaw leader had evidently come to the same conclusion. "Hold your fire!" he called to his men.

The glade grew silent and still, except for the drifting haze of gunsmoke. Jessie used the respite to break open the Smith & Wesson and replace the two rounds she'd fired.

"Hey, Barney! Old woman!" the leader shouted. "Throw away the guns and you come out of this alive!"

Barney snorted. "How about my sword? You want that too, young fella?"

Silence for a moment, and then the leader said, "Yeah, I want that sword, old man."

"I'll bet you do." Barney laughed. "How's that left paw of your'n, eh? Reckon there's any call for a one-handed outlaw?"

"My God," Jessie gulped. "Easy, Barney."

"Easy, my dead mule!" Barney whispered. "You don't know *everything,* girl. We got the cover, but this here's a Mexican standoff unless we can rile those owlhoots into doin' somethin' stupid." He winked at her and then yelled, "Hey, young fella! You want my saber, you come get it! I'll give it to you, you one-handed cripple! There's plenty more on you that I aim to cut off for messin' with my Dora!"

"Damn you!" the leader cried. He stepped out of concealment from behind a tree. His left arm was pressed against his chest. His hand was wrapped thickly in grimy, blood-soaked cloth.

Blood crusted the lapels of his bright green frock coat. The outlaw held a revolver in his right hand. "I'm gonna kill you, Barney. Then I'm gonna kill that old woman! Real slow..."

"We done the killin' so far, boy," Barney spat. "Them fingers don't grow back, y'know. You can join up with me. I got use for a cripple."

The outlaw's eyes were bright with hatred. I should have killed you right off," he spat. He held his maimed left hand before him the way a dog dangles an injured paw.

"You can always be a beggar." Barney laughed. "But your high an' mighty outlaw days have come to an end!"

"Now! Get them!" the leader screamed. He leveled his gun and began to dash toward Jessie and Barney.

Jessie was about to shoot the man, when a round kicked up dirt beside her, spoiling her aim. "Barney, get down!" she cried. "They've surrounded us!"

The outlaws were shooting at them from three sides. Jessie snapped off shots to her left and then to her right, over Barney's hunched form, but she was shooting much too quickly to take accurate aim.

The outlaws broke cover and charged. "Got to get at least *one,"* Jessie muttered. She took careful aim at one man running toward them from the right, but shots from the outlaw leader in front of her made her flinch.

"We been outflanked, girl," Barney whimpered.

There's no way I can shoot without exposing myself to their guns, Jessie realized. *But if I've got to die, I'll take that bastard in the green coat with me . . .*

She jumped to her feet, gripping the Smith & Wesson in both hands, and crabbed to one side. She ignored the outlaw aiming at her from her right, and drew a bead on the snarling leader of the gang.

A big man stepped into the clearing, a sawed-off, double-barreled shotgun gripped in his right hand. He aimed the shotgun at the man in green, and let loose one barrel. There was a deep *boom!* The outlaw leader was lifted off his feet and then slammed to the ground. He lay still, a gory, fist-sized hole in his gut.

The outlaw who'd been aiming at Jessie now spun toward the newcomer. Before he could fire, Jessie shot him twice. He fell back into the undergrowth.

The newcomer, meanwhile, was bringing his shotgun to bear on the wary outlaw throwing down on him from across the clearing. It was a tough shot for a sawed-off scattergun to make, and the newcomer evidently knew it. He took just an extra moment to aim, and then fired his second barrel—

Just a fraction of a second *after* the outlaw had pulled the trigger on his Colt.

The newcomer swore softly, slapping at his left thigh. He sank down onto the opposite knee, which caused the blast of his shotgun to go awry.

Jessie fired at the outlaw from the hip. Her round caught him in the side, staggering him, but he stayed on his feet and held on to his gun. The newcomer had dropped his empty shotgun and drawn his Colt. He aimed and fired, punching a hole in the wounded outlaw's belly. Jessie fired again. With three rounds in him, the outlaw crumpled.

Instinctively, Jessie brought her Smith & Wesson to bear on the newcomer. She stared at him for a moment, thinking that he looked familiar . . .

The big man grinned, dropping his Colt and raising his hands. "My name's Deke Tyler, ma'am. I mean you and Barney no harm."

The old man waved his saber. "How do you know my name, stranger?"

"I heard all about you and Dora last night, in Sageville." Tyler's craggy face darkened. "Mind if I put my hands down? This here leg wound I was clumsy enough to catch ain't serious, but it does smart a mite."

"Oh, of course," Jessie said, lowering her gun. She suddenly paled. "But there's one more outlaw!"

"No, ma'am," Tyler said patiently. "Three's all there was."

"Mr. Tyler," she said, "this morning there were six. You see here five bodies—or parts thereof," she added dryly. "There's a man still alive, I tell you!"

"If there was, he's long gone. There's only five horses back behind where these outlaws were holed up." He sat down and stretched his bleeding leg out in front of him.

"Here! Let me see to that wound," Jessie offered, going to him.

"Much obliged, ma'am," Deke Tyler said. "Anyway, last night, after hearing about what Jessie Starbuck did in Sageville, I left that town and rode all through the evening, hoping to overtake her. That's how I caught up with you so quick, I reckon. When I heard the shots, I circled around through these here woods to see what was happening. That's when I got to count the three outlaws and five horses."

"The last man just picked up and left?" Jessie mused aloud.

"Reckon so," Tyler replied. "Early on, from the looks of things. He's probably close to Roundpatch by now. They'll do that, these outlaw gangs. They'll stick together for a while, but when the going gets tough, a man or two will desert and head back to a place like Roundpatch to try his luck on another day."

"What if he brings back reinforcements?" Jessie worried.

"Heck, no." Tyler smiled. "These owlhoots wouldn't go across the street to help one another. I wouldn't fret about some outlaws coming to rescue their brothers in crime." He chuckled.

"I'm relieved to hear that," Jessie said. "Do you have a pocket knife?"

Tyler took one from his vest pocket and handed it to Jessie, who used it to widen the tear in his trousers where the bullet had entered. "Barney," she called out, "bring some bandages and alcohol."

"It ain't bad," Tyler said. "The bullet just grazed the muscle some. It wouldn't have happened at all if I wasn't getting so old. My reflexes must be slowing down."

"Nothing wrong with your reflexes," Jessie said absently as she worked on his wound. "But you ought to know better than to use a sawed-off twelve-gauge beyond fifty feet."

"Yes, *ma'am*," Tyler agreed. "You *do* know your guns, don't you, Dora? You shoot as fine as any gunhand I've ever come across, as well." Tyler reached out to tilt Jessie's head toward him. "And you've got lovely green eyes, Dora. Green as emeralds, they are . . ."

Jessie turned away. She hurriedly dug out her spectacles and put them on. "Don't see so good without these," she mumbled.

Tyler's seamed face split into a grin. "You saw pretty good when you were cutting down those outlaws, but who am I to argue with my elders, right, Dora?"

Jessie nodded, thinking, *I'm certain he knows!* But why is he just sitting there grinning? "There," she said. "Your leg's all done."

Tyler stood up and tested his limb. "Feels fine. I'm much obliged, Dora."

"What now?" Jessie asked, and immediately cursed herself for her phrasing. "I mean—"

"I know what you mean," Tyler said quietly. "You know how it is with old folks like us, Dora. We like to take our time, make sure we're doing the right thing."

Jessie stayed silent as Tyler thoughtfully stroked his chin. "Tell you what. These outlaws had themselves a nice campsite. There's a little stream over there. It's where I left my own horse. What say we all mosey over and take ourselves a little nap? I'm too old to ride through the night and then have a shootout, I'll tell you that much. Us three will rest a bit, and then I'll help Barney hitch up some of those outlaws' horses to his wagon. Those animals are saddle mounts, but I reckon they'll do to get that wagon back to Sageville."

"And then?" Jessie asked.

"And then we'll see," Tyler said firmly. He stretched and yawned. "I'm too tired to cross that bridge right now."

Jessie nodded. She too was exhausted from the day's events. "Come on, Barney," she called. "Let's get some rest."

"I ain't leavin' the battlefield," Barney declared. "I'm waitin' to hear from the General."

"These corpses don't make this clearing the pleasantest place to nap," Tyler pointed out.

"Don't care," Barney insisted stubbornly. "I ain't movin' till I hear from General Grant."

"Oh, Barney." Jessie sighed in exasperation. "I can't leave him alone," she told Tyler. "Not when he's lost in the past like this. You see, trouble causes his mind to wander. If I leave him alone, he could hurt himself."

"These corpses are stinking up a storm," Tyler said. "And the flies—"

"I know." Jessie looked about ready to cry. "But I can't leave him. Not until he comes out of his spell. I'm responsible for him, Mr. Tyler."

"I understand," Tyler said, looking at her with new-found respect. "Tell you what," he sighed. "I'll move these bodies and whatnot away from us, and then we'll all rest here."

"You'd undertake such a horrid task?" Jessie gasped. "Oh, thank you. I'll help."

Tyler shook his head. "You take care of the old fella." He smiled. "This is no job for a lady."

Jessie nodded gratefully. She watched as the bounty hunter set about accomplishing his grisly work. And she began to formulate a plan.

She would wait until Tyler fell asleep, and then she would gather up her clothes and her guns, and head off to the outlaw's campsite. She'd scrub off her makeup—the disguise's usefulness had just about run its course—take one of the horses, and ride in pursuit of the woman who was pretending to be her.

One way or the other, Jessie decided firmly, *this nightmare is going to end.*

★

Chapter 19

Ki opened his eyes. Above him was a water-stained, cobweb-festooned ceiling. He was lying on a gritty plank floor. Within his line of sight was a single window that was the source of the placid afternoon sunlight. Ki was not at all surprised to see that the window had rusty iron bars across it.

Well, it does make sense that an outlaw town's jail would fall into disrepair, he mused wryly. *I must be the first man to see the inside of a Roundpatch cell in quite a while . . .*

He tried to sit up, but the throbbing in his head laid him right back down. He took a deep breath and pushed himself up on his elbows.

"Don't!" Jessie scolded from behind him. "Lie back. You're not supposed to get up!"

Incredulous, Ki twisted around toward her voice. "Jessie? Is it you?"

She nodded morosely. She was sitting on the floor in a corner of the jail cell, her knees tucked up beneath her chin. She was wearing her denims and had a pan of water and a cloth beside her.

"They got me too," she said, approaching him. "Here, rest

269

your head on my lap." She dunked the cloth into the water and gently placed it across Ki's forehead.

"How long have you been here?" Ki asked.

"We'll talk later," Jessie said. "For now, I want you to rest. You'll have to regain your strength if you expect to help me break out of here."

"Jessie! I have to know what happened," Ki demanded.

"It's a long story," she cooed, stroking his cheek with her fingertips. "I escaped from Sarah, and I stayed free for a while, but eventually Seth Weeks's outlaws discovered me snooping around and locked me up in here. But I don't want to talk about that now!" She leaned over him, her long, reddish blond tresses forming a shimmering curtain around his face. "Ki, not being with you all this time has shown me how much you mean to me. I missed you so, Ki. I—I began to long for your touch . . ."

Jessie leaned closer to Ki, her lovely lips parting for a kiss . . .

Still feeling woozy, his head still throbbing painfully, Ki was mesmerized, frozen into inaction by Jessie's lovely, emerald-green eyes. He wanted to let go, to—

Her eyes!

Ki jackknifed up, out of Jessie's lap. He scuttled like a crab across the floor to the far side of the cell, where he crouched and stared at her. For one of the few times in his life, he felt true fear. In his youth, his homeland had abounded with folktales about *shura:* demons that could take on human form. Ki had never believed such childish stories. Until today . . .

"Ki? What's wrong with you?" Jessie demanded.

"Who are you? *What* are you?" the samurai challenged.

"I'm Jessica Starbuck, of course!"

"No!" Ki was adamant.

"Ki, stop it!" she begged. "I need you. Has that bump on your head driven you insane?" She stood up and took a step toward him.

Ki rose to his feet also, his pain forgotten now. "Stay away," he hissed. "You are not Jessie. You look like her, but you are not her. I can tell by your eyes!"

The woman stared at him for another moment, and then

shrugged. "Too bad, mate," she said in a flat Cockney accent. "It would have been nice between us." She licked her lips lasciviously, and then called out, "Lang? It's no use, lovey. 'E's on to me."

"I asked you not to revert to your old mode of speech," Lang said wearily, coming into sight from around a corner.

Ki stared as Birdy O'Hara and Seth Weeks joined the man in black whom he had earlier defeated. All three crowded around his cell, peering at him like a zoo animal.

"Let me out of 'ere," the woman demanded.

"Right." Seth Weeks reached into the pocket of his baggy overalls and produced a key. He unlocked the cell, allowed the woman to exit, and then relocked the door. "Well, Lang," the fat outlaw said, "your experiment failed. Now I'll shoot this Chinaman."

"He's not Chinese, but Japanese, and only partly, at that," Lang corrected him. "His father was as white as any of us."

Seth Weeks's flat black eyes blinked once. "You're getting to be a real pain in the ass, Lang, you know?" He reached into another pocket to produce a revolver.

Ki laughed. "I imagine you *would* find it hard to get a gunbelt to fit around that big belly of yours."

"Keep laughing, it's a good way to die," Weeks said pleasantly. He aimed his gun at Ki and thumbed back the hammer.

"Lang!" Birdy O'Hara whispered urgently. "You ought to talk with Ki before you have him killed. He knows more about Jessie Starbuck than any other man on earth!"

"Yes." The man in black nodded. "Yes, you're quite right, Miss O'Hara. Seth, put your gun away."

The elephantine outlaw hesitated. "You know, I'm not used to taking orders, Lang. It bothers me."

"That may be so," Lang answered coolly. "But you entered into an agreement with my superiors. If you wish to be paid, you will do as I say."

"A real pain in the ass." Seth Weeks sighed. But he put away his gun. "I'll deal with you later, Chinaman," he vowed.

"Go suck an egg," Ki replied. Then he turned his attention to Lang. "I must admit," he said, "you're an interesting man.

You fought well when we battled before. How did you come by such knowledge? And how is it that you've come to use it for such evil purposes?"

Lang smiled coldly. "Evil purposes? That's a matter of opinion," he said. "As to your other question, years ago I resigned a military command in my native Germany. I felt that there were others who would be willing to pay handsomely for my talents as a strategist."

"The cartel," Ki said. It was not a question.

Lang smiled again. "If you will," he said. "My new employers sent me to the Japans to study the *kakuto bugei*, the fighting arts. It took me a good many years to perfect my skills." He bowed his head slightly toward Ki. "Such as they are."

"Such as they are," Ki replied. "But why did the cartel go to such lengths? Did they wish to train an assassin to destroy Jessica Starbuck?"

"Hardly. They wished to train a samurai, who could *create* Jessica Starbuck. You see, my friend, while I was busy honing the skills that would enable me to emulate you, the cartel was busily searching the world for the other half of the equation: a woman who could impersonate Jessie Starbuck." He gestured toward Jessie's double. "They found such a woman in Beth Simpson. She's British, and worked as a barmaid in a pub in London. Her hair used to be brown, but in most other respects she was almost an exact physical duplicate of Jessica Starbuck."

"A duplicate," Ki agreed. "But hardly an exact one."

"Granted," Lang sighed. "But a good enough copy to fool most people. Admit it, Ki. Even you were briefly fooled."

Ki nodded. "Until I saw her eyes. Until I caught a glimpse of her soul."

"Blimey!" Jessie's impersonator scoffed. "Listen to the chink! 'E talks just like you, Lang. You both think that Starbuck bitch is the bloody Madonna!"

"Quiet, Beth!" Lang snarled.

Ki stared at the man in black. Their eyes locked for a moment, but then Lang looked away.

"Anyway, Beth's comments make an apt point," Lang continued. "We do think alike, Ki. That was the cartel's purpose

272

in sending me to your homeland for samurai training. The cartel felt that Jessica Starbuck could not have become so formidable an enemy if it were not for your guidance and assistance."

Ki understood. "So they created their own Ki to help develop their own Jessie Starbuck!"

"Precisely," Lang said. "I returned from the Orient ready to begin my task. Beth's services had already been contracted for. Her hair was dyed the exact shade of Jessica Starbuck's. Meanwhile, cartel operatives scoured the country for information on Jessie. No expense was spared. I was presented with a massive dossier covering every aspect of the Starbuck business empire and every aspect of Jessie's personal life. Beth and I went to a European estate where a duplicate of the Starbuck ranch house had been built. I began the lengthy task of transforming Beth Simpson into a walking, talking twin of Jessica Starbuck!"

"The 'ardest part was gettin' 'er speech down pat," Beth Simpson broke in. "Lang 'ere 'ad all sorts of speech coaches 'ave a go at me. It took a while, but finally I was able to talk just like Jessie."

"I took the opportunity to rid my own speech of its Prussian accent," Lang added.

Ki shook his head. "But why? Why go to such incredible lengths? Did you hope to substitute this woman for Jessie in order to take over the Starbuck empire? That would never work." He scowled. "You say she previously worked as a barmaid, and it shows. Her features have been ravaged by a sordid life. She would never fool anyone who truly knew Jessie."

"'Ere now, ducky," Simpson snarled, drawing her Colt. "It so 'appens I enjoy killing. I've 'ad to study about you for so long that I'm sick to death of you! I could shoot you now."

"Get hold of yourself, Beth," Lang ordered.

"I'm sick of you as well, mate! All your rantin' and ravin' about 'ow wonderful Jessie Starbuck is, and 'ow I'm nothin' compared to 'er. And 'ere I've been slavin' to please you—to make you notice me—all this time!" She paused, her voice tight. "Well, just remember, Lang, I'm the only one oo's truly essential to this plan."

"Of course, Beth, of course," Lang humored her. "But if

it's killing you have a taste for, shouldn't you take up your position on the far side of the pasture? Remember? Birdy O'Hara has informed us that Deputy Long will be approaching from that direction."

"Right." Simpson laughed. She looked gloatingly at Ki. "Too rich for your Chinaman's blood, am I, ducky? Well, I guess little red'eads like *'er"*—she jerked her thumb at O'Hara—"are more to your taste!" She turned to go. "Too bad you didn't know she was goin' to spill 'er guts to us when you told 'er everything. You as good as killed your friend Longarm by trustin' 'er!"

Ki endured the scathing attack, looking at Birdy O'Hara, who steadfastly refused to meet his gaze. Seth Weeks, standing beside her, looked as happy as a child on Christmas morning. "Longarm is going to die in my town! I'll be famous!"

Lang, meanwhile, had waited for Simpson to leave the jailhouse before continuing. "You're right, Ki. She is nothing but a coarse copy. Next to the real Jessica Starbuck, she would appear as inferior as a paste jewel next to a genuine diamond."

"Then you have failed," Ki said.

"Only partly," Lang replied. "I don't have to *replace* Jessie Starbuck, but only make people think they have seen her commit crimes. You see, the cartel's intention is not only to defeat Jessie, but also to destroy the Starbuck name and its reputation."

"They hate her that much?" Ki asked, astounded.

Lang laughed. "Her, and *you,* Ki. The two of you have foiled my employers so many times!" He shook his head. "It seems as if every time my superiors attempt to get a foothold in America, Jessie Starbuck and you arrive to spoil their plans. You and Jessie have cost far too many lives, and far too much money."

Ki nodded. "By framing Jessie, you have set the stage for her to be hunted down and then either shot on the spot or arrested."

"If she is tried in a courtroom, she will be found guilty," Lang continued. "Beth Simpson's bloodthirsty killings have created an overwhelming mass of evidence against her. Jessie will be hanged. Public outrage over her crimes will cause her business holdings to falter. My superiors will then be able to move in and buy up the Starbuck empire for a song. They will have won! On every conceivable level!"

"What will happen to all of you?" Ki asked.

Lang smiled. "I will return to my homeland a very wealthy man. My position will be assured, of course. Miss O'Hara's career will prosper as well. In addition, both she and Seth Weeks have been promised large sums of money."

The fat outlaw grinned. "With Jessie Starbuck out of the way, I can take over this whole state!"

"What about Beth Simpson?" Ki asked.

Lang seemed momentarily distressed. "I'm afraid her services will no longer be required."

"And I know how the cartel discharges employees," Ki said. "Any fool can see that the woman loves you."

Lang shrugged. "As much as she can love anyone. I had to motivate Beth to work hard, you see. We were asking so much of her. Money wasn't enough. Beth had to hate Jessie Starbuck as much as the cartel does, if she was to succeed. You know how a student can become infatuated with a teacher? When Beth became enamored of me, I encouraged her passion. At the same time, I did my best to make her jealous of the real Jessie Starbuck. I praised Jessie constantly, while I pointed out Beth's shortcomings. It worked. Beth grew to hate Jessie Starbuck. She wants the money, but she also wants to bring down her imagined rival for my affections."

"Imagined?" Ki echoed. "I don't think so, Lang. In your own way, you have devoted yourself to Jessica Starbuck nearly as much as I have. You have bound yourself to her." He extended a hand forward, palm upward. "Love," he said. He turned the hand palm downward and said, "Hate. The difference is as slight as the turn of a hand."

Lang seemed to stiffen a bit, though his expression remained impassive.

"Enough talk," Seth Weeks cut in. He drew his pistol. "I ain't got all day. It's time for me to shoot a smart-talking Chinaman!"

"No! You mustn't!" Birdy O'Hara cried out.

"It has to be done, sooner or later," Lang said dejectedly. "I know this man very well. He has been disarmed, but he's still capable of breaking free. Letting him live is a needless risk."

Lang was interrupted by the arrival of one of Weeks's bodyguards. "Boss?" the man called to Weeks. "One of the boys, Jimbo, just rode in with a crazy story. It seems that he and five others were messed up by Barney the drummer, and some old lady who—"

"Barney? And an old woman?" Lang interrupted excitedly. "Tell me, Seth! Has this old drummer ever shown an ability to fight back?"

"Hell, no!" Seth Weeks shook his head. "Barney ain't ever had a lick of gumption. He passes through my territory all the time. He's always been as anxious to please as a hound dog."

"The way Jimbo told it, Barney did some chopping with a sword," the bodyguard interjected. "But it was the old woman who did the shooting."

"I knew it!" Lang crowed. "I knew that old woman was Jessie Starbuck herself, in disguise! If only I'd had the time to make sure." The man in black turned to Seth Weeks. "You must send some men to capture her and bring her back!"

"I'll send some men, all right," the obese outlaw mayor scowled. "But to *kill* her!"

"You don't understand," Lang said. "I must see her!"

Seth Weeks shook his head. "Lang, I think that this Chinaman has you pegged. You've got Jessie Starbuck in your blood like a disease! I'm doing you a favor by having her killed."

"Damn you!" Lang thundered. "You do as I say!"

Seth Weeks's tiny lizard eyes grew even smaller. The pistol in his hand began to move from Ki toward Lang. "I kill any man who raises his voice to me . . ."

"Seth, I'm very sorry. Truly I am. Just listen," Lang implored. "Do as I ask. Bring Jessie Starbuck to me unharmed, and I'll see to it that you receive a bonus!"

"Bonus?" Weeks nodded, mollified by the thought of more money. "What about the Chinaman?"

"Let him live, for now." Lang said. "And see to it that Longarm is taken alive as well. Just imagine, Seth! You, the mayor of Roundpatch, can execute all three at once, right here in your own town. Why, you could even act as judge, sentencing them in front of your men! You'd become the greatest legend the West has ever known!"

Seth Weeks's blubbery form began to shake with emotion. "I like that," he laughed shrilly. He looked at Birdy O'Hara. "You'll write it up like that, for everyone to read?"

"Of course she will," Lang answered for the pale-faced reporter. "And meanwhile, Beth and your men could be robbing more banks. Remember, you're getting to keep all that bank loot`. . ."

"Yeah, okay." Weeks grinned at Ki. "Looks like I'm giving you a reprieve!" He turned to waddle out of the jail. "I'll do it the way you want, Lang." With that, the mayor maneuvered his enormous girth out of the door.

"If you'll excuse me, Ki, I've got to prepare my quarters for Jessie's arrival," Lang said, hurrying away. "O'Hara," he called over his shoulder. "You be careful," he warned. "Don't get too close!"

"Well, alone at last," Ki said as Lang left.

"Seems like you're always in jail and I'm always on the outside," Birdy said.

Ki nodded. "But this time you will not be bailing me out, I imagine," he said sadly.

"Oh, but I tried to, I really did, Ki!" she said fervently, her eyes wide. "I even threatened to quit if they didn't promise to let you go!" Her face fell. "But it was no use."

"You shouldn't have threatened them," Ki said. "If they think they cannot trust you, they will kill you."

Birdy sighed sadly. "No. They know they've got me. You must understand, Ki, when I threatened them, they warned me that they'd expose my past as a whore. I'd be ruined! No paper would ever hire me again! If I do as they say, I'll be rich, and become a powerful newspaperwoman. If I don't, I'll be back standing under that lamppost before I know it."

Ki regarded her silently.

"Stop looking at me like that!" Birdy cried out. "I warned you! I told you I was out for myself! I told you that rules are for crybabies!"

"You are happy, Birdy?" Ki asked softly.

"I'm getting everything I ever wanted!" the reporter shot

back, even as her eyes began to glisten.

Ki shook his head. "You always seem to be crying when you tell me that."

"I warned you!" Birdy whispered, and then ran from the jailhouse, the tears coursing down her cheeks.

Ki watched her go, then settled down cross-legged on the floor of his cell. The samurai tried to calm himself, but he was sick at heart.

There was Birdy's betrayal to mull over, and there was the safety of Jessie and Longarm to consider.

And there was the awful possibility that *this* time the cartel was going to *win!*

★
Chapter 20

Longarm rode for most of the afternoon before he caught up with Leroy Hoggs. The lawman was ready for anything, but when he finally confronted Hoggs, the prisoner was quietly sitting under the shade of a pecan tree, waiting for the deputy.

As Longarm rode up, Hoggs called out, "I surrender!" He displayed his hands to show that he was unarmed. "I'd put 'em up over my head," Hoggs said, "but the handcuffs make it hard."

Longarm nodded. He dismounted and walked over to the seated man. "Where's the derringer, old son?"

Hoggs gestured to his horse, standing tethered to a low branch of the pecan tree. "The gun's tied to the end of the reins," he said.

Longarm went and fetched it. "Damn, Leroy, you sure screwed things up this time!"

Hoggs nodded glumly. "Did I kill that old geezer?"

"Nope, but you'll have to stand for *trying* to." Longarm broke open the derringer. One round was spent, and one was live, just as he'd thought. "You haven't got any other tricks up your sleeve, have you, Leroy?" He paused, feeling pity for the little hombre. "I mean Smitty," he said gently.

Hoggs smiled up him. "I appreciate the way you've treated me, Longarm. Like I was a man. Nobody else ever has. Not that I deserve to be treated like one," he grinned. "I panicked back there. When I saw that jasper coming toward me with that hanging rope, I just lost control! I wish I could handle myself cool and collected, like you."

"Where'd you get this derringer, Smitty?"

"From that reporter, Birdy O'Hara," the little prisoner said. "She slipped it to me through the bars of my cell window, the day before yesterday. Right before you caught her lurking around that back alley behind the jail."

Longarm was perturbed. "Now why would she want to give you a gun?"

Hoggs shrugged. "She said it might come in handy. I reckon she wanted to butter me up to get a better interview." He laughed bitterly. "Too bad she didn't realize that giving me a gun was a sure way to get me killed!"

"Maybe she did realize that, Smitty. Maybe she did . . ."

"Huh?"

"Never mind that now," Longarm said. "You'd best understand how it is. You're going to have to stand trial in Sarah for the shooting. I'll testify that you were acting in self-defense. I'll do that for you, no matter what, Smitty, because it's the truth."

The prisoner nodded gratefully. "What about the bank-robbery charges?"

Longarm eyed him shrewdly. "That's up to you, old son. I think the time has come for you to tell me everything you know about this mess."

"Yes, sir," Hoggs said. He made a self-effacing gesture with his handcuffed wrists. "As usual, I don't have much to tell. I wandered into Roundpatch acting like a real tough hombre, but Seth Weeks's men took the starch out of me—and the money out of my pockets—quick enough. Then they told me to git! I begged them to let me stay. You see, Longarm, I had this dream that I'd learn to become a gunslick by hanging around with hard men."

Longarm frowned. "Why couldn't you have been content with your talent as a forger, Smitty?"

"Nobody's afraid of a fellow who's handy with a pen!" he sulked. "Nobody gets out of the way of a forger. I wanted the sort of respect a gunman commands!"

"What happened next?" Longarm sighed.

"Well, they let me stay on," Hoggs said. "Then this fellow named Lang showed up in Roundpatch. He was no outlaw, anybody could see that, but Seth Weeks himself was afraid of the man..."

"Seth Weeks, *afraid?*" Longarm scowled. "That doesn't sound reasonable. Any idea why?"

"Nope," Hoggs replied. "Except maybe because this fellow Lang had Jessie Starbuck with him—"

"*Leroy!*" Longarm interrupted, exasperated. "I *thought* you were going to tell me the truth!"

"I am!" Hoggs squawked. "I got no reason to lie! She was there! Big as life and pretty as a picture! Honest, Longarm."

Watching Hoggs, Longarm realized that whatever was going on, the man was not lying.

"This fellow Lang wanted some of Seth's men to ride along with Jessie during her bank robberies. Seth had to give in, but he wanted his men to think he was still top dog in Roundpatch. So he stuck Lang with me. His men thought it was a grand joke to play on Lang, and I guess they were right!" Hoggs became dejected. "I get my first chance to prove that I'm tough, and what happens? I get conked on the head, and my gang leaves me to rot in jail!"

"If you'll still lead me past Roundpatch's sentries, it'll even the score a mite against those jaspers," Longarm pointed out.

"I'll do that," Hoggs agreed, "on one condition."

"Now, Smitty," Longarm cautioned. "No more deals."

"What I want is for you to take these cuffs off me and give me a gun, so that I can fight with you, not against you," Hoggs said. "Those outlaws were no friends of mine. You're the closest thing to a friend I've ever had."

Longarm stared at the little man for a long moment. "I must be crazy. Hold out your hands." Longarm dug out the handcuff key and freed Hoggs.

"What about the gun?"

"Just mount up, Smitty," Longarm muttered, "before I change my mind about those cuffs."

It was well after sunset when Jessie made her move. She wanted to be absolutely positive that both Barney and Deke Tyler were sound asleep. Their three bedrolls were all closely grouped around a small campfire. Jessie patiently endured the passage of the hours, staring into the flames and making plans, all the while waiting for the two men's breathing to become regular.

The moon rose, the stars came out, the fire died down. Jessie thought it would take forever, but at last Barney and Tyler appeared to be asleep.

She got up and silently went to the wagon, where she retrieved her clothing, wrapped up the double-action Smith & Wesson and its extra ammunition, and hurried off toward the outlaws' deserted campsite.

As Deke had promised, his horse was tethered with the outlaws' mounts, and there was a shallow stream nearby. The first thing Jessie did was to discard her gray wig and those silly spectacles. She let down her hair, tossing her head to set her tawny, shoulder-length tresses flying. She quickly stripped off her soiled, pinned-together spinster's dress, and donned her own snug-fitting denims. Finally she knelt by the stream and scrubbed off every last bit of the makeup. When she was done, she dried her face with a scrap of the dress, and gazed at her reflection in the water by the light of the moon.

"Well, now, Jessie!" she giggled. "It's mighty fine to see you again!"

"It surely is," Deke Tyler said, stepping out of the trees fifteen feet behind her.

Jessie whirled to her feet. She drew the Smith & Wesson she had tucked in her waistband at the small of her back, pointing the gun at the bounty hunter.

Tyler held out his hands. "My guns are back at the wagon," he said. "Would you murder an unarmed man?"

"No," Jessie said. "But I won't be arrested for crimes I didn't commit."

Tyler nodded. "You can rest easy on that score. I'm a bounty hunter, but I don't bring in innocent folks."

Jessie tucked her gun back into her jeans. "You believe me?" she whispered.

Tyler grinned. "I knew it was you dressed up like your own grandmother as soon as I saw you. Not many women have big green eyes like yours, or know so much about guns. I was tempted to get the drop on you right then, but I got curious. I mean, if you were a bank robber, what were you doing here with an old man, fighting off some of Seth Weeks's men? Where was your gang? Then, when I saw how concerned you were about old Barney's condition—well, I just couldn't picture you being a bloodthirsty killer, that's all."

"So you trusted me?" Jessie marveled. "As far as coming after me unarmed, like you just did?"

"I knew you weren't a murderer. I guess I was willing to stake my life on it."

"Thank you, Deke." Jessie felt tears begin to flow, tears of relief. "I've been so alone!" Her shoulders slumped as she began to cry in earnest.

Tyler held out his arms, and Jessie ran to him. The big man held her gently, the way a father would comfort his daughter.

This is the way I'd be holding my own little girl, if she wasn't locked up in that hospital, Tyler thought as Jessie sobbed against his broad chest. *My daughter's beyond my help, but Jessie isn't. Not yet, at least . . .*

"Hush now, little girl," Tyler murmured as he hugged Jessie. "I don't know why you're in this mess, but I reckon we'll find a way to get you out of it."

"Oh, thank you, Mr. Tyler," Jessie managed to gasp. "I do need help—"

"You two! Put up your hands!" a harsh voice rasped from out of the shadows. "We got you covered. Now do it!"

"Play along," Tyler whispered to Jessie, gently moving her away from him, and then stretching his big hands toward the night sky.

Several men in long canvas dusters stepped out from behind the trees. The moonlight glinted off of the barrels of their revolvers.

"It looks like both of them are unarmed," one of the men wheezed, coming toward them.

With a sinking heart, Jessie recognized the ruined voice of the neck-scarred man who'd ridden with the false Jessica Starbuck at the Sageville mail robbery.

"I guess Lang was right," the fellow chortled hoarsely. "This here's the real Jessie Starbuck, unless there's *two* phonies around!"

"This here big fellow ain't Barney, though," another outlaw observed, watching Deke Tyler. "Any idea who he is, Dusty?"

The scarred man gazed at Tyler. Suddenly he grinned. "I surely do! That there's the one and only Deke Tyler!"

"The bounty hunter?" one of the outlaws exclaimed. "I'll kill him now."

"No!" Dusty ordered. "Seth will want the honor of killing Tyler. Bring him along with the Starbuck bitch."

While the two outlaws argued over Tyler's fate, Jessie sidled closer to the bounty hunter and whispered, "They haven't noticed the gun tucked into my jeans, underneath my jacket. Get ready to move—"

"No!" Tyler hissed.

"Get *ready*—" Jessie drew her pistol and aimed it at the man named Dusty. Before the surprised outlaws could blink, she squeezed the trigger . . .

And the hammer of her gun came down on an empty chamber. She fired again. Her gun clicked empty.

The outlaws, laughing nervously, regained their wits. "We're getting careless in our old age," Dusty muttered. He took away Jessie's gun and tossed it into the darkness.

"I took the liberty of unloading your guns during the afternoon," Tyler apologized to Jessie as they were led at gunpoint to the outlaws' horses. "You see, I was *pretty* sure that you were innocent . . ."

"Very clever," Jessie moped, swinging up into a saddle.

Tyler shrugged. "Except that I outsmarted myself!"

"What about Barney?" one of the outlaws asked as they made ready to ride.

"Forget him!" Dusty wheezed. "Starbuck and Deke Tyler are more than enough to make Seth happy."

The outlaws, with their prisoners in tow, rode off. A few moments later, Barney stepped out of the trees. The old drummer's eyes fell upon Jessie's discarded gray wig, but he seemed not to see it as he leaned on the point of his saber.

"What's that? What did you say, General Grant?" Barney muttered. "Yes, sir! I agree, sir! Them rebels can't be allowed to get away with kidnapping innocent Union citizens." He saluted and hurried back to the wagon.

"Don't you worry, Dora," the old man swore. "I'm comin'!"

Longarm and Hoggs left their horses hidden about a mile down the main trail, to approach within spitting distance of the lights of Roundpatch. Much to Longarm's surprise and Hoggs's chagrin, they'd not encountered a single sentry.

"I can't understand it!" Hoggs whispered as they huddled behind some trees which bordered a wide pasture. The faint sound of men laughing reached them, carried on the night breeze. "It used to be that Seth had riflemen posted as far as five miles outside the town limits!"

"Either you're lying, or Weeks pulled in his men for some reason," Longarm mused.

"I ain't lying!" Hoggs insisted.

Longarm nodded. "All right, then Weeks pulled them in."

"Or told them to let us go through unchallenged," Hoggs volunteered.

"Not likely, Smitty. How could Weeks know that we were coming? And what about that group of riders leading extra saddle mounts that passed by us a while ago? Nobody stopped them to exchange passwords. What would be the sense of making sentries stand outside all night if Seth Weeks meant for everyone to come through unchallenged?"

Hoggs thought about it, then shrugged. "Well, I guess it's a lucky break for us, right?"

Longarm didn't reply.

"Right?" Hoggs repeated.

"I wish I could have gotten a better look at those riders," Longarm mumbled. "It was too dark to tell, of course, but I could've sworn that one of them was Jessie." He hauled out his pocket watch and checked it by the light of the moon. "It's close to ten. We've been out here more than two hours. It's time we visited Seth Weeks."

Hoggs gulped. "What about that gun, Longarm?"

"Like I said, I must be crazy, but here." He handed Hoggs his Winchester. "You do understand, Smitty, that if you try and shoot me, I'll kill you?"

"Yes, sir," Hoggs replied quickly. "I'm on your side now, Deputy."

Lucky me, Longarm thought. "Let's go. Stay low until we're across that pasture. You go first, Smitty, and I'll be right behind you."

"I won't let you down, Longarm," Hoggs vowed, and then moved out, gripping the Winchester tightly.

Longarm kept his Colt at the ready, but he didn't expect any trouble until they'd crossed the stream that marked the actual beginnings of the town. The field was flat. It gave them no cover, but by the same token it afforded an ambusher no place to hide.

They forded the stream to reach the first of the buildings. "All right," Longarm whispered. "Where would Seth be?"

"Town hall," Smitty replied. "Leastways, that's his headquarters during the day. At this time of night, your guess is as good as mine."

"All right, then, town hall it is," Longarm said. "After you, Smitty—"

Both men froze as they heard a footstep behind them and then a whispered, "Longarm!"

Hoggs swung his rifle toward the sound, but Longarm pushed the Winchester's barrel off target. "Don't, Smitty!" he hissed. "I think that's Jessie!"

"Longarm! It's so good to see you!" Jessie gasped, running to him. "I've been snooping around for the last hour, trying to find Seth Weeks. I'd never imagined I'd be lucky enough to find you!"

Longarm embraced her. "At least you're alive!" He sighed happily. "But I ought to blister your tail for marching into the lion's den like this. Hell, you don't even have a gun."

"Yes I do, too!" Jessie said. "It's tucked into my boot."

"Don't trust her, Longarm," Smitty warned him. "I'm telling you, she's a murdering bank robber—"

"Quiet, Leroy!" Jessie spat. "Or else I'll—" She bent to draw her revolver from her boot top.

"Here now!" Longarm scolded her, reaching out for her pistol, but Jessie danced backward, out of his reach.

"Kill him, Longarm!" she demanded. "If you care for me, you'll kill him now!"

Longarm gazed at her. She had Jessie's voice, Jessie's clothing, the same green eyes and the same color hair—

But she sure isn't acting like the Jessie Starbuck I know, Longarm thought.

"Just how do you know his name is Leroy, Jessie?" Longarm asked. "You haven't met him, unless his story is true, and you've ridden with him to rob banks."

Before Longarm could finish what he was saying, several men stepped out of the surrounding darkness with their guns drawn. Longarm's Colt was taken away, as was Hoggs's rifle.

"I told you I wasn't lying," Hoggs said as Jessie kept them covered. "She's as bad as they come."

"You weren't lying," Longarm remarked, "but you *were* mistaken." He stared at the woman before them. "That's not really Jessie Starbuck."

"Hot damn!" rasped one of the outlaws. "First we bring in Jessie and Deke Tyler, and now we catch Longarm and another deputy!"

"I ain't a deputy!" Hoggs said. "It's Leroy, Dusty. You remember me!"

I figured he'd turn on me when the going got rough, Longarm thought. *Reckon I'm lucky he didn't try and backshoot me.* He glanced at Hoggs in disgust.

"I guess this here lawman forced you to bring him to Round-patch?" Dusty asked, fingering the scars ringing his throat.

Hoggs locked eyes with Longarm for a moment, then smiled. "Nope," he announced, "nobody forced me to do anything! Longarm here felt he needed a good man to stand by him, so he picked me!" The little man puffed out his chest. "Ain't that right—*Custis?*"

Longarm smiled back at the plucky jasper. "Couldn't have said it better myself!"

"In that case . . ." said Jessie's impersonator. She aimed her Colt at Hoggs.

"Wait now, Beth," Dusty began. He tried to step between the two, but before he could, the woman fired, hitting Hoggs in the chest.

The little man cried out, falling backwards to lie twitching and moaning. The woman shot him again. Hoggs moaned once, and died.

"Jesus, Beth," Dusty wheezed.

"You 'eard 'im say 'e was a lawman?" she demanded. "Besides, nobody cares about the likes of 'im, anyway."

"So your name's Beth, is it?" Longarm snarled, his voice thick with rage. "Tell me, Beth, what rock did they find you under?"

"'Ere now, ducky," Beth seethed. "You be polite to a lady." She stepped close to Longarm and abruptly swiped the barrel of her gun against his head.

Longarm sagged to his knees.

"That's right, ducky." Beth Simpson nodded. "You kneel before your betters." She used the tip of her revolver to flick Longarm's Stetson off his head. "And you remove your 'at in front of a lady."

"That's enough, Beth," Dusty rasped. "Seth wants him awake."

"'Ave 'im searched, and then take 'im to the jail," Beth Simpson decreed. "You can 'ave yourself a little reunion with your friends, Longarm." She smiled and then added, "Before the executions begin!"

★

Chapter 21

They took away Longarm's vest-pocket derringer, his extra
.44-caliber cartridges, and his folding knife. Then his hands
were bound in front of him and he was escorted on horseback
into Roundpatch by Dusty and the other outlaws.

Lang and Seth Weeks were waiting outside the jailhouse
when Longarm was brought in. "I've dreamed of an opportunity
like this for years." Weeks laughed.

"Me and mine aren't dead yet, fat man," Longarm scowled.

Weeks, blustering with rage, reached for the butt of the
revolver in his overalls pocket. Lang stopped him.

"Don't let him get the better of you," the man in black
counseled. "Remember your original plan—to execute them
all at once, for the sake of your legend."

"The only thing legendary about Seth Weeks is his waist
size," Longarm remarked.

"I would be very quiet if I were you, Deputy Long," Lang
said. "You are very close to dying."

"I've heard that before." Longarm yawned. "Where's Jessie—the real Jessie—and the others? That British tart you've
got *pretending* to be Jessie said they were here."

"They are." Lang grinned. "All of them are inside." He indicated the jail. "But not Jessie. She's waiting for me in my private quarters over at the hotel. We're going to have a late supper together."

"Don't tell me you caused all this aggravation just for a date?" Longarm asked sarcastically.

"Take him inside!" Lang snapped, turning to go.

"You heard the man," Dusty rasped. "Get off that horse." He thumbed back the hammer of his revolver. "And do it real slow."

"Don't forget to retie his hands behind his back," Seth Weeks added.

Longarm, his hands now securely bound behind him, was steered into the jail. He was led to the cell where Ki and Deke Tyler languished. Their hands were also tied behind them.

"Longarm!" Tyler exclaimed.

"Where is Jessie?" Ki demanded. "Mr. Tyler tells me she is here."

Dusty shoved Longarm inside the cell, then locked the door. The deputy eyed Deke and then joked, "I can't believe they got the drop on a pro like you."

Deke nodded. "These fellows don't miss a trick."

"Where is Jessie?" Ki repeated.

"Some jasper dressed in black says he's got her in his digs," Longarm replied.

"That would be Lang."

Seth Weeks strode into the jailhouse to confront Dusty. "Did you see to it that the sentries went back to their posts?"

"Sure, Seth," the outlaw wheezed. "I did it just like you told me. Our boys were heading back into position as soon as we got the drop on Longarm."

Weeks turned toward his three prisoners. "Well, gents, here's how it is. It's midnight now. In a few hours, at sunrise, Deputy Long and Deke Tyler can look forward to being shot! The Chinaman's got yet another reprieve." The obese outlaw licked his lips. "Lang's got Jessie Starbuck all to himself. I guess he wants the Chink alive to give him some leverage in case she don't want to spread her legs—"

"Seth Weeks," Ki interrupted softly, "I am going to kill you for that remark."

The outlaw leader shrugged. "When your time comes, Chinaman, I'm going to do the job myself."

The prisoners watched as Weeks and Dusty left the jailhouse. Longarm asked, "You have any luck picking these knots?"

Ki shook his head. "I have tried to untie Deke until my fingers were bleeding. It's no use. The knots are cinched tight, and are rock-hard."

"I figured as much." Longarm sighed. "Like Deke said, these boys don't miss a trick. Dusty had to cut the rope off me in order to retie my hands."

"We have no blades," Ki announced mournfully. "Lang knew of every place a samurai might hide a weapon."

"Well, they searched me pretty thoroughly," Longarm said, "but I still managed to slip a derringer past them."

Ki was astounded. "How did you do it?"

"After they took my Colt and pocket knife, and found the derringer I keep in my vest, they let up a bit," Longarm explained. "They must have figured they had all of my weapons, and normally that would be true. But today I happened to have an extra derringer buttoned up underneath my shirt."

Longarm grinned, pleased with his good luck. The extra derringer was the weapon he'd taken away from Leroy Hoggs.

"I don't suppose you've got a rescue posse underneath your shirt to go along with the gun?" Tyler asked.

"As a matter of fact, there *is* help on the way," Longarm said.

"Longarm," Tyler groaned, "please start from the beginning!"

"That's just what I was going to ask you," Longarm said. "For instance, who the hell is this Lang jasper?"

"For us to all exchange our stories would take some time," Ki said.

Longarm nodded and said, "Well, we're not going anywhere!"

• • •

The three prisoners talked through the night, comparing what they'd all learned, until a complete picture of the cartel's scheme emerged. In addition, Longarm explained how he'd come by the derringer, and how Marshal Farley had come by the extra men in the posse that was approaching Roundpatch.

"So Birdy O'Hara has been a cartel operative all along," Longarm frowned. "I expected as much when poor old Leroy Hoggs told me she'd slipped him the derringer through the bars of his jail cell. She obviously wanted to shut him up. Giving him the means to get himself shot dead in a jailbreak was a perfect way to do it."

"I feel compelled to speak on her behalf," Ki began. "She *did* save my life during the battle against the cougar."

"And she also knocked you out and turned you over to Seth Weeks," Longarm countered.

"She is being blackmailed, Longarm."

The deputy shrugged. "You can testify about that at her trial."

"Ain't we getting a mite ahead of ourselves?" Tyler asked sarcastically. *"We're* the ones who are going to be shot at sunrise!"

"Farley will get us out of this," Longarm assured the worried bounty hunter.

"Then where the hell is he?" Tyler demanded.

"You heard Seth Weeks say that he's re-deployed his sentries?" Longarm asked. "Well, Farley's got to take those guards out quietly, one at a time, if he's going to take Roundpatch by surprise."

"But only twelve men against Seth Weeks's fifty outlaws—" Ki began.

"Weeks's men are an undisciplined lot," Tyler pointed out. "Jessie had the same mistaken idea about these outlaws. When Farley rides in, most of these owlhoots will head out, interested in nothing but saving their own skins. No way will they stand and fight with Seth Weeks."

"I agree," Longarm said. "Weeks and Lang have maybe a half-dozen men who will stay loyal to them when that posse arrives."

"There is only one problem, gentlemen," Ki said, gazing

out the window of the cell. "Dawn has come. The time for your executions has arrived."

"Quick!" Longarm hissed to Deke Tyler. "Turn around and use your bound hands to get that derringer. It's right against my belly, underneath my shirt."

Tyler fumbled with Longarm's vest buttons for a moment before ripping the garment open. "Sorry," he said.

"I'll bill you, if and when we get back to Sarah," Longarm said. "But don't rip my shirt open. I don't want the outlaws to suspect I had anything stashed beneath it."

The bounty hunter painstakingly unbuttoned Longarm's gray flannel shirt and managed to ease out the derringer. He set the tiny gun down on the floor and quickly closed the buttons.

"All right!" Longarm said. "Give me the—"

Gray light flooded their cell as the door to the jailhouse was kicked open. Dusty and one other outlaw approached. The key to the cell was in Dusty's left hand. With his right he nervously fingered the scars around his throat. The other outlaw held a brace of pistols.

"Seth says it's time," Dusty rasped. "You two come with us."

While the other man kept his guns trained on Ki, Dusty unlocked the cell and ordered Longarm and Deke Tyler out. Then he relocked the door, drew his own pistol, and motioned for the two men to start walking.

"Wait!" Ki called out, leaping to his feet and pressing himself against the bars of the cell. "Dusty, do not do this! We can make a deal! Jessie could pay you handsomely if you and your friend sided with us."

Dusty shook his head. "Seth Weeks would hunt me down and skin me alive if I crossed him. Sorry, Chinaman. Anyway, I still ain't forgot how you knocked me out on the staircase yesterday afternoon. You killed my buddy, and damn near killed me, as well!"

"There was nothing personal in it," Ki replied.

Dusty's wheezing laugh rose up like steam clattering out of a cold boiler. "And there's nothing personal involved in our shooting these two lawmen. I'm just doing my job, Chinaman!" His wicked smile faded. "All right, you two," he addressed

Longarm and Tyler. "The time for gabbing is over. Start walking!"

Ki watched his two friends being led out of the jailhouse, and then the door was shut behind them. Dejected, Ki slumped to the floor.

A few moments later, the jailhouse door swung open once again. Ki waited, watching, until Birdy O'Hara appeared in front of the cell.

The reporter had been weeping. The whites of her blue eyes were as red as her carrot-colored curls.

"What do you want?" Ki demanded impatiently. "Have you come to gloat, to remind me that I was warned not to trust you?"

"Please don't," she sobbed. "There's no time now..."

"You are quite right," Ki remarked sternly. "There is no time. My friends are about to be—"

Ki was cut short by the sound of a shot shattering the early-morning stillness. A moment later, a second shot was fired.

Then there was nothing but silence...

Longarm! Ki thought. *And Deke Tyler! Can it be? Are they dead?*

Birdy tossed a knife into the cell. "Use it to escape!" she implored the samurai. "Remember that I love you!" she blurted, then turned on her heel to run out of the jailhouse.

Ki stared after her a moment, then retrieved the knife. He set to work using it to saw through his bonds, and then turned the blade against the lock on his cell door.

Longarm and Deke Tyler had caught a glimpse of Birdy O'Hara lurking around the jail. The distraught-looking reporter refused to meet Longarm's eyes, and Dusty's gun in the small of his back urged him on before the deputy could say anything to her.

"I knew that woman was trouble from the beginning," Deke Tyler whispered, as their two guards dropped back several paces.

"As I recall, you told me she ought to be paddled, not taken seriously," Longarm whispered back.

"I said she was trouble," Tyler replied, shrugging as best

he could with his hands tied behind his back. "I never said I knew *how much* trouble."

"You have the derringer?" Longarm whispered.

"I got it palmed," Tyler replied.

"This is far enough," Dusty rasped. "We'll do it here."

The outlaws had led their prisoners around behind a vacant row of storefronts. Longarm looked around. The area was deserted.

"Aren't we going to have an audience to witness our deaths?" Longarm asked, thinking, *Where the hell is Farley and his posse?*

Dusty shrugged. "Last night Seth broke open a few cases of whiskey to celebrate. Most of the boys are dead drunk. They're sleeping it off this morning."

"What about Seth Weeks?" Deke Tyler asked. "Doesn't he want to watch?"

Dusty shook his head. "Seth figures it's more dignified to stay in his office over at town hall. We'll report in when this is all over."

"Come on," the outlaw with the two guns demanded. "Let's get this over with."

"Right," Dusty rasped.

"Hey! Wait a second!" Longarm said quickly, hoping to stall for time. "Don't we get a last smoke?"

"Nope," Dusty said. "All you get is *killed!*" He nodded to his companion as he raised his pistol. "Now!" he rasped.

A shape detached itself from the interior shadows of an empty shop and rushed toward the outlaws from behind. Longarm saw it coming, but was careful not to give any sign that might alert the pair of executioners.

An instant later, even as the two outlaws were taking aim, there was a nasty, wet, tearing sound. Dusty gagged in pain as two feet of steel suddenly protruded from his chest. He sagged, revealing Barney the drummer behind him. Dusty fell the rest of the way to the ground, wrenching the saber out of Barney's grasp.

The other outlaw spun around and fired once, hitting the old drummer in the belly. Deke Tyler quickly turned sideways, aimed the derringer he had behind his back at the outlaw, and pulled the trigger. The little gun's .44 round caught the man between the shoulder blades. He nosedived forward, kicked once, and died.

Longarm used the saber sticking up out of Dusty's corpse to saw the bonds from his wrists. Then he drew the sword out of the body and cut Tyler free, and Tyler quickly knelt beside Barney. The old drummer was coughing up blood.

"D-Dora?" Barney called weakly.

"Is that the old jasper who Jessie's been traveling with?" Longarm asked. When Tyler nodded, the deputy asked, "You think he'll make it?"

"Not a chance," Tyler said. "He's a dead man."

"What's that, General?" Barney called. "Yes, sir! Dora will be saved!"

"I take it Dora is Jessie?" Longarm asked.

Tyler nodded. "But no matter who he thought he was saving, he was a brave old codger to come here. I wonder how he got past the sentries."

"Been here for hours, General," Barney moaned. "Want my Dora . . ."

"There's your answer," Longarm said. "He must have come into Roundpatch on your heels, and then hidden out."

"Before the sentries were re-deployed," Tyler agreed. "Come on, Custis, help me get over by these stores." To Barney he said, "You hold on, and we'll bring you Dora."

They made Barney as comfortable as possible, and then Longarm tossed Tyler one of the dead outlaws' three guns. The duo made their way toward the town hall. "It's my guess that if we can take Seth Weeks, the rest of these owlhoots will wave the white flag."

"Even if they don't," Tyler grumbled, "it'll make me happy to see Seth Weeks's weight increased by a couple of ounces of lead."

"Right, but try to keep things quiet," Longarm warned him. "So far, all Weeks could have heard were two shots. He's probably toasting our executions right now. We can take him alive if we get the drop on him."

"Well, that's the town hall, just across the street," Tyler

296

muttered. "You see the light coming from the third-floor windows? That's Seth Weeks's lair."

"Well, let's pay a visit to the mayor—" Longarm began, but then paused to look over his shoulder. "I hear horses, coming fast."

Tyler nodded. "A lot of horses." A joyful smile creased his weatherbeaten features. "That wouldn't be Farley, would it?"

Both men watched happily as Sarah's town marshal careened around the corner on horseback, his twelve-man posse right behind him. Longarm waved the newcomers over. "Keep it quiet!" he warned Farley. "We're trying to take Seth Weeks by surprise."

"Where is he? In there?" Farley asked, pointing up at the third floor of the town hall. His eyes narrowed. "Duck!" he shouted.

Both Longarm and Tyler hit the dirt as a shot was fired. A bleary-eyed outlaw was backlit in the windows of the town hall. "Seth!" the man yelled. "It's the law!"

"So much for taking them by surprise," Tyler grumbled. He aimed up at the outlaw and shot him. The man clutched at his throat, and fell back out of sight.

A barrage of gunfire rained down from the top-floor windows. The posse quickly dismounted, to scatter for cover. Their wild-eyed horses trotted off in all directions.

"Forget about all the other outlaws," Farley told his men. "Just keep that town hall surrounded! Seth Weeks is the man we want!"

"But you'll never take me, Farley!" Weeks shouted down.

As the posse watched, the long, thick snout of a weapon suddenly appeared in the center window. The men on the ground caught a glimpse of an arm cranking a lever. There was a harsh chattering sound as a volley of lead stitched pockmarks in the dirt and chewed up the clapboard of the surrounding buildings.

"He's got a Gatling gun up there!" Farley despaired. "He can hold us off for days!"

"Well, do what you can to keep him bottled up," Longarm said.

"No problem," Tyler replied. "That's the only door. We

can't get in, but he can't leave. Hey, Custis! What about Ki?"

"Farley!" Longarm called out. "Send a man to get Ki out of the town jail. I'm going after Lang. He's got Jessie with him. With all this shooting going on, there's no telling what he might do."

"So Jessie *is* here," Farley said.

Longarm nodded. "And this time she's got *double* trouble. Deke will fill you in, Marshal Farley."

With a gun in either hand, Longarm set out for Roundpatch's hotel. As he ran, he saw outlaws in various stages of dress— or undress—stagger out of their digs. To a man, they were cradling their hung-over heads in their hands against the noise of the gunfire, and to a man, they were totally uninterested in tangling with Farley's posse. Many of the outlaws were un- armed, and some of them hadn't even paused to struggle with their boots. Longarm saw a bunch barefooting it toward the stable in hopes that they might grab a horse and hightail it out of town.

Longarm was beginning to think things were going to be easy. That was when he ran into a trio of hard-looking men who *weren't* drunk, *weren't* running, *weren't* barefoot, and *weren't* unarmed.

"Get him!" one of the badmen called.

"You boys will git, if you know what's good for you!" Longarm warned them. The bullet whistling past his ear told him that the three men were not in the mood to accept advice. Longarm crabbed sideways, aimed low, and squeezed off a shot. The man in the middle went down, but the other two fanned out to both sides of the street. Longarm dove to the dirt as they blasted away at him. Both outlaws had good cover, and had managed to pin the deputy in an effective crossfire.

Longarm stared in frustration at the hotel just up the block. "Hell, Jessie," he muttered as a bullet kicked dirt against his cheek. "Looks like I'm going to be a mite delayed."

It had been all that Jessie could do throughout the night simply to sit still and listen to Lang's long harangue about how the cartel had finally won. She'd been separated from Deke Tyler as soon as they'd reached Roundpatch. Tyler, bound, had been taken to the town jail, and Jessie had been escorted to Lang's ground-floor room in the deserted hotel.

At least they didn't tie me up, Jessie thought to herself as she looked around at what had once been the lobby of the hotel. The cartel agent's quarters were like something out of Jessie's worst nightmares. The once handsome red carpets were now littered, and in some places rotten with mildew. The red velvet drapes covering the gaping, shattered windows had become the hunting grounds for countless scurrying spiders. In one corner, next to what had once been the reception desk, Lang had a narrow cot. Hanging from the wall behind the desk was a huge banner embroidered with the cartel's coat-of-arms. A cold supper of yesterday's beans and hardtack had been laid out across the desk, but Jessie, as hungry as she was, had refused to touch a bit of it.

The dirt and mold, the cartel's banner, and Lang's droning voice all combined to create in Jessie a feeling of suffocation, but what most horrified her were the waist-high stacks of files piled on the floor in the center of the room. The stacks leaned against each other like monstrous toadstools. Each pasteboard folder was embossed with the Circle Star brand, and each folder was thick with information about every facet of Jessie's existence.

Lang, his amber eyes burning with what seemed almost religious fervor, reverently laid his hand on one of the stacks, as if he were touching the Bible. "With these I've beaten you, Jessie. Admit it! I've studied you for years. I know you better than anyone on earth. Better than your friend Ki." Lang licked his lips. "Better than your lover, Longarm."

Jessie shook with anger. "And you're going to rue the day you began this obsession when Ki and Longarm get here."

Lang threw back his head and roared with laughter. "Obsession! Is that what you call my devotion to you? An obsession? Oh, you do treat me unjustly! I had everything a man could wish for in my homeland, but I gave it all up to undergo the rigors of a samurai's training in the Japans. Then I journeyed to this barbaric country to be near you, and all the while I studied these files." The man in black began to approach. "That night in Sageville, I saw through your old woman's disguise, Jessie. I knew it was you, but I spared you."

"Yes." Jessie was curious, despite herself. "Why did you, Lang?"

He looked away. "All these days spent immersed in your life. My nights spent dreaming about you. It is a final irony, perhaps, but really not so strange"—his voice faded to a harsh whisper—"that I have fallen in love with you."

Jessie stared at the man, too shocked to say anything. Finally she asked, "But, Lang, if that's true, why are you planning to destroy me?"

Lang straightened. He looked on the verge of clicking his heels. "I am a Prussian. I have my orders. I shall carry them out!"

Jessie sighed. "I don't hate you, Lang, but I do pity you. You've been driven quite insane by this horrid scheme. When Longarm and Ki arrive, I'll see to it that you're given proper care."

As Jessie spoke, Lang's look of love gradually shifted to a sneer of hatred. "Mad, am I? I'll show you how mad I am. It so happens that your beloved Longarm and Ki have already arrived!" He went to the hotel's reception desk and reached behind it to produce Ki's leather vest and Longarm's gunbelt.

"No!" Jessie cried, rushing across the room to give the items a closer examination. "They're not real!"

"Yes, they are," Lang said quietly. "You may look at them to assure yourself that they are real. Longarm and Ki are with Deke Tyler." Lang glanced out the windows at the slowly brightening day. "It is almost dawn. Tyler and Longarm have been condemned to death at sunrise."

"You've got to stop it!" Jessie pleaded.

Lang shook his head. "There's nothing I can do. Ki will be killed later on." He moved to the stacks of files. "These have turned out to be a more powerful weapon than any of Ki's blades, or Longarm's Colt."

Jessie eyed Longarm's gunbelt.

"Don't be foolish," Lang said as he quickly drew his own pistol.

As the two foes stood facing each other, they heard a shot, and then another. Lang smiled. "It's been done," he said. "Longarm and Deke Tyler are dead."

"Like 'ell they are!" Beth Simpson stood in the doorway of the room. "I saw the bloody bastards get the better of Dusty and the man with 'im. Longarm and Deke Tyler are loose!"

Now it was Jessie's turn to laugh. "I told you so, Lang! The cartel hasn't won yet!"

"Kill 'er!" Simpson demanded. "You've got to, Lang."

"No!" the man in black exclaimed. "It's not time! I—"

A burst of gunfire drowned out the rest of what he was going to say. The three people inside the hotel listened as confused shouts filled the air. Then came the deadly staccato rhythm of a Gatling gun.

"All 'ell's broken loose!" Simpson snarled.

"My files," Lang moaned. "We've got to save my files!"

"There's no longer any need for those bloody papers of yours," Simpson swore. "The game is over. You've got Jessica Starbuck right in front of you, and a pistol in your 'and. Shoot 'er!"

Lang stared into Jessie's eyes. His revolver remained pointed at the floor.

"You can't do it, can you?" Simpson sneered. "You love that uppity bitch! You love 'er, and all this while I've tried so 'ard to please you. But you never cared a lick for me. You only wanted the real Jessie Starbuck, not a copy."

"Shut up, Beth," Lang said dully. "I'm in charge here."

"Then kill 'er!" Simpson spat. "Do it! The cartel will pay us a fortune if she dies!"

Slowly Lang brought his gun to bear on Jessie. "I'm sorry," he told her. "But I have my duty."

Simpson glanced over her shoulder toward the street as more shots were fired. "Come on," she implored. "Get it done!"

Lang thumbed back the hammer of his pistol, gripping the weapon with both hands to steady his aim.

"I can't!" he suddenly cried in anguish. "I can't kill the woman I love!"

"I can!" Simpson laughed, drawing her Colt. "I can kill 'er and take the cartel's fee for my own!"

"No!" Lang shouted. He swung his gun toward Simpson and jerked off a shot.

His bullet went high, biting into the doorway in which Simpson stood. The bloodthirsty imposter reflexively brought her Colt to bear on Lang and squeezed the trigger, shooting him in the chest. The man in black sprawled backwards into his stacks of files. The folders cascaded down upon him, burying his lifeless body in an avalanche of Circle Star insignias.

Jessie saw her chance and took it, leaping for Longarm's gunbelt on the desktop while Beth Simpson stood paralyzed, just beginning to comprehend what she had done.

Jessie hauled the .44 Colt out of its waxed holster and aimed it at Simpson, but before she could fire, the imposter came to her senses and ducked around the corner of the doorway.

"It's not finished yet, Starbuck!" Simpson swore, and then she was gone.

Jessie had to get Beth Simpson. The nightmare would continue until her impersonator was brought to justice, one way or another. She ran from the hotel in pursuit of her double.

Longarm listened with alarm to the shooting that was coming from inside the hotel. There were still two outlaws keeping him from Lang's quarters. The pair of badmen were behind secure cover and had Longarm trapped in a crossfire, but the deputy was ready to run their gauntlet, regardless.

Got to take the chance, Longarm told himself as he rose up off of the ground in a crouch. *Jessie could've been wounded by those shots coming from the hotel. I've got to find out . . .*

He was about to begin his mad dash, his brace of pistols at the ready, when suddenly, for no apparent reason, one of the outlaws staggered out from behind a barrel, clutching at his side. The man collapsed into the street. His companion, directly opposite him, stepped out of his protective doorway to see what was going on.

Longarm fired from the hip. The outlaw fell back into the shadows of the doorway. Only his boots were visible, but they remained still.

As Longarm hurried toward the hotel, Ki stepped out into the street. A bloodied knife was in his right hand.

"You get that jasper just now?" Longarm asked.

The samurai nodded. "You looked in need of help. Hurry, we must rescue Jessie."

The duo dashed the rest of the way to the hotel. Rifle and pistol fire still filled the morning air, punctuated by rattling bursts of Seth Weeks's Gatling gun.

"One of Farley's men spring you?" Longarm asked.

"No." Ki smiled. "It was Birdy O'Hara."

Both men froze as they came face to face with Jessie, a gun in her hand.

Longarm and Ki exchanged wary glances. Longarm kept his guns angled downward, even as he thumbed back their hammers. Ki held his knife ready.

"Longarm! Ki!" Jessie cried out happily. Her smile faded as she surveyed their grim countenances. "What's wrong?" she demanded, her green eyes flashing emerald fire. "Don't you know it's me? Can't you *tell?*"

"Why don't you just drop that gun," Longarm began.

"Dammit, Custis! Lang's in there dead, and Beth Simpson is getting away!"

"Drop the gun," Longarm pleaded. "Until we can be positive!"

As Longarm and Ki watched, a sly smile appeared on the face of the woman before them. "So you'd like to be sure, eh?" the woman said slyly. "Remember the last time you visited, Longarm? We took the honeymoon suite of the hotel in Sarah. You sent down for a bottle of rye, and when room service brought it up, you poured it all over my—"

"Jessie!" Longarm crowed happily. A moment later he was locked in her laughing embrace.

Ki hurried inside the hotel. Jessie and Longarm, their arms around each other's waists, followed. The samurai was quite pleased to see his weapons vest, and hurriedly shrugged it on. He also discovered his bow and quiver behind the desk. Longarm strapped on his holster, trading Jessie his brace of pistols for his own .44.

"Beth Simpson's still on the loose," Jessie reminded the two men.

"We'll get her, sooner or later," Longarm said. "Meanwhile, we've got to help Farley bring down Seth Weeks!"

"Farley's here too?" Jessie laughed. "Well, I'm sticking with you, Custis, just until everybody knows that I'm the real me!" She glanced at the files strewn around Lang's corpse. "Those papers should be destroyed."

"You two go on ahead," Ki said. "I'll take care of this."

The samurai waited until they'd left, and then extracted a white *nage teppo* grenade from the pocket of his vest. The egg-sized weapon contained a substance that would burst into flame upon contact with the air. He hurled the *nage teppo* against the scattered files. A pillar of flame shot up to the ceiling, filling the room with a crackling roar.

Ki stood in the doorway long enough to be sure that the files were burning well. The flames had covered Lang and begun to spread along the floor and walls of the room when Ki finally turned and left the hotel. He knew it would only be moments before the entire structure was in flames.

The samurai caught up with Jessie and Longarm at Farley's command post, down the street from the town hall. The gunfire had stopped. Weeks's Gatling gun was silent.

"I think he's run out of ammo for that thing," Farley mused.

Birdy O'Hara was standing nearby, a pair of Farley's handcuffs on her wrists. She smiled up at Ki with red-rimmed eyes. "I guess you turned me into a soft-hearted sucker after all," she murmured, and then shrugged. "The funny thing about it is, I don't mind."

Ki nodded. "Jessie? Marshal Farley? Longarm? May I speak to you all?" The three gathered around Ki for a few moments, and then broke apart.

Farley stood with his hands on his hips, sternly regarding the redheaded reporter. "I'm told that you saved Ki's life twice. Once out on the trail, and once right here in Roundpatch." The town marshal rubbed his chin thoughtfully. "Since you ain't really hurt anybody, I'm persuaded to release you in Jessie Starbuck's custody."

Birdy O'Hara gave a yelp of joy, but then her blue eyes narrowed. "Just what does that mean?" she asked suspiciously.

"It means," Jessie broke in, "that I happen to be part owner of a newspaper back East. I want you to quit the scandal sheet you work for and join up with the *Sentinel*."

"The *Sentinel!*" O'Hara gasped. "Why, that's one of the finest papers going! I—I don't know what to say!"

Jessie smiled. "Say you'll accept."

Birdy stared at Jessie, and then at Ki. Her expression darkened. "I'd rather go to jail than accept charity," she declared scornfully.

"We do not offer charity," Ki brusquely said. "We offer you a chance to work your way up in your chosen profession. It is merely a chance, an opportunity. The rest will be up to you." The samurai paused. "What's the problem, Birdy? Are you afraid to try?"

The woman smiled. "Thank you, Ki, Miss Starbuck." She turned to Marshal Farley. "I accept."

"All right then!" Farley grinned. "Chuck!" he called to his deputy. "Take them cuffs off her!"

Jessie turned to Longarm and Deke Tyler. "By the way, how did you manage not to be executed?"

Tyler looked sad. "Old Barney saved us, Jessie. When those outlaws took me and you captive, Barney followed us into Roundpatch. He used his saber to kill one of the outlaws, but he got shot in the process."

Jessie paled. "Take me to him."

Deke Tyler started to escort her, but just then the town hall's Gatling gun resumed firing.

"Get down!" Farley shouted.

The door to the hall swung open, and out ran Seth Weeks, a gun in one hand, an ax in his other. He was moving quite fast for a man of his weight.

"That Gatling gun will keep us pinned down," Farley groaned. "Weeks is going to get away!"

Ki, armed with the knife Birdy O'Hara had given him, dashed toward the town hall. The Gatling gun tried to track him, but the sprinting, zigzagging samurai managed to outrun the bullets nipping at his heels. Then he was upon Seth Weeks, and the Gatling gun's operator had to stop firing unless he wanted to risk hitting the outlaw mayor.

"Damned Chinaman!" Weeks muttered, swinging his ax at Ki's head.

The samurai twisted his torso sideways, avoiding Seth Weeks's earnest attempt to sever his head from his shoulders. At the same time, Ki snapped out with a foot strike that jolted the pistol out of Weeks's hand.

The outlaw chuckled, tightening his grip on the ax. He began to stalk Ki, who kept Weeks at bay by brandishing his knife.

"Now's our chance," Farley whispered to several of his men as Ki and Seth Weeks circled each other. "You boys rush the town hall."

Weeks set up a series of roundhouse swings with his ax. His breath huffed out of him as he advanced upon Ki. The ax was now moving almost too fast to see. "I told you, Chinaman!" Weeks gasped. "I told you I'd kill you—"

Ki darted in close. Weeks, grinning triumphantly, swung his ax up and over his shoulder, meaning to cleave Ki in two. The samurai lunged with his knife, driving home the blade just beneath Weeks's ribcage. As the outlaw groaned in pain, Ki slid the knife across Weeks's massive girth, until the embedded blade was just above the man's navel, then sliced upward, until he hit Weeks's sternum. Whimpering in panic now, Weeks dropped his ax in a frenzied attempt to hold his split body together.

The attempt was futile. The obese outlaw had been split open like an overripe tomato, and he looked down in dismay to see his intestines exploding out of his sundered belly to fall in a steaming, bloody mound in front of him. He gave a drawn-out groan and tottered forward, slipping and sliding in his own entrails, then fell with ground-shaking impact.

One of Farley's men appeared in the third-floor window of the town hall, from which the Gatling gun had sent forth its deadly barrage. "It's all over!" he called down. "There was only two men left up here, and they surrendered!"

Farley nodded in satisfaction. The outlaw stronghold of Roundpatch had fallen.

• • •

Longarm and Deke Tyler escorted Jessie to the place where they'd left Barney. Jessie knelt beside the dying man and took his hand. She desperately wished that she had with her the gray wig and spectacles so that she could transform herself into Dora.

But there was no need for her to don a disguise. Old Barney's memories supplied the images his weak eyes wanted to see. "D-Dora? Hello, old girl. I knew you'd come. I knew it..."

"Barney," Jessie murmured, "I don't know if you can understand, but thank you."

"Hell, no thanks necessary," Barney told her, giving her hand a squeeze. "I'm jes' glad I had my Dora back, even if it was only for a little while..." He winked at Jessie, then closed his eyes and died.

"What do you think he meant by that?" Deke Tyler asked, more than a little awestruck. "Do you think he knew who you were all the time?"

Jessie was too busy crying to reply.

"Reckon it sort of speaks well for the old codger, either way," Tyler said.

"Reckon it does," Longarm agreed.

They could hear Farley shouting for everybody to regroup. "Fire!" the marshal was yelling. "There's a fire! Get your horses!"

It was true, Longarm realized, looking around. Off in the distance, the hotel where Ki had set the Starbuck files ablaze was now totally engulfed in flames. The breeze had carried burning sparks to other buildings, and now flames were licking toward the sky in half a dozen areas.

In a few hours Roundpatch would be nothing but a charred ruin and a memory.

★

Chapter 22

Jessie's big double bed at the Starbuck ranch was the finest place a man could be, Longarm decided. He wiggled his bare toes beneath the blankets. Beside the bed, on a nightstand, was a bottle of bourbon, and *in* the bed, beside Longarm, was a very naked, very lazy Jessie Starbuck!

"Hasn't this just been a wonderful two days?" Jessie sighed. "After all the excitement, I figured we deserved two days in bed." She giggled. "With each other!"

Outside, the late-afternoon sky was beginning to purple. Longarm hugged Jessie a little closer and said, "Tomorrow I've got to leave. Deke Tyler's waiting for me in Sarah. I've got to sign an affidavit that he deserves some of the bank's reward for his part in all this."

Jessie pouted. "I only wish we could make the bank give Deke the entire five thousand!"

"That amount was offered for Jessie Starbuck," Longarm reminded her. "And now it's being offered for Beth Simpson. You can't blame the bank for wanting to save itself some money. Anyway, Deke intends to set out after Simpson. Maybe he'll end up with the whole five thousand, after all."

"Maybe," Jessie agreed. "But I can't get that sad story you told me about Deke's daughter out of my mind. I wish he'd let me help."

"Deke won't take charity," Longarm said forcefully.

Jessie stretched her arms above her head. The blankets fell away from her lush breasts. "Birdy O'Hara wouldn't accept any charity, either." Jessie smiled. "But at least we've gotten her on the right track. Ki's with her in Sarah right now."

"Think she'll make it?" Longarm asked. Meanwhile he turned on his side to begin sucking on Jessie's pert nipples.

"Oh, yes— Oh!" Jessie squealed as her nipples tightened and swelled in response to Longarm's teasing mouth. "Anyway, Ki will *see* to it that she makes it." She wiggled in Longarm's embrace as his fingers danced down the length of her body, tracing the curve of her hip, and then tarrying on the silken swells of her round bottom.

As they kissed, Jessie reached out for Longarm, locking her fingers around his thick biceps as she pulled him down upon her. Longarm parted her legs gently. His callused fingers, upon the sensitive, syrupy folds of her center, were like fire.

Feather-lightly, Longarm began to stroke her wetness. Jessie's golden-red tresses fanned out upon the pillow like flames as her head rocked from side to side in response to his knowing touch. Her purrs and moans filled the bedroom.

She managed to writhe free, then to straddle him. First, Jessie tickled his erection gently with her fingernails until she'd set him throbbing. Next she blanketed it with the sweet warmth of her soft, flat belly as she slid down Longarm's body. Finally she sheathed his swollen member in the moist, fragrant valley of her cleavage. She used her hands to squeeze her breasts together, caressing and massaging him between her satiny globes.

"Custis," she cooed, while sucking and biting the taut skin of his lower belly, "if I weren't *me* right now, do you think you could tell the difference?"

"Up until now, I'm afraid not," Longarm confessed. "But *here's* how I'd tell . . ."

With that, he slid his agile body down Jessie's honey-sweet

length, until their tongues could intertwine. "Here's how I'd know," Longarm whispered during their long, wet kisses. "Somebody may *look* like you and *act* like you, but nobody can *kiss* like you!"

"Ya-hoo!" Jessie crowed. She rolled over onto her back and drew Longarm into her. His initial thrust brought forth a gasp of pleasure from her. Her buttocks gyrated against the bed while her inner muscles squeezed his marblelike firmness.

As Longarm rose and fell inside her in long, swooping strokes, Jessie lifted her legs to lock them about his waist. She set her luscious hips rolling to match his rhythm.

Longarm slowed his own movements each time he felt his orgasm growing near. He wanted to make this ecstasy last forever!

They rocked together for long minutes, cradled in each other's arms, joined together, tongue against tongue and sex against sex, until neither of them could delay their climax.

Growling, Longarm came. It was as if his spine had dissolved to form the spurts of blissful, molten sensation cannonballing out of him. Wailing, Jessie arched her back to swallow him up to the hilt.

They lay entwined until their breathing was once more steady and slow, and then Longarm rolled away from her and stretched out a weak arm for the bottle of bourbon. "How many was that?" he asked.

"Sixteen, I think," Jessie drawled. "But who's counting?"

"I believe I'm going to take a little nap." Longarm chuckled. He took a pull of the bourbon, then rolled over onto his side. "A nap ought to recharge me," he muttered. A moment later he was snoring.

Jessie gazed at him fondly. She couldn't fault him for falling asleep. Not after he'd worked so hard during the last forty-eight hours!

She, however, was not the least bit sleepy. She rolled out of bed and padded across the carpet to look out the window. The sun had set. The ranch was quiet and dark, except for the yellow light spilling from the windows of the bunkhouse.

Jessie decided to get dressed and go out for a walk. She'd

missed her ranch during the time she'd been away, and for the two days she'd been back, the only thing she'd had time to rediscover was Longarm's body!

Dressing quietly, Jessie pulled on her denims, buckled her Colt around her waist, and left the bedroom. The gun was an extra precaution she was taking on Longarm's account. He'd made her promise to wear it for a while, just in case Beth Simpson was still in the vicinity. That was something Jessie very much doubted.

She made her way downstairs and through the dark house to the kitchen. She went outside the back way, and paused to look up at the night sky and take deep breaths of the cool, fresh air.

Things had worked out pretty well, Jessie decided. It was true that the Starbuck reputation had suffered some slight temporary damage. But that always seemed to be the way it worked; nasty rumors spread like a prairie fire, but the truth took a lot longer. Marshal Farley and the town bank had sent wires across the territory, letting everyone know that Jessie was no longer wanted for any crimes. Still, Jessie guessed it would be a while before the whole mess faded from everyone's minds. *It would help matters if Beth Simpson was brought to justice,* Jessie thought. *If that woman has a lick of sense, she'll have taken up a disguise of her own and headed east, on the first leg of her journey back to England.*

Jessie didn't envy the woman when she got there. The cartel did not tend to give a warm welcome to agents who'd failed in their missions. Beth Simpson would be a hunted woman, no matter where she tried to hide.

Jessie found that her stroll had brought her near the stable. A young wrangler, just finishing his chores for the day, tipped his hat in greeting.

"Pete!" Jessie called. "Saddle me up a horse, would you? I'm in a mood for a ride."

The young wrangler looked puzzled, but he remained respectful. "Sure thing, Miss Starbuck," he said politely. He started back toward the stable and then paused and turned around. "Would the horse you just brought in be all right, ma'am?"

"What?" Jessie asked, startled.

"The gray gelding you just rode in, Miss Starbuck," the hand repeated. "Not more than ten minutes ago."

"But I didn't—" Jessie froze. "Never mind, Pete!" she called over her shoulder as she ran back toward the house.

"No, ma'am. I mean, yes, ma'am," Pete stammered, thinking that he'd most likely never get the hang of understanding women.

Jessie drew her Colt as she reentered the house through the back door and made her way through the kitchen. It made perfect sense, now that she thought about it, Jessie realized. Devising a double to replace Jessica Starbuck had been the most ambitious and expensive scheme ever attempted by the cartel. The plan's failure would infuriate the Prussians. They'd want a scapegoat, and Beth Simpson would be it.

On the other hand, if Simpson managed to kill me, everything would be changed. She would no longer be marked for death. Instead, she would reap a rich reward from the cartel.

Simpson has no choice, Jessie mused as she tiptoed her way through the dark main room of the house. *She has to try to kill me!*

Jessie caught up with her double at the staircase. Beth Simpson, her gun in her hand, was halfway up the flight of steps that led to the second-floor bedrooms.

She's still dressed exactly like me, Jessie thought. *Still fooling people into thinking that her actions are mine!*

Jessie raised her Colt. "Hold it right there, Beth!"

Simpson froze. She started to turn, but the sound of Jessie clicking back the hammer on her Colt stopped her. "You seem to 'ave me at a disadvantage, dear. 'Ow about a deal?"

"No chance," Jessie said. "Drop your gun, Beth."

"I think you'll 'ave a go at this deal, Jessie." Simpson chuckled. She slid her revolver into its holster and then turned around to stare down with imperious scorn at Jessie. "What do you say, lass? Are you good enough to beat me in a fair fight?"

Jessie, standing at the foot of the stairs, looked up at Simpson and smiled. "The situation we find ourselves in is simply too delicious to throw away," she replied coolly. "My word, it's like staring into a mirror and seeing my own reflection."

"I've studied you for so long, Jessie, I'm no longer sure whether it's you or me that's the reflection," Beth Simpson retorted.

Jessie nodded. "I guess there's only one way to find out." Slowly she let down the hammer on her Colt and slid it into her holster.

The two women stared at each other for a moment, studying each other by the faint light of the moon coming in through the bay windows of the main room.

We're like opposite sides of the same coin, Jessie thought. *The same, but so different!*

Beth Simpson slapped at her gun. Jessie's Colt found its way into her hand, and she managed to aim and fire a split second before Simpson's gun spat blue flame...

Crying out, Simpson clutched at her stomach and let her gun fall. The pistol clattered down the stairs. Simpson followed it. Her feet managed to skip down the first couple of steps before she lost her balance and began to tumble. Jessie jumped back as Beth Simpson's body came to rest at her feet.

Jessie experienced a moment of vertigo not unlike the one she'd felt the first time she'd encountered the imposter in the Sageville general store. She shuddered deeply as she gazed into the cold, vacant emerald eyes of her double. It was as though she felt the cold touch of death in her own soul.

"What the hell!" Longarm snarled. He stood crouched at the head of the stairs, naked as a jaybird, his .44 in his hand. He stared in consternation at the scene—two identical Jessies, except that one was lying dead at the feet of the other...

Jessie looked up at him. Longarm raised his gun.

"Maryland rye," Jessie said. "Room service. You poured it all over my—"

"Thank the Lord," Longarm sighed, his broad shoulders sagging in relief.

Jessie moved toward him, saying, "Tomorrow you might bring Deke Tyler back here. It looks as if he's going to get his five thousand dollars after all."

Longarm smiled as she stepped into his embrace, and said, "I'm sure glad that's over. One Lone Star lady is plenty for any man. *Two* of 'em is pure *murder!*"

314

Watch for

LONGARM AND THE JAMES COUNTY WAR

sixty-third novel in the bold
LONGARM series from Jove

and

LONE STAR ON THE OWLHOOT TRAIL

nineteenth novel in the exciting
LONE STAR series from Jove

both coming in March!

The hottest trio in Western history is riding your way in these giant LONGARM adventures!

The matchless lawman LONGARM teams up with the fabulous duo Jessie and Ki of LONE STAR fame for exciting Western tales that are not to be missed!

___07386-5 LONGARM AND THE LONE STAR LEGEND $2.95

___07085-8 LONGARM AND THE LONE STAR VENGEANCE $2.95

___07611-2 LONGARM AND THE LONE STAR BOUNTY $2.95
